SELFIE

SELFIE

KAY COVE

Page & Vine
An Imprint of Meredith Wild LLC

This is a work of fiction. Names, characters, places, and incidents either are the product of the author's imagination or are used fictitiously, and any resemblance to actual persons, living or dead, business establishments, events, or locales is entirely coincidental. The publisher does not assume any responsibility for third-party websites or their content.

The author acknowledges the trademarked status and trademark owners of various products referenced in this work, which have been used without permission. The publication/use of these trademarks is not authorized, associated with, or sponsored by the trademark owners.

Copyright © 2025 Kay Cove
Editing by Michelle at The Fiction Edit, Page & Vine
Proofreading by Judy Zweifel at Judy's Proofreading
Cover Design by K.B. Barrett Designs

All Rights Reserved.
No part of this book may be reproduced, scanned, or distributed in any printed or electronic format without permission. Please do not participate in or encourage piracy of copyrighted materials in violation of the author's rights. Purchase only authorized editions.

Paperback ISBN: 978-1-964264-08-0

This one is for every single woman who is living with the ghosts of past trauma,
suffering from wounds that never healed.

It's never too late to reclaim your voice, your story, and your stage.

The spotlight is waiting.

That spotlight is powered by self-love.

PROLOGUE

Spencer

My phone shakes violently in my hand as I stare at the send button. Once I do this, there's no going back.

With one eye cinched shut, I peek at the naked picture of myself I'm about to send. I didn't use a filter, but I did strategically angle my body to be more flattering. He won't be able to see *everything* from this photo, but still plenty. Way more than I'd show any other guy.

Nerves prickle every inch of my skin like a full-body tattoo. I'm blowing out short breaths like I'm preparing to dive into a pool of ice water. *Am I really about to do this?*

Shit. I don't know.

The last time someone got ahold of a nude picture of me, it nearly ruined my life. I swore I'd never risk it again.

After tossing my phone onto the couch to avoid an accidental finger-slip-send, I pace across the living room of the guesthouse. For the millionth time in five minutes, I glance through the big bay window to the main house. I know my boss isn't there. He's out of town but I can't stop glancing over to the main house like mere hope will bring him home. He still carelessly leaves the drapes open and lights on, making it so easy to see inside. The man has no concern over privacy. Then again, he has no neighbors nearby his massive private property.

But it's better this way. The clock is ticking. If I'm going to do this, I have to send this tonight while he's still away. I'd lose my nerve if I could see him right there, just across the pool.

"Let's weigh the pros and cons," I mutter to myself.

Con—It's too late. Nathan's over the back-and-forth. I missed my chance. I get fired, then my little sister and I get kicked out of this guesthouse.

Con—Another nude picture of mine gets released and it forces me to flee Las Vegas...again.

Con—He's actually horrified at the picture and will run for the hills once he sees me, exactly as I am without darkness to hide the flaws I've run from for years.

Pro? There's only one. After months of agony as this man's assistant, we finally give in to what we want. Work has been hell because my boss is a plague. The way he smells. The way he smiles. The way he tugs on his bottom lip with his teeth when he's thinking too hard. Every image and scent of him is deeply etched in my brain. I've deduced I have two choices to get Nathan Hatcher out of my mind—a lobotomy, or jump his bones. Either way I'll finally be free of my endless thoughts about him.

When I first started working for him, I thought the constant tension between us was mostly hate. I was near positive that my destiny was a spotlight feature on *Snapped*. But after all he's done for me, I know this is different than hate. More than a crush.

This is a deep-seated need I didn't know I had. I desperately wanted to be seen for who I really am, not who I'm trying to be. I'm praying once I show him, Nathan still wants what he sees.

My heart races and my fingers tingle with nerves as I pick my phone back up. Riding the adrenaline high, I send a few leading messages, but stall on the image.

Deep breath.

I tap and hold the send button, mashing my fingertip so hard against the screen that it flattens and loses color. I hold it there, savoring the last few seconds of peace before the excruciating waiting game begins.

The moment I lift my finger, everything happens at once. A cold wave of nausea replaces the butterflies in my stomach. The audible *swoop* tells me my image was sent. I watch the screen like a hawk, swearing if I blink, my whole world will come crashing down.

But he doesn't open the message right away. Nathan's read receipts are always on. He says it's for accountability, but I think it's because he likes for people to know when he's ignoring them on purpose.

I treat my anxiety-ridden meltdown with a whole glass of ice water and an aggravated pacing session that feels like a workout. By the eighteen millionth time I check my phone, I see the worst thing possible. Sometime in the last sixty seconds since I previously checked my messages, the little gray "Delivered" receipt turned into "Read."

Gripping the life out of my phone with one hand, I pop the very tip of my thumb in my mouth and clamp down with my teeth as I fixate on the screen. My eyes grow dry as my stare widens. I don't dare blink, as if any slight movement could scare away his response. Still as a statue, I hold my breath, willing those three stupid dots to populate.

But I'm met with nothing. He saw it and said *nothing*.

Maybe he opened this in a work meeting and had to shove his phone back in his pocket so no one could see. A meeting taking place at—I peek at the hanging clock on the far wall—10:15 p.m. *Okay, not likely.* Perhaps he's driving on the highway and can't respond until he's parked. Except, Nathan hates driving. He's the only man on the planet who doesn't salivate over Aston Martins and Ferraris. No, this billionaire doesn't collect cars, he collects buildings.

Well, there's always the possibility that he glimpsed the picture and got so turned on he had to handle the matter that *came up* immediately. He'll respond back to me once the blood returns to his brain. That'd be more ideal than the far-more-realistic scenario which is that Nathan is over me. He never wanted to see this image, and come Monday, I am going to have the most humiliating day of work ever.

I smack my cheeks rapidly, trying to wake myself up from

this nightmare. "*Fuuuck*," I howl in agony. What have I done? What in the actual hell was I thinking?

Shit, what if he's not alone? There was a block on his calendar tonight, but it was private from my view. When I asked him about it, he simply said, "Don't schedule anything over it." *Dammit to hell.* Of course that was a date. He probably met someone at the bachelor party last night and she's lingering the day after. It's past ten. I bet they are still sweaty in bed, sharing pillow talk until they are ready for round two.

I have no time to address the hurt I'm feeling. Humiliation is at the front lines of the current war in my head and I need to escape it. After grabbing the cozy faux-fur blanket from the living room couch, I march out to the pool deck. The custom resort-style pool is breathtaking. The palm trees are tall, surrounded by colorful tropical foliage. It's stunning at night, lit up by colored spotlights. But I didn't come out here for the view.

The lazy river flows by a stone water feature that trickles like a waterfall. Back in the bar area, the beverage fridge which needs maintenance hums loudly. After flipping the switch for the hot tub, I choose a lounge chair right by the edge of the tub. The jets are so powerful the water overflows from the hot tub and noisily crashes into the infinity pool.

I'm here because in the dead of night, the pool area is loud enough to drown out all my thoughts. Cozying up underneath my blanket, the sound of water splashing, crashing, and trickling finally lulls me to sleep.

And I swear I've only shut my eyes for a minute when I'm awoken by the god-awful sound of a metal chair scraping against concrete.

Before I can respond with a "what the fuck," I open my eyes to see *him* sitting right in front of me.

"Good. You're awake," he says flatly.

Nathan's eyes toggle between green and blue. Green when he's focused. They look more blue when he smiles. But right now, they look discolored—just dark and angry. His suit jacket that matches his gunmetal-gray pants is missing. The dress shirt he's wearing is untucked and wrinkled. His stubble is visible. He looks exhausted.

"You startled me." I shimmy out from under the blanket, letting it fall to my waist, then throw my hand over my heart to theatrically convey my point. The light evening breeze chills my skin through my thin, black pajama set.

"Now we're even." He shifts his weight to pull his phone out of his back pocket. To my extreme discomfort, he pulls up our text conversation, then holds the phone out in front of my face.

"I'm sorry. I didn't know how else to—"

"Why didn't you tell me?" he asks. I'm relieved when he sets the phone down by his thigh.

"Tell you what?"

"About Casey. I nearly ripped his head off tonight when I found out the real story."

"What do you mean—" I stop midsentence. "Wait. How are you here? You were in L.A."

For a split second he looks vulnerable as his gaze falls to his lap. "I drove...fast."

Nathan always takes a private jet from L.A. to Vegas because he can't stand the idea of being in a car for more than half an hour. "What time is it?" I ask.

He peers at his phone. "Quarter past one."

The cogs in my brain slowly start moving. That means Nathan saw the picture, immediately got in a vehicle, then drove like a bat out of hell in the middle of the night. He shaved an entire hour off a four-hour drive. "You weren't on a date?"

He looks positively disturbed. "Of course not."

"You had a private block on your calendar."

He hangs his head and nods. "The bachelor party got moved back a night. We found a better location. My dad has access to my calendar, I didn't want him to see and ruin the surprise."

"Oh."

His lips curl in a small smirk. "Why? Were you jealous?"

I'm not in the mood for our usual banter. I hang my head and nod solemnly.

"If you think for one second I'd get over you that quickly, you must not know how I feel about you."

"I thought I blew it and maybe you were trying to forget everything that happened between us." I force myself to meet his gaze. It's not enough to hear his reply. I want to see his genuine eyes, the ones that make me feel so safe and sure that I'm making the right decision.

"I couldn't forget if I tried. And I don't want to." He scoots forward, getting closer. "Where's Charlie?"

"A sleepover party she got invited to at the last minute."

"Good. I'm glad she's making more friends."

"Me too."

"Are you mad I pulled her on stage and asked her to perform at the charity event last week?"

"I'm not," I quickly tell him.

That catches him off guard. His expression softens, that little smile reappearing at the corner of his mouth. "You sure? Because this is a topic you get pretty huffy about."

My baby sister, Charlie, is only eleven. Singing prodigy or not, I don't want her swallowed up by the dangers of the music industry. Too many child stars have their lives ruined serving other people's greedy agendas. I want Charlie to have a childhood.

As if he can read my mind like an open book, Nathan says, "We share the same worries, Spencer. I promise. I would never put her in harm's way. Do you trust me?"

And I believe him. Truly. "I do."

His nod is small.

"I mean with everything," I add. "I want to tell you the truth."

Nathan lifts his eyebrows, his forehead wrinkling. "What does that mean?"

"There's something else that happened with Casey but it was hard to talk about." I take a steadying breath, preparing myself to explain, but something he said a moment ago dawns on me. "Wait, you said you knew the real story."

"Dawn slipped," Nathan answers.

"So you know about the real reason I left school?"

He wets his lips with the tip of his tongue but doesn't say anything. His silence is admission enough.

"And now that it's all on the table, how do you feel about me?" I brush the stray hairs away from my eyes so nothing is obstructing my view of his handsome face. "Tell me the truth."

"You first." Nathan taps his phone, but his stare is locked on me. "Why did you lie?"

The timer for the hot tub jets expired and now there's nothing but silence between us. For the longest time, we watch each other breathe. No words. Just chests rising and falling, wondering who is going to cave in this epic game of chicken we've had going on for months.

Me. I cave. But not because I'm the chicken.

I'm the brave one.

"Because I didn't want you to see my scars. I wanted you to see the good version of me."

"Spencer." He says it like it's a whole sentence, the look on his face is tormented.

When he doesn't continue, I force myself to ask, "Why did you leave me on read? That hurt."

He leans forward, his knee pressing into the side of my thigh. A faint whiff of his sweet, woodsy cologne tickles my nose. I've grown to love that smell—subtle, sensual, and leaves me missing it once it's gone. "Casey was there. I just found out what he did and stormed out of the party when you texted me. I damn near had a heart attack. I couldn't think straight. I got in the car and started driving. I needed to tell you in person."

"Tell me what?"

"That I know what this picture means. I know what it must've taken for you to send it after everything you've been through. I'll protect it. *And you.* You're safe with me."

After all the broody stares, eyerolls, and grunted one-word

answers, I can't believe this is the same man who caused me so much frustration, in every sense of the word.

"Okay." It's the only response I can muster and it comes out small and shaky. I don't think Nathan notices because suddenly his eyes are tiptoeing down my chest.

"It's a very nice picture." His voice is husky and low.

"Are you going to keep it?"

He glances up to grin at me. "It's already my wallpaper."

One moment we're both chuckling, and then his hand is on my shoulder. But that's not enough. Leaning forward in his chair, he slips his hand underneath the short sleeve of my pajama top and finds my bra strap. "This okay?" he asks as he pulls the thin strap down my shoulder.

I can only nod. It's too hard to speak with him touching my bare skin.

"Are you ready now?" Abandoning my bra strap, he grabs my hand and pulls my fingertips to his soft, cool lips.

"For what?"

"A truce. No more games. No more lies. Just us giving this an actual try."

A flood of warmth saturates my blood and bones. My whole body relaxes like I'm finally home. No more running. "You're going to finally start being nice to me?"

A playful grin appears on his face. "I didn't say that. I still plan on punishing you for teasing me with that picture." He lifts his brows. "You still have no clue what you do to me, do you?"

"I think I mostly infuriate you," I answer honestly.

He laughs as his face moves a mere inch from mine. "How'd we get here?"

"Where?" It comes out in a hush. I'm practically speechless with him this close.

He whispers right back, "With me needing your lips more than I need my next breath."

I praise myself for finding the strength to go after what I want for once. One picture summoned the unattainable man I've been pining for, for far too long. All I can think of as Nathan's lips close in on mine is how crazy this is.

How one selfie can change *everything*.

CHAPTER 1

Nathan

Three Months Prior

Barely two steps onto the construction site and my black dress shoes are coated with dirt, soot, and gravel. The air reeks of burning tires and liquor, but I'll deal with that later. Right now, I need to figure out why my dad told me his new purchase of a 28-story, three-million-square-foot hotel resort only needed an interior facelift. I'm clearly looking at a demolition.

I'm trudging toward the entrance when I'm stopped by a worker in a yellow hard hat. His cheeks are red enough to rival his neon-orange vest as he begins to shout at me in Spanish. I know some rudimentary Spanish, but he's talking too fast and is mostly drowned out by the background noise of construction. He takes a step closer, his finger stabbing the air aggressively around my chest area. His gesture is a glaringly obvious: *Who the fuck do you think you are?*

Before I can tell him that I own this building, another man in a matching orange vest comes jogging toward us. "Juan!" His voice booms over all the noise. When he reaches us, he smacks the man named Juan on the back of his helmet. "You tonto, are you loco? *This is el jefe.* Watch your tone." He turns to me and offers his hand. "I'm Frankie, the foreman here. I'm so sorry, Mr. Hatcher."

"What's he so upset about?" I nod toward Juan who has retreated several steps out of earshot, his head hung in shame.

"Juan's my shift lead. He takes safety very seriously. You're about to enter an active demo site and you're not wearing a hard hat. He'd be responsible if you got hurt. He shouldn't have shouted at you though. I'll write him up for that."

I nod in understanding. "Right. You're bilingual?"

Frankie nods. "Yes, sir."

"How do I say, 'I'm sorry, you're right. Good job,' in Spanish?"

With an odd look on his face, Frankie slowly translates my words. I walk up to Juan with my hand outstretched. He shakes it firmly, but there's fear in his eyes like he's worried he's about to lose his job. "*Lo siento, tienes razón. Buen trabajo.*" I must sound like a fool in my American accent, but I tried.

Juan relaxes, blowing out a big breath of relief. He taps his hard hat. "Always safety," he says in a thick accent. I pat his shoulder as a final gesture of approval.

As Juan disappears back into the jobsite, I turn to Frankie. "Don't write him up. Give him a raise. If it's not in the budget, bill my office."

Frankie laughs, seemingly more out of surprise than anything else. "Geez. Thank you. When suits come around here, they're usually assholes to my guys."

I half-smile. "I have my moments. Do you have protective gear I can use? My dad's inside. I need to speak with him."

"Right away." Frankie hustles off to a nearby trailer and returns with a bright yellow hard hat. The interior padding is holding on to a faint smell of sweat, but desperate times, desperate measures.

Dad's standing in the heart of the building. With all the rubble around us, it looks like he's in the eye of a storm, which explains the calm on his face. "Nate!" he thunders out. "Nice of you to show up, finally. You sleeping in these days?"

I check my watch. "It's seven thirty in the morning," I answer flatly. My dad is such an early riser, it could be argued he's actually a night owl. He continues to invite me to five o'clock sunrise hikes despite how many times I tell him to shove it up his ass.

"So, what do you think of this beauty? A fucking steal, right?"

I take in a panoramic view of the broken columns amidst the piles of rubble. Sludge is leaking from the fallen pipes and liquid is getting uncomfortably close to the coils upon coils of ripped-up electrical wires. "Are we looking at the same thing here?"

"All this space," Dad murmurs, spinning in place. "I'm thinking a manmade lake with a projected water show. Maybe burlesque dancers on giant floating lily pads." He waves his hands in the air like he's shoving off the idea. "But I'm not committed to anything yet, so if you've got something on your mind, jump in."

I blink at him. "Before we start talking about giant lily pads, can we discuss your definition of 'light facelift'? Because I'm looking at a flimsy house of cards, held together with thin toothpicks. Dad, you bought fifty acres of rubble. And what the hell is that smell?"

He rubs his hands together as he grimaces. "The sewage smell or the burning rubber?"

"What sewage smell?" I cringe.

"It gets stronger that way." Dad points over his shoulder. "We're not sure where it's coming from. Possibly a drain issue."

"Great." I stab my fist against my forehead. "And the burning rubber?"

"This building's been abandoned for a few years. There were some squatters. Looks like they've been burning tire scraps for warmth."

"Dad, up until ten minutes ago, I really thought you were the most savvy property investor in the world."

His grin is wicked. "And now?"

"Now I think you need a CAT scan before making any more business decisions." Right on cue, a light breeze brings a waft of the aforementioned sewage stink.

From what I understand, this was supposed to be a strip mall, and when the project went bankrupt, it was acquired by a new group of investors who attempted to convert the space into a massive hotel. The more costly the construction got, the more the investors lost interest in the project. Obviously, they cut their losses and abandoned ship.

"I looked at the bill of sale. We were already upside down before I saw this giant mess. You paid more than one hundred million dollars for the land alone—"

"It's a prime location."

"It's *not*," I argue. "It's too far west of the Strip. The only people who venture this far are lost, looking for Chinatown."

Dad lays his hand on his stomach. "Speaking of which, I could go for dim sum. Want to finish up here and make plans for lunch? I'll call Jules. She knows the best restaurants." He shoots me a pointed look. "Can I invite her?"

"I have lunch plans."

Fucking Julia. That's a whole other issue. My dad's current girlfriend is the epitome of a late-life crisis.

"You can't avoid her forever."

Watch me.

Eager to change the subject, I ask further about Dad's most recent harebrained purchase. "Who owns the lot directly behind this?"

Dad's grunt of irritation tells me all I need to know. "Who do you think? Senior."

Griffin Harvey Senior is Dad's biggest rival for property on the Strip. They're both heavy into real estate investments, and Harvey has a knack for swooping in and purchasing properties my dad has his eye on.

"We'd need it for a decent-size parking garage. A resort like this is not going to work without a parking garage."

"Yeah, well, if I make an offer to Harvey, he'll hold the property just out of spite."

"I thought your rivalry was a 'little friendly competition.'"

Dad licks his lips. "Let's just say it's gotten a bit heated over the past few years."

"Heated as in enough fire to burn bridges?"

He teeters his head. "You could say that. Aren't you friends with his grandson?"

"Somewhat." Finn and I used to be pretty close. We're both UNLV graduates and had the same friends. But a few years ago, we lost touch. Actually, I mostly lost touch with everyone. "I'll make a call and see what I can find out."

"Good." Dad closes the short space between us. Clamping on to my shoulder, he looks me head-on. "I asked her to marry me."

"Who?" I ask in disbelief.

He drops his hand and crosses his arms, looking annoyed. "*Ju-Lee-Uh.*" He enunciates like I'm a child learning my first word.

My only response is a dropped jaw and twitching eye.

"Come on, Nate. You can't be upset about this. You're thirty-three. Your mother and I have been divorced for ten years. She's been married twice since, and you never had an issue with that."

"One of those marriages was an accident and immediately annulled. The other was to a man *her age.*"

Mom and Dad didn't have a messy divorce. They just grew apart. Once I graduated from college, Mom left the country, becoming nomadic as she tried to reenact her personal version of *Eat. Pray. Love.* For a long time, Dad just worked. He dated here and there, but nothing serious. Then, one day, he meets a yogalates enthusiast and life coach, who is *thirty years* his junior.

I hold up my hands, looking at his expression that's a mix of pissed and wounded. "What do you want me to say?" I ask defeatedly.

"Congratulations."

"Fine. Congratulations," I parrot flatly.

"And that you'll make an effort to get to know Jules."

"Okay. I'll make an effort to get to know Julia." I definitely won't, but I'm trying not to be a dick to his face.

"And you'll be my best man."

Oh, hell. "Don't you think Uncle Mac would want to do it? I don't want to take that from him. I know how close you are."

Dad sucks air through his teeth, the sharp squeak echoing off the rubble surrounding us. "Uncle Mac?"

"Yes."

"The same Uncle Mac I speak to about once a year and only when he wants to withdraw a lump sum from his inheritance?" Dad oversees his little brother's allowance. It's a pain point between them. But after Mac almost spent a quarter billion dollars by commissioning the finest minds at NASA to build him a functional version of Optimus Prime, *to scale*, the entire family agreed he needed to be cut off.

"I'm happy. And Jules is wonderful in every way. She's the reason I bought this place."

"Not helping her case."

"She's teaching me to see the beauty in potential instead of focusing on the bottom line. We know how to acquire and sell and make more money than we'll ever know what to do with—but this?" He holds his palms up and takes a few steps back, gesturing to the condemned building like he's proud. "Let's bond over building something from nothing. I won't be here forever, kid. This is the kind of stuff you'll remember when I'm gone."

"You don't want to hire a project management team. You want to do this ourselves?"

His face is filled with the excitement of a kid in a candy store. "Yeah. From the studs. We pick the architects, the designers, approve the concepts, and do the walkthroughs. Let's get our hands dirty. A real father-son project."

I scoff. "It's a colossal undertaking." Typically our firm just deals with the numbers. When your corporation is worth billions, you hire people to hire other people. We sign the checks; they make the magic. I don't do site walkthroughs until the project is finished, or someone needs to be fired. Getting involved in the details turns one step into fifty.

"What do you say?"

A reluctant, "Fine," breaks through my lips. "Let's do it."

"What about being my best man?"

Agreeing to that would make it difficult to stay in denial about this marriage. But this is my dad... He's the best guy I know. He didn't give up on me during my darkest times. He was patient and supportive when I made decisions he didn't understand. I can't not do this for him.

I let out a deep sigh of exasperation. "Your bachelor party—strippers or no strippers?"

Dad laughs and pulls me into a rib-crushing bear hug. "Thank you, son. I knew I could count on you."

"Congratulations, Dad. I mean it." I wish I didn't sound so sullen. It's not only that I'm not particularly fond of my father's soon-to-be bride, it's also a painful role reversal. I asked my dad to be my best man, too. For a wedding that never happened. Three years later, it still hurts miserably.

He releases me with a broad smile on his face. "Great. I'll call Jules and let her know. She wanted me to tell you before she announced it on social media."

"That's considerate," I say dryly.

"Are you sure your lunch plans are concrete?" My dad lifts a brow so high it disappears underneath his hard hat. He doesn't even pretend to buy my excuse.

"Yes." I have to make my peace with this marriage...but not today. "Anyway, I have to get back to the office. You just dumped a shipwreck on my plate. Time to get started."

He chuckles. "All right, then."

I turn on my heel and head toward the building entrance as Dad calls out, "Before I forget, HR hired you another assistant. They start on Monday, next week."

I stop in my tracks and wheel around. "We talked about this."

"Nate, don't start with me." His voice grows thick with warning. He's a great dad, but he has a switch. You don't maintain a multibillion-dollar business without being a hard-ass when you need to. Just because I'm his son doesn't mean he hasn't chewed my ass out a time or two. "This is a massive endeavor, for both of us. Not to mention the wedding coming up. You need help."

"I don't," I say, clipped.

"Too bad. I say you do. HR had to recruit out of state to find a decent executive assistant willing to work for you. You're starting to get a reputation."

He's not wrong. I've been through seven assistants in the past year alone. One even placed her resignation letter on my desk with a yellow sticky note that read, *Attn: Asshole.*

"What's my reputation?" I take a few steps back toward him.

Dad strokes his chin with one finger. "We started offering exit questionnaires for corporate employees who resign. We ask them to give feedback, positive and negative, on the company and their direct managers."

"That can't be good."

Dad gives me a dry smile. "Your complaints are very well fleshed out. You only had one positive comment. It was from your most recent assistant who quit, Helen."

That's surprising. I barely spoke to her. I also didn't remember her name until Dad just mentioned it. "What was the positive comment?"

"'He didn't sexually harass me once,'" Dad recites from memory as he looks at me expectantly. "Do you understand what that means?"

"Not really."

"It means that out of a dozen assistants, the *only* positive comment anyone could muster is that you're not a sexual predator."

I bite down on my smirk. "That sounds like a win."

"Nate," Dad grunts. "Get your shit together. I'm serious. I've tolerated this for so long because after Elise passed, and they took Claire away, I knew you'd need time."

Hearing their names takes me back to the bad place. The hopeless place. I've been surviving for three years by not dwelling on this. "I am fine."

Sadness cloaks his face. He holds his hand out like he wants to comfort me, but he leaves a foot of space between us. When it comes to this, Dad is used to me pushing him away.

"You know I'd spend every penny I have to bring her back. I'd happily spend the rest of my life piss poor, under a bridge, if I could take this pain away from you, son."

There are some things money can't fix. I'm not sure if by *her* he's referring to Elise, or her daughter, Claire. Both are impossible situations. My fiancée is dead. Her daughter is kept from me by an army of legalities that not even the great Hatcher family can pay away.

I want to tell my dad I appreciate his sympathy. Maybe I even want to close the gap between us and let him hug me. But something stops me every time. Opening up about the greatest trauma of my life means *feeling* it.

"I'll make you a deal," I offer.

"Being?" The way he's looking at me, I know he's disappointed at my avoidant behavior.

"Get rid of the new assistant and I'll go to lunch with you and Julia today."

His eyes narrow. "I thought you had lunch plans?"

I pull out my phone and pretend to check the screen. "Look at that, they just canceled."

Pressing his lips together, he shakes his head in a clear sign of disapproval. "No dice. Your assistant stays. And just so you know, she was offered a contract and salary advance. You won't be able to scare her off by being an outright dick."

"Waste of money, Dad. I don't need a babysitter."

He levels a stare, a flash of condescension crossing his face. "Then quit acting like a baby." He smacks me on the back chummily as he strides past. "Jules and I will be thinking of your starving ass as we're enjoying the best dim sum Chinatown has to offer."

"Yeah, yeah."

He hasn't won. The new girl won't last. They never do. One way or the other...my assistants always leave me.

CHAPTER 2

Spencer

"Charlie, I've stalled as long as I can but if you don't get out of this car"—I glance through the rearview mirror at the blonde woman behind us and her vicious scowl—"Karen is going to exit her vehicle and slash my tires."

"How do you even know her name? We don't know anybody in Las Vegas." My little sister, Charlotte, pouts and folds her arms over her chest.

I roll my eyes and grumble. "I don't actually know her name. 'Karen' is an expression."

"I hate it here."

We've been in Las Vegas for exactly one week and this is Charlie's constant response. She's like a parrot that only learned one phrase. Our conversations go something like, *"Hey, Charlie, want the bigger bedroom in our new apartment?"* I hate it here. *"Hey, Charlie, do you want to go shopping for new school clothes?"* I hate it here. *"Charlie, how about I make your favorite food, Cubanos?"* I slow-roasted a pork shoulder for six hours, and even found a bakery that sells Cuban bread because I know my baby sister would appreciate a little taste of home. And what did she say to my labor of love? *I really hate it here.* I should've guessed her mood would not improve on her first day of school.

"Okay, grumpy." I flick on my turn signal to try to get out of the carpool lane. "Then I'm going to have to park instead and walk you in. And just so you know, I'm going to be the most embarrassing big sister in the world. Your cheek is going to be drenched from the big, sloppy kiss I give you right in front of all your little friends."

Charlie shoots me a look from the passenger seat. She's only eleven and really shouldn't be up front, but I made an exception to help boost her confidence today. I know it sucks to be the new girl. But she's not the only one going through it. Next week, it'll be me. I loved working for Hessler Group. My boss, Hank, has become more of a mentor than anything else. It broke my heart to resign and move across the country. It wasn't my first choice. In fact, it was my last resort.

"What's that look for?"

"I don't have any friends, Spencer. All my friends are in Miami."

That's an exaggeration. Charlie has one good friend named Halley and a handful of online acquaintances she plays Roblox with. But I still feel guilty that I ripped her away from our home and moved her all the way here in the middle of the school year.

"You're going to make friends fast. I promise." I pat her knee twice, ending with a little squeeze.

She grows quiet, and my heart twists as a single tear drips down her cheek. "Why'd you do this? We had a house in Miami. Now we have a crappy apartment. You broke up with Jesse even though he's really nice. And the worst part is we left Mom."

I flick off my turn signal and relax into my seat. Clenching my teeth, I try not to cry. I know Charlie doesn't understand what Jesse did and why we had to leave. She's way too young to understand I was protecting her. I can't even ask for her forgiveness for my big fuckup because then I'd have to explain to her that she's the product of an affair. An accidental affair, but still.

It's why we look nothing alike. I'm tan-skinned with thick, naturally curly black hair. Charlie has wispy-thin blond hair and blue eyes. Charlie is a prodigy when it comes to singing. I swear my shower curtain dies inside when I use my shampoo bottle as a microphone and belt out "Roar" by Katy Perry. We're so different, I get mistaken for her nanny more often than not. But I promised my mom I'd protect her secret until my dying breath. It wasn't to spare her pride. It was so Charlie never felt like she was an accident or unwanted. We were, and always will be, a family.

I'm doing my best to keep what's left of our family together. But every time Charlie says she hates Las Vegas, or hates me—which I pretend I don't hear—it's another tiny slash at my heart. It feels like death by a thousand paper cuts.

"Okay, missy, it's time. Either grab your backpack and hop out right now, or brace yourself for that big, sloppy kiss."

"*Fine.*" She unbuckles her seat belt and yanks up her brand-new purple backpack from between her legs with as much attitude as she can muster. "But just so you know, I'm running away after school. Have a nice life."

I act like her threat doesn't faze me, even though my little sister running away is among my top-five worst fears. "All right. Travel safely. I'm just bummed you're going to miss our epic fun plans for tonight."

She sneaks a glance at me through her peripheral vision. "What plans?"

"You said we don't know anyone in Las Vegas, but you're *wrong, wrong, wrong,*" I singsong. "Remember my old boss, Lennox?"

She scrunches one eye, trying to remember. I only worked directly for Lennox for a few months before she left Miami. "Purple-hair lady?"

"There's more to her than that, but sure. She's throwing a fancy birthday party for her friend Avery tonight right on the Strip."

"The Strip is for grown-up parties. You know I can't go." Charlie scowls at me, fury flooding her eyes. "So who is babysitting me, huh?"

"Well, Debbie Downer, guess what? Lennox rented out House of Blues and it's a private event. I already checked and you can come. But if you so much as sniff anything other than water or Dr. Pepper, *so help me God—*"

"I won't. *I won't*," Charlie whines. "Are Shirley Temples okay?"

I chew on the inside of my cheek as I debate. Shirley Temples look a lot like alcoholic drinks. It takes me slipping up *once* for Child Services to swoop in and try to take Charlie from me. I was only eighteen when I took legal guardianship for a six-year-old. Everyone, including our case worker, thought I'd fail at this, but I made giving my sister a wholesome and safe childhood my life purpose.

"You can order a Shirley Temple if they put it in a sippy cup."

She groans. "You're so lame."

"Or we could just skip it?" I lift an eyebrow warningly.

"No. I want to go. I'll be good." She makes a cross above her heart and holds out her pinky—our secret sister signal. "I swear."

Looping my pinky through hers, I squeeze as tight as I can. "Is that finally a smile?"

She rolls her eyes and nods, but her sassy expression melts into a warm, wide smile.

"I love you, Charlie. I know this is a lot of change, but I promise we're going to be okay. Everything I'm doing is for you. I need you to trust me, okay?"

She opens her mouth to say something but is cut off by a loud *hoooonk* from the car behind us, making us both jump.

"Are you fucking kidding me?" I screech out as I smack the steering wheel. I'm so peeved at the Karen behind me for ruining the only sweet exchange I've had with my little sister in weeks that the curse word slipped right out. "I'm sorry. Don't say that word."

She slides me a teasing grin. "Which word?"

I touch two fingers to my temple and rub in little circles like I have a headache. "You *know*. I am trying very hard to be a good role model for you. But I'm human, and very occasionally, bad words slip out."

She cackles as she flings the passenger door wide open. "Oh please, Spence. It's not even the first time you've slipped *today*."

I point through the door. "Get out."

After blowing me a kiss, she climbs out of the SUV and slams the door shut.

"Gentle," I growl under my breath, knowing she can't hear me. This is a really nice company vehicle. They said there was insurance on it, but I don't know if I'm liable for scrapes and dings. I don't want to show up on my first day of work having already wrecked company property.

I watch Charlie walk away with a little pep in her step. I don't leave until she's through the double doors of the school, disappearing into the crowd of students. We took a tour earlier this week. She knows exactly where to go for her first-period science class.

Right as I shift into drive, there's another loud honk from behind me. My blood starts to boil. I clench my fists so hard my knuckles crack. *Don't do it, don't do it.* I try to calm down, but... *fuck it.* I throw the car back into park and put my hand on the door handle, ready to go give this pushy asshole a piece of my mind, but suddenly, something deep inside holds me back.

I'm only twenty-three. No one would be surprised if I was a hothead and cursed this B out at the top of my lungs. I'm in Las Vegas. I should be going to parties on the Strip and getting so drunk I don't remember my name. But also, I'm not *just* a twenty-three-year-old.

I sigh and release the door handle.

I'm not only her big sister, I'm the only mom Charlie has now. Everything I do could create consequences for her. What if the jerk behind me is the mother of the only friend she makes today? Or worse, the mom of her first crush? I don't get to act on impulse. Since the day my mother died five years ago, it's been my job to think of Charlie before myself.

I suck down my pride and make eye contact through the rearview mirror. After flipping on my turn signal, I hold up my palm as an apology for blocking the lane too long.

"I'm trying, Mom," I say softly, looking up to the bright blue sky through the windshield. "I *promise* you, I'm trying."

CHAPTER 3

Spencer

"Anyone up for karaoke?" our server asks as she returns with our drinks. Charlie and I have been treated like royalty all night, sitting at the birthday girl's VIP booth. It's our first time ever getting bottle service. But in solidarity with my underage sister, I've only been sipping on Shirley Temples.

"Seriously? No one?" Our server wiggles a clipboard in the air, trying to coax a response from our table. "You're at House of Blues. Look at that lonely stage. Someone has to sing."

Avoiding my gaze, Charlie reaches for the clipboard with her grabby hands. Like a reflex, I intercept the clipboard and hand it off to Lennox sitting across from me. "Just our drinks, please." I shoot Charlie a pointed look.

"Regular Sprite for you," the server murmurs, handing Charlie her fizzy mocktail. "And this one's the diet. Just a splash of grenadine and no cherry." She places a black napkin in front of me and sets my drink on top of it.

The server proceeds to hand everyone else their drinks. Mai tai for Avery, the birthday girl. A Perrier for my pregnant former boss. And some sort of scotch, bourbon, or whatever top-shelf liquor excessively rich men like to drink, for their husbands.

Lennox and Dex have been my former bosses turned friends for two years. I only met Avery and her husband, Finn, a few hours ago, and they've already all adopted me and Charlie like family. I like having girlfriends that are older than me. I get to play the little sister for once.

"No karaoke for me," Lennox says, handing the clipboard back to the server. She tucks a strand of her long brown hair behind her ear. Charlie may know her as "purple-hair lady" but Lennox stopped dyeing her hair when she got pregnant. According to her, the all-natural, organic violet tint she's been using instead can't conquer the rich brunette of her hair. It smells nice though. There's a burst of spearmint every time she throws her head back and laughs.

"Good call," her husband, Dex, says with a slick smile. He rubs her round belly affectionately. "Jake startles easily," he adds.

Lennox responds by poking her tongue out. He's not wrong. I've heard her singing. "Startling" is an understatement. It's *almost* as bad as mine.

"Jake? You finally settled on a name?" I cock my head and study the sentimental look on Dex's face.

He nods but his eyes stay glued to Lennox's stomach. "Jacob. After my grandpa."

"That's sweet." I turn my attention to Avery and Finn. "Any baby plans for you two?"

"Hopefully soon," Finn responds. He plants a soft kiss on Avery's temple, and she cuddles into him a little closer.

"Not too soon, though." Avery widens her eyes at me. "Lennox has not made pregnancy look glamorous."

"Yeah, I won't sugarcoat it. It's a living hell." She gestures to her own chest like Vanna White. "But, silver lining, my boobs look huge all the time."

"Len," Finn says, nudging her. "Little ears." He nods toward my baby sister.

"It's okay. I know what boobs are," Charlie says proudly.

Mortified, I cover my eyes with my hand. *Fantastic parenting, Spence. Truly.*

"What're you drinking, Spencer?" Lennox asks. "That looks good. I think the baby's craving sugar."

"All yours." I eagerly slide my untouched drink over to her. "It's diet though."

Lennox looks around for the waitress that disappeared. "Oh, I can get one—"

"No, please! Take it," I urge. It's the least I can do.

Having such well-off friends is uncomfortable. I've had no choice but to let them pick up the tab tonight. They also insisted on paying for dinner prior to this party. Thank *God*, because I could not afford that steakhouse. I told Charlie we had to share a meal so we weren't too much of a burden. It worked out. Charlie was way too excited for the party to have an appetite, and lately, I've been trying to eat like a bird.

To the people at this table, a thousand-dollar dinner tab is nothing. To me, the McDonald's value menu is getting a little big for its britches. I spent all the spare cash I had on a birthday present for Avery. Even after scraping up all my spare pennies, no way could I afford a designer clutch for the birthday girl. I was slightly horrified when she opened her present in front of everyone at dinner. She gave me the biggest hug and immediately swapped out her Hermès wristlet to use her new brandless purse for her party tonight. Either Avery is the most genuine, humble rich person on this planet, or she pities me.

"Oh, that hits the spot," Lennox says after taking a swig of the drink. "He's already dancing in there."

I smile at her, pleased that my small gesture made her baby happy. It's such a tender moment until Charlie opens her mouth. "Spencer, are *you* pregnant?"

"*Charlie*," I hiss. "Why would you ask me that?"

"Because your boobs look huge, too. You're popping out of your dress."

My jaw drops as I make eye contact with Lennox, then Avery. They both stare at me wide-eyed, two deer in headlights. I glance at Finn, then Dex, who are both avoiding my gaze, and my apparently ample cleavage.

"That is *so* rude," I scold my sister. "Don't ever say that to people."

"But are you though?" Her eyes are twinkling with what

looks like hope. Does she honestly think a baby would be good news? I can barely take care of the kid I have.

I push back from the table and stand, trying to hold my head high. "Would you guys mind keeping an eye on my sister for a bit? I need a minute."

"Of course," everyone seems to murmur as one.

"Where are you going?" Charlie asks innocently.

I have to forgive her because she's eleven. But for fuck's sake, hell hath no fury like a preteen with no filter. Narrowing my eyes, I answer, "To the bar. For an alcoholic drink because I am most definitely *not* pregnant."

Feeling self-conscious, I pull up on the neckline of my dress for the millionth time as I lurk by the bar. The bartender has passed by at least a dozen times, but I can't get his attention at the far end of the counter. He's too busy tending to the mosh pit that has centralized around the beer taps. I'm unbothered. It's not like I'm in a hurry to get back to my table after the way my sister humiliated me.

She wasn't always like this. Her unleashed sass is a new development. Every time I want to smack her right across the face, I force myself to picture chubby, pink cheeks, twinkly bright blue eyes, and little blond pigtails. It's hard to stay mad at five-year-old Charlie. She was so damn cute. And I know that sweet little girl is still in there, *somewhere*.

I'm not even really angry at her overt curiosity. It was an inappropriate time to ask me if I'm pregnant, sure, but her question hurt because her observation was spot-on. This is an old party dress and it used to fit me much better. Now that I'm off my medication, I'm gaining weight. Evidently, it's noticeable.

But what choice do I have? Food, shelter, phones, internet, and school supplies are all more crucial than my pant size. It doesn't mean my expanding waistline isn't tormenting me. I'm dieting—and by dieting I mean, hardly eating. But every time I step on the scale, the number keeps creeping up.

"Can't get a drink?"

I'm so startled, I yelp like a puppy. To my left, a strikingly handsome—*oh screw the formalities*—a smokin' hot, sexy Adonis with golden-brown hair and deep blue-green eyes is staring at me.

"Where'd you come from?"

"Thin air, apparently." He smirks. "I thought you saw me. I didn't mean to scare you." For the briefest moment his gaze drops to my chest before snapping back to my eyes. It was so quick, it's possible I imagined it. Or maybe it was even unintentional. Either way, it summoned my self-consciousness again and I yank up on the neckline of my dress. The problem is I yank too hard, causing my miniskirt to ride up so high my underwear is exposed. Quickly overcorrecting, I hastily pull the dress down and I swear I can almost hear the *pop, pop* as my breasts break free from the deep V-neck. *Oh, dammit to hell.* With one hand clenched around my neckline, and the other fiercely gripping the hem of my dress, I silently vow to throw this outfit away the moment I get home.

"Are you okay?" He looks genuinely concerned for my sanity.

"You checked me out," I say, unclutching my dress. "My sister just told me I'm too fat for this dress and bursting out all over the place, so I..." I roll my wrist in a manner that says *etcetera*. I don't need to elaborate. He saw firsthand the awkward dance I just did.

"You have scratch marks on your chest."

"Excuse me?" His statement takes me completely off guard.

"I wasn't checking you out. You have red marks here." He pats his chest, illustrating the area of concern. "That's what caught my attention. It looks like somebody tried to grab you. Not to mention you're standing here alone by the bar, fidgeting, looking like you're about to cry. I was putting the pieces together."

"Oh, I must've accidentally scratched myself." I've been fussing with this dress too much. But I'm shocked at his observation. How long has he been watching me to come up with that hypothesis? "I'm perfectly fine. Outside of the whole sister-calling-me-fat thing."

"Sisters can be a pain."

Understatement. "So you get it."

He clamps one eye shut and grimaces. "Honestly? I'm an only child. But it seemed like the right thing to say at the moment."

Little beads of sweat form on my spine. *Holy hell. Here we go.* First I overheat, next comes the loud, dorky laughter, and if this man doesn't run right now, he's going to be lassoed by my incessant chatter all night. At twenty-three, I still haven't mastered flirting. Probably better not to risk it with a man this good looking. I see more humiliation in my future. Smiling, I turn around, hoping he gets the hint.

"And no offense to your sister, but she needs to get her eyes checked. Your dress is..." I spin back around when he trails off. His gaze is shifted to the side like he's trying to buy time.

"*Is?*" I prod.

"It looks nice on you." He lands on a safe answer, instead of something more provocative, and there's a little drop of disappointment in my stomach.

"You were concerned I was attacked. You're keeping a pretty safe distance between us. And you most definitely weren't checking out my rack. So, are you genuinely a nice guy, or is this all an act? Because if it is, *bravo*. You've really committed to the character."

He laughs heartily. "Before I came over here, for some reason I got the impression you were shy."

"Well now, don't you feel silly?" I beam proudly as I hold out my hand. "I'm Spencer."

"Nate."

As we shake, I notice two things. First, my thumbnail is already chipped from the manicure I gave myself this morning with the cheap drugstore nail polish. Second, he's wearing a two-hundred-thousand-dollar watch. I recognize the crown logo, the unique icy-blue dial, and triple counters. That's a collector's watch. I know this because the very same Rolex is on Jesse's vision board right next to a bright orange Lamborghini Urus.

I always dreamed of a family. Jesse dreamed of being filthy

rich.

"That's a beautiful watch," I say, carefully watching his reaction.

He tugs his cuff down, covering it up. "Thank you. I like your—" He stops midsentence, and noticeably surveys my ears, then wrist. He must be looking for jewelry to compliment, except I'm not wearing any. "Lips," he finally says.

Nice save.

The silent lull between us is quickly filled by a drunken slur over the loudspeaker. At first, it seems like someone's grabbed a mic from the stage and is trying to cause a scene. A verse or two later of butchered lyrics to Taylor Swift's "Cruel Summer" and I realize karaoke has commenced.

Nate and I wear matching horrified expressions. "Wow," I say, resisting the urge to cover my ears. "At least some people are cheering."

"I don't think we're as drunk as they are."

I laugh. "I haven't had anything to drink. Can't get the bartender to pay attention to me." I glance over my shoulder at the man in all black, still tending to the mob.

"Pull your dress down again. That might help our case." Nate winks at me, sending a quick tremor up my spine. I feel a little guilty for enjoying this. Jesse and I just broke up. But unforgivable lines were crossed. Trust was broken. We're done. How much longer do I have to mourn the death of our relationship?

I bat my eyelashes. "My breasts are safely tucked away. We'll have to think of something else."

He leans in close, and a whisper of his cologne envelops me. There's a hint of citrus, sweetening the smell of earth and musk. I'm lost for a moment. I don't know what the hell that scent is, but it's...it's...beguiling.

"I have bottle service at my table," he says in a husky voice.

"Then why are you slumming it at the bar with us common folk?"

He lifts his brows. "Why do you think?"

I shake my head. "I don't want to lead you on. There's no way in hell I'm going home with you. I came with my sister. I'm leaving with her too."

"You're getting ahead of yourself. I only offered you a drink."

"That's it?" I ask skeptically, folding my arms.

"That's it."

"Why waste your money on a girl who won't sleep with you?"

I hope the grin on his face means he appreciates my candidness. He pops his shoulders with nonchalance. "Because I have money to waste."

Cocky. Or maybe, *honest*? I don't know but my curiosity has me in a choke hold, so when he offers his hand, I take it. "*Just one drink.*" But I think I'm warning myself more than him.

Nate cups his hand with mine in what can only be described as platonically. It's the way a security guard would guide a celebrity to a table—just gentlemanly. By the time we get to the velvet rope blocking his circular booth, I'm concerned his ulterior motives have nothing to do with sex and instead I'm going to meet a gory end before he stores the pieces of my body in a chest freezer locked in his basement.

He unhooks the rope and gestures for me to slide into the booth, but my feet stay planted.

"Did you change your mind?" he asks casually.

"You're not a serial killer, right?"

He wets his lips before showing me a mischievous grin. "If I was, do you really think I'd tell you?"

I tilt my head like a puppy that just heard, *walk*? "I suppose, if you were a sloppy killer."

"Sloppy is not my style."

"So you're either a killer and a skilled liar. Or, you're luring me into a false sense of security and sex really is your endgame." He opens his mouth, but I hold up my pointer finger indicating I'm not done. "Or, you're actually a nice guy and I've officially watched too much *Dateline* which is why I live in a constant state of paranoia."

"You done?"

"Yes."

"Fourth option—I was in a serious relationship that ended abruptly and I'm still not over it. Maybe I like the fact that you're not so eager to jump into bed because I'm not dating right now and all I can handle is whatever this is."

Oh, geez. I jumped to serial killer before considering that maybe he's newly single and not trying to rebound. It's official. No more *Dateline*. "So just flirting?" I ask sheepishly.

"Is this flirting? When I used to meet women in bars, flirting seemed less...accusatory."

"I'm sorry. I'll be nice now. You know what? To make it up to you, how about I buy *you* a drink?" I instantly regret my words because what if he takes me up on that, and judging by his watch, the kind of liquor he drinks probably costs my monthly rent.

"Thank you. But if you stay, I'm buying. Nonnegotiable. I won't pressure you, though." He moves past me and slides into the booth before looking back at me. "Your choice."

CHAPTER 4

Nathan

I really expected her to leave. But I'm glad she didn't.

I'm only here tonight to talk to Finn Harvey. He's in town for one more night before he whisks his new wife off to Greece for a two-week vacation. I can't wait two weeks for an answer about the lot his grandpa owns. It's a determining factor on too many moving pieces for Dad's new project.

A simple call wasn't enough. I'm asking an old friend for a favor after dropping the ball on communication for years. At the bare minimum, I meant to buy him a nice wagyu steak, but he didn't have time for dinner. My only choice was to accept his invitation and catch him tonight before he leaves. But once I got here, I felt like an ass, crashing his wife's birthday party just to talk business. I was stalling when I spotted Spencer by the bar.

It all started out as a dare I made with myself. Dad is only forcing new executive assistants on me because he thinks I'm lonely. Maybe if I go on a date or two, that'll be enough to appease him and he'll let me work in peace.

Spencer's scouring the menu so hard you'd think she was choosing a permanent tattoo, not a drink that will disappear in ten minutes. "Nothing looks good?" I ask.

"The opposite," she answers, not looking up. "Everything looks good and I only get one."

She's cute. And so accidentally sexy. But I won't let my mind go there. I refuse to think about her rich complexion, or the beautiful contrast of her thick, dark hair fixed in loose curls, falling all over her tan shoulders. She's far from a stick figure, and I will absolutely not allow myself to imagine how her soft curves would feel in my hands.

It's been three years since Elise died. The first year, the topic of women was a nonissue. They didn't exist in my world. By the end of year two, I'll admit I felt lonely from time to time. On occasion I was tempted to bring a woman home purely for physical gratification, but the guilt always stopped me. A little guilt because I knew I only wanted a woman to keep me company for one night. And the deeper guilt because once I sleep with someone else, Elise won't be my last. The moment I cross that line, everything changes. Everything will fall apart. I'd just rather not have sex.

"I'm happy to buy you more than one."

"Oh yeah, hotshot?" She finally looks up with her big, brown eyes and winks at me. "Think you can afford it?"

"I'll move some money around."

Her chuckle is light and airy. She seems to have relaxed some. Her nervous laughter before at the bar sounded a bit like a horse whinny. "That's generous of you. But seriously, just one drink. I have to keep my wits about me tonight."

"Why?"

"There are lots of extremely handsome men here with indecent intentions." She waggles her eyebrows.

"Hey, I thought I was off trial."

"Sorry." She covers her eyes as she shakes her head. "That one slipped right out. I'm just teasing. This is nice, actually. I needed a break from my table. Plus we're so close to the stage"—she lowers her voice—"we can almost see the sweat on the performers."

"If you're calling this awful karaoke a performance, then forget the drinks." I grab the menu and slide it away from her. "You're belligerent and you need to be cut off."

"Ha! Be nice. They are trying. Some of them are...decent."

Clearly she's the kind of woman who likes to put a positive spin on things. "Are you going to get up there?"

"Oh yes." The look on her face is dead serious. "I'm the final act at closing. How else do you think they're going to clear out this party in a hurry?"

"Your singing is that bad?"

"Impressively abysmal."

I can't remember the last time I laughed this much. Definitely feels like a different lifetime. "Hey, can you scoot closer?"

Her smile fades as she folds her thumb into her fist for the umpteenth time. It's a nervous tic I'm starting to notice. "How close?"

"As close as you're comfortable with."

She moves a few inches toward the center of the booth, but we're still half an arm's length apart. After a brief pause, she sucks in a deep breath and shimmies closer until my thigh is pressed against hers. It feels natural, so I lift my arm above her shoulders. "This okay?" I check.

When she nods, I rest my arm around her, feeling how hot her skin is. If she's telling the truth and she hasn't had a drop of alcohol tonight, then this heat must be because I'm making her nervous. I like that.

I lean over to whisper against her ear. "I have an idea." She flinches when my lips touch her earlobe, then quickly steadies herself. "What if we order every drink off the cocktail menu but only take one sip of each? That way it's still one drink, but you don't miss out on anything."

"That's a pricey bar tab just to strike out."

"Obviously I'm hoping you're a lightweight and that one drink changes your mind. You know, indecent intentions and all."

I'm so close I get to feel her laugh, not just hear it. Her cheeks bounce and her body jolts as she giggles. "I don't think I've ever met a guy as sarcastic as I am."

"Then we were destined."

"Seems that way."

She claps her hands together. "Okay. I'm in. Eight drinks. One sip each. Maybe two sips from the pineapple mojito because that sounds divine."

"Done." I raise my free hand in the air and it takes a split second for the waitress to appear. She became extra attentive earlier this evening when I gave her my black card to open my tab. "One of everything," I say, tapping the menu.

"Beer too?"

I look at Spencer. She quickly makes a face before shaking her head.

"Only the cocktails. Thanks."

"Coming right up." The waitress retreats from the table and makes a beeline to the bar. She's smart. If she plays her cards right and does a good job, the tips she gets from the VIP tables tonight could probably make a couple car payments.

Spencer's phone lights up and she leans forward to glance at a message preview. Satisfied with whatever she received, she relaxes back. Instead of only tolerating my arm wrapped around her shoulders, she nuzzles into me. "I'm not trying to be too forward, but shit, you smell really good." She breathes in deeply to make her point.

"Really?"

"I'm not sure if I'm turned on, or I want to ask you where you bought your cologne so I can pick up a bottle for myself."

I ignore the pang of guilt twisting in my gut. *She's not coming back, Nate.*

I've taken a few women out on dates in the past year or so. Nothing even came close to a spark, until now. This is a good, small step. I have no intention of asking Spencer for her number. I'll never see her again, so maybe it's safe to toe the line.

"I'm pretty sure you're turned on," I rasp into her ear.

Her hand slinks onto the edge of my knee. Not high enough to be sleazy, but enough of a touch for me to translate it as an invitation. I pull her long locks away from her shoulder and behind her back. For the first time, I let my eyes fall to her chest, giving myself full permission to enjoy the deep crevice of her cleavage.

"Or, at least, I'm turned on," I admit.

She rotates her head, her cheek rubbing against mine, before her eyes are set on my own. We're so close our lips are touching. We're not kissing. Just lips grazing, waiting for someone to make the first move.

"I love this song," she murmurs, her breath tickling my mouth. "Do you know it?"

Of course I recognize the famous piano prelude. I'm already cringing for whoever is about to brutalize Alicia Keys's "If I Ain't Got You" on the karaoke machine. "I know it. I can play it too."

"You play piano?"

"Mhm." I don't elaborate. I've lost interest in anything other than succumbing to the urge to kiss her. I lean into Spencer, wanting to feel the pressure of her soft lips on mine, but the very moment the singer starts, she pulls away and her attention snaps to the stage.

I understand why. The singer is breathtakingly good. "I guess the birthday girl actually hired a performer for tonight."

"No, she didn't," Spencer chokes out. Staring at the stage, the color drains from her face.

Curious about what's spooked her, I follow her eyes. I'm shocked to see a little blonde-haired girl with the microphone. Based on the voice alone, I was expecting a woman in her thirties, seasoned, experienced. Her voice is rich and soulful. As the song progresses, she toggles effortlessly from the deep baritone to a melodic soprano with perfect pitch. She's singing like a talented professional.

"Holy shit, it's a kid?"

Spencer doesn't answer. Instead, her gaze is darting around the room. This little girl has commanded the attention of an entire club and silenced a mob of drunken partygoers. That's how spectacular she sounds.

"They're all recording," Spencer gasps. "Everybody is recording."

"Not a bad idea. I've never in my life heard a child sing like that before." I pull out my phone. Pointing it to the stage, I press record.

"Stop." *Whack!* She smacks my phone right out of my hand. It bounces off the table and I have to retrieve it off the floor. Straightening up in my seat, I toss my broken phone on the table, showing off the shattered screen.

"What is wrong with you?" It comes out harsher than I mean it to. I'm not upset about my phone. I'm so clumsy with it myself, I swear I have to get a new one every few weeks.

She runs her finger over the cracked ceramic. "Oh God. I broke it." Tears well in her eyes.

"It's new. I didn't get a chance to put a case on it. It's not a big deal. Are you okay?"

The song finally comes to a close, and amongst the loud clapping and cheering, a low rumble of "encore, encore" begins to fill the club.

"I'm sorry," she says as she breaks free from our embrace. "It was a reflex. I wasn't thinking. I'm so sorry."

I try to grab her hand but she's too quick. She scoots away out of my reach. I want to assure her I don't give a shit about the phone. I just want to know what set her off. Did I move too fast or pressure her?

"Spencer? Wait. What's—"

"It was nice to meet you, Nate." She doesn't even look back as she flees.

Stunned, confused, and a little pissed, all I can do is watch her disappear into the crowd.

What the fuck just happened?

I know better than to follow her. I should've known better and kept tonight strictly business.

This is why I don't date.

CHAPTER 5

Spencer

"Charlie, slow down," I call after my little sister. She's clumsily stomping up the concrete stairs to our third-floor apartment. She's going to trip and bust her lip out of sheer anger. "I don't want you to get hurt."

"Why do you care?" she snaps.

"Because you're my sister." Also, I'm not looking forward to paying the full deductible on our health insurance if we end up in the ER tonight.

Charlie stops and awkwardly pivots in the middle of the flight of stairs. She stumbles, her front knee buckling. Three steps behind, I throw out both arms as a reflex, waiting for her to fall forward, but she catches herself. "I'm *not*. I don't have a sister anymore."

Arms crossed, cheeks blotchy red, and a mean scowl on her face, she wants to look dangerous. But I know Charlie too well. It's obvious to me when she's trying to hold back tears.

"Well, that's just not true. I'm still your sister even when you're mad at me."

I panicked back there. I all but ripped Charlie off the stage at House of Blues, then threw her ass in a Lyft. I texted Lennox that I wasn't feeling well and needed to make an emergency exit.

My reaction was dramatic, but I saw all the phones recording and I know people's intentions. Charlie is an easy way to cash in on views. She's a phenomenon, and when she's old enough, I can't wait to see her take over the world. But, for now, in the age of digital danger all around, I have to protect her from being exploited online.

I seem to be the only one concerned about normalcy for Charlie. She already grew up without a dad. She lost her mom at age six. She had an eighteen-year-old signing permission slips and dropping her off at kindergarten. How much more can she go through? I read the stories about child pop stars and the atrocities they've endured in exchange for a life of fortune and fame. I refuse to let her life turn into an after-school special.

"Like I said back at the club, I am never speaking to you again."

"Okay. Starting when? Because you just spoke to me."

She stamps her foot, the thud echoing through the stairwell. "You don't get it, do you? *I hate you.* You never let me sing. You're just jealous because you sound like a dying cat when you try to sing."

Hurtful, but accurate. "I'm not jealous of you, Charlie."

At least, not in the way she thinks.

I'm jealous because Charlie doesn't worry for me. She's not scared of failing as a parent. She doesn't lie awake at night afraid that somebody could take me away. That's *my* job. Mom offered me an out when we found out she was sick. She was going to make arrangements for Charlie to be cared for by a distant relative, but I refused. I promised her I'd keep our family together and would protect my little sister. Except, talking is easy. Walking it out is much harder.

A hot breeze sweeps past us. Even at midnight, there's no relief from the heat of a Vegas summer. Drops of sweat bead on her forehead. Her jean shorts touch the top of her knees. I wouldn't let her wear a tank top tonight even though she wanted to. I made her put on a cropped cardigan so she wasn't showing too much skin. It was fine in the air-conditioned club, but out here, she's burning up. Maybe I'm overly protective of my little sister, but I'm terrified of Charlie being victimized and humiliated the way I once was.

"Come on. I'm tired." Reaching down, I pull off my gold,

strappy sandals that are starting to dig into my skin. I sigh in relief when my bare feet touch the concrete, my toes no longer strangled. "Let's go home."

I continue to ascend the stairs, past Charlie. When I don't hear her footsteps behind me, I stop on the landing and turn to see her glistening eyes.

"I'm not going." Her tears pool, armed and ready to drop to the ground like little grenades of frustration. In moments like these, I want to be her big sister, not her mom. I want to complain with her that it's not fair and Mom's just being overprotective for no reason. But I have to do what's right. Not what feels good.

"Charlie, move it. Mad or not, you're sleeping in your bed tonight. Not outside."

"But you said 'let's go home.'" She sniffles and paws at her face with the back of both hands, trying to control the tears that are now in full force.

"So?" I jab my finger up the final flight of stairs toward apartment 3F.

Instead of storming past me as I expected, she drags her feet softly. Her shoulders slump. She leaves a trail of tear splashes behind her. Quietly, so I can barely hear her, she says, "This isn't our home."

I didn't bark at Charlie to brush her teeth and wash her face last night. She was so upset, I let her slip into her room and shut and lock the door behind her. I'm sure her pillow is smeared with the glittery eye shadow I let her borrow.

Surprisingly, I fell asleep easily. The drama of the night took me out. Not surprisingly, I dreamed about *him*. Sexy, suave, sweet Nate who I absolutely blew my chances with.

As I whisk the pancake mix into my french toast batter, I scrunch my toes against the tile floor, reliving the nightmare of embarrassment. Within a split second I went from almost kissing

SELFIE

Mr. Too Hot to Handle, to smashing his phone and fleeing the scene. We didn't even kiss in my *dream*. He was shirtless and giving me a foot rub, though. While I, for some reason, had on a bright orange terrycloth onesie. I'm so out of touch with my own sexuality that even in my dreams I'm awkward.

Jesse would rarely ask for sex. I caught him several times satisfying his urges with his dick in one hand and cell phone in the other watching porn. He claimed sex alone was sometimes just quicker than sex together—simply a means to an end.

But I knew it was me. I was the problem. Sex was so ritualistic. I'd have to be perfectly shaved, freshly showered, and it could only happen at night under the cover of darkness. I only owned one pair of bikini-cut black underwear that actually made me feel sexy. If I were even slightly bloated, it was all off the table.

So that wasn't fair to my ex-fiancé. By the time he'd initiate intimacy, the poor guy would have to wait a solid hour for me to "get ready." And we both knew there was zero chance of him getting me off. I'd be too preoccupied with how much of my body he could see and what's jiggling or dimpled. The very *last* thing I think about during sex is having an actual orgasm.

I bet Nate's the kind of guy who is used to his dates screaming at the top of their lungs with their face buried in a pillow. It's good nothing happened between us. He would've been sorely disappointed. Unless he stayed for breakfast, in which case, I would've wowed him. What I lack in bedroom skills, I make up for in spades with my cooking.

The entire apartment is now aromatic with salty bacon and scrambled eggs, thick, fluffy french toast, and fresh-squeezed orange juice. But there's still no Charlie in sight. Rolling my eyes, I shove a fork into her eggs, grab her plate and glass of orange juice, then head to her room.

I'm amazed to find the door unlocked and the tiniest bit cracked open. Either she had to pee in the middle of the night and forgot to lock it back, or this is her peace offering. The effort we put into making up after a fight is a little unbalanced. I make her a beautiful full-spread breakfast filled with her favorite foods. She begrudgingly unlocks her door.

"Charlie?" Hands full, I knock with my elbow, sending the door wide open. She's sitting on her bed, covers draped over her lap, with a thick scrapbook open in front of her.

"I'm sorry." She hurries her words like she's been waiting to say them all morning.

"Me too." I hold up the plate and cup. "Peace offering?"

Her cheeks bunch up as she smiles, reminding me of five-year-old Charlie. A flood of both warmth and guilt washes over me at once. I quickly cross the room, set her food on the nightstand, then tackle her with a big hug. Charlie squeals as I plant kisses all over her head and cheeks, while tickling the ever-loving daylights out of her. It takes her a full minute to fight me off, pushing against my stomach with her heel.

"Stooop," she manages to whine, even though she's breathless between giggles. She makes a protective barrier with her body over the photo album. "You're going to rip it."

"Okay, okay. I'm done. What page are you looking at?"

Charlie straightens out, then falls backward against the cloth headboard. She taps the black album page with her toe. "Is this Mom's real hair or a wig?"

We have dozens of scrapbooks and albums. They're treated like bibles—holy and sacred. Scrapbooking was a hobby of Mom's, but when she got sick, it became an obsession. It was her mission to document as much as she could for Charlie. I was there. I got the memories. Charlie gets the pictures.

Hunching over, I study the four-by-six image of our mom at the beach. It's rare she's alone in a photograph. I must've taken this one. I remember this day because the sky was so peculiar. There was a purple haze over the entire shore. Mom and I stood awestruck in violet-colored sand, watching the ocean that looked like it was on fire the way the sun's final rays were cast in bright red strips.

"Real hair. It was before she got sick," I answer softly. Mom hated wigs. They were itchy and heavy, but she wore them after chemo took her hair, mostly for me, I think. So I wasn't so obviously reminded every time I looked at her that our days together were numbered. "She didn't know it yet, but she was pregnant with you in this one."

Charlie screws up her face. "How can you be pregnant and not know it? Don't you feel the baby moving in your stomach?"

There will come a day I'll have to explain the nitty-gritty of sperm, eggs, and implantation to Charlie. That day sure as hell is not today.

"She hadn't taken a test yet. You only know for sure when you take a test."

"Can I ask you a question? But don't be mad." Her cautious tone already warns me I'm not going to like this question one bit.

"Sure, but tread carefully. We just made up."

She folds her hands in her blanket-covered lap and taps the tips of her thumbs together. "Have *you* taken a test?"

I let out a tortured growl. *Again with this?* "Charlotte Riley, I swear—"

"You just said you don't know for sure unless you take a test."

My eyes fall shut and I pinch the bridge of my nose, breathing through my exasperation. If she were any other woman, I'd be tempted to smack her, but because she's my little sister, I have to spell this out clearly. "Do you understand this hurts my feelings? You don't ask a woman if she's pregnant unless you see the baby popping out. Even then, feigning a little surprise that she was growing a person is polite. It's girl code one oh one."

She squints one eye. "What's feigning mean?"

Did she even hear my point? I take a steadying breath, schooling my irritation. "It means faking. So yes, I'm gaining weight because I'm not taking my...*vitamins* anymore, and it's very hard for me. So you should *feign* support by not calling me fat, or bringing any attention to my body in front of our friends."

The color drains from her face as her eyes widen and her lips fall apart. "Is that why you got mad and left me at the club?"

"I didn't leave you."

She cuts me a look that says what she's not allowed to say out loud—*Bullshit*.

"Okay, fine. I didn't leave you for long," I add.

"You were gone ages," she snivels. "What were you doing?"

"Scoot." I gingerly close the scrapbook and set it aside on the floor. Pulling back the comforter, I wiggle in so close to my sister, I'm practically sitting on top of her. After covering us both back up, I nudge her knee with mine under the blanket. "I met a guy."

Charlie grows quiet for a moment as she stares straight ahead. "Was he cute?"

"*So cute*." Because she's way too young for me to say "rideable."

"Was he nice?"

I nod. "And polite, and considerate. Kind of funny, too."

She scowls at me. "Is he in your bedroom?"

"*What*? Of course not. I left him when I heard you singing. Speaking of which, do you realize how dangerous that was? How did you even give Lennox and Dex the slip and get on stage?" I thought I made my position quite clear when I snatched that signup form out of her hands.

"I didn't escape them. I told them you texted me and said it was okay."

"And they believed you?"

"I guess." She shrugs without an ounce of remorse on her face.

Rookie mistake. Always verify the text. Eleven is one of the worst ages for this nonsense. They are young enough they're still believably innocent, but smart enough to be very skilled at the art of lying.

Looking around the bedroom, it dawns on me how out of place Charlie looks in here. My new company owns this complex and offered us a furnished apartment at half the cost of normal rent. Of course I jumped. I wasn't sure how to split furniture with Jesse, so I left it all behind. This unit is decent. The shower is free of mold and mildew. There are no questionable stains on the carpet. All the blinds are intact and functional. But it feels like a businessperson's home away from home. Not a little girl's room.

"We should decorate," I announce. "What do you think? We can't paint, but how about a new bedspread and matching curtains? We could also get a cute nightstand and dresser."

There's a little twinkle in her bright blue eyes. "But you said we can't spend money anymore. We're poor."

"We're being frugal and trying to save money, but we're okay. We can afford some new furniture. Nothing too crazy. IKEA stuff. Let's at least add some color to this room." It's a partial lie. We really can't responsibly afford new stuff, but for this, I'll max out my credit card. Charlie deserves a room she loves.

She nods, her smile widening as she takes in a panoramic view of her space. I'm sure endless ideas are running through her mind. I hope she understands I draw the line at One Direction wallpaper. *Not happening.*

"Is this a good time for me to bargain?"

Charlie's question takes me by surprise. "Bargain? What do you mean?"

"If I tell you a secret and I promise not to lie ever again, could I get something I really want in return?"

My stomach drops as my heart starts to race. This can't be good. "What secret?"

She seals her lips shut and shakes her head.

"Fine," I grumble. "What exactly do you want?"

"A pet. A small one."

"What *kind* of pet?" Dear Lord, please do not let my little sister be in a reptile phase. I shudder thinking about Jesse's bearded dragon, Smaug, I had to tolerate for the two years we lived together. Smaug had eyes like the *Mona Lisa*; he was stone-still, but no matter where I was in the living room, his gaze was always *on me*.

Charlie holds her shoulders like she's bracing for impact. That's how bad she wants this. "So, I sort of made a friend at school yesterday. Claire."

I pat her knee excitedly. "On your first day? That's great. I told you you'd make friends quickly."

"Claire's in seventh grade. She's popular too, so she didn't have to sit by me at lunch but she did anyway so I wasn't alone."

"Aw, that's nice."

"Well, she has these guinea pigs, and her grandma says one has to go because they keep humping."

"They keep *what*?" Oh. This conversation just took a turn. Damn.

"Humping," Charlie says, again nonchalantly. "I don't know, that's what animals do to make babies. Right? Or is it just guinea pigs?"

Oh no. Oh, no, no. Immediate conversation dodge. "So you want one of her guinea pigs?"

Charlie presses her hands together as if she's praying. "The guinea pigs love each other but Claire's grandma says they have to split up. But if I keep one and Claire keeps one, then when we hang out, the guinea pigs can still play sometimes. That way they don't have to break up for real."

"And then Claire will want to hang out with you so her little pigs can see each other?"

Charlie shrugs. "That too."

I could lie and tell Charlie that our apartment doesn't allow pets. But haven't I put her through enough? "I'll need to talk to Claire's grandma, but I think we can make that work."

She gasps, then tents her hands over mouth and nose. I give her dramatic reaction a moment to simmer. "Seriously?" she finally asks.

"Seriously. But I want to know the secret now."

She hangs her head. "You know how you said I'm not allowed to be on TikTok or Instagram?"

My eyes narrow. "Yes."

"*I'm not*," she says quickly. "But I make singing videos and send them to Jesse. He made an account and one of the videos went viral. He texted me this morning."

A wave of fury takes me out of my body. My mind blanks as my limbs go numb momentarily. By the time I unball my fists, there are deep indents in my palm from where my nails nearly broke the skin. "Don't do that anymore, okay? I want you to stop texting Jesse or I'll take your phone away. Do you understand?" I try to keep my tone neutral, but I'm breathing fire and screaming atrocities on the inside.

"Yes."

"But thank you for telling me, Charlie."

"Can I still have the guinea pig?"

My eyelid starts to twitch. No matter how much I blink, I can't calm the little nerve down. "Fine. Now, eat your breakfast. I even got boysenberry syrup for you." Pulling off the covers, I swing my legs over the side of the bed. "I'm going to clean up the kitchen."

"One more thing," Charlie says as I near the door. She has no idea I'm in arm's reach of an aneurysm.

"Yes?"

"I don't think you're fat. I think you're the prettiest woman in the whole world. I just thought that if you were pregnant, it means you and Jesse would get back together. We could go home and be a real family."

I keep my gaze fixed on her sad eyes. I wonder if this is how Mom felt at times after my dad left. Did she feel the pressure to make us *whole*? I wish I could ask her what she'd do when her heart ached like this. Because no matter how much I sacrifice, and how quickly I force myself to grow up to be more of a mom than a sister, it's not enough. There's a hole in my little sister's heart that she's trying to fill with a greedy, materialistic snake.

"Charlie, we *are* a real family. Small, but real. We don't need a man and a baby to complete us."

She ducks her head. "Okay," she murmurs. I'm sure my words are in one ear, out the other. I close the door behind me and hurry to my phone in my bedroom.

With inhuman speed, I unblock Jesse. I consider a text

message, but it's not enough. Not even a slew of profanity in bold, capital letters can convey my anger.

He answers on the first ring. "Spencer?"

The background noise is near deafening. "Where are you?"

"Courthouse," he says. "One of my firm's divorce cases escalated to trial. We're dealing with a mess—"

"I don't care," I interject, cutting him off before he can continue rambling about work. "I'll make this quick. Stop contacting Charlie. End of story."

"What? I—"

"You put her on the internet, you psychopath! Have you lost your fucking mind?"

"Spence, calm down. I didn't put her face online. Just her voice."

"*I don't care*! I can't believe you're still doing this. She is not your get-rich-quick plan, you selfish asshole."

"Selfish? Spence, you've got this all wrong." The background noise quiets after a door slams. Jesse's voice is now echoing. "Everything I've done has been for us. I'm trying to take care of us."

I scoff so hard my throat scratches. "Bullshit. *Bull-fucking-shit.* You're filling her head with these asinine dreams of being the next Taylor Swift while you slowly drain every penny her dad left her. That's all she has, Jesse. No dad, no mom, *nothing* except a little money to help get through college and to adulthood."

"She has us."

"Wrong. She has *me*." Which isn't saying much because I'm the idiot who let Jesse trick me. "You lied to me. You manipulated me into signing everything over to you. And you know the worst part? I don't know who I hate more. You, for taking everything from us, or me, for being foolish enough to trust you."

"You're just too young and naive to understand. I have a plan. I'll get the money back, easily. This is insanity. You packed up your shit and just disappeared in the middle of the night with Charlie? You're so immature."

This has been the entire narrative of our relationship. Jesse calls me a child, and I shrivel because I'm scared he's right. I was always enamored that Jesse was older and smarter. He's a lawyer, for God's sake. I thought I found a good one. I didn't realize he spent four years at law school learning how to be even more conniving than he already was.

"You still there?" he asks after neither of us says anything for a solid minute.

"No," I answer. It kills me that he chuckles. I wasn't trying to be funny, but like it or not, sarcasm tends to be my primary communication style.

"I'm sorry. How do I fix this, baby? Come home and I'll do anything. You can't support Charlie and yourself on your own. You need me."

He almost had me. In a brief moment of vulnerability, I just wanted him to pull a hero move and make it right. But when Jesse says he doesn't believe I can do this by myself, he means it. The ledger against him is too long now. He treats me like a child. He doesn't include me in decisions big or small, like where we're going to live, or what we're having for dinner. The man proposed without a ring, twisting the story as if he couldn't afford the ring I deserved. I would've proudly worn a Ring Pop if it came from his heart.

If Mom were here today, she'd tell me to trust my intuition and to never ever let a man, or anyone for that matter, tell me what I'm capable of.

"Jesse, you can fix this by leaving my sister alone. The next time you contact her, I'll file a restraining order. Clear?"

I hang up before he can say another word.

He thinks I can't do this on my own?

Watch me.

CHAPTER 6

Spencer

On my first day of work, Charlie came through for me. She was up early—dressed for school, teeth and hair brushed. Opting for cereal, to save me the trouble of making breakfast, she even rinsed her bowl before putting it in the dishwasher. If she keeps up this behavior, I'll buy her a whole freaking guinea pig farm.

Claire invited Charlie to sit at the "cool table" and get pizza for lunch. Grade-school politics haven't changed. You still have to be *invited* to plant your ass on a particular cafeteria seat, but Charlie seems excited, so I'll call it a win. The school serves Domino's pizza at four dollars for a slice and a canned soda. I handed her a ten-dollar bill this morning just in case. Sweet as pie, Charlie asked me if I had enough cash left over for my lunch. I showed her my diet-friendly strawberry protein drink and told her I was all set, ignoring her look of concern.

My morning continued to sparkle from there. To my surprised delight, I have my own parking spot. There's a row of spots right by the elevator for all the executive assistants. I've worked for the CEO of a billion-dollar company before, but I never got my own parking spot. It's probably so we can be quick about errands, but still, it feels pretty glamorous parking my company car in a dedicated spot.

Maybe Las Vegas is actually an upgrade, not just an escape.

I literally whistled a happy tune in the elevator ride from the garage to the lobby of Brickstone Property Ventures. Overcome with first day nerves, I was really expecting a disaster this morning, but it's all smooth sailing as I enter the front lobby of the massive headquarters.

I weave through a cluster of businessmen all wearing suits and ties. I wore my most impressive black business dress with the cap sleeves, smart collar, and a gold-colored buckle in the front. There's something about how gold shines against black, making me look far more sophisticated than I am. Hell, I actually seem to fit right in.

"Good morning," I say as I reach the receptionist who is seated behind a large, wall-to-wall concierge desk. It looks more like a marble slab bunker than a work desk. "I'm Spencer Riley-Brenner. It's my first day working for Mr. James Hatcher."

She smiles and winks. "We all work for Mr. Hatcher, honey." I'm not sure if she's old enough to be calling me "honey." She barely looks thirty. Do I really look like a baby to everybody except Charlie? "Are you with the sales and customer service new hire class? Because orientation is in Meeting Hall A on the second floor. Let me grab you a map of the building." She swivels around in her chair, rummaging through pamphlets.

"I'm not in sales or service. I'm Mr. Hatcher's new executive assistant."

She spins back around, slowly. Her face is wrinkled with suspicion. "Who told you that? Because Dawn Pryce is Mr. Hatcher's assistant and has been for the past fifteen years."

Bile bubbles up in the back of my throat as I take in her perplexed look. We are in the midst of a huge misunderstanding, and I pray I'm not the one who's confused. I already got the company car and apartment, but I don't get my salary advance until thirty days into employment. If I don't have a job, I am so screwed. I emptied what was left of my checking account and put all the moving expenses and groceries on a credit card until I got paid. This entire move was a major, desperate leap of faith.

"The recruiter told me I needed to report to Mr. Hatcher at eight o'clock in the morning today. I already filled out all my employment paperwork online. I don't understand."

"One moment please." The receptionist flashes me an overly compensating smile before zeroing in on her computer. She types furiously, and after multiple rounds of pings that must be intercompany instant messages, she finally meets my gaze again. Except now her expression has gone from confused to worried.

"Everything okay?"

"Well, I figured out the problem. Rest assured, you *do* have a job here, and Dawn is on her way down now to take you to the other Mr. Hatcher."

"The other Mr. Hatcher?" I parrot back as if the words didn't quite permeate.

"Mr. James Hatcher's son, Nathan. James is the managing partner of Brickstone Ventures, which is a major property investment firm for a variety of industries. Nathan is in charge of commercial real estate investments, most of which are here in Vegas."

"Oh, well, that's fine. I'll work for whoever. I'm just relieved I have a job."

She grimaces as she shrugs. "That's one way to look at it."

I mean to ask for clarification because I don't like the way she's blinking at me, like I'm a mouse about to crawl into a cougar's mouth, but the sound of stilettos hitting the marble floor pulls my attention from her. A beautiful, middle-aged woman with a bright red bob approaches me in a direct path, like a rook on a chessboard. Our outfits are almost matching. Her dress is navy, mine is black, but they have a similar style. Although, judging by the red soles of her heels, noticeable every time she takes a step, I'm convinced her business dress is designer, whereas mine is most definitely from Nordstrom Rack.

"You're Spencer?" the woman asks as she nears me.

"Yes, ma'am." I hold my hand out. "Nice to meet you."

"Dawn." She shakes my hand firmly before releasing it. "Good grief, little girl. Who the hell did you piss off to end up with this job?"

My mouth falls open. "Excuse me?"

"Dawn," the receptionist hisses. "Don't scare her."

Consider me scared.

"Chelsea, I'm not scaring her. I'm preparing her." Dawn curls her fingers, beckoning me forward. "Come on. I'll show you to your desk and see if I can run a little interference in case Nathan's on the warpath."

"Warpath?" I squawk.

The women ignore me, talking right through me. "He's been extra edgy since James dropped the news about his engagement," Dawn explains. "Speaking of which," she tells Chelsea, "Julia will be here with a potential wedding planner at noon. If we're still in the earnings meeting, please escort them right up to James's office. Make sure she doesn't run into Nathan."

"Roger that," Chelsea confirms. "God, what're you going to do about the wedding? Nathan can't avoid his new mother-in-law forever."

Dawn covers her forehead, her middle finger and thumb pressed tightly against each temple. "If you value your job here, Chelsea, never use 'Julia' and 'mother-in-law' in the same sentence around Nathan." Dawn's bright green eyes snap toward me. "That goes for you too."

They both stare at me expectantly. "Um, I'm still kind of hung up on 'warpath,' so if we could just go over that briefly because the way you two keep exchanging glances makes me feel like I just signed an employment contract to work for Darth Vader."

Chelsea smiles. "Apt nickname for Nathan."

"Stop helping," Dawn bites out. "Come on, Spencer. You don't want to be late on your first day. He doesn't need any more ammo to hate you."

Dammit, I got too comfortable. I had such a good morning, I should've known I was skipping and whistling straight into a shitstorm. Dawn's already at the elevator bay, tapping the up arrow furiously. I'm midstride to obediently join her but Chelsea stops me.

"Spencer?"

"Yes?"

She smooths the top of her long, blond hair which is tied into a low ponytail. "Word of advice? Don't take anything personally. When in doubt, it's not about you."

I wet my lips. "Okay, that's the most grim send-off anyone has ever given me, but...thank you?"

She laughs. "If you're still here by one o'clock, I'll be really impressed. Stop by the front desk. I'll buy you lunch."

The elevator dings before the heavy metal doors peel open. "Spencer," Dawn calls out while snapping her fingers. "Come on, quick like a bunny."

I move toward the elevator with heavy steps. My high heels click off the marble tile but I'm treading so slowly, the floor may as well be wet concrete. I am that reluctant to meet my fate.

That's the bar Chelsea set? Not thirty days, not even a week.

She'll be impressed if I make it until *lunch*?

Fuck.

CHAPTER 7

Nathan

"Nate. Stay behind. I need a moment with you," Dad says as the rest of the finance team clears the meeting room. There's a low murmur of *oohs* from the team, mocking me as if I got called to the principal's office. It's all in good fun, except half of the executives in the room would probably love to see me topple off my pedestal. When you're the big boss's son, there's always target on your back. Unfortunately for them, I work hard and I'm good at my job. If they want control of the portfolio, they'll have to outperform me and my numbers. Good luck.

"What's up, Dad?" I ask as the final team member exits, closing the door behind them.

He pushes back from his seat at the head of the long conference room table and starts pacing. That can't be good. "Did you catch up with the Harvey kid this weekend? Any luck?"

I exhale deeply. "I tried. I stopped by his wife's birthday party but I couldn't catch him."

Dad stops in place before turning to face me. "He's pissed and wouldn't talk to you?"

"No, nothing like that. Finn invited me when I reached out to him. He was busy at the party, and I got...distracted."

"By?" Dad raises a quizzical brow.

Maybe I should admit I spent some time with a pretty woman at a bar. It'd make my dad happy to know I'm trying to move on. Except I'm not. I'm assuming that sometime before I die I'll succumb to primal urges. But as far as love goes? It was amazing while I had it, but now...I'm through.

"I had one too many," I easily lie. "I was too drunk to talk business."

Grimacing, he rubs the back of his neck—his nervous tic. "Dammit."

"There's no guarantee Finn can even help." From what I understand, Finn's pretty close with his grandpa but he graduated from UNLV with a bachelor of arts. He has no interest in commercial real estate investments. I can't imagine Senior is sharing his secret plans of taking over the Vegas Strip with his photographer grandson.

"Yeah, that crossed my mind," he replies distractedly.

"What's the problem?" I ask as I study Dad's strained brows and pursed lips, completing his vexed expression.

"I knew when I was considering purchasing the property there was already a buyer in line. So I had to be strategic."

Very few investors can match my dad's cash offers. When he wants something, he gets it, and everybody else has to settle for his leftovers. "By strategic do you mean you put your dick on the table and outbid the buyer?"

He averts his gaze. "I might've made a more generous offer. Anyway, I just found out from an insider in Senior's company that he was the original buyer. He tried to counter after my offer but couldn't rummage up the cash."

I lean back in my chair, pressing my lower back deeper into the lumbar support. "So? You won."

"*So*," he mocks like he's talking to a foolish teenager, "it means Senior had the same idea that I do. He wanted to flip the property and probably make a big investment into a new hotel-casino."

The puzzle pieces click into place. "Meaning there's no way in hell he's going to sell you the parking lot to help you execute the project you snaked from him."

"Snaked is a strong word."

"It's just business, Dad. He's a grown-ass man. He'll get over it."

Guilt washes over his face. "Or he might not. Let's just say in the past we've had a similar misunderstanding, and according to my inside source, Senior has no intention of forgiving me. I believe they have some R-rated nicknames for me over at Harvey Corp."

My phone pings, indicating some meeting or another I'm late to. What else is new? My schedule is such a fucking mess. As usual, I ignore it. "What inside source is feeding you all this information?"

"I might've *lent* Harvey an intern who has been feeding me some pertinent information necessary for business decisions."

My dad's glaring immaturity is a little entertaining. If these men, who are past sixty, continue to squabble and plot like grade-school rivals, I'm going to need popcorn. "You planted a mole in Harvey's company?" Smirking, I fold my arms over my chest. "And you wonder why Senior hates your guts."

"It was innocent curiosity—"

"*Innocent curiosity*," I repeat slowly. "That's a strange way to describe corporate espionage."

"Well, it doesn't matter anyway. I'm pulling Casey back. He resigned from his position at Harvey's office. He's going to be a project manager for this property—our right-hand man. He'll be back next week. Show him the ropes and take good care of him, okay?"

"As in kiss some major intern ass so he doesn't rat you out for spying on Senior?"

Dad lifts his arms in the air and gives me a buggy stare. "Whose side are you on, huh?"

I circle my finger in midair. "After this display of theatrics, I think Senior's."

"Hilarious," he responds flatly.

"Don't worry so much. I'll handle it. But can you make my life a little easier and keep things clean with Senior moving forward?"

He gives me a lazy, two-fingered salute, teeming with sarcasm. "Yes, boss."

Rolling back my chair, I stand. "All right, if there's nothing else, please excuse me as I get to work on cleaning up your mess."

My hand is on the door handle when my dad stops me.

"There's one more thing I need to talk to you about." The way he says it makes my stomach drop. His tone is completely devoid of humor.

"What?"

"First, I need you to promise me you'll stay calm." After taking a seat across the table, he gestures to the seat I just got up from.

I hold a poker face, pretending I'm unconcerned, but wild scenarios run through my mind. Is Mom okay? I talked to her last week, and she sounded in great spirits. Is Dad sick? He looks strong as ever—actually a little thicker around the midsection since he settled down with Julia.

"Say what you need to. I'm calm," I say as I slump back into the seat.

He folds his hands together and purposely stares at the table, not meeting my eyes. "ADA Trent Murphy and I golfed this past weekend. As a courtesy, he wanted me to let you know that Peter was released early from prison."

Shocked silence is all I can manage for what seems like eternity.

"Nate," Dad says sternly, his voice pulling me back to reality.

My mouth is so dry I can barely get the words out. "That's... what...six years early? He only served half his sentence. How did this happen?"

"On paper? Counseling, therapy, good behavior. In actuality, crowding issues."

My stomach lurches as reality continues to set in. How many more ways can I fail Elise? I wasn't there when she died. She held out as long as she could in the hospital, waiting for me, but I couldn't make it because I was stuck on the wrong coast. By the time I got home, Claire and all her belongings were swiftly removed from my home. *Her home.* She's not my daughter by blood, but I was more of a father to her than piece-of-shit Peter will ever be capable of.

"Somebody needs to warn Ruby—"

"Enough," Dad warns. "If you go near that family again, they will be granted the restraining order they so desperately want."

"Then *you* warn her. The first thing Peter will do is try to get in touch with Claire, which is not happening." My jaw clenches even picturing those two in the same room. It took Elise strength she didn't know she had to leave with Claire and press charges against the man who tormented her for so long. He doesn't deserve a relationship with his daughter.

Dad folds his hands together tightly. Suddenly, his eyes are pleading. "I haven't told you the worst part."

I lift my head, meeting his stare with daggers in my eyes. "What could possibly be worse?"

"Peter had a better chance at early release if he had a stable home to return to. He's living with Ruby and Claire now."

"No. Absolutely not—"

"Nathan, it's not your choice."

"*What the fuck, Dad?*" I bellow. "I told you all the stories. The living nightmare Elise escaped from. Peter's deranged and violent. He only takes breaks from snorting lines to prep a goddamn needle. He's not allowed near Claire. Not in this lifetime or the next. *I will not allow it.*"

Dad's patient as my breathing goes from the loud, growly grunts of a pissed-off bull, to a slow, calm cadence. I'm thirty-three and he's still parenting me by waiting until my tantrum is over to speak.

"It breaks my heart to say this, but she's not your child. This isn't up to you. It's Ruby's job to protect her grandchild."

I hate this feeling. Overwhelming dread at the imminent doom I can't do anything to stop. "If I killed him, she'd be safe. Elise could rest in her grave knowing her daughter won't be harmed."

"Perhaps." Dad ducks his head in a weak nod. "But what would Elise think about you locked away for a life sentence, even lonelier than you are now? Do you honestly think that's what she'd want for the man she loved so much?"

"That was slimy." My words barely come through my gritted teeth. "Don't use my tragedy against me."

"I'm for you, Nate. Not against you. *You* are not to involve yourself in this. You have a huge project to focus on. We can place a PI on it to give us peace of mind. If we see anything other than perfect behavior out of Peter, I'll personally ensure the LVMPD throws him right back into the garbage can he crawled out of. Can you trust me?"

I go silent again, listening to the loud ticks of the wall-mounted clock. I didn't notice it before. Now, the rhythmic *tick, tock* is deafening. A new realization hits me, and I toss Dad an icy stare. "You've known for a while, haven't you?"

"Hm?"

"The property, this father-son project... You just wanted me distracted."

He goes stoic. His lack of response isn't an admission or denial. "I love you, Nate. I'm here if you need me." With that, he rises. Dad makes a point to pat my shoulder before striding out of the meeting room.

Once I'm alone, his words echo off the walls, haunting me, because I know them so well. *I'm here if you need me.* It's the last thing I said to Claire three years ago.

Now she needs me.

And I can't keep my promise.

CHAPTER 8

Spencer

Rag in hand, I wipe at a thick leaf on the large bird-of-paradise plant in my new boss's office. I thought I spotted dust, but it was just a glare from the sunlight. The plant is already sitting by a floor-to-ceiling office window, ensuring plenty of sun exposure. I poke my finger into the soil to find it balanced—not soaked, but not dry. I only recognized the plant because Hank, my prior boss, had several of these in his office. After accidentally drowning two, I learned how to properly tend to them. Apparently, my new boss doesn't need my plant-care tips.

After pointlessly wiping a few more leaves on the already pristine plant, I look around to see what other menial tasks I can complete. *Nothing.* This place is spotless. I don't have access to Mr. Hatcher's calendar. Even if it wasn't ten in the morning, I don't know what I'm supposed to order him for lunch. Knowing my luck, I'd order orange chicken, unaware of his severe citrus allergy, and put my new boss in the hospital. According to my contract, I can only be fired for gross misconduct such as stealing or espionage. But I'm pretty sure accidentally killing my boss would also be classified as gross misconduct.

I have no choice but to sit and wait until Mr. Hatcher makes his way to his office this morning. Dawn told me he was in a lengthy finance meeting with her boss. After she led me to my assistant's desk, right outside of Mr. Hatcher's office, Dawn told me she'd check in before the end of the day. After ensuring I was set up in the company directory and could instant message her, she also programmed her number into my phone. Cryptically, she told me to contact her before *reacting* to anything, in case she could help.

I've obviously landed smack-dab in the middle of a *Beauty and the Beast* situation. Between Chelsea, Dawn, and all the pitying stares from employees this morning passing my newly occupied desk, I'm certain my new boss has tusks and a thick, shaggy mane. But here's what I've learned in my years of working as an executive assistant: Everybody respects a strong work ethic. I don't care how grumpy the *other* Mr. Hatcher is. I have nothing but good intentions here. There's no way he can hate me for merely existing if I bust my butt to do a good job for him.

After circling the large office one more time, I pause by the baby grand piano. For the life of me, I can't understand why someone would keep this in an office space. Surely they had to remove a wall to get this piano in here. No way it'd fit through the glass double doors. Unless you're a composer, what purpose does it serve? Outside of proving your wealth and sophistication. I roll my eyes even though no one can see me. It's pretty, but pompous.

I sit on the bench but leap like a startled cat when I hear something crack. Flinging open the piano bench lid, I assess the damage. The lid no longer opens and closes properly. One of the hinges is worn. It must've snapped under my weight when I sat.

Shit. Shit. Shit. I broke a seat.

Oh shut up, I mentally say to the impending body dysmorphic thoughts that are rearing their ugly heads. I don't have time to wallow and self-deprecate about my expanding waistline. Obviously this bench already had damage. Logically, my ass alone did *not* break this seat. But also, I'm skipping lunch today.

Dropping to my knees in front of the bench, I quickly run scenarios in my mind. I could shut the lid carefully, back away, and pretend I had nothing to do with this. *But that's a lie. No good.* I could be honest with my boss when he returns and beg for forgiveness. *Except he might impale me with one of his tusks.* No, I've got it. I will handle it. That's what a boss would want. I caused a problem, and I will fix it, quietly, without making a scene. I'll call maintenance and have this repaired before the boss man even notices. I'd rather present him with the problem *and* the solution simultaneously.

I pull out the small stack of sheet music lying in the bench to further assess the hinge, only to find a photograph hidden beneath the papers. A stunning, blue-eyed, crimson-haired woman is sitting cross-legged in a field filled with a sea of pink flowers. The sun is catching her hair, making it look like it's on fire. Almost an exact miniature replica of the gorgeous woman is seated right next to her. The little girl's legs are bent, her chin nestled into the space between her knees. They are both beaming. The girl is smiling at the camera as the woman smiles at who has to be her young daughter.

I don't know what possesses me to pick up the photo that is not mine to touch. It just makes me feel so warm and whole. The mother gazes at her daughter like she's the only wonder of the world. If I could sum up love in one photograph, I'd use this one. I know this look so well. It's how my mom looked at Charlie and me. Such a beautiful picture... *Why is this hiding in a bench?*

"What the hell are you doing?"

I know who it is before I turn around. Of course I recognize his voice, but it's the smell that gives him away. That sweet, sultry cologne that made me melt two nights ago at the club. *Nate* is Nathan. The piano...he said he played. I rise to my feet, trying to keep my knees together to avoid exposing myself in my skirt.

"You're kidding me. What a small world. I'm your new assistant." I'm grinning so hard it hurts. I was in my head about all the intimidating side comments this morning, but it was all a ruse. This man is no monster. He's sweet, sassy, and *sexy*. His black suit jacket is open, no tie, the first button of his shirt undone, exposing just a slice of his slightly tan skin.

I'm so lost in my Cinderella moment, bewildered that I accidentally stumbled right into my prince, it takes me a moment to register that while I'm all smiles, his eyes are narrowed. Based on the thick scowl he's wearing, he's not excited to see me.

"Why are you in here going through my things?" Nate zeroes in on the picture I'm still holding.

I'm always quick with my words but a haze I can't shake comes over me, jumbling my thoughts. I don't know where to begin. I have so much to explain all at once, I end up explaining nothing at all. "I found it," is all that manages to come out of my mouth.

"You found it?" he repeats, clearly unimpressed. "So you just take things you find, huh? Put it back."

My heart is now a thoroughbred at the Kentucky Derby. It's racing with all its might, and I think the finish line is me fainting. I'm so unnerved my hand trembles as I place the picture back at the bottom of the piano bench, replace the stack of sheet music, and gently close the lid. I grimace as it sits lopsided, evidence of my fuckup.

"I broke the bench. I'm very sorry. I'm on my way to call maintenance right now." *Oh, thank God.* That was a lucid sentence at least.

"It was already broken. That's not my concern. Why are you in my office snooping around?" He folds his arms across his chest. I have to divert my gaze because his glower is becoming too uncomfortable to endure.

"I wasn't snooping. I was trying to make myself useful. I thought it'd be nice for me to tidy your office, except it's—"

"Not necessary. I have a cleaning crew."

"Okay. Noted."

I'm still avoiding eye contact, but I can feel the heat of his disdain.

"If there's nothing in here you need"—he juts his thumb over his shoulder—"I believe your desk is that way. Don't come in here again uninvited."

He's not screaming or cursing at me. Nothing he's said is particularly cruel. I think the reason I'm holding back tears is because I fantasized about a fictitious character for two days straight. This isn't the man I met at House of Blues. They share a face, but that's all.

"Understood. My mistake." I hang my head as I stride past him. He turns, keeping his eyes on me like he's ensuring there's no funny business on my walk of shame out of his office. My fingers curl around the door handle. I'm almost free of this uncomfortable interaction. My better sense tells me to walk through the damn door and let it go, but...I have to know. Releasing the handle, I pivot to face Nate.

"I'm Spencer."

"Okay."

"You're Nate, right? Do you recognize me? House of Blues?" I could go on and ask if he remembers his lips grazing mine, or his eyes on my breasts.

My nerves flare up as he crosses the space between us. Now that I've jogged his memory, maybe he intends to pick up right where we left off. *Would I let him? Here?* I hold my breath as he reaches for me.

No, wait. Not for me.

Nate reaches *past* me, pulling the right side of the double doors open. Holding his palm a few inches from my midback, he guides me through the door without actually touching me. "I don't know what you're talking about," he says. "And I prefer Nathan."

He closes the door behind me, and I hear the distinct click of a lock.

I would've rather watched paint dry or grass grow than pass the time trying to avoid looking at *Nathan* through his large glass office doors. My L-shaped desk is positioned so I can see every move he makes. It would be ideal if Nathan would let me do my job, but he's been in and out of his office several times and hasn't acknowledged me once. His silent treatment is so effective, I'm beginning to doubt my own existence.

He has to remember me. Is he embarrassed? Nothing

happened. It was a flirty exchange and an almost-kiss. That's nowhere close to crossing the line. We can still be professional.

Maybe he's pissed about his phone—which would be petty and ridiculous seeing as he could probably afford to buy a brand-new iPhone daily without putting a dent in his bank account. But I guess if we're getting down to brass tacks, I did damage his property. I think I apologized at the club. *I think.* Perhaps it wasn't enough.

Or, maybe he really doesn't remember me. I'd like to think our little spark wasn't that forgettable, but there's a good chance he took another woman home after I fled the scene with Charlie. Either way, it's not my business. He's my boss. I'm done thinking about his piercing eyes and soft, warm lips. My bigger priority should be getting him to speak to me.

At exactly one o'clock, I peel myself out of my office chair. Dawn and Chelsea invited me to lunch and I'm looking forward to the only pleasant human interactions I have on my schedule for the day. I try to get Nathan's attention through the glass door. I plan on using charades to let him know I'm headed to lunch, but he doesn't look in my direction. Instead, I write a sticky note: *Off to lunch. Back at two. Here's my cell phone if you need me.* After scribbling down my number, I secure the note in the center of my desk before heading to the elevators.

Chelsea and Dawn are waiting for me in the building lobby, but they already have bags of takeout in their hands. As soon as they spot me, they wave and gesture to a seating area left of the front desk.

"I'm sorry, hon," Dawn says as I approach. "We promised lunch, but James got called to L.A. for an emergency meeting. We're boarding the jet in an hour, so we'll have to eat here."

"We're?" There's a hint of excitement in my tone. Then I panic. I can't leave Charlie to jet set to Los Angeles with a billionaire—even if it is for work.

"Not us," Chelsea explains in a pretend British accent. "We're not allowed on the jet, or the yacht. They leave the common folk behind when they travel."

Dawn rolls her eyes. "First of all, you've been on the jet."

"It was grounded," Chelsea complains.

"And James doesn't have a yacht."

Chelsea squints at Dawn, calling her on her lie.

"*In Las Vegas*," she adds.

Chelsea and Dawn begin to unpack the kraft paper takeout bags. We take a seat around the art deco coffee tables that are really not suited for lunch. The leather couches are too far away from the tables. It's clear this is going to be a plate-in-lap type situation.

"We didn't know what you wanted, so we just got a little of everything," Chelsea says as she takes off the lids of the takeout containers one by one. The savory smell of freshly sliced pepperoni and salami fills the air. My stomach churns with desire as Chelsea pulls out the crusty, buttery sandwich rolls. "This is the best deli in the city. We got a sandwich platter so you can try everything." She pulls out two condiment packets and waves them in my face. "Unconventional, but pair the brown mustard with the Italian dressing. It shouldn't work, but I swear"—she pinches her fingers together and kisses them—"pure perfection."

"Thank you." But I stay fixed in my seat while Dawn and Chelsea build their plates.

"What's wrong?" Dawn asks, looking over her shoulder. "Vegetarian?"

I pull my strawberry protein drink out of my purse and wave it in the air. I didn't bother putting it in the fridge and now it's room temperature. "I'm set." My game plan was to chug my drink, then order a dry salad wherever we went for lunch. I wasn't expecting this turn of events.

"That's your lunch?" Concern washes over Dawn's face.

"I'm trying to watch my weight. And I'm not that hungry." My stomach betrays me, groaning loudly for both women to hear.

I'm worried I've offended her when Dawn doesn't say anything. Was that rude of me? I didn't mean to be. I anxiously watch Dawn build a sandwich filled with sliced meat, cheese, and topped with a medley of veggies. She opens a small bag of potato chips and shakes half the package onto the plate. I'm filled with envy as I watch these slender women eat.

Something that's so complicated for me seems so easy for other women. It's simple. They eat at lunchtime because they're hungry. I can't put anything in my mouth without numbers flashing through my mind—calories, carbs, my weight. Rotating the bland protein drink in my hands, I scan the nutrition facts even though I know them by heart. One hundred calories, six net carbs, twenty grams of protein. Just enough to keep me alive...and miserable.

It wasn't always like this. I went through high school blissfully unaware that being the chubby, bubbly girl was something to be embarrassed about. I didn't have time to worry about popular girls or crushes on boys. My mom was dying. I didn't party on weekends. I learned to cook because Mom loved homemade food. She was a fantastic cook, but toward the end, she didn't have the strength to lift a pot and pan most days. In my free time, I took Charlie to parks and swim lessons because I knew how guilty Mom felt about her youngest daughter missing out on the things she couldn't do.

It wasn't until my freshman year of college that I was able to have my own life. I was riddled with guilt, leaving my family behind, but Mom wanted me to have a real college experience. She promised me she'd be okay until I got home...

It was the only promise she ever broke.

I didn't have time to process the trauma induced by how I lost my virginity in those first few days of college. My mom died. My sister needed me. There was no time to dwell on the painful humiliation of what that stupid football-playing prick did to me.

I rub off the label of the protein drink with the tip of my thumb as I'm taken back to the most gut-wrenchingly humiliating moment of my life. I still hear the *"moos"* behind my back. They said it was all in good fun. Just a game. *A princess. A jock. And a cow.* But what the hell kind of game traumatizes a girl for the rest of her life?

"Spencer, did you hear me?"

"Hm?" I look up and Dawn's crouching down so we're eye level. She's holding out the plate she prepared. *For me.*

She reaches for my protein drink. "Give me that. That's not food." I don't fight her as she pries the bottle from my clutches, then places the plate on my lap. She even goes as far as wrapping my hands around the sandwich. "Eat." She smooths my long hair over my shoulders, then sweetly brushes my cheek with the pad of her thumb.

Dawn proceeds to build another plate. Chelsea darts nervous glances in my direction, but doesn't call me out on the tears that trickle down my cheeks.

I sniffle as I take a small, hesitant bite of the sandwich. I only get the crusty edge of the bread. But it's enough to break the floodgates. *Fuck it, I'm starving.* Thick tears streaming now, I take a giant bite, filling my mouth with the perfect blend of soft bread, salty meat and cheese, and a burst of tang from the dressing-soaked veggies.

"Do you like it?" Chelsea asks.

I nod eagerly, keeping my mouth closed as I chew. But my response doesn't appease her concern. Her head is cocked, and there's still a cloud of worry in her eyes. I bet she thinks I'm crying because Nathan was awful to me just as they suspected he would be.

But that's not the reason.

I'm crying because the stunt Dawn just pulled is exactly what my mom would've done if she were here. If I had one wish, it wouldn't be for Jesse to have never betrayed me and Charlie. It wouldn't be a big diamond ring or walking down the aisle. Not money. I don't even need my new boss to be civil to me. None of that would fix the constant ache in my soul.

All I want...

All I need...

Is for Mom to be here.

CHAPTER 9

Nathan

On Thursday, I purposely arrive early to the office. I wanted to beat Spencer in to avoid the awkward walk past her desk. Admittedly, I handled that like shit on Monday.

Obviously, I lied. Of course I remembered.

I spent the entire weekend thinking about her. Sure, the indecent thoughts were speckled in here and there, but mostly I was trying to figure out what pushed me over the edge with Spencer. For three years, dating was as appetizing as burnt toast. I had no desire to pursue it. But something about Spencer coaxed the old me to the surface, even if for one night only.

It's not a good thing. I felt out of control that night. My thoughts and actions were far past the boundaries I'd clearly set for myself. Elise had my heart. *Has my heart.* And now she's gone. I'm so tired of these assistants that walk in here, cozying up to me, as if they can replace her. They're told I'm a billionaire bachelor, and they're shameless about taking their shot. I should've been nicer to Corrine. She was forty-eight, happily married, and as disinterested in me as I was in her. Or, maybe Timothy. He was dim-witted and utterly useless. He wore Velcro shoes and I'm still convinced it's because at twenty-two, he was incapable of tying shoelaces. In hindsight, both were better options. Now I'm stuck with the sexy, curvy, accidental-temptress who made me trip over my own two feet.

As I enter my office, I pull my phone and wallet out of my pocket and toss them into the silver bowl on my desk. A bright, red bow catches my attention.

Sitting on top of my laptop is a brand-new iPhone with a large Christmas bow secured to the box. A folded note is tucked under the bow.

Spencer asked me to give this to you. She didn't enter your office "uninvited."

-Dawn

P.S. Quit being a dick.

"Great," I mutter to myself. Spencer already has Dawn on her side which doesn't bode well for me. There are very few people brave enough to verbally tear me a new one. Dawn is at the top of that list, followed by my dad. She's been in my life since I was a teenager. She's more to us than an executive assistant or office manager; she's family.

I pick up the boxed phone, still secure in shrink wrap. Hm, maybe Spencer's more well off than I realized. I didn't get that impression from her behavior at the club, then again, she recognized my watch. Maybe she has some money if she can so easily buy an iPhone outright and hand it over as a gift. If so, why the hell is she working as my assistant?

I grab the receiver from my office phone and hit speed dial three. Dawn picks up on the first ring. "Dawn Pryce."

"What did Spencer say when she gave you this phone?"

"Good morning, Nathan. Might we start with pleasantries?"

"Sorry. Good morning. How was your flight?" Dawn accompanied Dad on an urgent trip to L.A. to address a funding issue on one of the complexes he's building. Somehow they already blew through the entire construction budget and the townhouses are barely framed. I almost feel bad for the project manager who took that ass-chewing.

"The flight was uneventful. I played a lot of Candy Crush.

How's your morning? Have you eaten? I'm about to pop out to grab a coffee and bagel for your father. Would you like anything?"

"No." I pause. "Wait. A bagel, please."

"Lox, no dill?"

"Yes."

"And a cortado?"

I sigh defeatedly. "Yeah. Thank you." This is why I don't need an assistant. I can do everything myself and Dawn's here to fill in the cracks.

"Okay. Give me thirty minutes."

"Thanks." I hang up the phone, then growl in frustration when I realize what just happened. I press speed dial three again.

"Yes, Nathan?"

"The phone. What did Spencer say it was for?" I wonder if she blabbed to Dawn about our encounter on Friday. It makes me uncomfortable. Dawn and Elise were close. I don't want her to think I was out acting like some sort of party boy hitting on loose women. I know she's gone. *I know, I know.* But this shadow of guilt follows me everywhere I go.

"Spencer said she accidentally shattered your screen. She felt bad and was trying to make it right. I also have the gift receipt if you want to exchange it for a more whimsical color." She cackles to herself, surely picturing me with an electric-blue phone which would be very out of character for me. My style is minimalist, blacks and grays, clean lines, no fuss.

"That's all she said? There has to be some ulterior motive."

She issues a sharp, exasperated sigh into the receiver. "You know, Nathan, she's a nice girl. And smart. While you're over here pulling an Elsa, holing yourself up in your lonely ice castle, the rest of us are enjoying the company of your very sweet new assistant."

"Mhm."

"In case you're confused, that was a reference from the movie *Frozen*—the first one, which is a masterpiece. The second one fell short."

"For you. I enjoyed it." Claire and I used to watch *Frozen* and

Frozen 2 on repeat. But that's when she was eight. I wonder if she even likes those movies anymore.

"My point is, cut Spencer some slack. So far she still doesn't have access to your calendar, you don't allow her in your office, and you haven't forwarded one email to her. She just sits there, rotting."

"I told Dad I didn't want another assistant."

"Yeah, and I don't want varicose veins at age forty-four, but life is what it is."

There's an awkward silence between us. "I uh..." I clear my throat. "Are those painful?"

"No. Anyway, Spencer needs this job. She's not a trust-fund baby. She has to work for everything she has. *So let her work.* You're not the only one who has faced real tragedy."

"What does that mean?" My mind starts to run in several directions. Spencer couldn't afford this phone? What tragedy? Why does she really need this job?

"It's not my place to say. I need to get going. I'm in no mood for your father's hanger. But first, I need verbal confirmation that you're going to speak to Spencer today. I don't care if it's a simple 'hello.' We're done with the silent treatment. *Capisce?*"

"And if I don't?"

"Then I will *ensure* the café burns your bagel to a crisp."

I smile into the phone. "You're a cruel, calculating woman, Dawn."

"Goodbye, Nathan."

I spend the next thirty minutes catching up on emails from the day before. I insist on being CC'd on everything. I can't keep up with the thousands of emails, but I do like receipts just in case. There's nothing that needs my attention except the mention of an introductory meeting with Casey next month. I'm reminded of how shitty this situation is. The least I can do is subtly warn Finn about the spy my father planted in his grandfather's business. I won't be asking Casey for any information about Harvey and his business plans. I intend to play fair. After grabbing my cell from the silver bowl, I shoot a message to Finn.

> **Me:** Hey. Sorry I missed you at the party. Dinner on me when you're back?

Finn: Did you show?

> **Me:** For a minute. How's Greece?

Finn: Incredible. Have you been?

> **Me:** No, not yet.

Elise had always wanted to go. I offered her a honeymoon there, but she said she'd rather make it into a family trip. Me, her, and Claire. *Dammit.* Why is she on my mind so heavily lately? I'd been doing okay for a while. Now, I see her everywhere. I nearly choked on my own spit when I saw Spencer holding her picture the other day. That's it, isn't it? This all got worse after the night I met Spencer.

> **Me:** I owe Avery a birthday present and you both a wedding present. What are you into?

Finn: Easy. Matching Lambos. Don't skimp on the upgrades.

> **Me:** *Hilarious.*

Finn: Kidding. No presents. It's just good to hear from you, man. You've been quiet.

Me: Yeah, been busy.

Finn's a guy's guy. He gets it. When a man says things are "busy," it just as easily translates to "dark."

Me: Saw you at the club though. You seem happy. Avery's a doll. Looks like you got a good one.

Finn: She's my angel. Crazy how a good girl can turn it all around, you know?

Finn: Shit.

Finn: I meant because of my ex. I wasn't trying to bring up anything.

Me: Don't tiptoe. I'm all right. Very happy for you. Steaks when you're back?

Finn: Yeah, definitely. But on me.

By the time I look up from my phone, Spencer's seated at her desk. She's not smiling today. In fact, she looks disheveled. If her lopsided ponytail and lack of makeup wasn't a tip-off, the fact she's wearing jeans is. Monday through Wednesday she was dressed to the nines, like business Barbie. Today she's wearing an oversized, black Rolling Stones T-shirt.

I grab the phone off my desk and head through the double doors. Spencer is glued to her computer screen. Her eyes scan left and right, furiously reading whatever she has pulled up. I have to tap her desk to get her attention.

"Christ," she gasps as her eyes grow wide as saucers. "I didn't see you."

I scan her head to toe. "The last Friday of every month is casual Friday. All other days we have a dress code."

Her nostrils flare as she inhales slowly. "I'm aware, thank you. I had an emergency this morning."

"What kind of emergency?"

Lips pressed tightly together, she gives me a disingenuous smile. "You're awfully chatty this morning. Are you done pretending I don't exist?"

I grind my teeth together to control my would-be smile. Something about her snark still intrigues me and I hate myself for it. "I'm returning this." I place the phone on the edge of her desk, then slide it within her grasp. She doesn't touch it.

"Go ahead. I believe Dawn gave you the gift receipt."

"I'm returning it to you. I don't know why you gave this to me." *Yes, I do.* But I can't admit that without owning up to the fact I'm well aware Spencer is the woman I was canoodling in the club last weekend. No way I can admit I still feel robbed of that first kiss.

Spencer shuts her laptop and swivels in her office chair to face me. Her big eyes become snake-like slits, sending a small shiver down my spine. "*Really, Nathan*? You don't know why I felt the need to replace your phone?"

"No." She clearly sees right through my lying. Only thing I can do now is double down. "You can't buy my affection with gifts, Spencer. It's inappropriate."

From snake to owl, her eyes pop wide as she fixes her unblinking stare on me. "Buy your affection? Are you freaking kidding me? I broke your phone in the club. I replaced it. That's it. My apologies in advance to your ego, but not every woman is staring at you with puppy-dog eyes begging for your *affection*." She flicks her fingers, sending the phone flying across the desk which skids to a stop right by my hand.

"Are you forgetting I'm your boss?"

"Are you though? I'm here to help, and you won't let me." She straightens her finger, the tip pointed at the box. "I thought if I righted my wrong, we could start over. I have thirty days to prove myself, and you haven't given me a chance."

"What?"

"You haven't given me anything to do." She speaks slowly, emphasizing the syllables as if I'm hard of hearing.

"And what exactly could you help me with today? Scoring front-row tickets to a rock concert?"

She shoves her hands under the desk, out of my view. I wonder if they are balled up in frustration. Maybe she's fantasizing about socking me in the face. "A pipe burst in my upstairs neighbor's apartment. I woke up to my closet flooded and all my clothes soaked. This is the shirt I slept in and the only dry pair of pants I had. I'll figure it out by tomorrow."

"Oh. Okay. That's fine."

She shuts her eyelids tightly, her thick top and bottom lashes mashing into one. "Gee, thanks. If there's nothing else..." She spins back around and reopens her laptop.

Is she dismissing me? What the fuck? "What did you mean by thirty days to prove yourself?"

"I'm on a trial period for thirty days. If I'm incapable of doing this job, my contract can be terminated."

"And after the trial period?"

"You're stuck with me."

She looks up when I let out a whispered chuckle. "Was it really wise of you to tell me that?"

There's not a hint of amusement on her face. "First off, I assumed you were already familiar with the employment contract *your* company offered me, so I didn't realize I was spilling secrets. Second off, I'm trusting that while you haven't exactly been pleasant, you're not actually plotting against me. I haven't done anything wrong...right?"

"Right," I confirm half-heartedly.

Sorry, Spencer. I have about a million unsolvable problems—

Claire's abusive father coming back into the picture, my father's impending marriage to a floozy, an overwhelming construction project with an impossible timeline. But in regard to all these unwanted feelings she's beginning to stir up? Suddenly, my whole assistant situation seems very solvable.

Less than thirty days to make her job impossible to complete? Yeah... Too fucking easy. I can definitely do that.

CHAPTER 10

Spencer

That can't be right.

I'm staring in disbelief at the digital numbers on the gas pump. My company car is a brand-new, sleek, black Lincoln Navigator. When I picked up the vehicle from the dealership, I was expecting a basic sedan. I believe my exact response was, "Squeeee," when they pulled the SUV around for me. The office manager rolled his eyes and mumbled something about trust-fund babies, but I was too elated to set his ignorance straight.

While the Lincoln is gorgeous, luxurious, and way more than a new executive assistant should be driving, it also gets about three miles per gallon and has a tank that could power a cargo ship. I'm going to go bankrupt on fuel costs alone.

"Freaking ridiculous." I tap my credit card twice to no avail before just forcefully shoving it into the chip reader.

"You're talking about gas prices, right?"

Peering over my shoulder, I try to find where the voice came from. There's no one behind me. I give up on the intrusion until a very handsome, black man steps into view from the other side of the pump. "Hi," he says, holding up his palm. He's filling up a dually vehicle that looks straight out of *Yellowstone*. Although his truck is more "monster" than "pickup," if you ask me.

He's beautiful. And I mean, knees-weak, butterflies-fluttering, thigh-tingling *beautiful*. "I suppose I shouldn't be complaining." I nod at his truck. "Do you need a second mortgage to fill that thing up?"

His laugh is so melodic. Is Las Vegas just full of gorgeous, eligible men? Not that I'm looking... Except I do look. There's a distinct tan line on his ring finger. No ring. But it's evident he's worn one for a long time. My stomach is suddenly uneasy.

"Just about," he answers. "It's a tax write-off, at least. Because of gas costs, I get to keep most of what I make."

"That's cool. What do you need a truck like that for?"

"Towing. I do horse and cattle transports."

"Oh. Nice."

I glance at my pump, deflated when it's already at forty dollars yet the tank is barely halfway full.

"I'm Caleb."

My smile is reticent. "Nice to meet you, Caleb."

He chuckles. "And you are?"

I steal one more glance at his lovely chocolate-brown eyes before calling him out. "I'm the woman who noticed you have a tan line on your ring finger. Any chance there's a wedding ring you stashed in your pocket?"

He widens his eyes, clearly surprised at my audacity. "Wow... that's...okay, fair observation. I'm divorced. About six months ago now."

"That's pretty recent."

"My thoughts as well, but my ex-wife is already remarried, so"—he shrugs—"in the court of public opinion, I'm well within my right to talk to pretty women at the gas pump."

"Sorry." I step onto the median between the pumps and hold out my hand. "I'm Spencer. Please excuse me while I try to unwedge my foot from my mouth."

He laughs again. "No, I think you're smart. You can make it up to me, though."

"How so?"

"Can you watch my pump while I grab some snacks?"

"Sure. Of course."

"Thanks. Be right back." He winks before jogging toward the shop.

The fuel dispenser's loud click indicates my tank is finally full. Fantastic. It only cost me a month's worth of groceries. I patiently wait for Caleb's side of the pump to make the same click. I don't know how watching his fuel pump is actually helpful unless his truck spontaneously bursts into flames and he needs immediate intervention. Morbid thoughts now stuck in my mind, I'm searching the premises for the emergency shutoff valve and a fire extinguisher when my phone rings.

Can't be Nathan. Now that I'm nearing the end of my second week of work, he's warming up to me a little. He's given me access to his calendar, but it's view only. I can't actually schedule anything for him. He grunts a simple "hello" on occasion when he passes my desk. But that's the extent of his warmth. This unknown number is doubtfully Nathan calling.

"Hello?"

"Good morning. Is this Spencer Riley?"

I omit correcting the woman on the phone. Legally, I'm Spencer Riley-Brenner. But seeing as I haven't seen or spoken to my dad since he left us when I was five years old, I don't see the purpose of carrying his last name. There's just the pesky task of starting a legal name change to drop the hyphen. Who has time?

"Speaking."

"Hi, dear." The *dear* tips me off to her age. Immediately, I know who this is even before she explains. "This is Ruby Barber, Claire's grandmother."

"Oh, yes. Hi there. Thank you for calling."

"Of course. From my understanding, the girls have planned a little sleepover this weekend. Are you okay with that?"

I sandwich the phone between my shoulder and ear as I pull the nozzle from my gas tank and replace the cap. "I am, I just won't be able to host. Building maintenance is working on repairs to my closet this weekend. I just don't want strange men in and out of the apartment while the girls are there. But I'm happy to host Claire as soon as it's fixed."

"Oh, don't fret. I'm happy to have Charlie here. I have a three-bedroom in Ellis Springs. There's a community pool where the girls can swim."

"Charlie will love that. She's such a fish. She'd live in the water if she could."

"I hope I'm not overstepping, but may I just say what you're doing is incredible?"

"Sorry?" A glimpse of Caleb in line at the register momentarily distracts me. Goodness he's muscular. I'm not a small girl, but I bet he could easily hoist me over his shoulder like a bag of potatoes. I shake the thought away. *Enough, Spencer.* The last time I thought I found a prince and almost kissed him, he turned into the icy toad that's now my boss.

I'm not ready to date again anyway. When I do start dating, I want it to be for real, not just to try to create as much space between Jesse and me as possible. I admit, that idea has occurred to me, and not out of spite. Just so I'm not tempted to run back.

"What you're doing with Charlie. I hope you don't mind, but Claire filled me in. You, so young, taking care of your baby sister. It's a tremendous sacrifice on your part."

"Thank you, that's kind. But I wouldn't have it any other way."

"You know Charlie and Claire have that in common—they both lost their mothers too young. I think that's why they're such fast friends."

"I'm very sorry for your loss. I can't imagine the pain of losing a daughter." I only know what it's like to lose a mother. It's hard to imagine anything worse, except losing Charlie, but my head can't even go there. I wouldn't survive it.

"Not my daughter," Ruby says, her chipper tone dropping just slightly. "Claire's father is my son."

"I'm still sorry. I think it's wonderful Claire has you guys."

"Thank you, dear. And also, while I have you, Charlie told Claire you guys are willing to take Spike. Is that true?"

I lean back against my car which nearly burns the back of my exposed arms. The scorching Vegas sun is unforgiving. It's a different kind of hot than Miami—dry and unrelenting. There's no water here to absorb the heat. "What spike?"

"No, his name is Spike. He's our male guinea pig."

"*Oh. Right.* Yes." I did promise Charlie that, and much to my dismay, she has not forgotten. "We'll take him. I'm just not sure what he needs."

"Don't worry, I'll write you a list and send over some supplies. He's a sweet boy, but a horndog, and I can't handle one more batch of babies. Babe has already had two litters of pups this year, and I suspect she's pregnant again."

Damn. Two pregnancies this year already? It's only summer. "How about we bring him home after the sleepover?"

"Perfect."

I'm eager to end the call when Caleb emerges from the convenience store. "It was really nice to chat, Mrs. Ruby. I have to get going to work, but thank you again. I really appreciate how nice Claire has been to Charlie."

After a sweet send-off, I hang up just in time for Caleb to reach me. "How'd it go?"

I step around the median and check his pump. His truck drinks diesel and his final cost is nearly double mine. "You might not want to look."

He laughs. "Good call. Here." He pulls out two plastic logs of Hostess Donettes. "Are you a powdered sugar or chocolate frosted kind of lady?"

I can't tell him neither, but absolutely no way I'm putting those in my mouth. Last I checked, the scale was up two pounds yet again. My diet this week is lemon water and hard-boiled eggs. "Hmm."

"Here, I wrote my number on both." He hands me both packs of mini donuts. "I'm just passing through Vegas, but I come through here often. If you ever want to get together and bitch about the price of gas, let me know."

I can't help my spreading smile. "Thank you. Maybe I will."

He pretends to tip a hat he isn't wearing. "Ma'am," he says with a cowboy flair.

I get back in my car and wait until Caleb peels out into traffic. The loud rumble of his truck only adds to his dripping masculinity. It was the perfect interaction. He was sweet, flirty, and didn't pressure me or grovel. That was an ideal meet-cute.

I check the donut packages once the coast is clear, and there it is, Caleb's name and number written in thick, black Sharpie. I'm about to program the number into my phone when a text pops up.

> **702-555-4322:** Good morning. It's Nate. Would you please stop by my office when you get here? I'd like your help with something.

> **702-555-4322:** Also, I got you a coffee.

My heart thunders in my chest as I shove the donuts into my oversized purse. I can ignore it all I want. And I'll continue to call my boss what he is—grumpy and callous. Obviously, I'm not remotely interested.

Except my fluttering pulse doesn't lie. It's racing at the tiniest glimmer of the man I met at House of Blues that night.

He needs my help. He got me coffee.

Oh, and he just called himself Nate.

CHAPTER 11

Nathan

Staring at my computer monitor, I scroll through the pictures again. The PI never gets Claire's face. All I can see is that she's gotten so much taller, and her fire-engine-red hair is down to her stomach. Picture after picture, all I can see is Peter taking Claire shopping. Peter taking Claire to the aquarium. Peter taking Claire for coffee and getting her a frappuccino drenched in chocolate and caramel syrup. Outside of the fact she shouldn't be having that much caffeine at her age... Nothing's wrong.

He ditched the beard. Post-prison, he's sporting the clean-shaven look and smiling in every picture. But I can't see Claire's face. Is she smiling too?

Picking up my cell, I dial Dad's PI on speaker.

"Hodge," he answers.

"I just got your email. What the hell is all this?"

"What's it look like, boss?"

"Do I sound like I'm in a playful mood? Or do I sound on edge like I'm willing to use every penny in my bank account to ruin a PI's life if he doesn't give me some legitimate answers?"

Hodge clears his throat. "Sorry, sir. These are the results of eight days of surveillance."

"Better. Where's Ruby?"

"The old lady?"

"Yes," I bite out. I don't have a long list of enemies. A few terminated employees who'd probably like to take a few swings. Business rivals, sure. But sweet old Ruby is the devil in disguise.

I know her true colors. Claire is a possession to her, and she's in total denial that her son is a monster. She saw Elise beaten within an inch of her life. Ruby is the kind of vile bitch who'd ask what the woman did wrong to deserve it. She has no right to raise Claire.

"From what I can tell, these are daddy-daughter dates. It looks like he's trying to make up for lost time. How long was he away?"

"Not long enough. And what does Peter do when he's not with Claire?" Truth be told, Peter is even-keeled when he's sober. It's when he's high or drunk that he turns into Mr. Hyde.

"He's squeaky clean. AA meetings, daily check-ins with his parole officer. He's even going to evening church services."

He can repent all he wants. Corrupt cops and wife-beaters go into the ground and stay there. There should be no salvation for evil men like him. I grab my takeout coffee, unaware of the tension in my forearm. Squeezing too hard, the coffee explodes, searing-hot cortado spilling all over my desk, shirt, and lap. "Shit," I hiss as I wait for the scalding burn to dissipate.

"You all right?"

"I'm fine." I snatch my phone up, holding it vertically so the coffee drips down off the broken screen. "Keep an eye on Peter."

"Sure thing, boss. How long?"

"Until I say." While others might be easily convinced of Peter's new sobriety, I'm not fooled. My command acknowledged, I hang up the call.

The whole office reeks of coffee now. I open a few windows to air out the space, then head to the hidden closet. I push against the cabinet and the door pops open. I keep a couple spare suits in here for shit like this. Sliding off my belt, I let it drop to the floor, then unbutton and kick off my pants. My shirt is probably fine, just a few wet spots, but I might as well change everything.

I grab two suits and their hangers from the rod. As I'm debating between black and dark gray, there's a shriek from behind me.

"Oh my God, I'm so sorry."

I turn in time to see Spencer whipping around, her long hair fanning out like silk around her shoulders. She starts to flee my office, but in her disarray she forgets the door is a pull from this side, not a push. There's an awful *thud* as she collides face-first with the door. She hits the glass so hard, she collapses backward.

I'm across the room in three long strides, my heart hammering hard, as I scoop her head up in the crook of my elbow. I normally try to keep distance between us. Holding her like this is too damn close to the line I so desperately don't want to cross.

"Oh, shit," I whisper upon the extent of the damage. Streaks of red are dripping from her nose.

"Am I bleeding?" Her voice is small, but clear, reverberating through my chest with each syllable.

"Yeah." No point in lying.

"Is it broken?"

I brush the hair from her face, away from the blood, allowing my fingers to linger longer than necessary near her temple. Very carefully, I press against the bridge of her nose, hyperaware of how her ragged breath is warming my skin. "How's that feel?"

"Not too bad." Her eyes lock with mine for a moment. A pleading look that matches my own. Like we both want to be put out of our misery. Her discomfort is probably a mix of pain and unnecessary embarrassment. Mine? The agony of wanting her.

"Then I think you're okay. C'mon. Up we go."

With my hands cupped around her elbows, I guide her into a sitting position. I'm going to completely ignore that her skirt has ridden up so high I can see her bare, upper thighs. Diverting my gaze, I temper my curiosity that's getting all kinds of stirred up. I force my gaze away from her supple skin. She's hurt. Now is *not* the time...

It'll never be the time.

As I move my hands to her shoulders, steadying her, Spencer presses her palms against both of her temples. "I might have a concussion. Suddenly the smell of coffee is really strong."

"No, that was me. I just spilled coffee all over myself. Hence why I was changing."

"Please don't give me a hard time about this. I had no idea you were almost naked in here." Her eyes flicker downward for a fraction of a second before snapping back up. She thinks she's subtle...she's not. I'm painfully aware of my state of undress, and how little fabric separates us. But the beast in my chest is purring with glee at the idea of Spencer checking me out. Maybe she is feeling what I am. "You said come to your office as soon as I got to work. The door was unlocked."

"I know, I know. Can you sit on your own?"

"Yes." She puts one arm down, bracing herself with one hand planted on the rug.

I hop up and fetch a fistful of tissues from the box on my desk. Returning to Spencer, still on the floor, I wad them up in a ball and press them gently to her nostrils. "Let's clean you up."

"I can do it," she insists, trying to take the tissues from me.

"Let me help," I answer softly. "I know you can do it, but I'm trying to be nice."

My words relaxing her, she sits as still as she can, letting me dab and wipe at her face, her eyes never leaving mine. It looks like she's still in disbelief and trying to savor the moment. The silence between us crackles with something unspoken, but we both understand. *Yes, we want it. No, we can't have it.* It's that simple.

When I'm satisfied with my handiwork, I meet her gaze.

"There. Back to pretty as usual." I regret the words as soon as they slip out. Partially because I just admitted out loud that the word I'd use to describe Spencer is pretty. Also, because she doesn't seem appreciative of the compliment. Her eyes flicker with uncertainty as the corners of her lips turn down.

"You are so confusing," she grumbles.

Yeah. I realize.

She clambers to her feet all on her own. Now she's lightly pressing against her eyelids. I'm sure her whole face hurts from that blow. Poor thing. "I think we should get some ice."

"I'll do it. You should get dressed." Her gaze roves down my

SELFIE

chest, lingering just a moment too long before snapping back up. "You have a meeting about the zoning permit in fifteen minutes." It's brief but unmistakable—the once-over she gives me, standing here in only my boxers. Her lips part slightly before she adds, "Gray, by the way."

"Excuse me?" I ask, my voice strained and distracted.

Spencer points to the suits I dropped in front of the closet when she collapsed. "Looked like you were trying to decide. Go gray. Just my opinion."

"I'll take that under advisement."

She nods, looking miserable. I want to blow off this meeting and ensure she gets ice and some Motrin. Actually, I want to give her the rest of the day off and take her home myself. But I bite back my inclination. Spencer is beautiful, smart, and witty as all hell. She'll find someone great, but she's not mine to save.

"Whatever you wanted to talk to me about, can it wait until this afternoon? I'd really like to leave with whatever dignity I have left and speak to you when my entire face isn't throbbing."

"That's fine." Now I'm in no hurry and really not looking forward to unleashing my clever plan to set Spencer up for failure. "Come back at two o'clock, after lunch?"

"Two o'clock," she confirms. She wobbles on her first step, then takes a steady second step to exit my office.

"Hey, Spencer?" I call out when she's nearly at the door.

"Hm?"

"Remember, pull, don't push." I let out a soft, pitying chuckle. Her back is turned, but I bet she's rolling her eyes.

I swear I hear her mutter "asshole" under her breath.

CHAPTER 12

Spencer

There's no denying it,
I noticed his bulge.
Also, while I'm being honest, I noticed the way his tan, defined six-pack was glittering in the morning sunlight like they were a Christmas present for me. I swear I only ogled him for a moment. Then I whipped around to restore his privacy.
Only problem was the damn door.
I was hopeful when I arrived at the office this morning the glacier-like work environment my boss worked so hard to create was finally melting. I'm a fantastic assistant. I could really help make his life easier if he let me. I don't see picking up lunch and dry cleaning beneath me. Acts of service is my love language. I learned when Mom's strength started to wane, the little things can make a world of difference. This was exactly the speech I intended to give Nathan when I burst through his office.
Except there he was in his black briefs that didn't leave much to the imagination.
By the time I get back to my desk from my humiliating encounter with Nathan, a takeout coffee has appeared on my desk. The cup is dwarfed by the kraft-brown sleeve; it's even smaller than a tall. *Geez.* The man is a billionaire, he could've splurged for a grande at least. Removing the ice pack I scavenged out of the break room freezer from my face, I take a small sip of the coffee. I wince at the brew that is most certainly lighter fluid.
Frantically, I check the sticky label on the cup and am

surprised when it reads, "cortado," not poison. Clearly Nathan and I don't enjoy the same type of coffee. I guess he likes this nonsense, whereas I prefer my caffeine not taste like torture. I don't actually drink coffee much anymore because I can't enjoy it the way I like—drenched in caramel sauce and a generous helping of cold foam cream. Back when I was on my weight-loss pills, I could survive a whole day off of one grande white chocolate mocha with a heavy dollop of whipped cream.

Selfishly, I miss them. The pills took the anxiety out of eating. It was like outsourcing the constant stress and fear I had when it came to food. Jesse helped me buy them from Mexico. He knew a guy who knew a guy. I should've known excessively taking pills that were a far cry from FDA-approved medication would've landed me in the hospital.

It scared the shit out of Charlie. My little sister is strong, but I think the scar of losing me, on top of everything else she's been through, would never heal. After a dramatic collapse, an overnight hospital stay, and the doctor threatening me with terms like gallbladder disease, pancreatitis, high blood pressure, and even cardiac arrest, I decided I couldn't continue to take them.

Now, I have to sit here and watch my body transform right back into what I really am. My mom told me I was beautiful and perfect every day of my life. She bestowed such confidence in me, I never saw the glass-shattering blow that was coming for me during my first week at UNLV. I might still see myself the way my mom did had nearly an entire college campus not seen me naked and publicly shamed me. Some people have that nightmare where they are caught on stage in their birthday suit, with all the people they're trying to impress shining a flashlight on all the parts of their body that are too big, too jiggly, too stretched and marked. It wasn't my nightmare...

It was my reality.

It's been five years since I quit school and returned home from Las Vegas. I managed to get my degree from a local Miami college. I busted my ass to finish school on time. I worked all day and studied. I started taking diet pills and lost all the wiggly parts I was teased for. I quietly fixed all my insecurities one by one, but it didn't make the trauma go away.

It's partly why I'm so paranoid about Charlie being on the internet and exposing herself to criticism. I don't want her teased and ridiculed like I was. It doesn't matter that she's a child, or beautiful, petite, blond-haired, blue-eyed, and sings like she's God's gift to humankind. The trolls have no mercy; they'll conjure up something. How can I console her the first time someone calls her a mean name, pokes at her appearance, or criticizes her talents when they are talentless themselves? How can I fix for her, what I never learned to fix for myself?

Coming back here, I'm also trying to face what I ran from. There were other jobs—admittedly, none paying as well as Brickstone Ventures, especially when you consider the perks. But I could've made it work elsewhere in Dallas or Denver, perhaps. Something called me back to Las Vegas... I'm still not sure exactly what.

After taking another small sip of the cortado—and regretting it—I sit down at my desk and open my laptop, mostly out of habit. Outside of the company-wide newsletters that go out on Mondays, my inbox is always empty. Except now there's a little notification. A bright red "1" on the email icon indicating I have a new message.

From: Nathan Hatcher
To: Spencer Riley-Brenner
Subject: Important Task

Spencer,

I'll have to cancel our meeting this afternoon. I'm headed to the East Coast to handle an urgent matter. I'll be back tomorrow afternoon. I'm emailing over instructions for the task I need you to complete. Please keep this confidential.

I'm sure you're familiar with Shaylin, the Grammy-winning pop sensation. She's considering a residency at our new hotel. I'm meeting her for dinner to discuss a potential deal.

I need a reservation at a chef's table.

I pause reading and roll my eyes. This is way too easy. Nathan's treating me with kid gloves. Fancy reservations are my calling card. I could get Hank a chef's table at Swerve, one of Miami's most exclusive steakhouses, easily. They don't even pick up the phone there. You have to leave a voicemail at least three months prior, pray they call you back, and when they don't (which they won't), you have to grovel via email a few times to be put on a waiting list.

I, however, once helped a random woman on the side of the road change her flat tire in a bind. Turns out she was the lead hostess at Swerve. She's now in my contacts list and Hank would always get the best tables. I never told him my little secret. My old boss just thinks I was *that good*.

But my cocky smile disappears as I continue to read the email.

To clarify, a celebrity chef's table, for example, Giada De Laurentiis, Gordon Ramsay, or Bobby Flay. Wolfgang Puck is my strong preference if he's free.

Thanks, Spencer. It's a very important meeting. We want to impress Shaylin. Don't let me down.

Before I forget, I need the reservation for tomorrow at eight.

Cheers,

Nathan Hatcher

Senior Partner, Brickstone Ventures

Consider me humbled.

A celebrity chef by tomorrow night? Did Nathan smoke an entire bowl before he wrote this email? How the hell am I even supposed to get in touch with Wolfgang Puck? Not to mention, do the chefs he listed even cook for guests? I always figured they just own the restaurants and film their cooking shows. This is absolute insanity. No way I can pull this off.

Oh.

It dawns on me. That's the point.

That's why he was being so pleasant. He was purposely luring me into a false sense of security. My boss wants me to trip over my own two feet, failing at his request. Perhaps he's hoping to write me up for failing to come through with an assignment. Although, if I brought this to HR, no way his case would stand. Any reasonable person would see this is absurd. No...I know exactly what he's doing. *The jackass.*

He wants to piss me off enough to quit.

A smarter girl would cut her losses and just find another job. My salary advance is generous, but it's not a lottery win. Surely there's another job in this city that would be a better fit than working for a sexy incarnation of Hades himself. But you know what?

I want to put this fucker in his place.

I'm *so* pissed off. Because he's pretending he doesn't remember me. Because he's weaponizing avoidant behavior. But mostly I'm angry because... I don't know. I still want the Nate I met at House of Blues—the one who had my heart skipping beats like it never had before. I'm convinced the broody jerk occupying the office in front of me stole Nate and is hiding him in a basement somewhere.

Not even Cowboy Caleb from earlier today was sending shivers up my spine. Even if he is scrumptious...he wasn't Nate.

I pull the mini donuts from my purse and tuck them in my top drawer. I'll let the little treats go stale, but Caleb's name and number is the reminder I need that not all hot, single men are evil.

All right. Now, back to the task at hand: outsmarting the

bosshole.

I grab my phone and scroll through my contacts. Las Vegas has all the celebrity chef franchise restaurants, but calling the reservation desks will get me nowhere in a little over twenty-four hours. I have to know somebody who knows somebody. I'm not rich or important, but I've spent the last few years of my life proving myself to very rich and important people who practically beg me to call in favors. Nathan made a grave mistake in underestimating me.

First call? The big kahuna—Dex Hessler. My prior boss's boss. My other prior boss's husband. And a bona fide billionaire good guy. As the phone rings, I press against the bridge of my nose which is still tender and aching. But that's to be expected.

When you go to war, you have to anticipate at least a little pain.

It's eight p.m., and Charlie is at least fed and in her room, on her iPad, while I'm banging my head against the kitchen table. Ten hours of doom after that email from him hit my inbox, I still have no solution to his "assignment." To make matters worse, I'm less than thrilled when Nathan's "name" pops up on my screen.

Bosshole: Checking in.

Me: Isn't it past ten at night where you are?

Bosshole: Yes. Is it inappropriate to be texting this late?

Me: Yes. What do you need?

Bosshole: I was wondering who you secured for tomorrow evening?

Me: Don't you want to be surprised?

Bosshole: Not particularly. Let me know if I need a backup plan.

Me: I believe I responded to your email informing you I'd handle it.

Bosshole: You did. And is it handled?

Me: Mr. Hatcher, surely you have more important things to do than micromanage me.

Bosshole: I'm a very hands-on boss.

I wish he were here so he could see the expression on my face. His glaring hypocrisy is impressive, really. I'm trying to think of the perfect witty reply. I don't want to poke the bear and cause a full-on attack. What's the sassy equivalent of giving a grizzly the middle finger?

Before I can think of the perfect reply, my phone rings. I actually drop to my knees on my kitchen tile thanking every god imaginable for Dex's name flashing across the screen.

"Hey, Dex. Thanks for calling."

"Of course. Is this a good time, or I can call back?"

"It's a perfect time. Why?"

"You sound out of breath. Are you working out?"

I snort at the idea. "Definitely not. The breathlessness you're hearing is from the rage-induced panic attack I've been having since ten this morning."

"Oh... Wait, what? Have you gone to the doctor, because—"

"It was a joke, Dex. I'm fine. I think... Actually, whether or not I'm fine is highly reliant on why you're calling. None of my other leads panned out."

I trill my fingers nervously against the hard floor, praying for good news.

"I have good news and bad news," Dex says.

"You sure it's not good news, and then slightly less good news?"

He laughs. "No, definitely a good-news-bad-news situation. Do you know the chef Tansy Haleen?"

Tansy, Tansy...so familiar. "Jog my memory?"

"She's the chef that cooks with pink pots and pans. She has her own show on Food Network, and she's a guest judge on—"

"Gah! Yes, *Final Cut*." I love that cooking competition. There's something about enjoying extreme stress when it's not your own. All the competitors on *Final Cut* have to cook with unconventional mystery food items that they can't see until the clock starts ticking. Brilliantly evil, especially when the surprise items are alive. One poor sap got his eye poked by a lobster. He cooked an entire four-course meal half-blinded, and they still eliminated him in the final round. *Savage.*

"Tansy and I go way back. She helps plan the menu for some of the fine-dining restaurants on our ships. I reached out and she got back to me."

"*Yes*! Amazing. Tansy will be perfect."

"She's in France right now and can't get back in time."

"Dammit," I grumble.

"But she's actually opening a brand-new restaurant right on the Strip."

"Great! I mean, that's a start at least—"

"It's not open yet."

I let out a shaky exhale through gritted teeth. "You're really playing with my emotions over here, Dex." *And my blood pressure.*

"Yeah, I'm sorry. I'll get to the point. I can't get you a celebrity chef in time for tomorrow night, but Tansy said her restaurant's soft opening is next week. The kitchen is fully operational and mostly stocked. It's yours if you can find someone."

Think, think, think. Okay, I have a restaurant, just not a chef. That's still something, right? "What's it called?"

"Viva."

"I'll take it," I blurt out as a sly plan quickly comes together in my mind.

"Great. I'll let her know. She'll have someone messenger over the keys. Sorry I couldn't do more."

"Are you kidding? Literally thank you from the depths of my soul. I can't tell you how many calls I made today." A lot of people tried to help me, and I'm so grateful. But Dex is the only one who came back with something tangible.

"Will this solve your whole boss problem?"

"Oh, you mean the Hydra I work for? No, I'll need Hercules and a thick sword to handle him. But this at least helps me keep my job, so again, thank you."

Dex laughs. "May I say, this guy is really bringing out the best in you."

"Sarcasm?"

"Absolutely. Why don't you just quit? Lennox and I can figure out something for you."

Swinging my legs around on the sleek, tile floor, I move my weight to my rear and scoot backward. There's a little clunk as I lean against a kitchen cabinet. The door won't fully close because my pots and pans are too big for this doll-sized kitchen. Honestly, I'm making do with what I have. Yes, the apartment is too small. No, we don't have a lot of nice things. But I'm trying to stay focused on what I do have—my sister, my health. A job, for now. Surviving means you're still in the fight, and that's something to be grateful for.

"I didn't want to be a mooch."

"I said we'd arrange a job, not a winning lottery ticket."

"But Hessler Group is in Miami. I didn't want to be there anymore."

"We have remote employees, Spence."

"None that are entry level. You require all your managers to be on-site. Your only remote positions are for board members and department directors. I'm not qualified for those positions." I looked into this when I found out Jesse drained Charlie's trust fund. High-level positions were not an option. I barely have a bachelor's degree, let alone ten or more years of experience. And I certainly couldn't work and live *on* the cruise ships. What would I do with Charlie?

"We could've created something."

"I didn't want to take advantage of my friends."

"Well, I know for a fact that Lennox sees you more as family than a friend. And just so you're aware, family absolutely takes advantage of family. It's in the fine print."

I smile into the phone. "Good to know."

"We're here if you need anything. If you hate your boss, quit. You're not alone, kid."

I know he meant it as a term of endearment, but that *word*. I hate it. A kid would expect handouts and someone to swoop in and fix their life. I can't be a kid... I have one. And I'm trying to set a good example for Charlie by showing her I can stand on my own two feet. I relied on Jesse to share the load that was mine to carry for way too long. Look how that turned out.

"Thanks, Dex."

"No problem. All right, I'm off to the grocery store for yet another late-night chocolate mint ice cream run. Three nights in a row, now."

I laugh. "Just buy a whole carton so you don't have to keep running out."

"Dude," he says. "I *am*. This baby eats like an offensive lineman, I swear. Don't tell Lennox I told you that."

We both burst out in laughter before ending the call.

I'll admit, I feel a little lighter after that conversation. It's nice to know I have a safety net if I really need it. It'd be the simpler solution, sure. Quit on Nathan, work for my friends. I can consider it... For now, I have unfinished business.

Next on my to-do list: Address Nathan's unanswered text.

> **Bosshole:** *S*till there? I need to know the plan for tomorrow night.

> **Me:** Eight o'clock at Tansy Haleen's up-and-coming restaurant, Viva.

> **Bosshole:** Really. How'd you pull that off?

> **Me:** It's better not to share details... just in case you get subpoenaed.

> **Bosshole:** Funny. Fine. Arrange a private transport to pick me and Shaylin up from the airport at 7:30.

> **Me:** Will do.

His response bubble populates a few times before ultimately it disappears. He must decide against "thank you" or "goodnight."

That's okay. His rudeness only adds fuel to flames, and at this point, I'm channeling my inner phoenix. I'm going to wipe that stupid, cocky smirk off of Nathan's face if it's the very last thing I do.

CHAPTER 13

Nathan

Holy shit, she's handsy. I thought I would be the one groveling tonight.

I'm not a fan of celebrity god complexes, but if anyone has earned an ego, it's Shaylin. She works harder than anyone in the industry. Her real name is Shaye Linda Colette, but the world knows the pop star by her stage name. Anytime I meet a person who only goes by one name, like a Madonna wannabe, I brace myself for narcissism. Instead, Shaylin has shown nothing besides humble and considerate since we got into the back of this car together. It's nice to see a singer-songwriter who is more passionate about her craft than her fame.

Her only crime is being a little more flirty than I'd care for. I've been tolerating her hand on my knee for the past ten minutes of this ride, but when her fingers tiptoe up my thigh, I make an excuse to hop into a seat on the other side of the stretch Escalade.

"Would you like some water?" I grab two flutes from a hidden compartment between the captain seats.

Shaylin's bright red lips curl into a mischievous grin. "I believe those are for champagne."

Right she is. Her sparkly, sequin dress reflects off the champagne flutes I'm holding. But there's no way I'm drinking in this back seat with a woman who is acting like she wants to mount me. "How about we stick with water for now? I'd hate for alcohol to influence your business decisions."

"All work, no play." She winks at me, still not answering my offer of water. That's probably good because I don't actually see any water back here. Just bottles of champagne on ice.

"This is a working dinner, right?"

She silently nods before tucking a loose strand of her long, blond hair behind her ear.

"The reason my dad and I wanted to reach out to you in the early phases of development is because, if you decide to commit to at least a one-year residency, we'd like to construct the stage to fit your needs. Your last tour had a water element. It was visually stunning. We'd love to recreate that energy."

"So, you're trying to steal my tour ideas?"

"What? Not at all, I just—"

She giggles. "Calm down, Nathan. I'm kidding. Thank you," she adds in a honey-smooth voice. "That's very considerate to offer me some creative say in the construction. Actually, the residency caught my attention because all the aggressive travel is starting to take a toll on my health. It'd be nice to settle down for a while."

"Sounds like this is ideal timing."

"Perhaps." She runs the tip of her pointer finger across her bottom lip. Maybe I'm imagining it, but she's giving off lioness vibes, and I may look like dinner. I really hope her endgame is a disgustingly large lump sum of money, and not getting into my pants. I'm stupid, really. You don't throw away a chance with Shaylin. She's worth almost as much as I am, and of course she's attractive, but my mind is on one thing right now...

What the hell does Spencer have up her sleeve? No way she got Tansy Haleen, or any celebrity chef, to cook a private dinner at a moment's notice. I keep checking my phone, waiting for her to wave the white flag and admit defeat, but it's been crickets.

The vehicle arrived at the airport right on time, and now we're headed to God-knows-what. Is Spencer more well connected than I realized? I thought this request was a slam dunk for her failure. By now I should've received a text or email, full of profanities, criticizing me for my diva-like behavior. Instead, I'm counting down the minutes until I get to call Spencer's bluff. Fuck, this is irritating. I don't like feeling this way, like I might not have the upper hand.

"When's the hotel going to be finished?" Shaylin asks.

"With divine intervention? One year."

"So, when you factor in the inevitable fuckups and inclement weather—we're talking at least two."

She earns a genuine laugh from me. "You know your stuff. But I promise you, if we agree on a firm timeline, we'll make it happen. I know how valuable your time is. I'll move mountains to ensure we hold up our end of the bargain. And as far as your payment—"

With a thick scoff, she holds her palms up. "Before you try to wow me with money, I'll go ahead and tell you the only thing that will get me to agree to your proposal. I swear on my life if you say yes to it, I'll sign paperwork tonight."

"Careful, Ms. Colette. You'll want your lawyer present to review all the fine print. I want to do everything by the book here."

She points to my chest. "You invited me out tonight. Your people went through great lengths to get in touch. Isn't this what you want?" She pauses to tug on her bottom lip with her top teeth. "Or did you have ulterior motives for this dinner?"

There's nobody I can complain to about this. *Oh, wah, Shaylin's overtly hitting on me.* If I had close buddies, they'd for sure punch me in the dick for passing up an opportunity of a lifetime.

"What's the one thing?" I keep my eyes fixed firmly on hers. There's no part of me that wants to savor a peek at her chest which is very exposed in her low-cut dress. Lately, I only fall victim to stolen glances around Spencer, which is another reason my assistant irritates me to high hell. She's a snake charmer who has apparently learned to exercise some control over *my snake.*

"I want an ownership stake in the hotel."

I can't hide my shock. "*What?*"

"Not for free," she clarifies. "I want to be an investor."

"You're kidding."

Her perky smile turns into a scowl. "You know what? I'm used to not being taken seriously, but my money is just as green as yours. I'm here to play."

"Oh, hey now." Risking being back within reach of her wandering hands, I hop over to the opposite chair right next to Shaylin. "That's not what I meant at all. I would of course respect you as an investor. I just don't understand why. Investments like this are heavy if you want an ownership stake, and it comes with a lot of risk. Your pay as a performer is guaranteed...and would be very generous."

"I'm twenty-six, Nathan. But I've been doing this since I was sixteen. I'm already so exhausted. I'm not going to be able to shake my ass on stage forever. It's time to think about branching out. I want to invest my wealth into something tangible that can take care of my kids, and their kids, and their kids' kids."

Smart girl. "I'll run it up the ladder."

Her talons clamp right back on my knee. "I thought you were at the top of the ladder."

"This project is a collaboration with my dad. I'd like his insight on this."

"Aw," she coos. "I love me a daddy's boy."

Good grief. I'm relieved when the car finally crawls to a stop. I all but jump out of the Escalade and hold out my hand for Shaylin. I hope she takes my eagerness as chivalry and not just a desperate attempt to put some distance between us.

Still, the instant her bright pink stilettos hit the concrete, her arm is looped in mine. Viva isn't embedded within a mainstream Vegas hotel, so it's only a few quick steps from the curb to the front of the restaurant. The walk isn't long, but it's plenty of time for the hostess, waiting for us underneath the entryway arch, to see me arm in arm with Shaylin and draw all sorts of wrong conclusions.

My stomach swoops when I realize said hostess is Spencer. She's dressed in all black and wearing an unmistakable frown at the sight of me and Shaylin.

"Good evening. I'm glad you two made it safely," Spencer

says in a sugary-sweet tone that doesn't match the kicked-puppy expression on her face. "Ms. Shaylin, you look stunning." She cuts me a look. "Mr. Hatcher...you're here."

Spencer has more poise than a seasoned ballerina, not appearing remotely starstruck by the pop legend on my arm. Speaking of which... I make an excuse to search my pockets for something and successfully detach myself from Shaylin.

"What are you doing here?" I ask Spencer, examining her scowl, that's pointed directly at me, for any hint of nerves. I didn't want it to go this far. I only wanted a text omission of failure. I don't want to embarrass the poor girl in front of famous company.

"Tansy asked for my assistance, since we booked her on *such short notice*. I hope you don't mind, I'll be your server tonight. The restaurant isn't technically open yet, but there's one table set for you in the middle of the dining room. Ms. Shaylin, there's a very nice bottle of rosé on ice at your table, but can I get you anything else to drink?"

"You are so lovely." Shaylin gives her a warm smile. Spencer looks just as surprised as I am when the pop princess grabs her by her shoulders and kisses both her cheeks. "I love rosé. That's perfect."

Eyes as big as globes, Spencer gestures through the door. "Right this way."

Shaylin takes the lead, allowing Spencer and me a brief moment, side by side.

"Anything for you, boss? A drink? Some bread? Or will you just be feasting on the shock that's smothered all over your face?"

Witty, this one. "So, when do we get to meet Tansy?" I ask.

Spencer clears her throat and smooths her black blouse. *Dammit, again.* Her ample bust creates an open space between the buttons. My gaze slips against my will...and now I know her bra is purple. *For fuck's sake.*

Shaylin seated herself, so I don't have to do the awkward shuffle of holding out a chair for a woman who is most definitely not my date. At least, not like that. Spencer waits until I'm sitting as well, practically blanketed with the oversized linen-covered table, to address us.

"Tansy is very excited for this evening," she starts.

"Great. Bring her out."

Spencer delivers me an icy glare. "Ms. Haleen would appreciate your discretion in the matter, but she just had a little work done." She waves her hand over her face and grimaces. "Her nose, chin, and ears... It's a bit of a bruised mess right now. She can cook but she's really not feeling up to company, so it's imperative you stay out of the kitchen to respect her privacy."

"*Of course.* I get it. When I got my nose done, I didn't even want my dog looking at me until the swelling went down," Shaylin enthusiastically explains.

I squint at Spencer, replaying her calculated excuse. "Nose, chin, and *ears*? Are you implying that Tansy got an ear-job?"

"Um." Panic briefly flashes across Spencer's face, then just as quickly evaporates. "Yes."

She can't honestly expect me to believe that. "Huh. Okay, then. Please wish *Tansy* a speedy recovery and thank her for cooking for us tonight, especially in such a delicate state."

Spencer flutters her thick, dark lashes profusely. *Well, ladies and gentlemen, there it is.* This is my assistant's tell when she's lying. She's either batting her lashes, or that's one hell of an aggressive eye twitch.

"What are we having tonight? I'm assuming it's a fixed menu?"

"Yes. Five courses," Spencer curtly responds to me.

"One of which involves Kraft Mac and Cheese?"

"*Nathan!*" Shaylin scolds me playfully. "Don't be rude. It's Tansy Haleen. Her food is art."

Oh please. I don't know who Spencer is hiding back there, but it most certainly is not Tansy.

"You know what? I'm going to let Ms. Haleen's food speak for itself. In fact, I'm going to head back to check on your appetizers." She points to the gold, five-armed candelabra on the table. "Would you like me to light that for you?"

"No," I answer.

"Yes, please."

Shaylin and I exchange a glance after our opposing responses. The last thing I need between the two of us is romantic candlelight.

"An open flame isn't safe on this tablecloth. I'd love to get you home burn-free, Ms. Colette." Sometimes the excuses just come to me. It's a gift.

"Fair point," Shaylin concedes.

"I'll be back in a moment with your humble pie." Eyes locked on me, Spencer theatrically open-palm pops herself on the forehead. "Whoops, slip of the tongue. I meant *hummingbird pie*. We're starting the evening with a touch of sweet."

"Ooh, how fun. We're starting with dessert? This is already arguably the best dinner I've ever been treated to."

Shaylin says something else, but it doesn't register. My stare is glued to Spencer's hips, swaying back and forth as she whisks away to the kitchen.

All right, sass queen. Go ahead.

I'm ready to be impressed.

CHAPTER 14

Spencer

Grabbing the bottom of my apron, I dab at the droplets beading on my forehead. Sweat is not an ideal garnish for this strawberry shortcake cream puff dessert I'm assembling.

I release a shaky breath. *It's almost over.* Just dessert left.

For the past few hours, I feel like I've been reenacting a scene right out of *Mrs. Doubtfire*, hiding in the kitchen, and toggling between waitress and secret behind-the-scenes chef. I have to keep my apron on in the kitchen so I don't get my clothes too messy. I know Nathan isn't buying this. His skeptical scowl is permanently glued to his face every time I set a new plate in front of them. But it doesn't matter because *Shaylin* is eating this whole ruse up. That's the point of tonight. If the dinner goes well, and she agrees to sign whatever deal Brickstone wants her to, this night was a success, and Nathan will have no reason to reprimand me.

Outside of the nervous anxiety, it's been fun to cook in a professional kitchen. I don't accidentally hip-check the counter every time I turn around which is already a major step up from my tiny apartment kitchen.

Most of what I made tonight was prepped at home. The hummingbird pie was my mom's recipe. The final touch was using small, heart-shaped cookie cutters to shape pieces from the center. It was such a waste of pie, but after a drizzle of caramel and dusting of confectioner's sugar, it looked like a bougie move a fancy restaurant would pull. Let's sacrifice a whole pie for two center-cut, palm-sized pieces.

Little do they know, the salad was from a bag, but I made the dressing fresh at least—a zesty lime vinaigrette that I googled. The filet mignon was also a little overcooked. I was going for medium-rare, but we got medium-well after they spent too much time in a butter bath. There's a good chance I'm my own worst critic, because there were zero complaints from the table. I actually watched in shock as Shaylin immediately cut a long piece of steak, the size of her whole thumb, and inhaled it like a barbarian. Good for her. It's refreshing when women actually eat on dates.

Dates. Ugh. It was supposed to be a business meeting, but let's call this what it is. Nathan's probably swooning over the slender, long-legged, blonde beauty that makes my annual salary in the blink of an eye. They're definitely going home together tonight, and I'm trying really hard not to think about it. I'm trying to think about the good parts of this evening, like when Nathan actually cracked a smile after biting into my Cuban egg rolls.

Those I will accept zero criticism on. They are my own personal twist on our beloved Cubanos. I slow-roasted the marinated pork shoulder all morning. I used Lumpia wrappers for extra crunchiness. While the spicy, dijon-honey glaze is a step away from authenticity, it balances perfectly. At least, that's what Mom used to tell me. These were her favorite. Even after she started chemo and her appetite vanished, she never said no to my Cuban egg rolls.

Ready to bring this entire evening over the finish line, I plate the strawberry cream puffs, and place a few halved strawberries on the side of the treat. Fighting the urge to drizzle, I dot the inside of the white porcelain dessert plate with homemade strawberry glaze. It looks fancier this way, and I'm pretending to be an award-winning chef back here. A tiny sliver of almond on each puff, then a light dust of confectioner's sugar, and... "Done," I exclaim out loud like I'm a contestant on *Final Cut* finishing my dish in the nick of time.

With a plate in each hand, I eagerly make my way through the double doors into the dining room. I did it. I actually fucking pulled this off. There's a bouncy pep in my step until I turn the corner of the dim-lighted restaurant to see Nathan's arm around Shaylin. They're no longer sitting across from each other. She's scooted her chair to him and is wearing his navy suit jacket over her bare arms. He's rubbing her shoulder affectionately. The moment he sees me, he drops his arm and shifts his gaze down as if he was caught doing something he shouldn't.

My stomach sinks, swallowed up by a black hole of utter disappointment. *Stop it, Spencer. You knew. This isn't a surprise.* I try to disappear as I approach the table. I slide their dessert plates in front of them silently and attempt to leave quickly.

"Why are you wearing an apron?" Nathan asks.

I look down and see the evidence of my slipup. *Fuck.* I forgot to take it off. "Dishes," I say quickly. "I was helping Tansy clean up."

He could easily pick apart my lie. There's stains on the clean white apron, colors from every single course. But instead, Nathan shows mercy. "I see."

"Hope you enjoy," I force out and spin around to leave.

"Wait!" When I turn back around, Shaylin's smile is so innocent. She has no idea she's hurting me right now. It's not on purpose. She has every right to go after a man like Nathan. Anyways, she can have him. I hate him. So. Damn. Much. "What is this? It's so cute I don't even want to eat it."

I'm exhausted. I just want to run to the kitchen, make a blanket fort, and fall asleep reading a good book with a bright flashlight. Adulting is too much sometimes. I miss being a kid.

"It's Tansy's take on a strawberry shortcake. Instead of a biscuit, it's an almond-liquor-infused cream puff with a whipped strawberry cheesecake filling. The glaze is a citrus-strawberry reduction."

Shaylin grabs the dessert with two fingers and takes a messy bite, cream spilling out of the casing of the pastry crust and smearing on her lips. "Mmmm," she moans. "Can I order about fifty more of these?" she asks, after swallowing. "It's seriously insane. Nathan, try this."

I die inside when she holds the second bite of her treat to his lips. He hesitates, but eventually his lips part and she shoves the pastry into his mouth. I've never seen a human chew slower. A sloth, sure. It feels as if Nathan is trying to drag out the torture he's not aware he's inducing.

"That's really good," he finally says. Something changes in his eyes. There's a sweet sincerity I haven't seen since the first night we met—just a quick flash of Nate. "Would you tell the chef she's incredible, and I'm very impressed. Good job."

I raise one eyebrow. "You want me to tell Tansy Haleen, '*good job*'?"

For a moment, nothing exists except us two. The romantic, dim-lit restaurant melts away. Shaylin dissolves into the abyss. It's only me, Nathan, and all our lies.

"Well, what should I say?"

"Just...thank you."

He nods in understanding. "Thank you, Spencer."

It's so obvious I'm caught, but who cares. Tonight wasn't about *winning* per se. It was about not giving up and not allowing any man to underestimate me.

"I'll let her know." With that, I turn on my heel and dash away before I'm trapped by further conversation.

My instructions were clear. I could use Tansy's kitchen, but I better leave it in the exact pristine condition in which it was handed over. I'm scrubbing a roasting pan so hard, it's past shining, and in dangerous territory of me scrubbing the metal coating right off. It's been about twenty minutes since I've been out there. Either they are lip-locked, or they're gone. I sincerely hope it's the latter.

If they left, I missed my opportunity. I should've gotten an autograph for Charlie. *Damn my pride.* She would've lost her mind. Thankfully, Charlie is at her sleepover at Claire's. If I would've had to bring her tonight, Shaylin and Nathan wouldn't have gotten a word in. Charlie would've crawled up in Shaylin's lap like a stray puppy begging for a new home. Maybe that's why I didn't get the autograph.

She took my guy. I don't want her taking my sister too.

"Ugh," I grumble out loud. Stupid, intrusive thoughts. *He's not my guy.*

"What's wrong?"

"Shit!" I squeal, the soapy sponge flying out of my hands, leaving a splash of bubbles all over the counter I just wiped down. "Dammit, Nathan. I told you not to come back here."

Advancing toward me, he is not remotely dissuaded by my command. "Call me Nate."

"Okay. I told you not to come back here, *Nate.*"

He's looking at me like an adorably huffy toddler. "Let me guess, Tansy had to run out?"

I glare at him through narrowed eyes. "Great guess. She had to excuse herself to go take her pain medication."

"Right. We wouldn't want her ears to start hurting." He flicks his earlobe coyly.

"What the hell do you want?" I'm not even going to try to hide my bitterness. It's too much effort. *Ah.* Let the lava of my rage flow free.

"You never brought the bill." To my surprise, he loosens his tie, then unknots it and lets it lazily hang free around his collar. Next, he frees two buttons on his light gray dress shirt. I don't think he's hypnotizing me on purpose...

But he is.

"There's no working register. She'll just send an invoice to the office."

"Makes sense."

He swaggers over to the other side of the counter where my Tupperware is neatly stacked. I couldn't tell by his perfect dictation, but the way he's walking gives him away. Long, lazy strides, like he's moving but has nowhere to be. He's tipsy. The restaurant bar is already stocked. I wonder if he helped himself. I make a mental note to tell Dex to tell Tansy she may need her restaurant to bill us for what I'm assuming was a very expensive bottle of liquor. While Nathan isn't ostentatious with his money, he also doesn't strike me as a hooch kind of guy.

"What're you doing?" I ask as he removes the blue lid from the Tupperware holding the remaining egg rolls. There's only a couple left. I wanted to bring them home to Charlie.

"These were my favorite. Everything was superb tonight, but these were..." He blows out a deep breath, seemingly unable to come up with an adequate description. "Did you try them?"

I shake my head before nodding to my protein drink on the far counter. The flavor is awful. Leave it to Protein Milk Extreme to ruin vanilla cupcakes. "I'm dieting."

He scrunches his face in a mixture of disdain and confusion. Yet, at the same time his eyes sweep over me in a way that makes heat radiate across my skin.

"Why?"

I match his befuddled expression. "Usually people diet to lose weight."

"Yes, believe it or not, I'm aware of that, Spencer. I'm asking why *you* feel the need to lose weight?" There's something hazy and warm in his eyes—like they've feasted, and they're satisfied. It makes me feel suddenly self-conscious but also...*seen*. When's the last time a man has looked at me *like this*?

Hovering my hands over my body from my shoulders to my knees is my only response.

"It's confusing to me," he mumbles as he removes the lids from a smaller container filled with the mustard dipping sauce.

"What is?"

"You're so clever and intelligent. Yet you don't see what everybody else does." He dunks the egg roll into the sauce and crosses the kitchen with purpose. Cupping his hand underneath the coated end, he holds the egg roll to my mouth. "One bite won't ruin your diet." His eyes lock with mine, at first. Then they fall back down to my lips.

"No, thanks."

"Spencer. It's life-changing." He flashes me a wicked grin that's lined with flirtatious energy, jolting straight to my core.

"No," I repeat, scrunching my toes to try to keep myself steady. He's too damn close. I'm going to lose it. The way he smells...the way he's looking at me... All I can think about is what his lips taste like.

"Your boss is giving you an order," he says in a low tone that pulls me from my haze.

"How about one task at a time, hm? I'm still finishing the last order my boss gave me."

"Try. It." He pokes me with the egg roll, smearing sauce all over my top lip. "Boop."

I inhale slowly, then exhale even slower, trying to exercise some gentle parenting techniques. I don't shout at him. I don't deck him in the face. "You're not tipsy, you're drunk, aren't you?" I accuse, before chomping down on the egg roll just to get him off my back. I tried to *accidentally* nip his finger, but the jerk is too fast.

He basically force-fed me, but *damn* does real food feel good. I chew, savoring the medley of flavors in my mouth. I'm so distracted by the relief of real food in my mouth, I'm completely caught off-guard when Nathan swipes a finger over my top lip, clearing the sauce. He pops the finger into his mouth, releasing a soft, rumbly moan.

"See? So good." Nathan's wearing a smug smirk as he watches my jaw sweeping the floor. *What the hell is he playing at?*

He continues nonchalantly, "I'm not normally a fan of fusion food, but this is something else. And here I always thought a Cuban sandwich was made with ham."

I want to take the rest of the egg roll from his hand and shove it down my throat, whole. My stomach churns in misery, begging for more solid sustenance before I go back to restricting myself to liquid protein. I also secretly want to bathe in this sauce and see what else he's tempted to sample. More than anything, I hate how he has this hold over me. *Hate it.* I want to be as impervious to Nathan as I am to any other man because logic tells me not to want what I can't have. It'll end in heartbreak.

I quickly redirect the conversation. "My dad would make them with mojo-brined roasted pork *and* ham. You need both for a real Cubano. He'd hate this sauce, though. Plain mustard only."

"You're Cuban?"

"A quarter. My dad was black and Cuban."

"Was?" Nathan asks softly. "I'm sorry."

"Oh, no, he's alive...I think. I don't know. He left us when I was little and"—I pop my shoulders—"he just never looked back."

"And your mom?"

I pause for a moment, feeling the sudden weight of the conversation. "My mom *was* fair-skinned, with platinum-blonde hair and light blue eyes. She was my dad's polar opposite. She died five years ago."

"Oh." He doesn't say "sorry" again. Instead, we make our peace with the uncomfortable silence. What could he possibly say? An apology never fixes it. All the empathy in the world doesn't bring her back. But I appreciate the torn expression he's wearing. It's probably in my head, but I get the feeling he'd like to embrace me. Except that reminds me, I'm not the woman he's interested in taking home tonight.

"Should you get back to Shaylin?" *Dammit.* The question comes out with an edge of jealousy I've been keeping locked down.

"I ordered her a car and sent her home," Nathan answers, plainly.

My whole body relaxes at the surprisingly good news. "But I thought..."

"It was a business dinner. We talked business, now it's over."

I could make a comment about how their cuddling didn't look like *just business* but I don't want to ruin this moment. He's actually acting human, and I don't know how long we have until he turns back into a toad.

"Want some help with the dishes?" Nathan reaches for my sponge, his fingers brushing mine for a beat longer than necessary. The brief contact sends a flutter through my chest.

"Very nice of you to offer." My smile grows, heat rising to my face as I notice his gaze dropping south of my lips. *It's an obvious invitation, right?* "What do you want in exchange?" I mean it to be a little flirty. I keep playing hopscotch with this line of hate and longing, my body refusing to align with my better judgment.

He deadpans, "For you to quit."

I'm stunned into momentary silence. If it weren't for the suddenly stone-like stare on his face, I'd think I misheard. "Excuse me?"

"I can't fire you without risking a wrongful termination suit, which I think you're clever enough to file. So, I'd like you to quit."

"Why?"

He tilts his head ever so slightly. "Spencer, come on. We're not going to work well together. Why do you need such a serious job, anyway? I looked at your employment file—you're twenty-three. Still a baby. You're in Las Vegas. Bartend at a cool club, or deal blackjack or something. Party every night. You have plenty of time to grow up. Office jobs aren't going anywhere. Be a kid while you can, you know?"

That word again. My heart is now racing for an entirely different reason. I snatch the sponge out of his hand in a dramatic show of rejecting his help. "You have a gift, Nathan."

His deep blue-green eyes look dark and sleepy. Maybe from the travel, followed by a long night. Or, maybe it's the booze. The smell of him—the one I crave—is currently overpowered by something sweet and sharp, like sugary gasoline.

"What do you mean, a gift?" he asks.

"Everything that comes out of your mouth is accidentally insulting." Clamping my eyes closed, I shake my head. "You lie like it's your native tongue. You're a jerk without even trying. It's impressive, really."

A small smirk starts on his face but quickly dissipates when he sees I'm not joking. "I was only trying to say—"

"You don't know anything about me or my life, which is fine. I don't want to share a single part of me with you. But I am a great assistant. I'm sorry you don't want me here. Too bad for you, I'm not going to roll over and die just because you asked me to." *Oh no.* I have to leave right now before the tears start. They're more out of frustration and fatigue than anything else, but Nathan *can't* see me cry.

I yank off my apron and chuck it to the side of the counter, the movement causing me to brush against him. Just that little touch, and my clothes are on fire.

"I'm going to the restroom, then I'll finish cleaning up the kitchen." I pause to give him an opening to apologize, or maybe even just explain. I would happily settle for an explanation as to why this *jackass* is so put off by me.

But no. He stays quiet. There's remorse on his face, but nothing else comes out of his mouth. His eyes tell a different story, dark with something that looks dangerously like desire swimming in his frustration. Maybe he's as fed up with our situation as I am.

"Please don't be here when I get back."

I barrel through the doors, and my tears start to pour, my body still humming from the conflicting feelings. Every time this man seems in reach...

He slips away.

CHAPTER 15

Spencer

"For the love of all that is holy, Spike! Shush!"

Monday morning, I sink deeper into my living room couch, praying for a swift, painless death to take me. That's how drained I am. I'd rather suffocate, face buried in this stiff couch, than go to work this morning. Partially because I don't want to see Nathan's stupid face. We haven't spoken since Friday night at the restaurant. But more concerning, I don't think I'm coherent enough to pretend to do my job today. I have lost two nights of sleep in a row now due to a plump, lovesick guinea pig who has endless endurance for squealing at all hours of the day and night.

Spike continues to cry as I chug hot coffee, not even feeling the heat in my throat. I'm so tired, the nerves that are supposed to warn me when my flesh is on fire have officially shut off.

Unable to take another second of his screeching, I peel myself off the couch and force my legs to move. After grabbing a baby carrot from the fridge, I shove it through the wire of his cage. "Here, you little chubster." I'm a few more glugs into my coffee before I drop to my knees so I'm eye level with his cage that's resting on the coffee table. "I was *not* body-shaming you, by the way. You're supposed to be round and chubby, and it looks great on you. But if chubby is a trigger for you, I can say fluffy moving forward."

"Oh my gosh, did you just apologize for body-shaming a guinea pig? You've officially gone cuckoo for Cocoa Puffs," Charlie sasses, entering the living room. She maneuvers around the edge of the couch and drops to her knees next to me. She stares at Spike like a proud mama. Except I'm the one feeding him, cleaning his cage, and getting him fresh water. I'm also apparently the only one affected by his incessant whining. Charlie has slept like a baby all weekend.

Examining my little sister's face, I see way too much glitter. There's a light brush of blue on her eyelids. She also smells like sickeningly sweet peaches. I'm too tired to have this argument with her right now. Once I get a good night's sleep, she and I can go a few rounds about my minimal-makeup rule.

"Did you give him another carrot?" Charlie asks accusingly.

"Obviously," I snap. "He's not screaming at the top of his lungs, which must mean he's eating."

"He's not supposed to have more than one or two pieces of carrot a week, Spencer. They're too high in sugar. It's going to hurt his belly."

"I'm going to hurt his belly," I mumble under my breath. I just threatened a three-pound piggie-rodent. Sleep deprivation has me unhinged.

Ignoring me, Charlie opens his cage door and scoops him up into her arms. She sweetly nuzzles him and he's instantly calm. Whenever I pick up Spike, he goes straight Wolverine, trying to escape. I have the scratch marks up my forearm to prove it.

"Did you decide if you're renaming him? I'm a big fan of Snickers." I'm not only referring to the candy bar. Spike is a Ridgeback Abyssinian guinea pig. Charlie made me sit through an informational special on guinea pigs. Guess how many different types there are? Way too freaking many. The piggies are usually classified by their hair patterns. Ridgebacks make it look like he has a little mohawk, which is I think why they named him Spike. It's not a terrible name, but his mohawk is understated these days, and his coat is a blend of rich, dark chocolate, warm caramel, and stripes of vanilla cake. He should be named after a dessert.

"We're not renaming him."

"Why not?"

"Because he's two. He already knows his name, don't you, my sweet boy?"

Oh good Lord, Charlie. If you love him that much, change his bedding every now and then, hm? "Guinea pigs don't know their names," I tell her.

Charlie cradles Spike in one arm, then whips out her phone from her back pocket. She waves it in my face menacingly. "Wanna bet? I'll ask Siri right now."

It's hard for me to believe that a little creature who seems to prefer his food bowl be half pellets, half droppings could really recognize his name, but whatever. "Spike it is, then. Go get your backpack. We're going to be late for school if we don't leave soon."

"I'm not going to school today."

"Uh, yes, you most certainly are."

"No, I'm not."

Dear Mother Theresa, Gandhi, and Julie Andrews in the *Sound of Music*, please give me the strength not to punt an eleven-year-old across my apartment. Massaging my temples, I ask, "Why do you think you're not going to school today? Which you are, by the way."

"Spike will be lonely. It's his first week away from Babe. He needs support."

Babe... The randy little minx that got us into this mess. Apparently these two can't keep their furry paws off each other. If they aren't in the same cage, they roll over, play dead, and screech for their lives—some real Romeo and Juliet bullshit.

When they are in the same cage, they're quiet, but they reproduce. *A lot.* Not only that, but the babies are incestuous, so poor sweet Grandma Ruby was basically living in a guinea pig sanctuary for far too long. She eventually got rid of the babies, but after the vet told her there was a good chance Babe and Spike would die if they got spayed and neutered, the only choice was to put them in separate households.

And that is the story of how this squeaky, little, Snicker-colored asshole became the third member of our family.

"Charlie, he's going to be fine." Or more accurately, we won't be here to hear his squealing.

Her eyes growing wide, she shakes her head slowly. "No way, Spence. I am *not* leaving him when he needs me most."

"How about we return him to Ruby and Claire? Voilá. Problem solved."

"You can't," she hisses. "Spike was my good behavior present and you can't take him back. Jesse has texted me *twice* since you said he couldn't, and I haven't responded at all. I earned Spike."

Welp, it seems as good a day as any to murder my ex-fiancé. He's lucky I'm busy this morning dealing with a condescending punk of a boss who I'm sure is waiting to punish me with more silent treatment or another impossible task. I still stand by what I said to him in Tansy's kitchen. It was the raw truth. If I get fired for holding up the mirror, so be it.

"Charlie, the bottom line is you have to go to school because I have to go to work. Put Spike back in his cage."

I was expecting more lip, not for Charlie to burst out in spontaneous tears.

"Are you kidding me right now?" I ask in disbelief.

"He's hurting because he misses Babe. Try to have some compassion."

Compassion? She's starting to use her English class's weekly vocabulary list against me. Last week she told me a boy at school told her he liked her but she found him to be a *fatuous* jock. I had to go look the word up.

"How did you feel when we left Jesse?" Charlie asks.

Relieved, free, elated, like I could finally think clearly. Charlie's still adapting to the idea of life without Jesse, so I curtail my honest reply. "Sad, at first."

"Right. So Spike is sad, and he shouldn't be left all day at home by himself."

I squeeze my lids shut so hard, my eyes water. "Level with me because we're running out of time. Any chance you're going to drop this? Or are you going to dig in your heels?"

"Consider my heels dug."

Ugh! The way I'd like to mentally unsubscribe from my morning right now...

"Get me his travel carrier and his little diaper. I'll take him to work with me today."

My actual game plan is to bring Spike on a quick field trip in dropping Charlie off at school. If we leave right now, I'll still have enough time to return home, pop the piggie back in his cage, then head to work. I'll scoop him up before picking up Charlie. Problem solved.

It's not lost on me that lately, the solution to my problems has been desperate, blatant lies. Gotta say, I'm not sure if I'm loving the new me in Las Vegas.

While Charlie looks on the cusp of accepting my plan, she still hesitates, squinting one eye. "You're going to pet him, hug him, and give him lots of positive attention between meetings, right?"

"I'm going to keep him alive, Charlie. Don't ask me for more than that. Now, skedaddle. Go get his carrier and your backpack."

"Fine," she grumbles as she puts Spike in my arms, then darts down the hall.

Still calm from the prior embrace of his preferred mama, Spike snuggles against my chest. I stroke from his little nose over the slant of his forehead. "Are you that sad, buddy?" He responds to my voice, lifting his head so I can see his adorable pouty bottom lip. "If you could just keep it in your furry pants, you could live with your girlfriend. You did this to yourself, you little horndog."

Mweeep. Mweeep. Based on the look he's giving me, I'm pretty sure his squeaks are guinea pig for "screw you."

I pet him from head to rump anyway and he melts under the attention. His little butt is wiggling with glee. I use my arms like an elevator, raising Spike up so I can kiss the top of his head. "But thank you for making my sister so happy."

There was an unexpected plot twist.

Due to heavy construction on Baker Street that I was most definitely not expecting, there was no time to drop Spike off at home. Chelsea didn't say a damn thing when I greeted her at the front desk with a pet carrier in hand. As soon as I got to my desk, I stowed Spike away underneath my desk. He's out of anyone's sight line, and I can nudge his carrier with my toe if he gets too vocal. Luckily he's been mostly silent all morning, probably distracted from all the new sights and smells.

"Look, Spike," I say, tapping the side of his cloth enclosure with the point of my high heel. "If you just behave until lunchtime, I promise you a small pile of fruit when we get home. Our little secret. Just don't go ballistic with your whining...*please*."

As usual, my inbox is empty except for the Monday company newsletter. It should be easy to slip away a smidge early for my break today.

Ping!

Or so I thought.

An email from Nathan arrives right at 8:00 a.m. It's a quick request. Apparently I'm to call a construction company and ask for a detailed breakdown of an invoice to be sent over immediately. Easy enough. I glance through the glass doors into Nathan's office. It's empty.

All right, well, let me knock this out really quick. I reach for my desk phone when there's another email alert. At 8:02 a.m., there's another request from Nathan. This time I need to reschedule a finance meeting for ten o'clock this morning. *Hm, that's an exec meeting.* Definitely takes precedence. Abandoning the phone, I compose an email to all the senior finance executives and their executive assistants to at least let them know of the cancellation.

I barely have a greeting typed out when another email comes in. The time stamp reads 8:04 a.m. Another request for a same-day bakery order for a senior partner's retirement party today. There are no other instructions other than, put it on the company card, and make sure there are no nuts due to some allergy sensitivities.

By the time another email comes in at 8:06 a.m., I finally get it through my thick skull that this is Nathan's revenge. He tried to smoke me out of my job by an impossibly difficult task. It didn't work. Now, he's relying on volume.

Nathan scheduled all of these emails. Ten more arrive in two-minute intervals. By half past eight, I'm sitting with an entire week's worth of tasks that all need to be done *right now*. Fists balled, I growl in frustration. He's such a dick. I could just walk out. *I really could.*

I have other options. Nathan doesn't deserve me as an assistant or a friend. But something very stubborn, deep inside me just can't admit defeat. He wants me to quit, which is why I won't. At this point, I'm acting as childish as he is.

I allow myself two minutes to fantasize about standing up, kicking back my chair, and waltzing out of here with my head held high, while giving Nathan the bird. *God, that feels good.* But once the two minutes is over, I get my ass to work.

By the time Nathan walks into the office, well past ten, I've already ordered the retirement party cake, contacted the construction company about the missing invoice, rescheduled the finance meeting, and knocked out about three other mindless tasks.

I try to ignore him as he walks past my desk, pretending to be buried in my laptop and far too busy for morning pleasantries, but to my dismay he stops. I have no choice but to acknowledge him, which I do with a disinterested stare and a muffled, "G'morning."

"You look busy," he says in a monotone, devoid of any emotion.

"That I am." I try to match his lifeless tone.

Damn, he looks good today. His white dress shirt with the subtle yellow and blue pinstripes fits a little more snug than his usual shirts. It hugs the curves of muscular shoulders, broad chest, and well-defined arms. It makes sense. Vampires have to be alluring to trap their unsuspecting victims.

"Did you get my email?"

"Oh, yes. All of them."

He shrugs with one shoulder. "Look, I heard you at the restaurant. You wanted to help? Here it is. If you can keep up, then maybe..."

"Maybe, what?"

Nathan diverts his gaze. "I don't know. I'm taking it day by day, as you should too. Really think about if you're happy here and even want to work for me. Being my assistant isn't a cakewalk."

"I can handle it," I say defensively.

"Fine. Did you get to the email about the residential complaints? You'll need to contact each of the property management liaisons for the PINs to the voicemail boxes."

I pivot in my chair to face him. "I did get that email. But a little context would help. What exactly am I looking for?"

"There's an issue with a property management company we employ. One former tenant is threatening a major lawsuit, saying that the property management company is retaliating on excessive maintenance requests by forcing tenants out of their units, whereas property management is saying tenants are refusing to pay rent and breaking their contracts, so they're unable to help. I'm not a fan of 'he said, she said' situations. I want to get to the bottom of it quickly. There's a secure voicemail that tenants can use to anonymously report concerns, issues, and complaints without fear of backlash."

"Ah, almost like a tip line."

"Exactly. The only problem is, no one has checked those voicemails in years. I need you to sift through and take notes for me. I have to make a decision on whether we'll be firing the company or we're going to fight the tenant in court."

"Easy-peasy," I chirp.

"I'm estimating there are close to one thousand voice messages in there between four mailboxes. I need you to listen to every single one and I want the information on my desk by Friday."

My jaw drops. "*A thousand by Friday?*"

He lifts his brows as a triumphant smile claims his face. "Is that a problem?"

"Nope." I pop the *p* sounding cocky as shit, while mentally I'm cracking under the pressure. "I'll get it done."

"Great. Oh, and feel free to come into my office whenever you need to for measurements."

"Come again?"

"Did you get the email about my office redesign?"

"Um, yes." I glance through my periphery at my open inbox. The fucking notifications are still coming in. I thought we were done, but there's a fresh batch of unread emails. Subtly extending my arm, I close my laptop so Nathan can't catch me in my lie.

"The email didn't really state what you were looking for." It's just a guess.

"I was hoping you could fill in the details," Nathan explains. *Holy crap—lucky guess.*

"You want me to arrange a remodel of your office without knowing what you want?"

He flashes me a devilish smile. "That's half the fun, right? Guessing what I'll like." He chuckles cruelly. "I trust your taste. Just make it look more lively. Right now my office looks—"

"A little *American Psycho*?" I very helpfully finish his sentence.

"Bland," he corrects. "Just freshen it up." He pulls out his wallet and retrieves a black card. "My only request is that you don't touch the piano. Otherwise, whatever you need, put it on here. New furniture, painters, storage items. I don't have a budget for this, just get it done. This is your company card."

I pluck the credit card from his hand and admire it. I flip it over to see my name etched into the back. "You went through the trouble of having a company card made for me? Wow. Thank you. It feels so official."

He nods slowly. "Don't worry, I can cancel it at any time."

This is his MO. He's determined to ruin every moment

between us that dares to be pleasant or promising.

"Noted." I swivel back around. In my haste, I accidentally kick Spike's carrier and he lets out a startled, *mweep.*

"What the hell was that?" Nathan's face fills with worry. "Sounded like a mouse."

"I didn't hear anything," I fib.

He shudders. "Call maintenance just in case and have them get in touch with pest control. Tell them to come immediately. If there's a mouse in the building, I want it gone yesterday."

Mweep, mweep. Nate freezes when he hears Spike's pleas once more. He probably wants out of his carrier. I roll my eyes as I loop my fingers through the soft cage handle and place Spike, home and all, on my desk. "Before you call in the SWAT team, it's not a mouse. *I'm sorry.* I meant to drop him off at home this morning but I hit traffic and didn't want to be late for work. I can't leave him in a hot car until lunch."

I'm busy explaining myself, so it takes me a moment to register the color has drained from Nathan's face. "You brought a giant rat to the office?"

"It's a guinea pig...a common household pet." I scoop Spike out of his carrier. One hand wrapped around his belly, the other securing his rear, I present him to Nathan. "He's harmless."

To my shock, Nathan takes a large step backward. His jaw is clenched, his breathing strained, as his wide eyes stay locked on Spike as if the little guy were a deadly cobra. He points to the carrier. "Put it away."

"What's wrong with you?"

"I have a thing with rodents," he says, his voice tight. "It's fine. You're not in trouble, just get rid of it."

"I'm not going to kill my sister's guinea pig."

"I didn't mean..." He shakes his head, looking positively rattled. "Take him home. *Now.*"

"Wish I could, but I have a lot of work to do. I can't sacrifice the whole morning."

"Take your laptop. Work from home," Nathan quickly

suggests. "Anything you need to be in the office for, just ask for Dawn's help."

"You're that scared of guinea pigs?"

He flashes me a warning look, his masculinity questioned. "Not *scared*. I just don't like rodents. The beady eyes. The weird paws that look like frog hands mixed with talons. Not to mention the tails."

"Oh, guinea pigs are tailless." I spin Spike around and show Nathan his furry butt. My boss flinches at the sudden movement. "*Wow*. That bad, huh?"

He hangs his head in shame, and it takes everything in me to remain respectful and not burst out in laughter. Clamping his eyes shut, he pinches the bridge of his nose. "Spencer, please take it home."

"Okay. I will." I carefully deposit Spike into his carrier. Nathan visibly relaxes.

"Call me if you need anything." He makes a beeline to his office. With his back turned, I finally unleash my smile.

Oh, silly, silly Nate. We're at war, boss.

You shouldn't have shown me your Achilles' heel.

CHAPTER 16

Nathan

"How was Greece?" I ask Finn right as he pops a generous piece of steak in his mouth. I have to wait for him to chew and swallow.

"Unlike anything you've seen," he finally replies. "I'm kicking myself for not having gone sooner."

The restaurant I picked feels a little too romantic for a guys' dinner. There's a soft glow on Finn's face from the flickering candle between us. Between the crystal chandelier right above our table, the butter, which is carved into tiny roses, and the private table with a plush, velvet curved booth, it's as if one of us is about to drop down on one knee.

"Mind if I put this out? It's distracting."

Finn lets out a rich chuckle before licking his fingers and pinching the flame. It sizzles, then leaves a pencil-width tail of smoke. "Thank God you said something. I was concerned this whole evening was you putting down the moves. No judgment or anything, but I'm a married man."

"You jackass. I'm way out of your league, anyway."

Finn smirks. "Oh please. I could have you if I wanted you."

I laugh. "Steak is damn good though, right?" That's why I picked Lumeere. Best dry-aged wagyu in the city. Not to mention the largest selection of scotch I've ever seen.

"So good, I'm ordering one for my wife to go." He holds up his hands. "On my dime."

"Not a chance. I would be more than happy to buy Avery

dinner. It's the least I can do. I uh..." I hesitate, running my hand down my face and bracing for an uncomfortable conversation. "I never got the chance to apologize for missing your wedding. I didn't deserve an invitation to begin with, and then bailing last minute, I just..."

I RSVP'd to Finn and Avery's wedding. For a long time, he was one of my closest friends. But after I lost Elise, guess I was determined to lose everyone. I stepped out on our friendship, and Finn honestly shouldn't be as cool with me as he is right now.

"You don't need to apologize. I didn't expect you to come."

Pulling in my lips, I bob my head. "So we both already knew I'm shitty."

"No." Finn crosses his arms and leans back. He examines me like a shrink would a patient in denial. "I don't think you're shitty. I just imagine weddings are a trigger for you."

"Only weak men are triggered by their friends' happiness."

"Or honest men. It's not my happiness that puts you off, Nate. It's that you were robbed of yours." He exhales a heavy sigh. "Sorry, forget it. I didn't mean to bring it up."

I rub my cheek, feeling the short stubble I need to shave. "You know what? It's fine. It happened three years ago. I should be able to talk about it."

"You sure?" Finn's tone is rightfully skeptical. "I've been known to ignore all texts that ask, "Are you okay?" or, "How are you feeling?" or even, "Is there anything I can do?"

"Yeah."

"So, how've you been?"

"I was doing all right. But lately shit's been stirring up." I omit telling him about my almost-kiss with Spencer at his wife's birthday party. It feels unfair to admit it to him, when I still won't admit it to Spencer. But after assailing me today with that rat-pig, I'm not sure I ever will. I didn't touch it, but I swear I can still feel it on me. "Peter got out of prison."

Finn's expression flattens. "You're fucking kidding me. After what he did?"

"Overcrowding. And Elise isn't here to contest it."

"*Jesus,*" Finn breathes out. "Where's he staying?"

"With his mom and Claire. Supposedly he's clean now, but we have eyes on him just in case. If he hurts Claire, I'll..." I don't know how to finish that sentence out loud in public, because the end of my thought is, *I'll go to prison for the rest of my life for murder.*

Finn shakes his head, disgust painting his face, and I'm reminded of why I should've kept in touch with my friends. It's comforting to know Finn gets it. I don't have to explain that I'm fucking angry, scared, hurt, and out of sorts. He was there through the worst of it. He understands.

"Have you seen Claire at all?"

"Not since the day they took her," I admit softly.

I still hear Claire's bloodcurdling cries. I feel the sting on my knuckles. Powerless to fight it off any longer, I hang my head as the painful memory consumes me.

Three Years Prior

"Shh, shh," I coo, rubbing the enswell gently under Claire's eyes, alternating after each stroke. "I know, I know."

The iron tool is used for boxers between rounds to calm the swelling in their face. Claire's been crying so hard for nearly twenty-four hours straight. There are pock marks around her eyes where tiny blood vessels burst, blending in with her red freckles. Her eyes are nearly swollen shut.

Claire collapses against my chest, her tears dampening my shirt. Her mental breakdown is the only thing holding me steady. I need her to need me so I can focus on something other than the pain. Once I'm alone with nothing to do, I'll fall apart to pieces.

"Maybe it wasn't Mommy," Claire whimpers. She pushes off of me, and desperately finds my gaze. "Did you check?"

I didn't know a nine-year-old would go through the stages of grief just like an adult. I almost don't want to pull her from denial. At least in denial, there's hope.

"I saw her, honey. It was Mommy." My voice cracks as the image of Elise, so still and cold as ice. Her bright red hair in contrast made all the blood look dark as mud. They swore they called me mere moments after the cars collided, but she was gone on impact. I never got to say goodbye. Twenty-four hours later, I still don't remember the last thing I said to her. All I can vividly think of are the things I should've said, but didn't. And never will. "We lost Mommy."

Claire throws herself back into me. I swivel the locket I'm wearing around to my back, the golden chain now wrapped around my neck like a noose. I never take it off, but right now I don't want the hard metal to bore into her head as she rests her head against my chest.

I try not to show her how much I'm hurting because it sets her off ten times worse. Before I know it, she's back to dry heaves as if she's run out of tears and can only shake and convulse in my arms.

"Shh, we're going to be okay. I'm here." I kiss the top of her head, my tears now flowing into her hair. "I love you."

She does her best to say it back, but the words are broken and distorted through her fits of sobs. We hold each other tightly for minutes, hours, all day...hell if I fucking know. Time passes eerily slowly after the death of a loved one. Everything goes by in slow motion as you drift and float, waiting for something worth grasping on to, to bring you back to reality.

Pound, pound, pound.

It's only when there's an aggressive knock at the door I realize Claire and I must've dozed off. I lay her backward on the couch. I'm careful not to jostle her too much, but she's so exhausted, now that she's asleep, I know it's a deep sleep. And the asshole at the door who almost disturbed her slumber is about to face my wrath.

Who the fuck even made it past the security gate? Dad's been calling. I asked him to give me a day or two to get Claire settled. Maybe he couldn't stay away.

"What?" I bark as I pull the door open.

Dread seeps into my pores, not when I see the uniformed officer on my doorstep, but the vile woman trying to hide behind him.

Ruby. "Get the hell off my property!" I shout at her. "You're not welcome here."

Ruby cowers, playing the victim, but I see through the facade. She had so many opportunities to be a protector, a role model, a mother when Elise didn't have her own. Instead, she remained an enabler, making excuse after excuse for her son as she watched him break an innocent woman down almost to nothing. How dare she come here to offer her condolences.

"Are you Nathan Hatcher?" the officer asks.

"Yes. And this is *my* residence." I point to Ruby's forehead. "She's trespassing. Remove her immediately."

Ignoring my demand, the man continues, "I'm Officer Reynolds. Is Elise Maynard's daughter, Claire, here?" He takes a step forward but I extend my arm across the doorway, blocking his advance.

"Of course she is. This is her home. Where else would she be at nine o'clock at night?"

Suddenly unable to meet my stare, Officer Reynolds ducks his head. "Mr. Hatcher, I'm sorry this is so abrupt, but we're here to collect Claire, immediately. Legally, she can't remain in your custody."

Now the panic spreads. The tremor of nerves starts in my neck and pulses through my entire body like living electricity. "Wh-wh-what... I don't..." Unable to form a coherent thought, I shake my head, saying no, but looking at the gun in his holster, the severity of the situation seeps in slowly.

"Luckily, Claire can skip the discomfort of staying with Child Protective Services. Her grandmother"—he looks over his shoulder at Ruby—"is here to take her home."

My heartbeat thumps in my temples. "What the hell are you talking about? This *is* her home. She's lived with me for over a year. We painted her room together, for fuck's sake. This is where she's staying."

"That's not up to you anymore," Ruby cuts in. "Now that Elise is gone, I'll be taking care of Claire."

There's more rage inside me than my body can contain. I'm going to erupt any moment. "How dare you speak her name?" I turn my attention to the officer. "Do you know this woman left her daughter-in-law practically for dead as she helped her son escape the state? And you think I'm letting her anywhere near Claire?"

"Oh, screw you. That's *not* true. Yet another story Elise invented. I haven't seen Claire in years because that witch kept my only granddaughter from me. Do you know how bad that hurts?" Her smile turns sinister. "You're about to," she whispers.

"Witch?" I ball my hands into tight fists. "She's not even in her grave yet. You miserable, evil—"

"Mr. Hatcher," Officer Reynolds interjects. "According to the law, Mrs. Barber is next of kin. I'm sorry, truly. But you need to surrender the child."

"Dad?"

My throat tightens when I hear Claire's small voice behind me. I do my best to use my frame to block her from view, but Ruby pushes past me.

"He's not your dad, sweetheart." She opens her arms for Claire, but she steps away. "Don't you remember your real daddy?"

"Dad?" Claire sidesteps Ruby and puts her hand in mine. "Why is Mrs. Barber here with the police?"

"I'm your *grandma*, Claire. Don't call me Mrs. Barber."

"See? She's basically a stranger to Claire." I'm begging the officer to see reason. "She belongs with me."

There's an unmistakable snarl on Ruby's lips. She smooths her gray bob-cut hair behind her ears. "Claire, where's your room? Let's grab your toothbrush and pillow for tonight. We'll come back for the rest later."

She makes her way down the hallway, but I don't stop her. Hopefully she gets lost in my mansion and keeps herself busy exploring all the things I gave my girls that her son never could. She can take whatever she wants. I squeeze Claire's hand tightly. I'm holding on to the only thing that matters to me.

"This isn't happening," I tell the officer. "You need to wait while I get my lawyer on the phone."

"Mr. Hatcher, please understand that this is above you and me. I really am sorry, but you're not Claire's biological father nor her legal guardian. There's nothing to justify her staying here."

"What about the fact I've been providing for her and her mother for years now? What about the fact I love her? How can you do this? Her mom died yesterday! How can you attack us like this while she's in mourning?"

As understanding sweeps over Claire, she clings to me with both arms. "*No, no,*" she whimpers. "I don't want to go. Please don't make me go."

Ruby returns to the foyer empty-handed. "I couldn't find your room, but it's fine. We'll buy you new things, honey. Come on, it's time to go."

When Claire refuses to release me, Ruby intercedes, roughly removing my daughter's arms from me, one by one. It takes everything in me not to strike her across the face. Every part of me wants to. But I don't hit women. I'm not her son.

"Daddy, *please*. I don't want to go. I want to stay here." There's fear and panic in her eyes. I know in my heart this is inevitable. I always meant to adopt Claire officially after I married her mom. The date was set... We just didn't make it. Hot tears burn tracks down my face as I do the only thing I can right now, which is to not make this worse.

"You can at least give us a moment," I snarl at Ruby. "Get the fuck out of my house."

"I'm not leaving without her." Claire winces when Ruby tightens her grip around her wrist.

"Let her go before I remove your hand from your body," I

growl.

"You see?" Ruby directs at Officer Reynolds. "He's *violent*."

"You gaslighting bitch. You know who the real monster is." I never use language around Claire, but I've lost control.

"*Stop*," the officer roars. "Mrs. Barber, you're escalating the situation unnecessarily at this point. Please wait in your vehicle. I'll bring Claire out in a moment."

Disgust painted across her face, Ruby reluctantly acquiesces and releases Claire. She points between my eyes. "You two had no right to keep her from me all these years. This is what you get. Make sure when you say goodbye, you mean it. You won't see her again, I'll make damn sure of it."

She storms off, leaving Claire hysteric in her wake. As soon as I squat down, her arms are shackling my neck. "If I sleep over with her tonight, you'll come get me tomorrow, right? Just bye for tonight...*right*?"

I so badly want to lie to her to make it okay. But is that fair? "Claire, look at me." She pulls away just enough to meet my stare. "I will do everything I can to bring you home. Okay?"

She nods. "Tomorrow?"

I bite my lip so it doesn't tremble. "I don't know."

"Then I'm not going."

"Here." I pull the golden chain over my head and drop it over Claire's head. It's way too big for her, and the heart-shaped locket dangles almost to her belly button.

She touches the heart. "But it was a gift." Elise didn't love again easily after her abusive ex. Trusting me with her daughter took even longer. But the first Father's Day we really felt like a family, they gifted me with this little picture locket. Elise on one side, Claire on the other. They signed the gift tag, "from your girls."

My girls.

"Exactly. This is the most valuable thing I own. I wouldn't give it up without being sure I'll get it back. Keep it safe for me. I want it back when you come home."

She nods emphatically, believing me with her whole heart.

I pray I'm not a liar. Ruby's threat circles through my mind and I pretend she has no power. *But does she?*

"Okay, time to go, sweetheart," Officer Reynolds says.

"I'll walk with her." I rise, Claire's hand in mine.

Officer Reynolds holds his palm against my chest. "Mr. Hatcher..." He looks almost as tormented as I feel. "In my experience with these situations, it's best if you say goodbye here. We don't want to stress Claire out any more than necessary."

With his hands around Claire's shoulders, he guides her through the door. Her fingertips glide against mine one final time as he pulls her away from me.

"Claire," I call out.

She freezes, allowing the officer to get a few steps in front of her. Slowly she turns around, like she barely has the strength. It kills me that she's staring at her untied sneakers. She doesn't want to look at me, like out of instinct she's detaching. "I love you, Nate. I tried to say it back earlier, but couldn't. *I love you.*"

Putting us out of our misery, the officer doubles back to escort Claire away, down the path to the wraparound driveway. He gently shuts the door behind them.

It must be shock. Grief. Fury. Fatigue. I don't know, but I can't actually move my feet. All I can do is drop to my knees. I listen quietly until the low rumble of car engines completely dissipates.

I need to get to my phone and jump into action. This is all a misunderstanding. The lawyers will clear it up. Claire will come home. *We need each other.* To grieve. To heal. She's the only part of Elise I have left. She can't just be gone.

Move, Nate. I have the power to wake up our entire legal team in the middle of the night with a snap of my fingers. But for some reason, I still can't move my legs. All I can do is replay Ruby's threat in my head over and over again.

You won't see her again. I'll make sure of it.

It's not until I hear a crack that I realize I'm punching the floor with all my might. Swing after swing, my knuckles bleed and bruise, but I ignore the ache and sting.

I keep punching harder and harder, falling into a rhythm.
Pushing past the pain...
Just trying to stay focused on the task at hand.

CHAPTER 17

Nathan

"Where to, boss? Home?" my driver asks me as we sit in an idle car.

"I, um... Give me a minute." I don't know where I want to go. It's not home. After rehashing all that traumatic shit at dinner, I don't want to go back to my home and sit alone with the ghosts of my should-be family.

I dragged out dinner as long as possible with Finn so I wouldn't have to face my grim thoughts. But when he opted to skip dessert, I know he just wanted to get back to his wife with her dinner while it was still hot. He promised he'd check in with Senior about the parking lot, and I very subtly told him to warn his grandpa about possible spies in his company. Of course I didn't tell him my dad was behind the whole debacle, but I felt a warning was the decent thing to do. What are they going to do? Find Casey and fire him? From what I understand, he already put in his resignation. I just want to ensure no bugs were placed or important documents are missing.

"I can't wait here much longer, Mr. Hatcher. We're half-blocking a fire lane and a cop keeps circling. He's bound to notice. Should I pull into a parking garage?"

Still not answering, I release a deep sigh. My chest slowly rises and falls like the emotional exhaustion is inhibiting my breathing. I'm not sure what to do. For three years straight, I wanted to be alone. But now, when I'm dreading it, I don't have anyone I can call. Or, do I?

It's past eight on a Friday night... I shouldn't call my assistant. It's creepy. But, then again—she didn't get the reports done I asked her to. Maybe that's excuse enough.

Finding Spencer in my contacts list, I press the green call button. She answers on the first ring.

"I *know*," she snaps. No hello, or what do you need. She was expecting my call, and probably anticipating some form of verbal discipline.

"You know what?" I ask, playing dumb.

"Oh." She sighs into the phone. "Sorry, what are you calling about?"

I picture her big brown puppy-dog eyes, probably thinking she dodged a bullet. *Nope.* "I'm calling about the fact I asked for the voicemail notes on my desk by Friday. As far as I'm aware, *it's Friday.*"

"Nathan, I tried my best. I got everything else done on the list. I've been listening to voicemails in the car, on speaker while I shower, and basically every single waking moment. I've only made it through about half. I don't know why you think one person could get this done in time. I sent you an email earlier with my progress and the spreadsheet."

I've been at dinner with Finn. I haven't checked my email in a few hours. "What spreadsheet?"

"My old boss, Hank, was a data guy. I became quite the whiz at Airtables while I was working for him. I figured you wouldn't want to read through hundreds of pages of my call notes, so I made a spreadsheet organized by property location, complaint type, and severity. There's even a column in the spreadsheet about profanity level, scale of one to ten."

"Profanity level? Impressive."

"That's actually a pretty useless column. They are mostly all nines and tens. Go ahead and assume everyone calling these lines is beyond irate."

"What are the tenants so pissed about?" I look up and meet my driver's stare through the rearview mirror. He widens them in a look that asks, *What the hell are we doing?*

"*That's the thing*," Spencer says, surprising me with her sudden enthusiasm. "The great thing about spreadsheets is it's easy to identify patterns. I listened to about half of each property's voicemails and for Midlake Townhouses and Falcon Crest Apartments, the complaints are pretty varied. Some legitimate, some bogus, but there's a good mix of various issues. Now, with Lakeshore and Graystone apartments, that's where it gets interesting."

I relax in my seat, enjoying the sound of her voice. We're talking about work, but suddenly I don't feel so alone. "Well, Nancy Drew. Sounds like you're on a trail. Fill me in."

"Nancy Drew? As in you're calling me a child?" Her question has a bitter edge.

"Spencer, I'm ten years your senior. Please believe me, when people in their thirties call a young twentysomething a 'kid,' it's a compliment, and out of pure envy."

She laughs. "Okay, I'll take it. Anyway, I live at Graystone."

"You do?" I cringe. Those are mostly corporate housing apartments in desperate need of a facelift. We get an obnoxious overhead return on those units because they were cheap as fuck to build, yet because of the location, we can charge about triple what they're worth. From a businessman's perspective, it was a fantastic investment. Knowing Spencer is living there leaves a bad taste in my mouth.

"Yes. Remember a couple weeks ago when my closet flooded? It's still not completely fixed. Building maintenance came through and put up new sheetrock where the water leaked, but the plumbing issues in the unit above us are still ongoing. I overheard the maintenance team complaining to each other that the plumbers were purposely dragging out the job for more billable hours."

I shrug as if she can see me. "Not ideal, but that's common in the industry. They have to feed their families somehow."

"Well, yes, except one of the maintenance guys said that his brother was licensed and bonded and could have the pipes repaired same-day, except... And this is where it *really* gets interesting, boss."

"You have my full attention." It's the truth. I'm enjoying playing into her skit. She seems very proud of herself.

"Graystone and Lakeshore apparently have an exclusive agreement with one plumbing company—Ottman Plumbing. They won't call in anyone else to do plumbing repairs so all the residents have to wait on that *one* team."

"Again, Spencer, not to burst your bubble, but that's not uncommon."

"Bup, bup, bup—let me finish," she chirps. "Remember how you asked me to get that detailed breakdown of the invoice from the construction company? The office manager warned me they'd be switching plumbing providers before the final construction because they didn't like how *Ottman Plumbing* makes their clients sign an exclusivity agreement saying if they do the initial installation, they are the only ones who can service the plumbing for a minimum of *fifteen years*."

"Fifteen? Nothing in plumbing is under warranty for fifteen years as far as I'm aware."

"Exactly!" she exclaims with glee. "Don't you get it? They are purposely doing shitty jobs during construction, banking on the plumbing failing, then they reach into your pockets again for the repairs. Not to mention, they are also half-assing the repairs for more billable hours."

"Holy shit—"

"And guess who was contracted for plumbing at Lakeshore and Graystone apartments?"

"Ottman."

"Yup. And guess what kinds of damages almost all of the voicemails for Graystone and Lakeshore are about?"

"Plumbing?"

"And the fallout from shoddy work. Water damage, mold, warped floors, mildew odors. Boss, your complexes are basically giant soggy boxes of cardboard. I'd move if I could afford to."

I spring up in my seat, pressing the phone tightly to my ear. "So it's not the tenant or the property management company's fault. We need to take the plumber to court."

"Precisely."

"And you have a paper trail?"

"I think so? I have detailed documentation with time stamps, and just in case, I made sure to save every single voice message I listened to."

I could kiss her right now. We'll need the documentation to bury these corrupt fucks. She's so smart for keeping it. "Spencer, you did amazing. *Good girl.*"

"I...uh...okay. Thank you." She clears her throat like she's uncomfortable, and I can't for the life of me understand what suddenly tripped her up.

"You said there's still more messages?"

"Yes, I was actually still listening when you called."

And now I'm the asshole who has my assistant working late on a Friday night. My brilliant assistant who might've just saved my company hundreds of millions of dollars in the way of lawsuits.

"Have you eaten?" I ask.

"Huh?"

"Meet me at the office. Run me through your spreadsheet and I'll help you listen to the rest of the calls. We can order a late dinner. Breakfast too if we pull an all-nighter. I want to get my legal team as much ammo as possible to build a strong case. We're going to bury these assholes, immediately."

"I would, Nathan. I want to help. But I can't leave my apartment."

I scoff. "What, you got a hot date over there or something?" It's a joke, but my stomach churns at the idea of Spencer with a guy. I realize she's not mine. But also, *she's mine.* If I'm going to give her a fair shot as my executive assistant, she really doesn't have time to be talking to any other guy.

"My sister is underage and I don't have a babysitter."

"Oh."

"But I'll keep plugging away tonight and will report to your office first thing on Monday after I drop Charlie off at school."

No. I want my lawyers on this now. And also, every bone in my body is aching to see Spencer. *Tonight.*

"Do you like Chinese food?"

"Yes, but I'm still on my diet."

"Oh, fuck your diet." If I weren't her boss, I'd tell her it'd be a travesty for her to lose even an ounce of her curvy hips or plump tits. I'd happily bury my face between her beautifully thick thighs and suffocate there. It's a crying shame she doesn't see what I see when she looks at herself. "I'm going to pick up dinner, then I'm on my way. I'm not far from Graystone."

I ate, so this is mostly for Spencer. I just don't want to show up empty-handed. Breaking bread together is always the best way to start a truce.

"Spencer, is that all right?" I ask when she doesn't say anything. "I won't if it makes you uncomfortable."

She hesitates for so long, I'm certain I overstepped. I'm doing mental gymnastics, trying to figure out how to rescind my offer with my dignity intact, when she finally answers, "Charlie likes orange chicken, but not spicy. I like pork lo mein and hot and sour soup. We're in apartment 3F."

"Attagirl. Give me a few, I'll be right there."

"Hey, Nathan?" Spencer asks.

"Yeah?"

"Thanks for being cool about me being late with this project. I'm so relieved. I thought you were calling to yell at me."

"Of course."

The call ends and I instruct my driver to head toward Lucky Buddha near Graystone. Spencer's words bounce around in my mind as we pull into traffic. *She thought I was going to yell at her? Am I that far gone?*

I get my past assistants didn't like me. Admittedly, I never gave them a chance.

But Spencer? I don't understand. If she thinks the worst of me, why has she stuck around? Is her stubbornness and determination honestly about the job?

Or is it about me?

CHAPTER 18

Spencer

What in the actual fuck?

My boss is coming over.

I'm trying to wrap my head around the conclusion of the conversation I just had with Nathan. But it's really hard to focus because the butterflies in my stomach have erupted into synchronized choreography in my gut. Those fluttery little creatures are telling me he has ulterior motives. Never once in my entire professional career has a boss asked to come over this late at night. Not even under the guise of an urgent work project.

I could've easily said no. Mr. Billionaire, who people bow to with the snap of his fingers, could've told me to report to the office, or could've demanded he stop by and confiscate my work laptop for the data. But no. He *asked*. And he's bringing dinner.

My phone lights up the darkened living room as a text from Nathan populates.

> **Bosshole:** Sorry, terrible memory sometimes. Charlie's orange chicken—you said spicy or not spicy?

The butterflies are ricocheting off the walls of my stomach now because not even I can deny it. The only time a man cares to get the details right is when he's trying to make a good impression. So here we are, with my ass of a boss turning a new leaf. This man is a professional shifter going from toad to prince, every other day.

Me: Not spicy.

Bosshole: Got it. Be there in twenty.

I shake out my fingers, releasing a trembling breath. *Okay, okay.* It's fine. I'm fine. Butt on carpet, back against the couch, I stretch my arms overhead, trying to relieve my body of some nervous tension. And that's when I get a little whiff of the pits. *Uh-oh.*

Okay, it's really not bad. It's what any woman smells like after working a twelve-hour day—not exactly powdery fresh. But my hot boss is coming over and I need to smell nothing short of a bubblegum-candy meadow. I recheck my phone. He said twenty minutes. *Shit!*

Scrambling on to my feet, I haul ass to the bathroom and nearly topple over Charlie, who, with the worst timing in the world, has emerged from her bedroom wearing her pink, unicorn fluffy robe, carrying not one, but two bubble bath bombs, one in each hand.

Briefly, I'm distracted because those suckers cost about five dollars a pop and I've told her time and time again—use sparingly. This girl is going to bankrupt us on glitter and bubbles. "What do you need two for?"

"This one is strawberry, this one is banana," she says, holding up her left hand, then the right. "I'm going to have a strawberry-banana-smoothie bubble bath. May I borrow your pink, gel eye mask? Also, would you be a lamb and make me an iced chai tea latte? Not too much whipped cream."

"No!" I shriek.

"To which part?" Charlie screws up her face, offended by my outburst.

"All of it! No chai tea, no eye mask, and no bath. I need the shower right now."

"Um, no. Dibs. I already have all my bath stuff ready. You can take a shower when I'm done."

"In three hours?" I ask, completely aghast.

"Perhaps." She shows me a wicked smile. "Why do you need a shower so bad?" She leans in and sniffs me. "You smell like you normally do."

I think she's insulting me, but I don't have time to dissect that. "Charlie, my boss will be here any minute to work on a very important project. He's bringing us Chinese food. Isn't that nice?"

"Orange chicken?"

"Yup. So please, please be a sweet sister and let me hop in the shower before he gets here. You can take your bath after, as long as you like. Just make sure to lock the door and get fully dressed before you come out."

I have never seen a creepier look on my little sister's face. A sinister smile curls the corners of her lips. "How come you wanna smell so good for your boss? I thought he was a butthead."

"Charlie, *please*." The clock is ticking, and I don't have time to explain how sometimes you can want to punch a man right in his jaw, while simultaneously wanting to see him and his generous bulge in his tight, black briefs again.

"I don't know," she singsongs while taking a menacing step toward the only bathroom in the apartment.

"I'll tackle you if you take one more step toward that bathroom."

"I will scream and make a very big scene," she deadpans.

"All right, I don't have time for this. Name your price."

"Anything?" Charlie cocks her head to the side, smile still crazy, looking like the Riddler right before he tricks and backstabs Batman.

"Not more pets, but otherwise, *anything*."

"I want Drunk Elephant."

I blink at her. "Come again? You want to get an elephant drunk?"

"No." She rolls her eyes the only way an eleven-year-old can, needlessly dramatic. "Drunk Elephant. It's a skincare line. Holly Garcia in my geography class says her skin is so glowy because she uses sunshine serum drops and a polypeptide cream. But she said I probably couldn't afford those things even though I need them because my skin is so dull."

These are the new grade-school insults? It used to be fat, skinny, flat-chested, or whispered sneers about acne. Now we're stooping to dull versus glowy skin? Good God, bullying has really leveled up.

"Babes, listen to me." Forgetting the urgency for a moment, I grab my baby sister by both her shoulders. "The only kind of woman who comments on another woman's skin, hair, nails, weight, is someone who is really insecure about themself. Holly's face may be glowy, but her personality sucks. And you, little sister, are beautiful." I stroke her cheek with my thumb. "Your skin is baby soft and has plenty of shine. One day, you're going to get acne, there's no stopping it. But guess what? You'll still be beautiful inside and out. So the next time Holly tells you that your skin is anything other than radiant, know that she's talking about herself. Not you. Okay?"

Charlie drops her head and stares at her toes. "Okay."

"How about instead of a complicated skincare regimen you definitely don't need, we do a spa day instead. Tomorrow. We'll get our nails done, maybe a facial. Sound good?"

"Mani *and* pedi? And can I get gel polish? Ooh, and can Claire come?"

"Fine, fine, *fine*, Charlotte. Yes to all. Now please, let me hop in the shower."

"Hold on," she grumbles. "Let me get you a couple shower fizzies so your shower smells extra good. I like pairing strawberry and vanilla." She disappears into her room.

"A couple?" I call after her, knowing the shower fizzies are even more expensive than the bath bombs. "What do you mean 'a couple'?"

Tween bath products. Highway-freaking-robbery.

※

I slip out of Charlie's room with an empty paper plate in hand. She inhaled her food, leaving me feeling guilty that I don't buy her enough of the "good stuff." I wonder if she's suffering because of my incessant dieting. I make a mental note to have "fun food Fridays" from now on.

Nathan isn't where I left him. He slinked on to the floor in front of my laptop on the coffee table. He has one knee hiked, the other leg outstretched. He even took off his socks and shoes. He's so sexy when he's relaxed.

My boss arrived about fifteen minutes ago with too many takeout bags. He was obviously confused and thought he needed to bring enough Chinese food for the entire defensive line of a professional football team.

"Is your sister hiding because she doesn't want to meet me?" Nathan asks.

"No. Not at all. I bribed her to leave us alone."

"With what?"

"Unlimited screen time, and a promise to take her and her bestie to a spa day tomorrow, which I can't afford." I still have one more week until my salary advance hits my bank account. Even then, I shouldn't use that money for treats. Half is for paying off my credit card and other living expenses. The other half is to replenish Charlie's trust fund. I'll need to work at least another few years before I can fully replace what Jesse wasted.

Nathan is smiling, but it doesn't quite reach his eyes. "I still feel bad taking over your apartment."

Placing my hand on my hip, I raise my brows. "Do you want me to demand she and Spike come out?"

"Spike?"

"You two met, remember? Our guinea pig."

He's trying to act unbothered, but his body visibly stiffens.

"Forgot about that thing. They can stay in there." He points to Charlie's door as I burst out in laughter.

"Terrified of guinea pigs. That might be my favorite thing about you, boss." Well, second-favorite thing, but I'm not telling him what his taut muscles do to me.

"Terrified is a strong word," he says plainly before changing the subject. "I'm scouring this table, and you did a fantastic job, Spencer. I'm really pleased. Thank you."

I curtsy. "All in a day's work. Well, a week's work. Anyway, you get it. Thank *you*."

"For what?" he asks.

I lift my shoulders barely an inch and release them in a tiny shrug. "For saying thank you."

His eyes drop to the cheap carpet like he's ashamed. "I'll do that more. Promise." He's wearing a smile when he looks up. Patting the carpet next to him, he asks, "Ready to dive back in?"

"Yep. I just need to find my phone. I have the voicemail numbers stored in there." I pat myself down as if I accidentally stashed my phone in my sexiest, black, matching camisole-and-capri pajama set. Obviously I didn't. The silk set has no pockets.

"Here, I'll call it." Nathan pulls out his phone and dials. It's right when my phone rings from between the couch cushions that I remember how he's stored in my phone. Unfortunately, Nathan has the same realization almost simultaneously. Unwedging my phone from the cushions, he peers at the screen. Then his jaw drops.

"You found it," I murmur uncomfortably.

He levels a stare. "Just so I'm clear, is 'bosshole' a combination of boss and asshole?"

I lace my fingers together and twiddle my thumbs. "I mean I wouldn't say asshole per se."

To my surprise he erupts into a hearty belly laugh. He throws his hand over his chest like he's trying to prevent his heart bursting from the hilarity. He must feel his movement is restrained, because he proceeds to undo the top button of his dress shirt. It's immediate hypnosis when I glimpse his smooth, broad chest.

"Okay, come here. Let's talk," he finally says.

I drop down at least an arm's length away. With my back braced against the couch, I tuck my knees to my chest.

"You smell nice." Nathan steals the very words from my mouth because I was about to say the same thing about him. He's wearing that cologne again. The one that turns me into a heat-seeking missile. "What is it?"

"Shower fizzies. Strawberries and cream. It kind of smells like—"

"Strawberry shortcake," Nathan finishes for me. "That's what it is. Yours was the best I've ever tasted, by the way."

I don't know what to say. Suddenly I'm so nervous. But good nervous, like I'm at the tip of a very high diving board getting ready to jump. Below is an intimidating Olympic-sized pool. If I don't execute my next move with precision and tact, my body will break when I crash into the water.

"The cream puffs?"

He nods. "Wish I had one right now."

My head knocks back against the couch cushion. "You knew I was lying the whole time."

He cackles. "Big-time."

"Why didn't you call me out on it?"

He looks ahead, staring at the plain wall. "Why are you trying so hard to impress me?"

"You're a smart guy, Nate. Why do you think?"

He wets his lips, buying time before he has to respond. The waiting is agony. It's only a few seconds, but seconds when time stops is still an eternity.

"There's a good chance you're holding on to something that doesn't exist."

There he goes again. Cryptic. Dismissive. An edge of condescension. I know what he's thinking: silly girl and her little boy crush. "Message understood," I reply curtly. "Let's work at the dining table. More space."

I rise, but quick as a flash, he grabs my hand and yanks me back down. He swivels his hand so our embrace goes from cupped palms to interwoven fingers. I know he can feel my trembling but I can't help it. All I can do is breathe, ensuring oxygen gets to my brain so I know this is real and not some fantasy I concocted.

With his free hand, Nathan grabs his phone and shows me his broken screen. "I didn't fix it because it reminds me of that night."

Here we go. Finally, an admission. *Prince or toad?*

"What are you talking about?"

He swallows hard, like the words are difficult to taste. "Eight drinks. One sip each... I remember, Spencer. I liked everything about that night except the part where you got away."

Prince, prince, prince.

"Why didn't you say anything? You had me questioning my sanity."

I regret opening my mouth when he releases my hand. He raises both knees, resting his elbows on the top of his thighs while he buries his head in the lap-cave he's created. "You met a different version of me that night. I didn't want you to get the impression that he often makes an appearance."

"You were faking that night?"

"No." His answer is sure and finite. "Not that. It is a part of me, just a very small, often absent part of me."

Boldly, I scoot a little closer. There's still an inch between us, but I feel the heat from his body. "And who is here tonight? Nate or Nathan?"

His smirk is small. He's trying to appreciate the inside joke, but heavier things must be on his mind. "Who would you prefer?"

"I want the guy who's nice to me. The one who makes me laugh and smile. The one who apologizes when he offends me."

He cinches his eyes closed and grimaces like he's in pain. "Okay, give me your phone."

I don't think, I just react. Obediently, I unlock my phone before handing it over. Nathan plucks it from my hand and turns the screen so I can't see what he's doing.

"There." Finished with his mission, he hands my phone back.

"What'd you do?"

Wordlessly, he picks up his own cell and dials with one tap on the screen. My phone rings loudly and vibrates in my hand. I glance down at the caller ID which now reads: *It's Nate. I'm sorry.*

My shoulders shake violently as I laugh. A genuine laugh that has my heart tightening, and my lungs working hard. "Every time you call, it's an apology?" I manage between breathy huffs.

He looks so satisfied, like the sound of my laughter is a reward. "I have some apologies to make up for and it's best to get a few in the bank ahead of time, just in case bosshole rears his ugly head."

"Good call."

He slinks his arm around my shoulder and pulls me against his chest. I'm transported right back to House of Blues when the charming man swept me off my feet in his VIP booth. It had nothing to do with his money or status. It was *this feeling*. I barely nibbled at my Chinese food, not wanting to derail my whole week with one cheat meal, yet I feel so damn full in his arms. A satiating warmth that pulls all my defenses down and makes me beyond vulnerable. But somehow, for no good reason, I trust him to hold me steady.

With his free hand, Nathan curls two fingers under my chin. He strokes the tip of my nose twice with the pad of his thumb. "I'm sorry for being so hard on you."

I smile at him, getting lost in his almost-turquoise eyes, the blue and green blending in a spectacle of color. "And I'm sorry for calling you all those names."

"That's okay. I'll survive 'bosshole.'"

"Oh bosshole was the tip of the iceberg, my friend. I've used a lot of creative names for you over the past few weeks."

"Really? Such as?" He tightens his grip around my shoulders, drawing me closer as his eyes narrow dangerously.

"Nothing noteworthy. Just know I'm sorry."

"Come on, sassy-mouth. Let's hear it. I can take it." He squeezes even harder, unintentionally showing me his strength.

"No, thanks."

"You have no qualms talking back to me. In fact, you do it with every breath you take. Why so nervous now?"

"Because if you squeeze me any harder, I'm going to squeak like a rubber duck." Actually, I love the way he's holding on to me desperately, like he's afraid I'm going to slip away. I'm drowning in his scent, a heady blend of citrus, amber, and a hint of leather. I pretend to try to wiggle away, but it's just for show. I want to be glued to every hard angle of this man's perfect body.

"Am I scaring you?" We're so close that when he whispers, his breath tickles my lips.

"A little," I lie.

"Oh, baby, don't worry. I'd never ever hurt you."

"I know." I'm shocked I can muster a coherent response because this Adonis of a man just called me "baby."

He leans in close, we're touching nose to nose, so I have a front-row seat when he widens his eyes in warning. "I am, however, going to tickle the shit out of you."

In the span of a heartbeat, I'm lying back on the carpet, my boss on top of me, squealing, laughing, and writhing against the floor as I try to fight him off with my heels. I'm no match, but I don't care. Because after weeks of angsty confusion, *finally*...

Nathan's hands are all over me.

CHAPTER 19

Nathan

Our eyes widen in tandem as the next voicemail plays on speaker. I hope by eleven o'clock at night, Spencer's young sister, Charlie, is fast asleep in her room, because the profanities are not only aggressive, but creative. There's a lot of background noise, things zipping and slamming, like someone is angrily packing bags. But this message isn't a tenant complaining. The woman on the voicemail mistakenly dialed the number, evidently ignored the outgoing message, and proceeded to deliver a detailed, verbal dissertation on exactly how she's going to dismember her cheating boyfriend.

Spencer clasps her hand over her mouth when the mystery lady gets to the part about dipping her—I'm assuming now *ex*-boyfriend's penis in lye. "I feel like we should check on D'Anthony."

"When was the message left?"

She squints one eye, as if doing quick calendar math. "About three weeks ago?"

"Oh, it's way too late for D'Anthony. He's gone now." It's a joke. The woman sounded far too drunk to be dangerous to anyone but herself. "But save that voice message, in case we get subpoenaed in a cold case."

Spencer's laugh dissolves into a wide yawn. She does her best to cover it, but her eyes are watering, her shoulders slumping. Poor girl is exhausted.

"You're tired. I should go."

"I'm okay. I'm down for a few more." She nods toward the

laptop where her clever spreadsheet is pulled up. "Mark that one down as profanity level ten."

"I don't think my legal team will need that message for anything." I nudge her shoulder with mine. She sways, then knocks right back into me. Side by side, sitting on her stiff sofa that feels like hospital furniture, Spencer and I are glued together. Ever since I crossed the line of tickle torture, we've made no apologies for touching each other—her hand on my leg, mine on her back. She smoothed my eyebrow, and I answered by tucking her long, dark hair behind her ear. The touches are innocent, and hesitant, like we're trying to navigate this new intimacy between us.

When Spencer tries and fails to cover another giant yawn, I tap the tip of her nose. "Bedtime, miss."

"Awfully forward of you, Mr. Hatcher. But okay." She bats her eyelashes. I can't tell if she's teasing, or she actually wants me to take her into the bedroom and fold her like a lawn chair.

"You're playing a dangerous game," I caution.

She answers by making a finger gun, holding the tip of her pointer finger to her lips, and blowing out the pretend smoke. *Fuck, why is that so sexy?* Everything she's done tonight has me fighting a hard-on. The crazy part is she's so completely unaware of the lure of her body, she'd probably believe me if I told her I wasn't stealing glances at her full tits all night. It's not my fault. Her little spaghetti-strap, deep-V camisole is practically serving them up on a platter, begging me to partake.

So why haven't I?

Because the minute Spencer showed me the spreadsheet in front of me, I realized she's so fucking smart, and a rare Gen-Z unicorn who actually has a strong work ethic. I may want her help more than I want to get between her thighs. Though, at the moment, those are fiercely competing desires.

"Who are you calling?" Spencer glances warily between me and my phone.

"My driver. He's been sitting in the parking lot for over three hours."

Spencer drops her jaw in shock, but he's fine. I ordered him food at Lucky Buddha. Knowing Byron, he's fallen asleep in the driver's seat with a full belly and an audiobook in the background. I pay this man generously to nap.

"You have a driver who follows you around and just waits on you wherever you go?"

"Yes."

"When you come to work every day, he just hangs around until you need a ride?"

"Yes."

"And that's his whole job?"

I shrug. "Pretty much."

She rubs her thumb against her bottom lip and smiles like a light bulb just went off in her head. "How much does that pay?"

"Why?"

"Because I'm thinking I should've applied for *that* job. It would've been much more straightforward and far less face time with you."

"Did we not learn our lesson earlier when I tickled you so hard you were squealing like your guinea pig?" I make a claw and she curls herself up into the fetal position, anticipating more torture.

Instead, I hover over her, lingering a moment too long before I step past her. Covering her eyes like the words are difficult to speak, she asks, "Why are you in such a hurry to leave? I'm having a good time. Aren't you?" There's a twinge of nervousness in her voice. I hate to admit it, but I like it. The way she averts her gaze when I look straight into her eyes. How she flinches at my touch before relaxing. I like the idea that she's as affected by me as I am by her. I just have a better poker face.

"I'm enjoying your company a lot, which is why I have to go. Any longer and I'm going to tear those silk pajamas right off your body, throw you on the bed, and fuck you in every position imaginable. So, it's best I go now."

"Okay," she answers softly. Her voice is steady, but her

eyes betray her. They are the size of saucers at my admission of attraction. It baffles me that she's surprised I want her. Can't she see I'm constantly on the brink of losing control almost every time I'm around her?

A little horrified at my confession, I suck in my lips and head toward the door, but Spencer stops me. Arm like a whip, she grabs my hand before I'm out of reach. "No, I meant okay to the... positions and such."

I squeeze her fingers twice before dropping her hand. "Spencer, if you want me that bad, I don't get it. Why'd you run out on me the night we met? What changed? Considering you call me bosshole, getting to know me surely didn't help the matter." I was getting close to crossing that line with her when we met. There was a part of me that was angry when she so quickly pulled me out of the shell I'd been hiding in for years, only to abandon me.

She points over my shoulder to the door, indicating I should leave.

"All right, I'll go," I say with a defeated shrug. This conversation is giving me whiplash.

"No, I'm pointing down the hallway." She angles her finger more so she's clearly pointing at the middle of a bedroom door. *"My sister* is why I left that night."

"What?"

"Remember the singer on stage when I left?"

"The little girl with pipes like Céline Dion?"

Spencer juts her outstretched finger toward the door again. "That's Charlie."

"Sister?" I hold out my hand at hip level. "The little *blonde* singer, yay high."

"I don't like using the term half sisters," Spencer explains. "When Charlie was little and people would say that, she thought it meant I only loved her half as much as a normal sister. So, we don't say that. But to clarify, we have different dads, and we're twelve years apart."

"You're raising her by yourself?" I'm shocked I didn't know

all this, but then again, she never offered and I never asked.

Spencer nods sullenly. "I'm trying."

"What does that mean?" I grab the knit blanket thrown over the sofa chair and drape it over Spencer before sitting back down next to her.

"I've had Charlie on my own since I was eighteen. Most days it feels like a blind-leading-the-blind type situation." She cuddles deeper under the blanket, exhaustion sweeping over her.

"Just the two of you guys, huh?"

"Well, there was Jesse for a couple years. Charlie's still angry at me for that one." She covers her mouth, shielding yet another huge yawn.

I scoot over to the far side of the couch and hold my knees together to create space for Spencer to use me as a pillow. Pulling on her shoulder, I guide her to rest her head in my lap. She lets out a low hum of satisfaction when I stroke her hair. "Who is Jesse?"

"My ex-fiancé."

"Engaged so young?" I pull up the blanket to cover her bare shoulder, then go back to playing with her thick hair that sends a burst of sweet strawberries into the air every time she shifts positions.

"I'm embarrassed to admit this, but I was going to marry that man and I'm still not sure if I really *loved* him. I mean, I cared about him a lot and we had plenty of good times together. In hindsight, I think I wanted to marry Jesse more for Charlie than myself."

"They got along well?"

"I think he just accepted us for what we were. Most guys my age were put off by the idea of staying in on Friday nights and playing board games. Or the fact I don't drink much because I have to keep a clear head for emergencies. They didn't like that I always had this little shadow with me wherever I went. But Jesse was older. He understood the life I was living."

"How much older?" I rarely consider the age difference between Spencer and me because she's so grounded and well-spoken. But the truth is, I own bottles of scotch that are older than she is.

"Quite a bit older. I met him when I was twenty. He was twenty-six."

Six years? Our age difference is almost twice that. "Why did it end?"

"My goodness. What's with the third degree?"

"You said at the restaurant last week that I didn't know anything about you or your life. I'm trying to remedy that." It bothered me to my core when Spencer told me off. Because it was damn true. I'd made so many assumptions about her and they've all turned out to be wrong.

"Oh my God, Nathan," Spencer says so loudly, she's practically shouting. She sits up, the blanket falling into her lap. "I can't believe you're taking me and Charlie to Disney World tomorrow on the private jet!"

I look at her like she's lost her marbles. I mean, I guess I could do that, but that was a very un-Spencer-like way to ask. "Um, I—"

She puts her finger to her lips, effectively shushing me as she turns her ear toward the hallway. "I'm just making sure she's not eavesdropping. She would've burst through her door like the Kool-Aid Man if she thought we were going to Disney World."

My chest bounces with light laughter. "She's never been?"

"Have you?" Spencer asks.

"Every single Christmas from age five to about fifteen. I used to think my parents were the most over-the-top amazing parents in the world for planning a Disney World vacation every holiday. But I think it was just my mom's way to get out of elaborate Christmas dinners with her in-laws."

"That bad?"

"My dad comes from money and his family loves to show it off. Everybody walks into Christmas dinner wearing about a pound of jewelry. They purposely leave their new Bentleys parked right in front of the house so they're seen. My mom came from humble beginnings. Her parents had a family cleaning business that barely put enough food on the table. She got one small gift on Christmas morning, and the rest of the day was about staying in pajamas, movie marathons, and simply enjoying a day off work. My parents are divorced, and I think that's why they didn't last. They were too fundamentally different. Mom never loved being rich. She didn't like what money brought out in people."

Spencer pokes me in the arm with two fingers. "I get it. That's similar to what went wrong with me and Jesse. He's not rich or anything, but he craved it in his bones, you know? I look at Charlie and see this innocent little girl who is almost clueless about how much baggage she's carrying around. I see someone who deserves everything, yet has had so much taken away from her. But Jesse... he looks at my little sister and sees an opportunity."

"Because of her voice?" I intuit.

Spencer nods sullenly. "Jesse tried to talk me into seeking out talent agents and even reaching out to record labels. I am not deaf. I know Charlie has a unique gift, but I've become an internet sleuth when it comes to child stars in the entertainment industry. Far too many of them end up the same way—as addicts, mentally unwell, depressed from the vicious public bullying. And those are the straightforward cases, the children who were coerced, threatened, overworked, or sexually abused. Those aren't scars you can erase. It shapes the rest of their lives. I always ask myself when I hear these tragic stories—how did this happen? Where were the parents? I promised myself that won't be us. Nobody will ever ask where I was. I'm here, right by her side."

"And Jesse wanted to sell Charlie off for a big advance?"

"Pretty much. Charlie...well, she doesn't know this part." Spencer holds up her pinky. "Promise not to say anything?"

I can't remember the last time someone asked me to make a pinky promise. I chuckle at the sentiment, even though Spencer's face is dead serious. Looping my pinky finger around hers, I clamp it tightly until she feels secure enough to continue sharing. "Promise."

"Charlie is the product of an affair that my mom did not

know about. Mom was pregnant by the time she found out he had a wife and children. She was devastated, but she wasn't thinking about herself. She was thinking about his family and how much she unintentionally hurt them. I don't know if it was the right call or wrong call, but she told him to forget about her and the baby and to just do better by his family."

"Oh shit. And so that was that? He just walked away?"

"Yeah. Maybe it was just to absolve his guilt, but he left Charlie a quarter million dollars for whatever she needed. When my mom passed away, I became Charlie's legal guardian, meaning I could withdraw from the fund for Charlie. I..." Spencer trails off, wetting her top, then bottom lip. It takes me a moment to see she's trying to compose herself because she breaks out into tears.

"What's wrong?"

"I'm so embarrassed. I haven't admitted this to anyone really."

"Your secret's safe with me." I successfully keep so many of my own, it'll be no problem to keep a Spencer secret buried, too.

Her eyes stay straight ahead. "I don't know much about investments. Jesse told me if I pulled out some of Charlie's savings, he could triple her money, and we'd be able to give her a nicer life. He's a lawyer. I thought he understood this stuff. I didn't ask questions when we moved to a nicer apartment, Jesse got a new car and new clothes. I kept making withdrawal after withdrawal, draining every penny, believing him when he told me—"

"That he was doing exactly what he said he was going to do?" I roll my eyes, almost growling under my breath. I'm not agitated at Spencer. I want to strangle the asshole who took advantage of a woman who quite clearly thinks of everyone before herself. "Spencer, you're not to blame. If I were in your position, I would've thought the same."

She finally looks at me, shaking her head. "No you wouldn't have. You're a smart man, Nate. You would've asked for receipts. You would never have been dumb enough to take a greedy man's word at face value. I was a fool. That's why I moved out here in such a hurry. I just wanted to fix my mistake as quickly as I could."

"Why didn't you demand he give the money back, or sue him?"

Spencer scoffs. "Yeah, the only lawyer I could afford is Jesse—as in, for free. And not only is he pretty mediocre, but I doubt he'd take himself to court." Laughing it off, she shrugs. "It was my fault for trusting him. It's my job to repair what I broke."

No. Enough. "Spencer, look at me." She pivots, her knee pressing against the back of the couch as she faces me head-on. "You need to change the narrative, because you're a victim, shaming yourself. You didn't *allow* Jesse to trick you. He chose to be selfish and mislead you. It's unfortunate, and he left a mess of a situation behind him, but trusting someone you love is nothing to be ashamed of. You shouldn't be embarrassed because you weren't aware of his true colors. You should be very proud you had the strength to leave once you found out."

The way her eyes latch on to mine, I know she's hearing me. Hanging on every single word. Spencer said her mom died five years ago. That means she was only eighteen when she had the weight of the world dropped on her shoulders. Eighteen is still a baby. She needed her mom. Instead, she had to become one. Not to mention her only companion was a snake.

Spencer wraps her arms around me and buries her face in my neck. "Thank you. *Really, thank you.* Because I didn't know how badly I needed to hear that. I've felt so guilty."

This time as I'm hugging her, there's nothing sexual going through my mind. I brace her against my body just trying to be something solid she can melt against. I'm patient as she holds on to me as long as she likes. Mentally, I'm making plans I know I shouldn't.

Call my accountant and set Charlie up with a savings account. Get them out of this apartment and into a home with a backyard... maybe they can release that rodent back into the wild. Plan a Disney World trip for three next time I can steal away from the office. I'm inserting myself into something I have no business to, but I'm powerless to control it.

"Do you want to stay?" Spencer sniffles and pulls away. It's only when she wipes the side of my neck that I realize my skin is damp from her tears.

"For sex?" I ask point-blank.

A touch of pink highlights her cheeks. "Well, I don't exactly take you for a cuddling type of guy. I'll settle for what I can get."

It's the admission she didn't mean to make. Spencer doesn't necessarily want to have sex right now. Not like this, after cheap Chinese food she barely touched, in this shitty apartment. She just doesn't want to be alone.

"You know what they say about assuming."

She smirks. "Are you saying I'm an ass?"

"I'm saying I'm a cuddler." I stand, holding out my hand. "Come on, kook."

Surprise washes over her face, maybe a touch of relief, as she puts her hand in mine and lets me lead her to her bedroom. It's not hard to find it. Her entire home is about the size of my master bathroom and closet.

"Pink sheets, hm?" I quirk one eyebrow and show her a teasing smile. "How very Barbie princess of you."

"Excuse you." She sits on the edge of the bed and folds a corner of the comforter down, showing off more of the feminine linens. "These are dusty rose. Far more sophisticated than pink."

"Mhm." I pull out my phone and text Byron, dismissing him for the evening. After placing my phone on the nightstand, I undo my belt, sliding it out of the belt loops slowly. "I don't know what the protocol is here, so I'm going to keep undressing until you say stop."

In a show of charades, she pretends to zip her lips shut, lock the corner of her mouth, then throw the key over her shoulders.

A soft, amused chuckle escapes my throat. "How long has it been since you had sex?"

Her eyes roll up as she searches her brain. "Six months, I think?"

"I thought your breakup was more recent than that?" I

unbutton my sleeves, one by one.

"Yeah, we weren't the kind of couple that stayed locked in the bedroom." Her lips twist into a grimace. "Full disclosure, I've only been with two guys. I lost my virginity to some asshole football player in college. It was so awful it put me off to sex for a while. The next time was Jesse and he wasn't exactly a testosterone-fueled guy. I'm probably not as experienced as you. I um... I hope that's not a problem. I'll try to keep up."

"Keep up? What exactly do you think I'm into?"

"Well, you said you wanted to have me in all these different positions. I'm not one hundred percent sure how bendy I am. But I'll try." She gives a slight shrug, her expression unreadable. "You said at House of Blues you just got out of a serious relationship. How long has it been for you?"

I'm certain I never said my relationship ended recently. But I let her draw her own conclusions because I can't go there. I can't think about Elise. If I do, I'll go bolting from this room, leaving Spencer all sorts of confused.

"Longer than six months," I answer simply.

"Really? But you're so hot," she blurts out.

I grin at her compliment as I casually unfasten the top few buttons of my shirt. "Thank you. Is there a certain sex quota 'hot people' have to hit that I'm unaware of?"

She laughs freely, breaking a little of the tension. "No, I just figured hot people go at it like bunnies. If I were as good looking as you, I could probably bring a different man home every night if I wanted. Not that I would."

"Good. Don't do that. But you know what I think?" I pull off my shirt and toss it aside before undoing my pants button. That catches Spencer's attention. She freezes, averting her gaze.

"What?" She fists the top sheet, bunching it in her hand like she's trying to brace herself.

"I think you're so fixated on your sister, you don't notice people noticing you. You're not as 'good looking' as me, Spencer. You're way out of my league."

She rolls her eyes, unwilling to accept my flattery. "If you're trying to earn sex, Nate, I already offered."

It's my turn to laugh again. A deep, throaty chuckle rumbles from within me as I drop my pants and kick them to the side. "How about I stop here?" I ask once I'm in my underwear.

"Should I—" She tugs on the hem of her pajama top. "I mean, do you want me to?"

"Lie down," I command as I cross the room to turn off the overhead light. The bed squeaks as she shuffles. Once she's flat on the mattress, I climb into the other side, silently cursing the cheap, lumpy mattress. I mentally add, *new bed* to my list of to-dos. Grabbing Spencer from behind, I pull her against me, her back to my chest. I sigh in pleasure at the warmth of her body. It's been a long time since I've slept next to someone. I forgot how nice it is to not feel so alone.

She reaches behind and her hand goes searching, but I quickly catch it and gently place it back in front of her. I wrap my hand around hers, holding her curious fingers in place. "We're just cuddling." I'm not only speaking to Spencer, but also my cock which seems determined to spring to life.

"Don't you want to?" she asks.

Yes. But also no. I underestimated what this means to me. Wanting someone and caring about them are two different things. Sleeping with my assistant has evolved into a situation with much bigger consequences. Between her college mishap and lazy-sounding ex-fiancé, one more lackluster guy in the sheets might turn her into a nun. I have to approach this with a little more tact.

"Of course I do. But sleeping next to you is a novelty, too."

"I guess you weren't kidding about being a cuddler."

I smile into her hair. "I want to take you out first. Spoil you rotten for a night. Let me earn it."

She turns over in my arms. "I'm not high maintenance, Nate. You've been a great friend all night. That's already *earning it*."

Fuck, it's tempting. The way she smirks at me, the scent of sweet fruit and flowers, and the way her hips swing every time she walks away from me, was enough motivation. But feeling her soft, warm body against mine has me craving my assistant at ten times the intensity.

I roll her back over, punctuating my rejection with a sweet kiss to her temple. "Be high maintenance, Spencer. Don't settle for what you can get. Demand what you're worth. Now go to sleep."

She makes a joke about being unable to sleep with my massive weaponry poking her in the back. I'm sporting a partial, so if she thinks that's massive, she's going to be unnerved when I let go of self-control and she really sees what she does to me in its entirety.

In only a few minutes, she's breathing deeply, chest rising and falling in a pattern.

"You awake?" I whisper. Trying to gauge if she's faking slumber, I trace the curves of her body from her shoulder, down the slope of her waist, over the curve of her hip. She doesn't even flinch. Assured she's sleeping deeply and won't hear me, I part her hair around her ear and rest my lips right by her earlobe. "Spencer, it scares me how much I already like you."

CHAPTER 20

Nathan

I slowly pry open my eyelids, feeling the warmth of the bright, morning sun pouring in through the plastic blinds. Spencer's still in my arms. We're both a little damp with sweat. I remember it being hot last night. We kicked off the covers but were apparently unwilling to let each other go.

Carefully, I pull my arm out from under her, trying my best not to jostle her. I don't think it matters. She's sleeping like the dead.

Her mouth is open as she silently sucks in heaps of air. Her big hair is disheveled in every direction, making it look like she's sleeping underneath a mop. She slept in her makeup, so her eyeliner is smeared and her blush has faded from rubbing against the pillow.

She'd probably hate me to see her like this, but I stare because it's beautiful. She's sleeping so hard because she felt safe with me last night.

Rolling over, I reach for my phone. It's still early. Seven on a Saturday morning. I should lie back down, but I need to make a few calls. First my dad. Then the lawyers. Finally, The Orchid Spa. It's a luxury spa that Dawn loves. I get her a gift card every year for her birthday.

I pull on my pants but leave my belt behind. I don't want the clanking to disturb Spencer. I'm pushing my arms through my dress shirt as I sneak out of the bedroom and take the two steps to the living room.

"Oh, hello," I say when I see an unsuspecting girl sitting at the kitchen table with a giant bowl of cereal.

Her jaw drops as she peels off her bright blue headphones with rainbow-colored cat ears. She pauses whatever's on her cell phone and closes the scrapbook sitting next to her.

"Hi," she squeaks.

I button up my shirt faster than humanly possible. Thank fuck I had the good sense to put my pants on before coming out here. I almost forgot Spencer and I weren't alone.

"Charlie, right?"

She nods and points at me. "You're my sister's grumpy boss, right?"

I grin. "Or feel free to call me Nate."

We both stare in awkward silence for a beat. I actually consider fleeing back into the bedroom right before Charlie breaks the ice.

"I have a little left of the good cereal. I was going to have another bowl but you can have it if you want," she offers.

I near her, examining her cereal-dyed milk. I smell the sickeningly sweet scent of fake fruit. "Fruit Loops?"

She makes a disgusted face. "Trix with marshmallows, you animal."

"I'm an animal for liking Fruit Loops? They're the same thing."

"So wrong," she mutters under her breath before hopping up to fetch me a cereal bowl and spoon. Do I want children's cereal this morning? Not remotely. But I'd be a fool not to see this for what it is. An offering, but not of food, of friendship. I'd be willing to bet every penny in my bank account that if Charlie doesn't approve of me, Spencer's interest will dwindle quickly.

Charlie proceeds to fill my bowl with the last of the cereal, dumping crumbs and all into the bowl which barely fills it halfway. Next, she grabs the half gallon of milk from the fridge and slams it onto the table. Setting my bowl in the space across from her, she drops the spoon in the dry cereal and looks at me. "You want me to pour your milk for you too, or you got it?"

I chuckle softly. Apparently, snark is a family trait. "I think I can manage." I sit down in the seat Charlie chose for me. After splashing my cereal with just enough milk to coat the fruity shapes, I stir the cereal with my spoon.

Charlie's looking at me like I just committed a gruesome crime. "You can use more. We can always get more milk."

"I like my cereal crunchy. Too much milk and it goes soggy."

"Oh. I like mine soupy."

I flick my spoon, drying it the best I can, then hold it out to Charlie. "Cheers."

An excited glint in her eye, she rips her spoon out of her half-eaten cereal, then licks it clean before clanking it against my spoon. One bite in, it dawns on me how natural this feels. I just touched my spoon to Charlie's spit-spoon like a natural reflex. I used to never share food until Elise and Claire came into my life. I loved my family so much, all my boundaries crumbled.

"Did you spend the night?" Charlie asks.

I take my time chewing my large bite of cereal, trying to stall as I come up with a reasonable explanation. "Sort of."

"You can't sort of spend the night. You either did or didn't."

Dammit, Nate. That would've worked on a five-year-old. Charlie is much older. "Your sister and I are just friends."

"You sure?" She shuts one eye while tilting her head. "I don't think Spence likes you very much."

"Oh? Why do you say that?"

Charlie stirs her cereal, turning her milk into a whirlpool. "Well, she tells all her friends that you don't pay her enough to put up with you."

I chuckle. "That's probably true. What else?"

"Some other stuff I'm not allowed to repeat. We left our swear jar in Miami, but she still keeps tally in her head." Charlie rolls her eyes so hard, her light blue irises completely disappear for a split second. "But if you have money on you, I'm open to betraying her for the right price."

"I like you, Charlie. But unfortunately, I don't have any

cash on me," I say between breathy huffs of laughter. I'm curious though. Spencer's haughty insults are kind of a turn-on. I just want to *handle* that sassy mouth of hers. I wonder if Charlie would take Venmo.

"So, I heard you sing at House of Blues."

At that, Charlie perks up in her chair and beams. "Was I good?"

"Way better than good. Where'd you learn to sing like that?"

She shrugs. "My mom said I just came out singing like a bird. I really love it. Spencer doesn't let me sing in public, but as soon as I can get a job and afford my own cell phone, I'm going to get TikTok and post on there."

"Spencer doesn't let you have social media?"

Charlie shakes her head, wearing a bitter expression. "Nope." She shows me her phone in a pink Hello Kitty case. "She blocked everything except music, games, and YouTube Kids. So annoying. All my friends at school have TikTok."

"That's not a good thing. Your sister loves you very much. She's protecting you."

"*I know,*" Charlie says, exaggerating the syllables. "That's why I put up with her."

Spencer's logic makes more sense as I get to know Charlie. While she's smart, charming, and talented, she's also impressionable. Not to mention she's eager to show off her skills. Getting tangled up with the music industry at her age would be like dangling a baby seal above chummed, shark-infested waters.

"That song you sang that night though, it was beautiful. I almost got married, and that was supposed to be our wedding song. It was nice to hear it again."

Charlie's face goes blank as she sucks in her bottom lip. Something set her off. Wordlessly, she goes back to half-heartedly poking at her cereal-sog.

"What's wrong?" I ask.

"If you're married, why are you spending the night with my sister?"

"I said I *almost* got married. We're not together anymore."

"Why, what happened?"

I duck and dodge every time someone brings this up. The only people I mention Elise to are the people who were part of our life before the accident, and even then, I rarely make exceptions. There's something so earnest about Charlie. Today, I don't feel like telling one more lie.

"Same thing that happened to your mom."

"Oh." She hangs her head and I'm worried that was too insensitive. But then she adds, "Cancer?"

"Car accident. It was very sudden."

"Oh, that's better I think."

I blink at her, completely befuddled by her thoughts. "Why would you say that?"

"I'm sorry," she murmurs. "I didn't mean to be mean. I'm sorry about your friend." She reaches for her headphones in the middle of the table, but I place my palm over them.

"Charlie, I'm not upset. I just wanted to know what you meant."

"Um, well..." She takes her hands back, abandoning the headphones, setting them in her lap instead. Her gaze is fixed on her fingers underneath the kitchen table. "Sometimes I wish I didn't know my mom was sick. Goodbye is really hard and it felt like we were waking up every day and saying goodbye. If it was sudden, then we'd only say goodbye once and the rest of the days would've just been normal."

"I never thought about it that way," I muse.

I was always angry I didn't get more time to prepare with Elise. I kick myself that we didn't just get married, and instead we spent so much time planning the perfect day. She didn't have a wedding with Peter, so a wedding would've been a first for both of us. I wanted it to be huge and extravagant. I wanted Elise to have the fairy tale she deserved. Had we gotten married, I would've had a legal claim to adopt Claire. For as long as I can remember, I've blamed the suddenness of losing Elise as the core issue to everything, but what would waking up every day and knowing I was going to lose her feel like? How do you live each day with looming tragedy casting a shadow on every step you take?

"How long was your mom sick?"

"Since right when I was born, I think. A really long time. Do you want to see her?" Spencer taps the scrapbook. Another offer of friendship I'd be a fool to refuse.

"Yes, definitely."

She narrows her eyes. "Put your cereal bowl up first."

"You were eating with it open a moment ago."

"I know, but I'm *really* careful. I don't trust you yet."

"All right," I grumble, picking up my half-eaten cereal. I grab Charlie's bowl too and place them both in the sink.

Returning to the small, glass kitchen table, I pull my chair around so I'm sitting right next to Charlie. She brushes a few crumbs away, ensuring the space is clean enough for her precious book. She opens the first page which consists of three four-by-six photographs. The first is a picture of a blonde who looks way too young to have a little kid. But a five- or six-year-old Spencer is standing next to her, clutching onto her leg with a big, toothy smile. The caption reads: *Remember Us.*

The next picture is the same blonde in a hospital gown, holding a swaddled bundle—the baby she just gave birth to. Nobody's looking at the camera. The woman and Spencer—about the same age Charlie is now—stare at the baby, looking like two proud mamas. The caption scribbled is: *Never forget.*

In the final picture, I recognize Spencer as the woman she is today. Her mother looks rail thin, and there's a bandana wrapped around her head. She's smiling but it looks like it's a strain to do so. Charlie, maybe five or so, has watery eyes and her cheeks are blotchy, like she just mopped up her tears and someone told her to smile.

"Why is Spencer holding a suitcase in this one?"

Charlie examines the picture. "That's the suitcase she took to college. I didn't want her to go."

"I see," I offer distractedly as I take in the caption: *Always here.* "It must've been hard to say goodbye to your big sister."

"She wasn't gone long."

Tears stream down Charlie's cheek, and in a knee-jerk reaction I can't control, I reach out and wipe her tears away with the back of my hand. "It's okay," she says, sniffling. "Spencer says crying is good. It's how you let the feels out, otherwise they get trapped and make you miserable. When you cry, you feel better afterward."

"That makes sense." I think. Actually, I've never tried that.

"I don't remember exactly. It felt like longer, but Spencer says Mom died just a little bit after this picture was taken. She came home from school to take care of me."

Remember us. Never forget. Always here. The words repeat over and over in my mind, and it's strange to me. The only picture of Elise and Claire I keep around is hidden in the broken piano bench. I can't even fix the damn lid because Claire broke it when we were playing "floor is lava" in my office one night while Elise ran an errand. It was the very first time she trusted me enough to leave me alone with her daughter. I had one mission: keep Claire smiling and laughing, broken furniture be damned.

I've buried every precious memory deep in my soul, and yet here Charlie and Spencer spend time with their memories. They cry to feel. They embrace their tragedy instead of running from it. *Am I doing this all wrong?*

"Do you like cake pops?" Charlie asks.

The dramatic shift in conversations catches me off guard. "From Starbucks?"

"Yeah."

"They're fine, I guess." I think I've only had one in my entire life, and I don't remember caring much for the texture.

"I get my allowance tomorrow. If you let me know when you're coming to hang out again, I can get us some. Spencer used to eat them with me, but not anymore. She can't eat anything now that she's off her skinny pills."

"Skinny pills?"

"Sometimes pills, sometimes shots. But she was more fun back then. Jesse used to take us to Dave and Busters and we'd eat fries and wings and stuff like that."

All I can think of as she tells me this is that it was actually *Charlie* who was funding their family outings. "Now Spencer doesn't eat anymore?"

"No. She got really sick from her medication and passed out one time..." A haze comes over her as she falls silent. It's like she got caught on an unpleasant memory. I stay quiet, giving her time to process and finish explaining because in one conversation, she's helped me put so many pieces of the Spencer puzzle together.

"What happened?" I eventually ask.

"She wasn't responding. I had to call nine-one-one. It was really scary. After she stayed in the hospital overnight, she promised me she'd stop taking all that stuff that made her sick. She weighs herself like fifty times a day now though. Sometimes I wish she'd go back on them so she'd have fun again."

"Fun as in eating cake pops with you?"

Charlie nods. "And Flamin' Hot Cheetos because those are the *best*."

Outside of the heartburn, yeah. But I don't say that because it makes me sound old as dirt. "I like those too."

Her eyes sparkle as she beams at me. "I bet I'm going to like you even more than Jesse."

Thump.

It winds me. Such a sweet sentiment, but now it's crystal clear why Charlie is pouring me cereal, showing me her precious scrapbook of memories, and offering to buy me cake pops. Spencer is playing the role of the mother she lost, but there's still a piece missing.

I imagine Spencer doesn't easily bring men home because her little sister gets attached. She didn't even tell Charlie the real reason she left Jesse, probably not to tarnish her sister's memories and hurt her any more than necessary. Spencer has to think in every direction with every decision she makes. Everything she does impacts her sister. So the fact she asked me to spend the night last night...

She's ready for something a lot more serious than I am.

I'm prepared to dip a toe in the water. But Spencer and Charlie are already in the deep end, waiting for their knight in shining armor to dive in. This is history on repeat, and I can't go through it again.

Falling for my assistant. Loving her kid... Losing them both.

I won't survive it.

I push back from the table so fast, my chair nearly topples. I catch it in the nick of time and scoot it in on the opposite side of the round table. "Charlie, it was nice to meet you, and thank you for sharing your cereal. I have to go, but will you tell Spencer I said bye?"

"I can go wake her up," Charlie says.

"No, it's okay. Let her rest."

Byron isn't even here yet, but with my wallet still in my back pocket, and my phone tucked in the front, I have what I need to go.

"Okay." Charlie's response is clearly disappointed, but I can't linger. There's no way to make this right. My chest is about to burst from my rapid heartbeat as my brow dampens. "Will I see you again?"

I wordlessly shrug before reaching for the front door handle, because I don't want to tell her the truth...

No. Probably not.

CHAPTER 21

Spencer

Lennox groans loudly, entirely unsubtle about the ecstasy she's currently experiencing.

Avery reaches over and pats Lennox's knee. "Hon, we don't need an invitation into your bedroom. Now we all know what you sound like when Dex is on top of you."

Lennox cradles her ballooning belly, which the white, fluffy spa robe can barely contain. "You really think Dex is on top these days with this thing in the way?"

Avery looks across to me, Dawn, and Chelsea all seated on the other side of the row of pedicure thrones. "I sincerely apologize for my best friend's endless need to *overshare*."

Chelsea releases a sharp cry of a laugh. "Oh, please. My best friend comes with me to get my butthole bleached. No need for shyness here."

Dawn plucks the cucumbers off her eyes one by one. Lids still shut, she exhales heavily. "And that, ladies, is what *real* oversharing sounds like. Chelsea, maybe enough Bellinis, hm?"

"Nathan rented this place out until closing. I'm going to finish at least another three...pitchers. I'm going to get so drunk I'm going to tell everyone about that time we were in Memphis and you rode the mechanical bull commando."

Dawn leans over and snatches the champagne flute right out of Chelsea's hands. "No. That's enough for you. Just shut your lips and enjoy your pedicure."

"Where are the little girls?" Avery asks, looking around the room.

"They're doing a cereal bath soak in the zen room." From what I understand, there's a giant in-ground soaking tub down there for mud baths and such, but they cleared it out and made a tween-friendly spa experience when Nathan called. The girls are being treated to a warm, oatmeal-honey bath that has a bunch of bath bombs in the shape of Fruit Loops. I was invited in and firmly said no to that chaos.

"I'm trying to be in solidarity, Spence, but it's really hard to hate your boss right now." Lennox groans again as the nail technician resumes massaging her swollen feet. "I mean, I'm on Team Spencer but—*oh, God. Yeah, right there.*"

Encouraged by her moaning, the nail technician grinds her knuckles into Lennox's arch.

"What Lennox is trying to say between orgasms is that this was really nice of your boss to rent out the entire spa for a day. Seems like he's trying to impress you."

I try to curb my enthusiastic smile, but Dawn notices how I light up. She waggles her eyebrows at me. "We came to an agreement last night," I tell them. "I think working together will be smooth sailing from here."

Nathan slipped out on me this morning. I woke up alone to a text from him that informed me he had to get our project notes over to his legal team, but I should call all my girlfriends and tell them to drop what they were doing for the day. I didn't mean to complain when I told him I couldn't afford my spa day promise to Charlie. But it slipped, and he took it as an opportunity to be the hero.

When I promised Charlie a spa day, I meant mani-pedis at a local nail salon that was running a BOGO deal, then a stop at Target for more animal face masks. The sloth one smells like grape cough syrup, but the rest of them are actually decent.

Nathan didn't just one-up me. He made my plan look pathetic. The Orchid Spa has a waiting list months out. Somehow, my boss was able to shut the entire spa down for a day, get them to reschedule all their preexisting Saturday appointments. That was probably expensive enough, but add on the charcuterie trays with actual caviar, the endless mimosas and Bellinis with top-shelf champagne and prosecco, and last but not least, spa services to our hearts' desire. Let's just say I'll be rewarding my boss in a really big way. Being sweet to me earns him sex. But being so kind and considerate to my baby sister? I'm going to read the *Kama Sutra* and take some notes before I see him again so I can show him my full gratitude.

"Dammit, I'm sorry," Lennox says to her nail technician. "Can we pause? I have to pee again. Had I known this spa day was coming, I would've had them install a catheter so I could sit in peace for more than ten minutes."

"Good grief," Avery mumbles as she lifts her feet out of the foot soak and dabs them on the towel next to the bowl. "I'll come with you."

"Same," Chelsea says, following suit. "I'm four Bellinis deep, meaning not only do I have to pee, but I also am too tipsy to find the bathroom on my own in this gigantic place."

With most of our party excusing themselves, the nail technicians and masseuses seize the opportunity for a quick break.

"We certainly know how to clear a room," I say to Dawn.

She laughs as she reaches for a piece of cheese on her appetizer plate, sitting right beside her on a beautiful, stained-glass end table. The entire spa is decorated in a Venetian style. Statue replicas of famous art pieces, marble columns, and Murano glass chandeliers dimly light the slightly jagged terrazzo tile, making it feel like you've transported straight to Venice. This place is the kind of luxury I *read* about, not experience.

"Did you try the caviar?" Dawn asks. "Nathan splurged on catering."

Stunned, my mouth falls open. "He even got this catered? Goodness. My old boss, Hank, gun to his head, could not tell you which deli I got his daily Reuben from." If I called out sick from work, I'm convinced he'd just starve. Hank *needed* an assistant. I feel like Nathan just tolerates one.

"Nathan's always been self-sufficient. He's just overworked."

"He can't tell his dad he needs a break?"

Dawn tightens the twisted towel on her head. She got some kind of conditioning treatment on her hair that needs to saturate for at least another hour. "He's a self-induced workaholic. Believe me, James has the same concerns I do. The only person he ever let take care of him was Elise."

"Who's Elise?"

Dawn gives me a sharp glance. "Nathan didn't tell you about Elise? I thought you said he spent the night."

"He did, but nothing happened." I'm petrified as a sickening realization squeezes my throat. "Dawn, is Nathan single? Because I swear if he's not, I didn't know—"

"Oh, calm down, honey. Nathan is single. Elise is the last assistant he had that he actually let in. After her, the brooding barricade that locks up his human emotions went up. Let's just leave it at that for now, okay? I'm not above gossiping, but only when they're my secrets to share."

I nod in understanding, as the questions rip through my mind like a bullet train off the tracks. I want to know about Elise immediately so I can see whose shoes I'm trying to fill.

"So, is caviar calorie dense?" I respectfully divert the conversation. "I've never tried it before."

"Did you just say caviar and calorie dense in the same sentence?" Dawn lifts a perfectly sculpted eyebrow. I make a mental note to ask her if that's permanent makeup, because her brows are always flawless. I have to tweeze almost daily to keep my thick caterpillars in a feminine shape. "Still on this diet, then?"

I sigh. "I was on weight-loss injections for years. They were more expensive than I could afford, but selfishly, I just..." I shake my head. "It's hard, you know? Charlie is the living embodiment of my mom. And my mom was *gorgeous*. Effortlessly slender and beautiful, light hair, light eyes. She turned men's heads wherever we went."

"So you took weight-loss drugs to look more like your mom and sister?" Obvious concern pools in Dawn's eyes.

"No, it was more like after my mom died, I became really aware of how I was the odd one out. I'd take Charlie around and people would assume I was the nanny. They'd compliment Charlie, telling me her parents were in trouble because she was going to grow up to be a heartbreaker and her daddy would have to beat the boys away with a stick."

"Ah, I see." Dawn's intuition is spot-on, because she proceeds to explain like she's reading the lines from my own mind. "If Charlie and your mom were always noticed for their beauty, and you were told you were their polar opposite, that means—"

"I was the troll."

"You're not a troll, Spencer. Not even close. I don't mean to speak ill of your mom, but did she pressure you to lose weight while you were growing up?"

"*God no.*" I actually laugh at the sentiment. "All we did was cook and eat together. She didn't let me have coffee until I was sixteen, but other than that, she restricted nothing. She told me I was royalty every day of my life. I was blissfully unaware that I was considered 'thick' or 'big-boned'—actually I think they're calling it 'big-backed' these days. I don't know, I just didn't feel insecure growing up. My weight obsession started after what happened in college."

Reaching between her legs, Dawn turns off the jets in her foot tub, and it grows eerily quiet. "What happened in college?"

I chew on the inside of my cheek, wondering why in hell I decided to pick at this scab today. Dawn has a presence. She's sassy, like me, but also powerful and commanding, like I want to be. I guess I already see her as something more than a colleague to look up to. "It's kind of difficult to talk about because it's so embarrassing."

"You don't have to. But it might make you feel better. Honey, I don't care how embarrassing the story is, you're with a friend who would never laugh at you."

I hear the metaphorical locks unlatching, the secret boxes having their lids snatched off, the sound of a shovel digging deep into the frozen ground. That's what I have to do to unearth one of the most defining moments of my life that I've tried and failed for years to bury and forget.

"It was a stupid hazing ritual for the senior football players... I was a virgin."

Dawn drops her head. "I don't like where this is going."

"It wasn't like that. It was consensual. Um..." I have to pause for a moment as my voice cracks and my breath goes shaky. "The seniors had this game they'd play—a scavenger hunt. During the first week of school they'd have to sleep with a princess, a jock, and a cow."

"A cow?" Dawn asks, her eyes stretching into wide circles.

"Not an actual cow. A princess was considered someone else's girlfriend. A jock was more aptly named—any starter at school on a sports team. And a cow, a...fat girl."

"For the record, I've always been a big supporter of trade schools. I feel like college these days is teaching boys to become predators. But all in good fun, right?" she asks with bitter sarcasm.

"Believe me, school administration and authority were very unaware of the tradition. The football team was pretty strict about confidentiality. I believe the rule was: Snitches die."

"*Jesus*," Dawn hisses.

"Anyway, I was a dumb college freshman full of foolish confidence my mom instilled. I happily ate it up when the starting quarterback asked me to come hang in his dorm room. We turned the lights off, sat on his bed, watched a movie... You can guess what happened next."

"Did he hurt you?"

"No. I mean, it was uncomfortable. It was my first time, and I was nervous. He kept saying I felt good, so I thought I was doing what I was supposed to. He even let me stay the night and walked me back to my dorm the next morning. He texted me later that afternoon, full of emojis, asking how I felt."

"Did he know you were a virgin?"

I nod solemnly. "I thought that's why he was being so nice and checking on me. I actually thought for a whole two days I was dating the starting quarterback. I felt like hot shit, let me tell you." I chuckle, but not because it's funny. I can clearly see now, five years later, how suspicious his behavior was.

"So, what were you? You weren't the princess because you were single, right? Did you play sports?"

The shame rolls over me like a heatwave. This time I don't try to escape it. I just want to share this with someone, *anyone*. It's been so lonely carrying the painful burden of this betrayal all on my own. "He asked me a day later to send him some sexy selfies. I tried a few with my underwear on, but that wasn't good enough. He wanted me completely naked. I did it. Within twenty-four hours, hundreds of posters with my nude photos were plastered all over campus, with 'cow' written on every single one."

"Oh, Spencer," Dawn gasps. "Oh my God, I can't believe that. Did you go to the dean?"

"I didn't have to. They saw the pictures too. Campus security pulled all the posters down and sent an email to the student body that anyone caught distributing the lewd images would be suspended or expelled." It didn't stop the bullying. I got moo'd out of the dining hall. Someone snuck hay into one of my textbooks with a sticky note that said "afternoon snack." I wanted to die.

"But what did they do *for you*?" Dawn asks. "Did they promise disciplinary action? Did they offer counseling? Was there talk of legal action?"

I think back on the hours I spent in the dean's office. It was all such a blur. I couldn't make eye contact with any of the administrators or faculty because I was humiliated. They'd all seen me butt-naked. The most sacred parts of me strung out for the world to see like a carcass in the road.

"I remember one counselor stating they wished my birthday hadn't gone by yet because if I were underage, they'd have a case for distribution of child pornography. That could've put a lot of asshole football players in jail. But the case as it stood... I don't know. I was in shock, I think? All I know is I wanted to talk to my mom about it. I called her a couple times but chickened out. I was ashamed. She'd raised me better than that."

"Better than what?" Dawn's feet are fully out of her foot tub now. She's resting them on either side of the large, tinted glass bowl. I keep mine submerged. My feet are beyond pruney, and the nail tech is going to have one hell of a time getting gel polish to adhere to my soaked toenails, but the water is grounding me. I swish my feet back and forth in the water, creating small waves that crest and break at the top of the bowl.

"Mom told me to wait for someone special. Someone who treated me well. I blew it on the scum of the earth."

Dawn exhales sharply. "Did you know I'm a mom? I have a daughter a little younger than you. Her name is Cora. She's actually studying abroad in Germany right now."

"Wow." Well, I hope she has a better college experience than me.

"It's every mother's living nightmare to see her daughter ridiculed and traumatized. But let me tell you something that I know in my bones: Every piece of advice she gave you was because of tough lessons she'd learned herself the hard way. We strive to shield our babies from the pain we experienced, but also, the twisted irony is we're mighty enough to protect our children because of the hell we've already endured. I know Cora will face immense heartbreak in her life. It's my job not to prevent the inevitable, but to tell her she's strong even when she feels weak. I'll stand through the fire with her, but I have to let her live her story."

My words are caught in my throat. I choose not to speak because I know I'll become overwhelmed with emotion. In response to my silence, Dawn rises from her lounger and embraces me. She kisses my forehead two, three, then four times. And that's when I melt. Tears pour down my face as I suck in short heaves of air.

"I never got to tell her," I say into Dawn's shoulder. "She died late the next week. I left school and pretended like it didn't happen. I focused on what Charlie needed. I just wanted to move on."

"But did you?" Releasing me, Dawn steps back to let me catch my breath.

I crash-dieted for a while after it happened. My body adapted and not even starvation was enough to keep my weight down. I became obsessed with BMI. I wanted to be in the *normal* range. *I just wanted to be fucking normal.* I wanted to look like Mom and Charlie. I wanted to belong. When I stumbled upon weight-loss medication, the weight came off so easily. I met Jesse, and he was instantly enamored. I'd been through so much pain, I really thought being smaller opened the doors to happiness.

"I guess not," I finally answer. Hearing the distant voices of Avery, Lennox, and Chelsea getting louder, I clean under my eyes and pat my cheeks, trying to hide the evidence of my breakdown.

"In hearing that story, the only opinion I would trust is your mom's. Believe the woman who told you you were beautiful every day of your life. She's right. What those kids did to you was *wrong*. The school should've done more to stand up for you. That boy who took the most vulnerable moment in a woman's life and made a mockery of it should have a boot clamped around his dick. You have nothing to be ashamed about, Spencer. Do not forget that."

I sniffle and nod hurriedly as the girls get closer. Avery and Lennox are quickly becoming the best friends and big sisters I never had. Chelsea is my friendly face at the office and constant comic relief. I trust them, but I can't rehash the story again today. I'm tired and ready to just enjoy Nathan's spa day present. Now that I've shared this with Dawn, who speaks to me just like my mother would, I feel like all the extra weight just fell off my body.

"What was his name?" Dawn asks in a hush, intuitively picking up on the fact I don't want to continue the conversation once the rest of our party has returned.

"Why?" I ask.

"I just like to name all my voodoo dolls before I torture them. Did he make it to the NFL? If so, I'll be starting a very defaming anonymous Reddit thread, just so you know."

I burst out into giggles. "No, I don't think he played past college. His name is Casey Conrad."

"Well, fuck you, Casey."

Yeah, I couldn't agree more.

Fuck you, Casey.

CHAPTER 22

Spencer

It should be illegal to drive after an entire day getting spoiled rotten at a luxury spa. Honestly, I shouldn't get behind the wheel. I'm so relaxed, I'm borderline high. I got massaged, had my face exfoliated with dead sea minerals, and even ate caviar for the first time—*ahem, first and last time*. I don't understand why a small tin of ocean-flavored popping boba balls is worth hundreds of dollars, but maybe I'm not fancy enough to appreciate the elegance.

But it's not like I'm going to make a habit of this. I promised myself today was a one-and-done situation. This was a treat for Charlie which is why I made an exception, but I'm not going to take advantage of Nathan's wallet ever again.

I'm waiting in the front lobby for Charlie and Claire. It's late and the spa is near closing. Everybody else collected their things and made their way to the parking lot. They actually let Lennox leave in her robe, to her great delight. I, however, am stuck waiting on the tweens who don't want this day to end.

"Hold up!" I shout when they come barreling by the front desk, heading in the opposite direction of the exit. "Girls, I told you, it's time to go." I tap the outside of my wrist where a watch would go. "Claire, I told your grandma I'd have you home in...five minutes ago. Chop, chop."

"Sorry, Ms. Spencer. It's my fault," Claire says. Her thick, red hair is fastened behind her back in a long ponytail. Her scant freckles are sparkling like stars in the night sky after the rainbow sherbert facial she opted for. Charlie got the ice cream sundae facial, and for the past twenty minutes they've been loudly comparing notes as to which smelled better.

"What's wrong, sweetie?"

"I lost my locket. I took it off when we put our swimsuits on and I can't find it anywhere. Charlie's been helping me look."

"It's here!" A lady in a black blouse and black palazzo pants comes jogging down the hallway, the clickety-clack of her high heels echoing off the walls. She holds out a long, gold chain with a thick, heart locket dangling like a pendulum. "You left it in the locker, honey. We found it," she says in breathless relief.

Claire hugs the lady, thanking her more times than I can count.

"Okay, Charlie," I say, holding up my car keys, "take your bags and put them in the trunk. Get in, get buckled, and I will be out shortly. Okay?"

For once she doesn't pry, too wrapped up in the company of her best friend. They go back to discussing the pros and cons of their facials. Come on, it's a no-brainer. Sherbert over ice cream sundae, all day every day.

I watch Claire's long ponytail sway behind her, once again having the strangest feeling of déjà vu, like I've met her before in a different life. It happened the first time I met her after their first sleepover. I was a little distracted by Spike, who was screaming like a piggie gladiator, hell-bent on vengeance when we separated him from Babe. But still, I had the same feeling that I do now... I just still can't quite place her.

"I'm Margaret, the spa director," the woman says, outstretching her hand. "Did you and your party have a good time? Was everything up to your standards?"

"My standard for a pedicure is *not* getting stabbed with nippers or going home with foot fungus, so please believe me when I say today was one of the most memorable days of my life."

She chuckles. "Well, I'm glad you had fun. I hate to be so candid, but do you have any idea if today was up to Mr. Hatcher's standards? Our gratuity is based on your experience, so as long as it's honest, your glowing report would be helpful."

"Ah, I see. Um, yes, I will let Mr. Hatcher know it was fantastic. Better than superb. I will actually invent a new adjective to properly describe the utter euphoria that today was."

She clasps her hands together and bows her head. "Thank you so much. There isn't anything we wouldn't do for the Hatchers."

And their money, I add mentally. Nathan doesn't act like an arrogant, rich elitist. It's only through subtle tells that I really understand the magnitude of his wealth. The watch he wears, how all his designer suits are perfectly tailored to his body, or the fact he has full-time employees whose job it is to just wait around on him all day.

"Um, is the register closed?" I point to the wall of skincare products, neatly displayed on the built-in shelves.

"What would you like?" Margaret asks with a wide smile.

"Something for my sister. Just a cleanser, a moisturizer, and maybe a toner or serum. Do you have anything without too many chemicals? Her skin is still so young."

Margaret points to the other side of the wall, with rows of bamboo bottles and jars with dark blue writing. "This is Azure, our cleanest line. Very safe for young skin. And it smells divine." She grabs a test bottle and unscrews the lid before holding it to my nose. The scent is light and refreshing, a blend of ocean sea salt, tangerine, and mint.

"Wow, that's incredible. Okay." I draw in a deep breath. "This is the part where you tell me these cost hundreds, right?"

"Don't worry," she says, waving me off. Stepping behind the register, she pulls out a large gift bag and begins to stuff every Azure product she can reach. My stomach drops like an unhinged elevator. *Shit*. She thinks because I'm friends with Nathan that I'm also rich. This is going to be embarrassing, but I have to tell her I can't afford all this.

"Margaret, I appreciate it, but I can probably only buy one or two—"

"You're Spencer, right?" she checks.

"Yes."

She hands the bag over. "Two sets of the entire skincare line. Directions are on the boxes. Anytime you need a refill, or a service, stop by and give the front desk your name. It's on the house."

I try to hand the bag back. "I feel so bad. I wasn't trying to get free stuff. There's no way I can take all this from you." I hold up the heavy bag, knowing this is probably over five hundred dollars of retail.

"It's not free." She winks. "Mr. Hatcher gave us very strict instructions to take good care of you. You and your sister are going to love these products, I promise."

"Are you sure?"

"Just let Mr. Hatcher know you had a nice time today. That's all we ask." I could continue to resist, but there's not an ounce of hesitation in Margaret's honey-smooth, calming voice.

"Thank you so much."

I tuck the gift bag into my tote filled with a change of clothes, tennis shoes, and my wet swimsuit. I want to surprise Charlie later.

I can't wipe the stupid smile off my face as I head to the Lincoln. The girls have the cabin interior lights on, and I already hear Tate McRae blasting through my speakers. I bop my head along, appreciating the sassy tunes of today's new Britney Spears.

Pulling out my phone, I call Nathan but he doesn't answer. After two rings it goes straight to voicemail. I'm actually kind of surprised he hasn't called or texted to check in since this morning. It's probably best not to turn into a paranoid, stage-five clinger the very day after he slept over for the first time. I don't want to scare him off.

I bet he's in a meeting with his legal team as we speak, making plans to take down the corrupt plumbing company. In lieu of a voicemail, I pause outside my closed driver side door, letting the girls jam out for a little longer, and send him a text.

> **Me:** Today was incredible. I don't even know how to thank you. You are officially Charlie's favorite person on the planet.

The read receipt goes from delivered to read immediately. His response bubble populates, then quickly disappears. His text follows shortly and I giggle at his contact name every time it pops up on my phone.

> **It's Nate. I'm sorry:** You're welcome. It was my pleasure.

> **Me:** Are you busy?

> **It's Nate. I'm sorry:** Somewhat.

> **Me:** About that date... When do I get to see you again?

> **It's Nate. I'm sorry:** Spencer, today was a gift of friendship.

> **Me:** Meaning?

> **It's Nate. I'm sorry:** Last night was crossing the line. Starting Monday, I'd like if we could go back to just being professional. I promise I will be a better boss moving forward though.

I stare at his words, trying to breathe through the unexpected sucker punch to the gut. What the hell? I know Nathan isn't my boyfriend, but is he already breaking up with me?

> **Me:** What happened? I'll be home within an hour. Can we at least talk? I'm so confused.

> **It's Nate. I'm sorry:** I don't have time tonight. Sorry.

> **Me:** Please?

I feel weak for practically begging, but at least it's honest.

Again, the read receipt is immediate. But this time Nathan doesn't respond. I bite on my tongue so hard it hurts. I don't know why, I guess to subtly express the pain I'm feeling inside. All the weight Dawn lifted earlier today with our heart-to-heart talk jumps right back into my body, like Flubber finding its rightful host again.

I force myself to slap on a smile. Opening the car door, I throw my tote into the front passenger seat, and join Charlie and Claire in belting out the chorus of Tate's "run for the hills."

I should've listened to the song lyrics more closely and took her advice.

In the case of Nathan Hatcher, I should've run for the hills the very first moment he first looked in my direction.

CHAPTER 23

Nathan

On Monday, I texted Spencer asking if she'd like a coffee from the local spot, and if so, what kind? She ignored me. I bought her one anyway and left it on the edge of her desk. By lunchtime, I couldn't resist the urge to check. Lifting the coffee up, it was clear not a drop was consumed. She sent me a curt email informing me that Dawn needed her assistance on a project and she'd be away from her desk for most of the day.

I wanted to put my dick on the table and tell her she'd need my approval before she loaned herself to another employee, but something told me to stop digging my own grave. So I let that one go.

Tuesday rolled around and I was determined to break the ice. I even looked up dad jokes, for fuck's sake. I used: What do sprinters eat before they race? *Nothing. They fast.* She stared at me like I'd sprouted rainbow-colored horns. I know for a fact the not-pissed-at-me Spencer would've found that cute at least. When the joke didn't work, out of desperation, I texted her that I left my belt at her place and needed it back. I prepared myself that when I got her alone in my office, I was going to shut the door and tell her the truth. I'm just not ready for a relationship, and I'm very sorry I led her on.

A part of me feels like I should mention how much I still want her, and how my cock hates me because I want to strip her down and bend her over any surface she'd let me. I'm worried she thinks this has anything to do with her. It's me. It's all my ghosts.

But the excuse didn't matter. I walked into work on Wednesday to my belt, in a neat coil, already placed in a small, white box.

By Thursday, I'm determined. I strut into work this morning ready to pull rank. *Like it or not, Spencer. I sign your paychecks, so when I think we need to talk, we're going to talk. End of story.*

The first thing I notice is that Spencer's wearing something odd. Normally she's all business skirts, dresses, and slacks. Spencer always dresses like she's about to enter a courtroom. But today, her thick hair is pulled back into a sporty ponytail, and she has on...overalls?

They are black overalls with silver button hooks. *What in the world?* It's only when I'm about a yard away from her desk that I notice the enlarged rat that pops its head out of her pocket. And suddenly the overalls make sense. She's using the giant chest pocket to kangaroo-mommy that *thing*.

"Spencer," I say as I near her. "It has to go. I told you I don't want rodents here."

She swivels around slowly, stroking Spike's head with one finger, looking like a Disney villain. "Funny thing. Did you know guinea pigs can be registered as emotional support animals and are permissible in the workplace as long as you have HR approval?" She taps a tri-folded piece of paper next to her. "This is a letter from HR recognizing Spikey here as my new desk buddy."

"Are you trying to get a reaction out of me? Look, we need to talk."

"Spike isn't here for you, he's here for me," she argues.

"Really?" I roll my eyes. "And what does he support?"

"Mostly my anxiety, which is stemming from one main source," she says, narrowing her lids.

"Point taken. And you're right. I owe you an explanation. Step into my office and let's talk privately. Now."

"Fine," she grumbles as she rises.

"Leave that thing."

She taps her paper again. "Take it up with HR, boss. Where I go, he goes. So, I'd choose your meetings sparingly if Spike terrifies you so much."

Great. We're back to her calling me boss which is pseudo-respectful because I know when she verbally says *boss*, she's mentally saying *ass*.

I watch the guinea pig's fidgety nose twitch back and forth, debating if I can learn to live with this. But I can't stomach it. I resist the urge to shudder. "Not terrified, I just don't like them. Spencer, seriously. Enough. This isn't the way to get back at me."

"I'm not getting back at you, Nathan. I'm not anything with you except just...done." She sits back down and reopens her laptop. "Would you excuse me? I have a lot of work to do."

I bite back my irritation at her stubbornness and try to keep my tone warm. "How are the office remodel plans coming?"

"Fine," she answers without looking at me.

"So, it'll be done by the time my project partner shows up next week?"

"Yes. Furniture will be delivered this weekend. The designer asked that you please leave your office unlocked."

"Okay, I can do that. Is there anything else you need feedback on?" I know she can't tell, but even me being within eyesight of that chunky rat is a testament to how much I like Spencer and how bad I feel about how this all went down.

"I'll email you if I do." Her eyes are still attached to her screen. I should've never started this cold-shoulder war with Spencer. She's even better at it than I am.

"All right, well, you know where to find me."

I trudge to my office, defeated. My mood is further worsened when I open my emails and see another fresh set of images from the PI, Hodge. Grabbing my desk phone, I dial him immediately, and as usual, he picks up on the first ring.

"What am I looking at?" I ask, staring at the picture of Ruby, looking disheveled, meeting with a suspicious-looking man in an alleyway.

"I don't know, boss. I thought I should bring it up. I've been tailing Peter, but like I said—he's squeaky clean. I got a gut feeling I should follow the old lady one day, so I did. The man she's meeting with is a known drug dealer."

"Ruby bought drugs?" I peer more closely at the image. No money or packages seem to be exchanged.

"Nah, boss. They were just talking. I've got nothing else. I can keep tailing her if you want?"

"Keep following your gut feeling. I want you focused on Peter, but if Ruby starts acting outside of the norm, dig up whatever you can. And if you ever suspect Claire is in danger, the police are your first call. I'm your second. Clear?"

"Yes, sir."

"Thanks, Hodge, I have to go," I say as I see my dad hovering at Spencer's desk. To add insult to injury, Spencer's smile is wide and toothy. She's clutching her chest, laughing hard at something my dad said. He turns around and to my horror he's holding her guinea pig in his arms, looking at it like a brand-new baby. Okay, so obviously my rodent phobia doesn't come from my dad. We make eye contact through the closed glass doors of my office and Dad waves. I hold up my palm and he hands Spencer back her rat-pig and makes his way into my office.

"Your assistant is *delightful*. Sweetest little thing. Did you know she's part Cuban and black? I asked her where her pretty complexion came from."

"I'm aware," I bite out. "You're engaged. Should you be describing other women as sweet and pretty?"

He slumps into the chair opposite my desk. "First of all, Jules doesn't have a jealous bone in her body. She knows where my heart is. Second, what's wrong with you? Still feuding with your assistant? Because if you'd stop with the silent treatment, you'd learn she's a gem."

I want to tell him it's the opposite, actually. Spencer's the one with the icy demeanor lately. But I'm not in the mood to explain myself. "What's up?"

"Legal contacted me this morning. What you unearthed about the Graystone and Lakeshore properties was impressive detective work."

"That was all Spencer. She went through those voicemails and put the pieces together." If anyone deserves credit, it's her.

"*Smart girl.* Give her a raise," Dad says firmly. I don't have the heart to tell him that at the rate we're going, she's probably going to quit on us the moment she finds a comparable job.

"Anyway, I've had inspectors in and out of those properties all week. Lakeshore is fine. It's salvageable with repairs, but Graystone is pretty much condemned."

"Condemned?" I push away from my desk, folding my arms over my chest. "Isn't that a little dramatic? I was just there and the apartments are functional."

Dad brushes against the top of his lilac button-down, probably getting guinea pig hair all over my office. *Great.* "It's lipstick on a pig," he explains. "My concern is safety. The plumbing isn't up to code, the electrical has suffered because of it. I want to gut the entire thing, rebuild properly, and then offer all the tenants we displace the first opportunity to sign up for our brand-new, rent-to-own condominiums."

"Dad, if we force an evacuation, we're on the hook for relocation assistance, we'll have to return all deposits, and we might have to reimburse portions of leases. It'd be a major financial loss. There's no other way to do the repairs."

Dad rubs his hands together, palm sliding across palm. "Nate, some decisions aren't about money. I'm not willing to risk the tenants' safety. Yes, we're going to take a major financial loss. But we're going to sleep in peace knowing a newborn isn't going to have damaged lungs from inhaling mold, or the ceiling isn't going to concave and crush a family. This is the only way to stay ahead of accidents we aren't anticipating. We're closing the complex. That's my final word."

I finally nod in agreement. "So be it, then."

"Get on the phone with the property management company. We're also issuing them a formal apology for putting them in this situation. I also want a thorough investigation of all our construction partners. Moving forward, I want to make sure all our partners are squeaky clean. No more crooks."

I cock a brow. "Does that mean you won't be placing any more spies in Harvey's employment?"

Dad clears his throat, trying to swallow down his smirk. "I sent Harvey a very nice gift basket with smoked Alaskan salmon and rare truffles."

I slip him a sly smile. "Because truffles absolve your deviant behavior."

"Pretty much." Dad rises. "All right, I'm headed to a meeting. I meant to ask you about Santa Barbara this weekend. Are you available?"

"Why? Are you in the hunt for yet another project?"

"No. I invited Julia's parents, her siblings, their spouses, and their kids to the beach house for some bonding time. It'd mean a lot to us if you came."

"Oh, I uh..." There's so much on my mind between my newly recharged feud with Spencer, Ruby meeting with a drug dealer, and all the work on my plate, it's hard to sift through the clutter of my mind to find a good excuse. "I have plans."

"What plans?"

"Some landscaping things at my house. They're measuring the pool, replacing the fridge, and installing a new built-in grill. It's a whole thing. I need to be there."

Dad blinks at me. "Your excuses are getting lazy."

I hold up my hands like I'm caught and surrendering. "Then why do you ask, Dad? I'm happy for you and Julia. And I want you to get along with your new family. I'm just not interested in cozying up to strangers right now."

Dad's face morphs into disappointment. "She made you soup. It's in the break room."

"Huh?"

"Julia makes a bone broth soup with homemade egg noodles. She swears it's a magic cure."

"For what?"

"For every five events Jules invites you to, I only ask about one. I'm trying not to overwhelm you. I keep telling her you're sick so as not to hurt her feelings. I've used that excuse so much, she thinks you're dying from mono. So, she made you soup. Even though you reject her over and over again, she still has hope and extends blind kindness to you at every turn. It's getting harder not to see your behavior as deliberate."

I tuck my chin to my chest, feeling weighed down by guilt. "I've been an ass."

"You sure have."

"Fine. I can't do this weekend, but I swear on my life, my answer to the next invitation is yes."

Dad makes his way around my desk to clamp his hand around my shoulder. "Thanks, Nate."

"No problem." He's at the door when I stop him. "Wait."

"Yes?"

"Tell Julia her soup is delicious."

Dad cocks his head. "You haven't even tried it yet."

"I know, but it's nice to say. Just tell her thank you."

He nods once more before he's through the door. My view is no longer obstructed and I see Spencer's empty desk. An idea sprouting to mind, I march to her work area. After ensuring the rodent carrier under her desk is empty, and the guinea pig is nowhere in sight, I snag the pen off her desk. *Sticky note, sticky note.*

She stores a set here somewhere…

I open the top desk drawer which is empty except for a hole punch, a collection of pens, and other office supplies rarely used in this day of digital communication. I open the second drawer to see a rainbow collection of sticky notes. *There we go.*

I'm jotting down a note to her on a pink sticky, inviting her to lunch with me in the break room—Julia's homemade soup. She's been so clipped to my texts and emails, maybe a handwritten note will warm her up to me again. It at least shows some effort.

I'm signing my name, *from Nate*, when other contents

of her drawer catch my attention. Cheap mini donuts seem out of character for Spencer. I pick up the pack of powdered sugar Hostess Donettes to see a name, Caleb, scrawled in black permanent marker. Next to it, his phone number. The chocolate glazed donuts have the same.

A beast of jealousy screams and tries to claw its way out of my chest. If there were any doubt about my feelings for this woman, I am immediately humbled. I'm furious at the idea of her getting another man's number. I hate how she laughed so easily with my dad, yet every time she looks at me it's with daggers for eyes. I'm even more pissed at myself, because I had her and I let her go. I should've just talked to her more that night. I should've explained everything that happened with Elise. It's Spencer, she would understand. She'd be patient as I worked through my shit. But opening up about my grief is a Mount Everest I can't seem to climb.

I know this sticky note won't do. It's not enough to invite her to lunch. I bunch up the note and chuck it in the wastebasket. I have to leave Spencer alone until I'm ready to tell her the truth and lay all my messy tragic baggage on the table. Until I can do that, logically she has every right to talk to other men...

But not today and not donut guy.

I casually toss the packaged donuts in the trash, one log at a time.

Sorry, Caleb.
She's mine.

CHAPTER 24

Spencer

Oh shit. I look around Nathan's office, filled with regret. The bubblegum-pink wallpaper is so bright, it's giving me a slight headache.

I arrived at the office this morning to examine the remodel. Nathan said there was no budget, so I hired one of Vegas's most prominent interior designers and offered her a rush fee. I told Lynette I wanted Nathan's office to look like Barbie and Tinkerbell had a baby girl and this was her nursery if they had the budget of a Kardashian. I thought she'd realize it was a joke. Or maybe, I've been so angry... Was I hoping my retaliatory prank would make a big impression?

Either way, looking at it now, I fear I went too far.

The entire office looks like a replica of the Flamingo Las Vegas, and much to my dismay, I'm counting at least six different shades of pink. Charlie would *love* this space. This is a dream office for an eleven-year-old girl who still secretly watches reruns of *Hannah Montana*, even though she swears she's too cool now. She has no idea I can see her YouTube watch history through parental controls.

But while this is a perfect office for a preteen, it's wildly inappropriate for a grown man and real estate professional running a billion-dollar business. *Oh my God.* I tent my hands over my mouth and nose as the panic sets in. *He's going to kill me.* This is borderline gross misconduct. This could be seen as a waste of financial resources, intentional insubordination...even vandalism.

My advance just hit my bank account this morning. The trial period is over and I was supposed to walk into work today finally able to breathe easy. Why would I risk this? Nathan's so unpredictable, there's a good chance he'll get rid of me over this. I'm easily replaceable. All he'd have to do is put up an Indeed listing: Unbelievably sexy, broody, billionaire boss seeking a docile assistant that causes him no stress and doesn't throw adult temper tantrums when he admits he doesn't want to date her.

If he posted it now, that position would be filled by lunchtime.

I really, really fucked up. Maybe there's still time to fix it, though. The new pink, crushed-velvet furniture can easily be replaced by the plain black leather sofas. The sheer pink curtains can come down. There's nothing I can do about the wallpaper, but I can at least take this faux-fur pink rug out of here before Nathan arrives—

"*What the fuck?*"

Oh, no. Too late. I don't even have to spin around to gauge my boss's response. His words lash out like a whip, tension-ridden and full of anger. I can already see his furrowed brows, burning glare, and balled-up fists before I turn around.

"Um, what do you think?" I ask, shriveling in place. I wore my best office dress this morning, the black one with cap sleeves, a sharp collar, and the waist belt with a golden buckle. I even paired it with my black, closed-toe Jimmie Joos—the most expensive knock-off brand I can afford. I wanted to feel powerful and confident this Monday morning, but lo and behold, I've never felt more defenseless, like I just entered a lion's cage naked, with two thick ribeyes strapped to my stomach.

"You did this?" When I finally spin to face him, his expression is somewhat unreadable. He's not happy—clearly. But I'm not finding any signs of an impending explosion.

"Well, in a way. I did say feminine-forward, but this is more pink than I could've ever imagined. There are some tweaks we can make. I'll call the designer right now and—"

"It's fine, Spencer. It's...colorful." Nathan takes a few more steps into his office, observing all the intricate details, like the pink flamingo statue by the sitting area, his new blush-colored executive chair, and the fuzzy magenta throw pillows sitting on the sofa.

"You're not mad?" Now pure confusion is my dominating emotion. Why isn't he yelling?

"No." He looks like he's about to choke on his clipped, one-word answers.

Assuaged by his obvious effort to maintain calm in a disastrous situation, I actually feel bad about my behavior. "I can make any changes you like," I say. "I think the rug is a little too much."

Nathan nods. "Let me stew on it."

"So you're going to work here today?" I still can't hide the surprise painted all over my face.

He presses his lips together so hard they lose color. They smack when he opens them again. "This *is* my office," he answers. "Also, Spike rolled himself to the elevator bay. You should grab him before he accidentally ends up in the lobby."

Even more curious. He called Spike by his name, and not "gross rat" or "chubby rodent." He seems to do better when Spike is in his gerbil ball. Perhaps he feels safer with the sphere of plastic protection.

"Right. Well, I'll go get him, then."

"Fine."

I waltz right past him, but his footsteps thud behind me. As soon as I reach the exit, he grabs my wrist and pulls me to the right of the see-through glass doors, out of view of passersby. Suddenly my back is against the wall as Nathan makes a barrier with his hands planted on each side of my head. I'd have to duck under his muscular arms to flee.

"Do you feel better?" He leans closer, a dangerous look in his eyes. "Is this what it takes?"

I'm suddenly breathing in gasps. My head goes fuzzy with his lips this close and his tantalizing smell surrounding us. "What?"

"Are we even now?"

"I don't understand."

"If you're pulling a stunt like this, it's because you're angry. Go ahead and take it out on me, Spencer. I can handle it. But I need to know at the end of this, when you're done acting out, you'll come back to me."

His words break the haze and only infuriate me further. I push against his hard chest, savoring the split second where my hands were on his body. Where they should be. Where we could've been had he not tossed me aside like a dirty dish rag. I don't push him hard enough to move him, but he backpedals, understanding my request for space.

"You can't go back to something you never had. Quite frankly, Nathan, I'm sick of being played hot and cold. I don't know what you want, I just know it's not me. Leave me alone and let me do my job in peace."

"Then why are you still here? If you're so done with me, why haven't you quit?"

"Quit the job that gave me a car, home, health and dental insurance, and a year's salary up front? Use your common sense. Not all of us have a bank vault like Scrooge McDuck's. If you think I'm still here to get your attention, your ego is steering you wrong."

There's unmistakable hurt in his eyes. "Spencer, I'm really sorry." He folds his arms over his chest, but it doesn't look authoritative like it normally does. It looks more defensive than anything. "I meant what I said. I wanted to take you out but..."

"But what?" I've been craving this answer for over a week now. Nathan obliterated my feelings when he went cold and put an end to our brief entanglement. All I can think of is he spent the night, held me, touched me—even if it were only PG. Then the next day he wanted nothing to do with me. He got a taste, and realized he didn't want me after all. There's no other plausible explanation.

"I'm sorting out some stuff. Can you give me some time?"

Is this because of Elise? I want to believe him. I really do. The way his eyes look soft and light today, more blue than green. There's heavy drops of sadness in them, and I'm dying to know why. But I also know how this ends. I'm tired of trying to see past his concrete-hard exterior. I don't have time for these games.

"You can have all the time you need, because whatever you're sorting out has nothing to do with me. Let's keep it professional, like *you* requested." Shaking my head and forcing out a sharp exhale, I fight off the glimmer of hope. I'm sure whatever excuses Nathan has in his arsenal would probably have me weak-kneed and ready to forgive him. Which is exactly why I don't want to hear them.

"Fine," he murmurs.

"Fine," I parrot back.

I walk purposefully to the elevator to retrieve my lost guinea pig. I find him ramming himself into the elevator doors over and over, like a Roomba that's malfunctioning.

"Spike, you goofball," I say, scooping him up. I look into his little black eyes and he settles down, finding my gaze. "You do recognize your name, don't you? You're smarter than most people think."

He sniffs the air, lifting his head and showing me a peek of his overbite and his pouty bottom lip. "So what's your opinion?" I ask quietly as we make our way back to my desk. "Was I too hard on him?"

Arms secured around the plastic ball, I clamp my lids shut briefly, trying to shake off my feelings of guilt. It's not my fault. I didn't start all this. So how come when I close my eyes, all I can see is the cloudy look of sorrow on Nathan's face?

And why do I feel responsible?

CHAPTER 25

Nathan

After two hours of punishing my body in the pool, my arms ache as I hoist myself out. Water soaks the concrete ledge as I shut my eyes, waiting for the world to stop spinning. I need water. Forcing my legs to move is like walking through Jell-O. I'm trying to take my sexual frustration out in the pool. It's futile. I could go and find a one-night stand, but let's be honest. Only one woman can scratch the itch I have.

I make my way to the outdoor kitchen and grab a bottle of water from the beverage cooler. It's barely cold. My lies are catching up to me. I told my dad I couldn't travel this weekend because I was getting this fridge replaced, turns out it actually does need to be replaced.

Halfway done with my water, I glance at my phone sitting on the granite countertop by the sink. I catch the tail end of a call notification but miss the actual call.

Snatching up my phone, I'm horrified to see I have thirteen missed calls from Spencer. I don't give myself enough time to thoroughly run through scenarios in my mind. Is she hurt? Where's Charlie? Did they get into an accident? I dial her back as the sobering reality settles over my body, making my legs feel bionic. I'll run to her if she needs me.

"Spencer?" I ask as soon as the ringing stops and the line connects. "What's wrong? Where are you?"

"Your front gate," she says, clipped. Her tone both does and doesn't surprise me. I thought she was calling with an emergency, so the annoyed edge in her voice makes me relax. It's nice to know she's her normal self. Obviously she's fine. "Your security guard won't let me through. Why haven't you been answering?"

"I was swimming. I'm back by the pool. How do you know where I live?"

"I'm your assistant. Your home is the billing address for my corporate card."

"Oh, well, I'm flattered you're borderline stalking me." I mean for it to be flirty, but I think I've pissed her off further.

"Real funny, Nathan. Are you going to let me in?"

"Right." I don't ask why she's here. I don't care, actually. I'm just happy I get to see her. "Hand your phone to the security guard."

Wordlessly, she obeys. "This is Russell."

"Russ, it's Nathan. The woman in front of you is my personal assistant, Spencer. Put her on the approved list. Let her in anytime she wants moving forward."

"There's a kid with her, sir. Should I—"

"Yes, both of them."

"Roger that," Russell says, then the call ends.

My head of security is not one to mince words. He ends conversations when he's done retrieving information. The man wastes no time on pleasantries. He'd never survive in sales, but he's one hell of a bodyguard.

I finish off my water, pondering why Spencer has chosen to grace me with her sassy presence this Saturday afternoon. I don't have to wonder for long. Before I know it, Spencer, dressed in blue jean shorts and an oversized T-shirt, is barreling through the patio doors, then charging toward me, a pink piece of paper crumpled in her fist. Waiting for her by the edge of the pool, I flex my midsection, hoping my bare abs have some effect on her.

Her stare is intimidating. She's makeup-free today, which is a new angle. I'm used to seeing her all dolled up at the office, but this woman is naturally beautiful in every sense of the word.

"Where's Charlie?" I ask once she's in earshot.

"Waiting in the car. I take it you're a strong swimmer?" Her scowl deepens if that's possible.

"Yeah. Why?"

Without another word she shoves me hard, sending me flying backward, crashing right back into the pool. I hold my breath as the water engulfs me with a massive splash. I had no time to be graceful about anything. I swim to the ladder, climb out of the pool, then pinch the sides of my swim trunks, trying to wring them out while they're still on my body.

"That was uncalled for," I say with a smirk.

"No, it was very, *very* called for. You're having me evicted?" Spencer's practically shrieking, waving the pink paper in her hand. "How could you do this? Talk about petty. I told you I'd fix your office. You didn't have to boot me and Charlie out of our home."

I shake out my hand, sending water droplets flying, then pluck the piece of paper from her grip. A cursory read tells me Dad wasted no time in delivering the evacuation notices. "It wasn't personal—"

"How is this not personal? You're retaliating because of Spike and your Barbie Dreamhouse office. Maybe you should hop down off your high horse and accept the fact that *you* started this. I *liked* you. I really liked you. You strung me along, whispering all these sweet nothings, then threw me away like a candy wrapper. Now you're kicking me out of my home. Fuck it. Maybe I should just quit."

"Hey now." After closing the space between us, I grab her wrists and hold them gently by her side, so she can't throw me into the pool again. "The building is dangerous. It's condemned. That's why we're closing it. Everybody is getting evicted, not just you. We pulled at a string and the entire tapestry came loose. It happens."

She presses against her temples tightly, like she's trying to keep her head intact. "What am I going to do now, Nathan? I could barely afford this place to begin with."

"There are other apartments."

"This one came furnished, and your company was subsidizing

half our rent. Utilities were a flat fee. It's only ten minutes away from Charlie's school. I just started over. I don't know how I'm going to do it again." Her attitude lowers to a simmer, and I can see how overwhelmed she is.

"I'll help." I release her wrists once I'm certain she's not going to surprise attack me again. "What do you need? I can cover your rent wherever you want to go."

"No." She shakes her head. "No handouts. I don't like owing people when I'm not sure if I can ever repay them."

"Gifts don't have to be repaid, Spencer. Just tell me how much you need and it's yours. I'll take care of you guys."

The sun is behind me, so she squints when she looks up at me. She planks her hand over her forehead to block the blaring rays, forgetting there's sunglasses resting on the top of her head. "I'm not your puppy. You don't take care of me."

"Then why are you here?"

She lifts her shoulders and drops them. "Charlie and I were on our way to the community pool. I guess I needed to yell at somebody. Sorry. I should go. The AC is on, but it's so damn hot today, I don't want to leave her in the car too long."

"Swim here." I nod over my shoulder. "We can fire up the grill."

"No, thanks. As much as Charlie would love this pool…" She spins around, taking in a three-sixty view of my property. "You really are a billionaire, aren't you? This is a resort, not a pool."

"You say that like it's a bad thing." A diabolical plan suddenly forms in my mind. I point to my left. "This was meant to be a pool house, but wires got crossed during construction. They built it with two rooms and a full kitchen. It's about fifteen hundred square feet. Bigger than your apartment, right?"

She scrunches up her face. "Double the size."

"Great, so it's settled. It's yours as long as you need it."

"Move in with you?" Spencer issues a shrill cackle. "Have you lost your mind?"

I fold my arms over my chest and angle my body so the sun

isn't cooking the broad side of my back anymore. "Why is that so crazy?"

"Would Tom move in with Jerry? Would Peter Pan bunk with Captain Hook? Simba and Scar sure as hell aren't sharing the Pride Lands."

I smirk at her. "Clever. But just so you know, while you think you're innocent, between you accosting me at my home and then trying to drown me, I think you're more Captain Hook than Peter Pan."

"I didn't try to drown you," she mumbles.

In the five seconds since I suggested it, I've grown very attached to the idea of Spencer living here, always in arm's reach. An entire security detail between her and any other interested donut dudes. This is when I choose to be ruthless in getting what I want.

"Spencer, I really can't afford for you to be distracted at work. Finding a new home, moving, the new commute—I can't give you time off for all that." I jut my thumb toward the guesthouse. "If you want to keep your job, you'll move in. Plain and simple."

"You can't make me by threatening my job."

I close the space between us and hover over her, puffing myself up like a bear. "Watch me."

"What?" she squeaks, tilting her head back to peer up at my gasoline-fueled gaze.

"All the shit you get away with at work is because I let you. It's entertaining, really. But make no mistake, when I want my way, I get it. So unless you want to find a new job along with a new apartment..." I flash her a wicked grin. "Let me show you your new place."

"You are criminally insane."

"Not the first time I've heard that." I wink at her. I don't give her any time to protest, because quite frankly, now I'm dead set on this whole plan. Had it come to me before, I would've taken a sledgehammer to Spencer's apartment myself.

"I don't know." She sneaks a side glance at the guesthouse

and I swear there's a brief flash of relief.

"You're welcome."

"Huh?"

"Oh, my mistake, I thought you said, 'Thank you, boss, for saving my ass.'"

Her glare returns. "I most certainly did not."

I playfully pop my shoulders. "I'm going to go give Charlie the good news."

Spencer crosses her arms. "As in you're going to bribe my sister by showing her all your fancy shit, so it's two against one?"

She's spot-on. I am fully banking on Charlie chaining herself to a pool chair, demanding that she and Spencer stay. "And here you thought you were the cleverest in the room." I tap her nose. "How's that reality check feel?"

"I didn't agree to anything. And I told you, Charlie and I have to go. We're on our way to the pool."

I point to her up and down, gesturing to her casual ensemble. "You have a swimsuit on underneath this?"

"Yes. Why?"

"Are you a strong swimmer?" I ask before scooping her up, one arm under her knees, the other arm supporting her shoulders. She squeals and flails but it's far too late. I toss her with all my might, so she lands safely away from the concrete ledge of the infinity pool. She drops in with far more grace than I did.

She resurfaces, wiping her face with one hand as she treads water. "I'm...going...to...kill you," she growls out.

"Mk, pumpkin. Towels are over there." I point to the neat stack of striped beach towels by the cabana. "There's water and soda in the fridge. I think some piña colada mix too. Help yourself. I'll be back."

"Nathan, you're a dead man," she shouts as I walk away.

But with my back turned, I'm smiling ear to ear knowing damn well how this is going to go. It's a win-win. Spencer can stop stressing so much about money and providing for Charlie. And as for me?

Well, now I'll have someone to come home to.

CHAPTER 26

Spencer

"Two bathrooms! Two *whole* bathrooms!" Charlie squeals. "I am a freaking princess. Look at my pool!" My bedroom door is open, so I hear Charlie first loud, then fading away like a car passing as she blazes from one end of Nathan's luxe guesthouse to the other.

It all happened so fast. One minute, I was swearing up and down I'd never move in with my bosshole. Four hours later, after a symphony of Charlie's pleas and crocodile tears, we were packing up our little apartment. I've never seen Nathan look more satisfied. He shamelessly manipulated Charlie, even luring her further with the promise of piano lessons. He has a baby grand at work, but a full grand at home. He might as well have pulled up in a windowless van and offered her candy. In less than twenty-four hours, the smug bastard ultimately got his way.

I took the slightly smaller bedroom, much to Charlie's delight. It was an easy win to give her, the bedrooms maybe have a ten-square-foot difference. What I chose not to mention to Charlie is that my closet is double the size of hers. It's better this way. With more closet space, she'd want more clothes to fill it up.

Nathan's guesthouse is much nicer than the home I was raised in. Not to mention his freaking castle is a stone's throw away. I don't want my little sister getting too used to this. I will never be able to provide her with this life, and I'm going to have to be the bad guy and rip her away from this fantasy in a couple weeks when I find us a new place to live.

"Charlie?" I call out. "Can you come in here, please?"

I hang up my last work dress, zip up my suitcase and tuck it in the corner of the massive closet. I made a big to-do about Nathan leaving us alone to unpack. He offered to hire movers, which he apparently can get at the snap of his fingers, but we didn't have any furniture or big items to bring over.

Charlie appears in my doorway, her hand on her hip. "Hey, can I borrow your lip gloss?"

"I don't have lip gloss."

"Then how come your lips are always so shiny?"

Aw, that was sweet.

"Is it because you're greasy?" Charlie asks earnestly.

Mmk, less sweet.

"I use tinted lip balm, Charlie. Good grief. Now, why do you need makeup?"

"Nathan's taking me to the grocery store to pick up some stuff we'd like to eat."

There are so many things wrong with that statement. First off, Nathan is not to take my sister anywhere, anytime without my permission. Second off, how does Mr. Billionaire even know where the grocery store is? Doesn't he have people for that? I'd sooner believe he *owns* a grocery store than fathom him doing his own food shopping. This is exactly why I need to explain things to my sister.

"Okay, Charlie, sit down." I point to the bed.

Rolling her eyes and scoffing like she's trying to cough up a hairball, she plops down on the king-sized mattress. "*What*?" she ask-whines.

"I will take you to the grocery store in a little bit." I sit down next to her. "I don't want you thinking that just because Nathan has so much that it belongs to us too. You're not to let him buy you presents, pay for food, or take you anywhere on his dime, because that's taking advantage."

"You're *so* grumpy," she bellyaches.

"What's that supposed to mean?"

"Nathan wants to share, and you're the one who hates him for no reason. He's really nice. And he even said we can pick up some things for Spike."

I look at her with wide, questioning eyes as my mouth gapes. "Things like what?" A blowtorch and skewer sticks flash through my mind.

"Like an auto-feeder and a much bigger cage."

There it is. A bigger cage that Spike can get in and *stay in*. I make a mental note to buy another rodent ball as soon as possible. He cracked his by the elevator bay, and I'd like to ensure Spike has extra mobility around the guesthouse. He's my little furry boss repellant.

"All right, Charlie, listen to me—" I stop short. "Wait. Did you hear that?"

"Hear what?"

"Where's Spike?" I try to breathe quietly because I swear I just heard something in the house.

"In his carrier, napping. He had two lunches today, so he's sleeping it off."

"He might be up." And I'm probably being paranoid. New places stress me out, no matter how nice they are. "All right, anyway... The thing about Nathan is that while he's nice and generous, he's not ours to keep. I don't want you to get attached and then get your feelings hurt. It was hard enough for you to let Jesse go."

"Nathan's way better than Jesse. I can see that now."

"Charlie." I smooth her hair behind her ear. "Nathan and Jesse are apples and oranges. I loved Jesse, but Nathan is just my boss."

"But he spent the night. I know you think I don't know what that means when adults sleep over. He really likes you."

I'm terrified to ask her to clarify an "adult sleepover," so for now, I sidestep it. "Do you know what catch and release is?"

"No." She falls backward on the bed. I follow suit and wrap my hand around hers. It's not teensy anymore. Reality sets in when

I realize our hands are almost the same size. She's growing up so fast, and I'm so stressed out about giving her a good childhood, that I'm missing it.

"Catch and release is when people fish just to see what they can catch. As soon as they get what they're after, they throw the fish back. They never mean to keep them. It's just a game. The only thing that interests them is the chase. Do you understand what I'm saying?"

"You're saying Nathan is playing catch and release?"

"Exactly." Oh, thank fuck she gets it. My feelings are still raw, and I don't want to dive into how foolish I feel, swooning over my boss, forcing some fantasy with a guy who is so far out of my reach, he might as well be living on the moon.

"That's nice of him," Charlie says so casually.

"What?" I pop up into a sit, and blink at her. "How is that nice?"

"Well, if we're talking about fishing, what's the alternative? That he catches you, kills you, and puts you in a fry pan. Releasing you is a nice thing to do, isn't it?"

Did my little sister unintentionally impart some form of profound wisdom on me? "Fish and people are different, Charlie."

For a moment, she's silent. She stares at the ceiling fan as the white blades circle slowly. I lie back down, enjoying the cozy moment. It's almost perfect, except with the size of this bed, there's a noticeable empty space on the other side of me, like our family is almost whole, but not quite.

"I'll talk to him for you if you want? Ask him if he likes you," Charlie offers in a hushed tone. "I'm really good at it. Last week I asked Taylor B if he liked Madison, and he said yes. They're dating now."

If it were only that simple. *Enjoy it while it lasts, sister. These are the last few years of your life where boys will make sense.* At this age, they wear their hearts on their sleeves, and are somewhat willing to tango with something called the truth.

"I'm okay. Thank you though."

"Because you're scared he'll say no?" she asks.

"It's because I'm scared he'll say yes." And I know for a fact Nathan Hatcher doesn't like me the way I like him. I'm a toy at his mercy. An easily manipulated plaything. Something to catch, then release.

She holds up her hand. "On Mom, so you can't lie... Do you like him?"

I raise my palm, matching her gesture. It's our most serious command whenever we say, "*On Mom*." I'm powerless to lie. "Very much. But don't worry about it. It'll fade. If you want to go shopping with Nathan, that's fine, but grab some cash out of my purse and that is your *budget*."

"Knock, knock," Nathan says as he physically knocks on the door trim. He's wearing nice light jeans and a plain navy T-shirt, looking more casual than I've ever seen him before.

Frazzled, I fly up into a sitting position again, as if I'm caught. No way he heard all that, right? *Shit*. "When did you get here?"

"Just walked in." He shrugs, unbothered. I'm alarmed, but he's not. *Phew*. He didn't hear a damn thing. "You settling in okay?"

"Yeah, everything's great. Except I think there's a pest control problem." I smirk.

"I agree, but you call that rat a pet, so who am I to argue?"

I try so hard to hold in my laugh, but it breaks free of my lips like river rapids against a paper-thin barricade. Nathan's smile crinkles the corners of his pretty eyes. His peculiar blue-green eyes are dressed in a naturally thick layer of lashes any woman would envy.

"I was talking about bossholes with no leash who think they can enter houses uninvited."

Nathan fakes a gasp. "Your boss is entering a structure on his own property that he paid for? How riotous."

"Completely unacceptable," I agree with a widening smile.

"Don't you worry, miss. I'll ruin his life in your honor."

"Good."

Scoffing again, Charlie scoots off the bed. "Yeah, you two

like each other," she mutters. Heat fills my cheeks, but cool as a cucumber, Nathan ignores her side comment.

"You ready?" he asks her.

"I just have to go get cash. Spencer said I could take sixty dollars." She cockily pumps her brows at me, knowing she has me backed into a corner.

"Forty," I offer, compromising.

"Fifty," she sasses back.

"Could be zero."

"Fine. Forty," she grumbles, marching past Nathan like forty bucks is a disappointment. That's two allowances for this week.

Nathan doesn't follow Charlie out. He leans against the doorframe, one foot in two boats. He's half in my room, half not. I don't know why I have such strong nervous butterflies. I slept next to him. His underwear-sheathed dick and I are acquaintances. But I'm still not used to it when he stares at me like this. So intently. Like he's trying to read my mind.

"You need something?" I ask.

"I'm sorry," he says simply.

"There are worse things than being forced to live in a palace." I roll my wrist and gesture to my temporary room.

"Oh, not about moving you in. I feel pretty good about that." His weak chuckle is unenthusiastic. "I meant I'm sorry I didn't ask you first to take Charlie shopping. It's been a while since I've been around kids her age, and I should've respected you as her parent before offering. But her hopes are up now, so..."

"She can go. I trust you."

His brows lift in surprise. "You do?"

"To protect my sister?" I nod. "Yeah, I do."

"And what about you? Do you trust me to take care of you?"

I tuck my legs in, folding one ankle over the other. "Am I giving off the impression that I need protecting?"

He runs his finger over his bottom lip, a pensive look on his face. "One of my many character flaws is that I like to be needed."

"I do need you," I snap back. "I need you to *not* use this

opportunity to spoil the shit out of my sister."

"Why not?" he challenges. "I'm not sure if you're aware, but I'm not exactly hurting for cash. You guys have been through too much for too long. You deserve to feel safe and spoiled every now and then instead of always looking up, wondering when the sky is going to fall. So, with your okay, I'm going to go buy Charlie some really expensive, unnecessary shit today."

Stupid prince. I wish he'd go back to being a toad. He's so much easier to resist when he's a toad. "How unnecessary are we talking?"

"Unfathomably ridiculous. Like I know a dude who custom builds six-foot bubblegum machines."

"Hm, if they have one in pink, that would be the perfect finishing touch for your office."

He shifts his gaze up with a heavy sigh. "I actually forgot about that for a moment."

I release a rich belly laugh, feeling genuinely happy. Maybe this can work for now. Nathan and I can find a way to be friends. Maybe this crush will become a silly thing of the past. "All right. Offer accepted. Spoil my baby sister. Thank you...for everything."

He ducks his head in a humble nod. "One more thing," he says, pulling a flat, square box from his back pocket. He takes three steps forward into the room and balances the box on my knee. "I said you both deserve to be spoiled." He leans over and gently flicks my earlobe. "You never wear earrings, yet your ears are pierced. I just figured..." He shrugs.

I gape, trying to find words. The box on my knee might as well be a thousand pounds, pinning me in place. I can't speak, I can't move...I can't think. *What is this?*

"Nathan, I—"

"Let's not do the awkward dance of you refusing them, me insisting, you refusing again, me threatening your job. We'll still get to the same end result."

His domineering assholery sobers the moment. "Being?" I ask.

He grins. "My way."

I roll my eyes. "You're like a defective Sour Patch Kid. Sour on the outside, and then just more sour on the inside."

"Maybe so. Just wait until I leave before you open those."

"Why?"

"So I don't have to see the disappointment on your face if you don't like them." He turns to leave.

"Nate, wait." I scoop up the flat box, cradling it to my chest. "No one has ever bought me jewelry before."

"But you said you were engaged."

I shake my head. "No ring. Just promises. *Broken* promises."

"You're kidding me," he almost whispers. Returning to my side, he kneels down in front of me. He gathers the box from me and opens the lid, revealing a pair of beautiful pink diamond studs. "I'm glad you left him. Don't settle for a guy who tells you he loves you. Choose one who shows you."

He leaves me speechless. Not just because of these precious earrings, probably worth more than I'll ever care to know. But it's the thought behind it. Is this Nathan showing me...more? Does he think about me as much as I think about him?

"Thank you." I can barely manage the words. I think I said them. If nothing else, I screamed it from my mind.

"I could've gone bigger, but I thought these would fit you better. I know you're not into ostentatious things. Sometimes the rarest beauty shines brightest in subtlety."

"You should go. It looks borderline gory when I ugly-cry. I don't want you to see me like that." I sniffle hard to convey my point.

Nathan laughs lightly. He slowly rises, as if reluctant to leave my side. But when Charlie shouts, "Ready!" at the top of her lungs from the living room, the moment's over. All the unspoken words fall between us as the spell breaks and the haze is lifted.

He pauses one more time near the door, looking over his shoulder. "And just to clear the air—when it comes to fishing, I'm a catch-and-keep kind of guy."

Disappearing from the doorway, Nathan leaves me confused for the briefest moment. Then, it dawns on me. It wasn't a restless Spike I heard earlier. It was Nathan entering the house. He must've heard every word, including when I told Charlie, *on Mom*, how much I really do like him.

CHAPTER 27

Nathan

Charlie and Spencer have been living with me for almost two weeks, and sharing the internet, so now my entire social media feed is guinea pig advice. It's a living nightmare. All the hairy pigs on my screen, I mean. Not the part about having company at home. That's been heaven.

Since Spencer and Charlie moved in, I've been treating every night like it's an eleven-year-old's birthday party. We've done pizza by the pool almost nightly. Crumbl cookie deliveries every other day. To my great pleasure, Spencer actually ate with us. She's smiling more. Her sass has skyrocketed, but that might just be because we're getting more quality time with each other. I think snark is her native tongue. My favorite part is the earrings she hasn't taken out of her ears since I gifted them.

She keeps saying she loves how beautifully understated they are. In a way, I agree. They are a subtle pink, each earring barely over a carat. What she doesn't realize is these are natural pink diamonds from one of the most revered rare-jewelry providers in the world. There's about fifty thousand dollars sitting in each of her ears. It's probably best she doesn't know that. She'd have a heart attack.

Charlie's also a freaking riot. She has a sharper mouth than her sister, but a heart just as sweet. We have a standing cereal date every morning before she goes off to school. We've become cereal connoisseurs, ranking all the top contenders by flavor, crunch, and most importantly, sog-resistance. Well, important to me.

Charlie likes her cereal to look like pig slop.

After glancing over to Spencer's empty desk, I check the time. Almost nine. She drops Charlie off by seven fifty-five. Her school is about ten minutes away. We've been drinking coffee at home together. This morning, after telling me she felt extra exhausted, she downed three cups, so I know she's not on a latte run. *Where the hell is she?*

Me: I have some concerns about Spike's rodent ball.

Spencer: For the love of God, Nate. Let it go. He can't hurt you. I'm getting ready to go Fear Factor on your ass.

Me: Huh?

Spencer: Lock you in a cage with a thousand guinea pigs to help you conquer your fear.

Me: Literally the only thing you could do to get yourself fired.

Spencer: What's the problem with the rodent ball?

Me: According to all these internet articles, you're not supposed to put him in a plastic ball. Something about hurting their spines. Apparently guinea pigs don't bend like hamsters.

She doesn't respond right away, and I know she's online

researching my claim.

> **Spencer:** Well, shit. I didn't know that. I thought I was giving him a little freedom and exercise at the office.

> **Me:** Oh please. Give it up, woman. You thought a rat in motion would freak me out more than one in his carrier.

> **Spencer:** Moving on... Should we take him to the doctor?

> **Me:** *Guinea pig vet... Lamest medical degree imaginable.*

> **Spencer:** There aren't piggie-specific doctors. Surely you're familiar with veterinarians.

> **Me:** Nope, never heard of them. I think Spike's going to be fine. Just no more ball. Even better idea—quit bringing him into the office.

I already tolerate that little punk in my home. It helps that he stays locked in the guesthouse with the girls. I bought their pet a two-story rat castle to play in. I upgraded his food. He drinks pH-balanced alkaline water now. He should have no need to leave his oasis.

> **Spencer:** I just looked up alternatives. Would you have issues with a medium-sized acrylic pen by my desk?

> **Me:** Big problems.

> **Spencer:** So you'd be mad?

> **Me:** Yes.

> **Spencer:** How mad? Like I'll-lose-my-job mad?

> **Me:** Like I'll-bend-you-over-my-desk-and-spank-you mad.

Shit. That slipped right out. Sometimes when I'm moving too fast, I text exactly what I'm thinking. I'm typing out an apology when Spencer replies.

> **Spencer:** I'll risk it. I'll buy padded underwear.

> **Me:** Who says you get to keep your underwear on?

> **Spencer:** Now I'm feeling like you have ulterior motives with this spanking.

> **Me:** Fuck around and find out, Spencer. Buy that cage. I'm begging you.

I have to adjust my slacks as my cock twitches uncomfortably. It's a constant problem I'm having lately. The flirty texts are just the beginning. Spencer is very unaware of when her thick nipples are showing. I'm not. Every time she's in a swimsuit or pajamas, I literally have to picture Spike and his beady eyes to calm my intrigue.

So why haven't I made my move?

Because she said she liked me. I heard her talking to Charlie the day they moved in. All the haughty attitude, glacier stares, witty comebacks... It's Spencer trying to fight her feelings because she thinks I want to sleep with her, then toss her aside. *Catch and release.* Which is why I'm determined to prove her wrong. The only way I can do that and prepare myself for something more permanent is little steps.

I've been practicing on Charlie.

Eleven-year-olds *love* keeping secrets. Charlie's good at it, especially when I tell her it's for Spencer's benefit. She'd do anything for her big sister. So, she is now my confidant. I share bits and pieces, a little at a time. I told her how Elise also had a pretty voice. She didn't have Charlie's vocal range, but she was still talented. I'd play piano, Elise would sing along.

I ask Charlie about her grief, too. We swap stories about the realistic dreams we've had where it felt like our lost loved ones were back. We admit how painful it is to wake up and realize it wasn't real. But the great thing is, Charlie's patient. When I can't bear another step down memory lane, and have to change the subject, she doesn't push. Either she has the attention span of a guppy, or even at her young age, she's so emotionally intuitive, she's recognizing my limits.

Ten minutes go by and Spencer doesn't respond. She's now late for work, and as any other amazing boss would do to their OCD, perfectionist assistants, I give her hell.

> **Me:** You're officially late. Now, I can either write you up with a warning, or you can pull down your panties and bend over my desk. A couple swats and all is forgiven. Your call.

I'm expecting a polished, sass-studded response from the great Spencer, but instead...

> **Spencer:** I don't think I can make it today. Are you okay without me? The Johnson contracts are printed out and on your desk for review.

> **Me:** No I can't make it a day without you. Get your ass to work, lazy.

She responds with a picture of a thermometer reading. One oh three. I could playfully accuse her of grabbing that picture off the internet, except her bare toes are showing. I recognize her pink, chipped polish. The color matches the train wreck of an office I'm still working in. If I spend too many more days in this pink prison, I'm going to have to forfeit my man card, but *damn*. I rock back and forth in my blush, cloth executive chair. This thing is really comfortable and the lumbar support is awesome. And who is going to have the balls to make fun of the boss's pink office, hm? I'd have their head.

> **Me:** You were feeling fine this morning. You dropped Charlie off at school, right?

Spencer: I was trying to power through. If I act sick, Charlie's suddenly extremely sick too.

Me: Ah, so fibs are contagious.

Spencer: Use that in my eulogy, if the guilt doesn't kill you first.

Me: Aw, double funeral. That's kind of sweet.

Spencer: Great. Not even in death can I get rid of you.

Me: Ha. Jokes aside, what're your symptoms?

Spencer: Pounding headache, body aches, so tired, cold sweats, nauseous and some other stuff I'm not going to share with you.

Me: Meaning you're spewing from both ends? Well, pumpkin, that's the flu.

Spencer: Did you just say *spewing*?

Me: We're all adults here.

Spencer: One of us is.

> **Me:** I'm on my way. Are you a Tamiflu or Xofluza kind of girl?

> **Spencer:** What?

> **Me:** NyQuil, then?

> **Spencer:** I'm fine, Nate. Just let me sleep it off. Please? Your new project manager is starting today anyway. Dawn told me to put a block on your calendar. You can't miss that meeting.

I tap her photo and hit the call button. Spencer answers with a disgruntled, "What?" Her voice has already changed from when I saw her a couple hours ago. Whatever she has is escalating fast. She said she was extra tired. That's probably what she's been puking up, all that coffee.

"I can miss any fucking meeting I want. I'm coming home to take care of you...just as soon as I pick up a hazmat suit."

"Hilarious," she grumbles, devoid of actual mirth in her tone. "Out of curiosity, could you get a hazmat suit?"

"Easily."

"Such a humble billionaire."

"Aren't I though?"

"Do you need anything else?" Her last question sounds more like a plea than her usual snark. Now, I'm worried.

"No. Seriously, what do you need?"

"Just some rest."

Hmm, I'm not buying it. I get that she's a suffer-in-silence type, no surprise there. Spencer is much stronger than she gives herself credit for. She carries the weight of the world on her back, and even when it cracks, she keeps moving. The thing is, she's not alone anymore. She can put away her brave face. I want her to need me as much as I need her.

"Okay, get some sleep. I'll check in with you the minute this meeting is over."

We end the call, just in time for Dawn to enter my office.

"My oh my, you're looking dapper today."

Dawn holds out her arms and spins around, showing off her ruby-red A-line skirt with the bow around her waist. It complements her new hair color, which is now a deep red brown. Over the years, Dawn has sported every color in the book—red, jet black, platinum blonde. But she's stuck within the spectrum of red the longest.

She freezes, examining my office makeover. "Still looks like a Powerpuff Girl threw up in here." She holds up her hands before I can answer. "Is Spencer taking over this office now?"

I roll my eyes as I exhale. "No. She's not."

"Then she got you good."

"It was somewhat deserved." I shrug.

She curls her lips in amusement. "Glad you're so self-aware these days."

"Mhm."

"Anyway, why am I here? I got your email requesting I grace you with my presence." She pulls out the chic pink-colored, golden-legged chair across from my desk and flutters her lashes. "I'm here. I'm gracing."

"How close are you with Julia?" I ask right away.

Dawn's brows lift into wide arches, surprise painting her face. "Much closer than you are."

"I'm trying to fix that. I've been a little—"

"Cold? Distant? Rude? Spiteful?" she *helpfully* supplies.

I level a stare. "I was going to say busy."

"I think my suggestions were more accurate."

Are all the working women in my life so lippy? *Goodness fuck.* "Anyway, I want to do something nice. I need a big gesture that can begin to make up for my behavior. Any ideas?"

Dawn crosses her legs and leans back in the chair. She's quiet as her high-heeled foot bounces in place. "Her charity event," she finally says.

"Huh?"

"Didn't you get your invitation? It's this weekend. Julia is hosting her first big charity event for post-prison rehabilitation."

"No." By no, I mean I haven't checked my mail in weeks. There's a mound of envelopes by the entry table I have yet to open. "I wonder why Dad didn't mention it to me?"

"Probably gives you too much time to plan an excuse. I think his new strategy is confronting you the day before. Your support would mean a lot. They're trying to raise twenty million dollars in one night. It's a huge undertaking and she's nervous."

I place my forehead in my palm. *Dammit.* I've been the worst son. "I'm going. I'll definitely be there. I'll buy Julia a big congratulatory present for hitting her goal." If she can't hit the number on her own, I'll cover the rest. "What kind of cars is she into? Do they still make Ferraris in pink?"

Dawn gives me a look that screams, *you dumbass.* "Maybe try the Barbie dealership and see if Mattel can make you one to scale."

"Ha-ha," I deadpan.

"You know what Julia would really like?" Leaning forward, she taps the edge of my desk. "Quality time. She just wants to be friends, Nathan. Despite what your incorrect intuition is telling you, she's not marrying your dad for money."

I exhale deeply. "It's weird though, right? A thirty-year age gap? I mean ten or less I'd understand. But what the hell do they see in each other?"

Dawn shows me a knowing smile, the same one she wears when she's about to mother me. "It's not about what they see. It's about what they *feel*. When they're together, they're happy. That's all that matters to them. Or have you forgotten how good 'happy' feels?"

My lips twitch into a grin, my poker face betraying me. "I've been a little happier lately."

"Hm. I wonder why?" Dawn asks with such sarcastic flair.

She purposely glances at Spencer's empty desk. "Where is your assistant today?"

"Sick. I was thinking of taking off work and making sure she's okay. She sounded pretty rough on the phone."

"That's a good idea. Love sickness has no cure. You can only treat the symptoms." Dawn winks.

I flatten my expression. "Careful with the L word. That's...not what this is."

"Then what is it?"

I take a moment to consider. "To be honest, I don't know."

"What's holding you back?" Dawn folds her fingers together like a professor who is quizzing me and already knows the answer.

I wet my lips, preparing myself for the dreaded question I've had in my mind since the moment I met Spencer. "Do you think the closer I get to another woman, the more I'll lose Elise and Claire?" I tap my temple twice. "I made Spencer an Arnold Palmer the other day. I brought it to her by the pool and said, 'I made your favorite.' She had no clue what I was talking about—"

"Because that was Elise's favorite drink."

I nod sullenly. "Memories are starting to get muddled the more time I spend with Spencer. I don't think I'm ready to...lose them."

"Nathan," Dawn says, leaning forward once more. She reaches over the desk holding her hand out, asking for mine. I place my hand over her warm fingertips and lightly squeeze. "I promise I'm not saying this to hurt you, but you already have. *You lost them.* And it's awful and unfair. But when you accept that, you can start to heal."

I try to pull away but she grasps on tighter. "Don't," I demand.

"You lost love, but there's more to find. And remember, every day you keep those barricades around your heart up, you're depriving someone of *you*. The real you. The 'you' we all miss. The 'you' we've seen glimpses of now that Spencer's come around. You've always been a selfless guy. If you can't try for you, then try for *her*."

The best part of me wants to yank Spencer into a fairy-tale romance and see her eyes light up when I tell her I'm never letting her go. The worst part of me is bitterly angry that lately, when I close my eyes, I don't see Elise's big, emerald-green eyes. I don't see her light freckles. Sometimes I forget what she looks like. But every curve, dimple, and angle of Spencer's face is etched into my mind in crystal clear high-definition.

I rise, pulling myself free of Dawn's embrace. I hold my breath as I make my way to my piano bench. I'm relieved when I lift the lid and it still stands lopsided. Pushing the papers aside, I find the photo I took of Elise and Claire on the day I proposed.

Returning to my desk, I place the picture on top of my desk, then retrieve a roll of tape from my top drawer. Of course all my office supplies have been replaced. Even my scotch tape is now in a glittery-pink dispenser. *Damn, Spencer is thorough.*

I tape two corners. Satisfied the picture is secure, I look up to meet Dawn's stare. "There. Now I have a reminder."

"Okay," she says simply, flashing me a tight smile. I can't tell if she's proud of me, or disappointed.

"I'm still going to go check on Spencer though. Could you see if my dad could take the meeting with Casey at ten? Today's his first day. I don't want to ditch him entirely."

She nods. "James's schedule is open this morning. I'll let him know." She gets up, takes two steps, then spins around. Planting her ass right back down, she looks me dead in the eye. "I need to tell you something."

I wave her off. "My dad already told me about his dirty dealings with Casey. Don't worry, I fully intend on setting him straight—"

"No, Nate. I saw Claire a couple weeks ago at that spa day. Charlie invited her best friend to join us."

I nearly choke on the silence between us. A medley of emotions rips through me. Fear, excitement, jealousy...but anger most of all. "Why didn't you tell me?"

"Is it my job to?"

I glare at her, clenching my jaw. I take a few calming breaths and remind myself that my anger is misplaced. Dawn didn't take Claire from me. Ruby did. Purposely warming my icy tone, I ask, "How is she doing? Did she ask about me?"

"She didn't seem to recognize me."

"You were a platinum blonde when Elise died."

Dawn bobs her head in agreement. "But she looked happy and healthy. She and Charlie get along really well."

Shock still trembles through me in waves, like the aftershocks of an earthquake. "Charlie and Claire...I..." How did the PI not inform me of this? Probably because he's only tracking her deadbeat father and conniving grandmother. "Does Spencer know who she is to me? Does she know about Elise?"

"No. It wasn't my place to say. But it's going to come out eventually, don't you think? Better she hears this story from you."

I nod. I've put this off for so long, but now it's inevitable. It's time.

"Nathan, I know what's going through your head. Just try to think of how this impacts Charlie."

"Charlie?" I question, my face screwing up in bewilderment. "What does that mean?"

"Imagine how hurt Charlie will be if she thinks your friendship is just a ploy to get close to Claire. Take it from a mother of a daughter, girls her age are like crows. They'll take grudges to the grave. You understand?"

She effortlessly reads my mind. Admittedly, the first thing I thought of was telling Charlie she should invite her best friend over to her cool, new house. But Ruby would never allow that. In fact, if Ruby knew Charlie was living with me, she probably would take Claire away from Charlie. Ruby's favorite thing to do is wait until a powerful bond is formed, then hack away at it with a machete.

"I understand."

"Good." Dawn rises again, this time smoothing out her skirt. "I'll get that meeting on the calendar. I'll email the new guy too and let him know what's going on."

"Thank you," I say distractedly, eyes fixed on the little redheaded girl in the photograph.

"What's his last name? We have about six Caseys in the directory."

"He's probably not in the directory yet. Casey Conrad." When I finally pull myself away from the photo, Dawn is staring at me with wide, panicked eyes.

"Conrad?" She's not blinking. "Do you happen to know if he played football in college?"

"No clue. He graduated from UNLV about five years after me. Yet another reason Dad thought we'd hit it off. Why?"

"No reason. It's just strange." Dawn suddenly looks weary. Like a fresh wave of worry just capsized her boat.

"What's strange?"

She lifts one shoulder. "I'm praying it's a coincidence, but I have a voodoo doll named Casey Conrad."

I quirk one eyebrow. "Aren't you a little old for voodoo dolls?"

She cuts me a look. "Did you just call me old?"

"What? *No.* I said, aren't you a little old *for voodoo dolls*? As in childish revenge." She answers my question with more silence and more of that piercing, unblinking stare. "You have a Nathan Hatcher voodoo doll, don't you?" I cringe.

"Yes. But don't worry, I don't poke him much." She shows me a villainous smile. "I have work to do. Tell Spencer I hope she feels better."

With that, Dawn rushes out of my office the same way she always does when she's setting off to put out a fire.

CHAPTER 28

Spencer

I wake up, startled, the tail end of my own snoring jostling me from my deep slumber. I wipe the corner of my mouth where the drool has dried. Sniffing with all my might, I try to suck in oxygen through my nostrils, but they're far too stuffy.

"Ow." I wince as I try to sit up. My arms are stiff, my torso made of lead. Every bone in my body has pins and needles stabbing through the marrow. I got hit by a full-speed train, masquerading as the flu.

I want to sink back into the pillow and let the world go dark again, but...

Wait! Shit!

I glance through the blinds, not even a streak of sunshine is visible. *It's motherfucking dark out!* I feel around for my phone but it's nowhere in sight. Summertime in Las Vegas, the sun doesn't disappear until after eight, meaning I left Charlie at school. Tears form in my dry, stinging eyes.

Oh my God. Oh my God. I kick my legs off the bed, hoping my body will catch up.

Unfortunately, my panic-induced adrenaline doesn't override the severity of my flu symptoms. The room spins as the nausea overwhelms me. I try to grab on to something so I don't fall over, but the lamp on the nightstand is even less sturdy than me. I topple to the ground, bringing the lamp down on top of me. The light bulb shatters against the nightstand drawer, shards falling onto my head.

"The fuck?" Nathan shouts, magically appearing in the doorway. "I was gone for two minutes. What happened?"

I try to sit up, but before I can fail again, Nathan's thick, firm bicep is supporting my neck. "Charlie," I say. Her name comes out like a feeble croak. I pat my throat aggressively and try again. "I left Charlie at school." I force out the words, setting my throat on fire.

"I picked up Charlie from school, remember?"

I shake my head.

"Yeah, not a surprise. You're probably still high as a kite off medicine. I did not realize NyQuil was like ten percent alcohol when I gave you that double dose."

"You asshat," I shout. Moaning in pain, I cradle my raw throat.

"You see?" Nathan asks, wearing that stupid smirk. "That's what you get for shouting at the man who has been your bedside nurse for the past ten hours."

I try to roll my eyes, but I can't even muster the strength to show Nathan how annoying he is. "Where is she?"

"I put her in the main house for tonight. She's on her iPad right now. She ate. She already took a shower. Hair, braided. Teeth, brushed. I checked her homework but I don't know when the hell sixth-grade algebra got so complicated. I had to take her word that she did it right."

I smile. "Good. Now bring her home."

"You're too sick and contagious, Spencer. Charlie's safe from your germs in the main house."

Great. Charlie's going to infest Nathan's home like bedbugs. Once she's in, there's no getting her out.

"Then why are you here braving my germs?" I peer at his bare chest and realize how sick I am. I must be delirious if I didn't immediately notice his hard chest and perfectly sculpted abs. "And why are you shirtless?"

"Risking it," he says nonchalantly. "And you soaked through my shirt."

"What do you mean I soaked through it?" Dread sweeps over me. *Please say sweat, please, please for the love of God say sweat.*

"Your fever is so high you're sweating," he explains.

Oh, thank God. "You held me?"

"Through thick and thin. And by thick and thin, I'm describing all the logs you were sawing." He flashes me a devilish smile. "You've got some pipes on you. That was impressive snoring."

I'm too wiped to be anything other than relieved. My sister is safe. I'm alive...for now. And Nathan handled everything.

I bury my head in the crevice where his muscular arm meets his strong chest. I'm sure if I could smell anything, he'd smell amazing. I hum in appreciation when he wraps his arms around me, cuddling me close. "Go away."

He strokes my damp hair, completely unbothered. "That is the literal definition of mixed signals."

I turn my head and peck his bare chest with hot, dry lips. "I hate you."

His chest bounces lightly as he chuckles. "Still going."

"Seriously, thank you. For taking care of Charlie." I wince again.

He scoops me up, managing to go from his knees, to his feet, without faltering, lifting my dead weight. I try to flex my stomach as if that could make me seem lighter, but I've apparently lost control over my limbs. Nathan lays me gently on the bed.

"Did you hit your head when you fell?"

"No. But I broke your lamp. I'm sorry."

"That's okay, I'll add it to your bill." He taps my nose, then scrunches his.

Why is he so playful and cheery? I think he's enjoying helpless Spencer way too much. He did say he liked to be needed. I definitely need him now. I don't know what I would've done if Charlie and I lived alone. Would I have woken up if she called me from school? Could I even drive? I'm not sure if the room is spinning because I'm *that* ill, or if I'm drunk from my so-called nurse overdosing me.

Nathan secures the covers up to my chin. "There you go. Cozy?"

I nod. I'm thankful for the comforter blocking out the room-temperature air that feels like ice at the moment. "May I have something to drink?"

"Of course. How about some broth?"

"Ice water, please." I want to douse out the fire in my throat.

"I want you to try to eat something. You already don't eat enough, and now you're so weak you can barely keep your eyes open."

"Just water."

"*Spencer*. Just a couple sips of soup. It'll make you feel better."

I summon all the strength in my body to roll my eyes. It wasn't my pupils' finest performance, but it gets the job done. "Fine. Where's my phone? I'll DoorDash some ice water."

That should've made him laugh, instead a dark flicker of agitation crosses his face. "In the kitchen, charging."

I glance to my side and see the empty charging dock on the nightstand. If he thinks I'm too sick to be suspicious, he wildly misjudged me. "Why?"

"Your phone was going off. *A lot*." There's a sharp edge to his tone I don't appreciate. "I didn't want it to wake you."

"Bullshit."

Nathan lifts his brows, like he's surprised I used a curse word. He sits down near my feet. "Not bullshit. Want to know who was incessantly texting you?"

I wrack my fuzzy brain and can't come up with anyone who would cause this reaction. "Who?"

"Your ex." He presses his lips together before sucking them in. It's like he's trying to swallow down a more serious reaction. "I handled it."

"What do you mean you *handled* it?"

Nathan huffs in disbelief, surprised I'm put off by his possessive behavior. "I told him you were sick, didn't want to talk to him, and you never wanted him to contact you again."

"*As me?*" Oh, screw my aching throat. I'm about to get shouty.

"So?" he asks. "He stole from you, Spencer. He disrespected you. He used Charlie. You're done with him. Why are you upset? I did you a favor."

With great strain, I wrench myself up to a sitting position. I hold up my thumb. "You took my phone. *Red flag.*" I straighten my pointer finger. "You texted my ex, pretending to be me? *Red flag.*"

"After everything I've done for you and your sister, this is all I ask: Don't talk to other men while you're living in my home. It's a slap in the face."

"Have you lost your goddamn mind?"

"What?" he snaps.

"You're leveraging your generosity to control who I'm allowed to talk to?" My middle finger joins my other two outstretched digits. "That's a red flying billboard in the sky, pulled by a fucking blimp. Not okay. I'll talk to whoever I want."

Nathan narrows his eyes. "So you're still in touch with Jesse?"

"Shouldn't you know? Were you reading through all my text messages while I was sleeping?"

"No. But it's my responsibility to make sure you don't—"

"Stop!" I shriek. "I'm not your responsibility. You're my overly flirty boss who gets pleasure from tossing me around like a beanbag in a cornhole game. Back and forth, *back and forth*. You're overbearing."

Grunting out of exasperation, he throws his hands in the air. "Isn't that what women want? A protective guy?"

I pinch the bridge of my nose, feeling my throbbing headache between my eyes. "Only *if* your intentions are pure."

His fist lands on his thigh. "What the fuck does that mean?"

"I might be able to forgive your boneheaded move of *invading my privacy*, if it's coming from a place of jealousy. People do stupid shit when they really like someone. But do you? Do you want me? Or is it just fun to keep me dangling at the end of your pole? You said you're a catch-and-keep kind of guy, but I don't feel kept."

"You don't feel kept? I adopted you into my home. My

company overpays you. I put those diamonds in your ears. I watched multiple episodes of *The Baby-Sitters Club* with your sister. You don't see what's going on here?"

"Then how come after you spent the night, you pumped the brakes? Is it... Did you see something you didn't want to see? Are you not attracted to me but wish you were?"

He grabs my feet under the blanket, squeezing gently. "Spencer, it's not like that."

"Then what is it?" I curse myself as the tears escape the corners of my eyes. They are hot tears of fatigue—half from this constant push and pull with my boss, half from the flu that's equally as tormenting. "Is this all about Elise? You're not over her?"

He releases my foot. Ducking his head, he peers up at me with a new look. A look of disdain. If I weren't already sitting, this very look would seat me, sending chills down my spine. And I know I've made a mistake in bringing her up.

"Who told you about Elise?"

I shake my head. "You did. You said at House of Blues that night there was an abrupt end to your relationship. Dawn mentioned her name, but didn't tell me anything else." I swallow the painful lump in my throat. "Did she hurt you? Because if you're not ready to talk about it–"

"You're right," he says. "I don't want to talk about it."

I let the thick silence between us fill the room, because I'm scared to ask for clarification. I went too far. I pushed too much. But then again, so did he.

He finally continues, "I think maybe you're right about everything. I'm leading you on to nowhere. I'm not ready for this. I want to be...but I'm not."

"What?" Except I know what. The weighted words can only mean one thing.

"Not today. Not this week. But when you're feeling better, I'll help you look for nice a place to live. Don't worry about money. I'll take care of all of it. But this...you here... I can't do it." He shrugs in defeat.

Well, I found his self-destruct button. A giant red button with the word "Elise" in big, white block letters. It was so shiny and inviting, I couldn't help but press it. If I had the strength, I'd pack my shit this instant. Or, maybe I'd leave it all behind. I should be getting used to fresh starts by now.

"Fine. As soon as I'm not contagious, I'll call my friends." I wouldn't even have to ask. Lennox would put us up in a heartbeat. That'll buy me some time to figure out my next move. New home. New job.

"I just said there's no rush."

"You know what? My mistake."

Remorse overtakes his face. "Look, I'm sorry. Maybe I need to cool down, and we can talk when I'm—"

"No, I meant, *my mistake*. When I told you I was done with you, I should've stayed done. I won't make the error twice. Get the fuck out."

He opens his mouth like he's ready to protest. Nathan could easily make the argument that this is his house. But something stops him. He clamps his jaw shut and stands. Staring at the broken light bulb, he says, "I'm going to go get the vacuum and clean that up. I don't want you cutting your feet."

"I know where the vacuum is. And I don't want your help." Lying down flat, I pull the covers over my head. I hold my breath, waiting to hear the sound of a door slamming, but I don't. Nathan treads silently through the guesthouse and there's only a soft click as the front door closes.

I normally can't sleep when I'm angry. Unresolved fights like this keep me up at all hours of the night. But tonight, the flu is my friend. I'm too weak to think, too tired to care, too hurt for hope. I let my ailment pull me into a deep slumber, falling asleep to the sound of Mom's voice.

I'm here, baby. Don't cry. I'm right here. You're going to be okay, kiddo. You'll survive this one too. I love you.

Tears stream down my cheeks. I weep shamelessly, shielded by my blanket cave. I know it's not real. Tomorrow I'll be strong.

I'll rebuild everything. But tonight, in my dreams...
    I let myself break.

CHAPTER 29

Nathan

What the fuck just came over me? I went too far. She's not going to forgive me for this one.

I sit on the pool ledge with my legs in the water. Even at night, with my shirt off, it's too fucking hot. The pool is warm and doesn't offer any real relief from the arid heat. I'd be far more comfortable inside my air-conditioned house. Except, I'm stuck. She told me to leave, but how can I? I'm halfway between my house, where I should go, and Spencer's bedroom, where I want to be. I'm in my own personal purgatory.

It shouldn't be this hard.

Spencer, I care about you a lot, but I never dealt with the grief of losing the woman I loved, and the child who called me Dad.

I skipped denial, dove into anger, dabbled in bargaining. Depression is where I really shined. I showcased my despair by isolation and assholery, as Spencer would call it. But somehow everything fell off the rails at acceptance.

Spencer, I'm scared if I let myself fall for you, like I know I could, I'll lose what's left of Elise.

I shouldn't be happy, replacing my family with a new one. I don't deserve it. Not when I failed Elise in every way imaginable. Not when her daughter is being raised by one of her sworn enemies.

Spencer, I—

Mweep.

Puzzled, I look up to find the source of the squeak. *What the shit?*

Spike stands at the edge of the pool, clear on the other side. His eyes are down and he's ducking his head trying to touch his nose to the water. He can't quite reach.

"Spike," I command. "Back up."

He ignores me because...well, he's a guinea pig, and as far as rodents go, Spike is not the brightest. I watched him once as he chewed on his paw, screeching in agony as he inflicted his own pain.

Ducking his head again, he tries to lap at the water.

"Spike! It's chlorinated, you dodo bird."

By now his paws are wrapping around the ledge, showing off his creepy hand-talons. *Gross.* I pull myself up, deciding who to alert to this potential disaster. Spencer would probably like to see me floating face down in this pool at the moment, so I opt for Charlie. I bet she's still awake. We're going to have a serious talk about double-checking that Spike's cage is locked. Then again, he's probably only out because I accidentally left the front door of the guesthouse open when I was bouncing back and forth all night between taking care of Charlie and Spencer.

I steal one more glance at the multicolored rat-pig as I yank my feet out of the water. He's not wearing his diaper. "You shit all over my pool deck, didn't you?" That would be the perfect insult to the injury of this night.

It's going to be fine. As soon as Spencer's feeling better, I'm going to beg her on both knees to stay. I don't know what dumbfuckery came over me, but the last thing I want is for Spencer and Charlie to leave. I'm not a perfect man, but no one else has made me want to do better. Around Spencer I feel jealous, on edge, constantly confused and out of control, but the point is *I'm feeling*. And for that, I should go fetch the moon she hung.

My back is turned, and I'm on the bottom step leading up to the main house when I hear a distinct *plop*. I whip around to see a small, dark shape floating back to the pool surface. *Guinea pigs can swim, right?*

Spike breaks the surface just long enough to let out a few

mweep, mweep, mweeps, before he's swallowed up by the pool again. He doesn't resurface this time.

Oh, fuck me. Jeans still on, I sprint to the edge and dive into the pool. Opening my eyes in the chlorine water, I ignore the momentary burn. *There he is.* Almost at the bottom, I scoop Spike up before he hits the pool floor. Kicking as hard as I can, I hold him above my head to get him oxygen as fast as possible. Hand around his belly like a claw, I keep him above the water until I can get us to the closest ladder.

After setting him down on the pool deck, he collapses. His belly is swollen, probably having taken a few glugs of water, but I think I got to him in time. *I hope.* I'm on my knees growing impatient, waiting for him to breathe. But his eyes are closed and he's too still.

For fuck's sake, do not let tonight be the night Charlie's beloved pet dies. She'll never forgive me.

"Spike," I growl. "Get up." I poke his swollen belly hard with two fingers, trying to see if I can push the water out. "*Please.* I swear I will never insult you again. I will find a ten-acre strawberry patch and make you the king. Just please for the love of God—"

Mweep.

Music to my fucking ears. "You dumb little daredevil—" I stop, remembering my promise as Spike begins to sneeze uncontrollably. Or maybe he's coughing. I don't know but he's alive.

Setting my disdain aside, I pick him up and hold him against my bare chest. He's shivering, trying to shake off the excess water. Using my finger, I squeegee around his eyes and nose to help clean him up. His little heart is going berserk, probably knowing how close he came to death. Certain he's okay, I try to set him back down, but he clings to me, desperate to stay in my embrace.

"Ah!" I hiss as his sharp nails scratch up my chest. "Fine, fine. You get two minutes, a thorough blow-drying, then you're going back in your cage. We're not ever going to tell Charlie what happened here tonight."

I lie down on the concrete, letting Spike nestle onto my chest. It's not long before his panicked breathing slows and his pulse calms. It's like he's steadying himself against my heartbeat. Curling himself up, his breathing falls into a steady rhythm and I can't find it in me to disturb him.

I relax against the concrete as the pool lights switch to night mode. With everything low-lit, I can almost see the stars. I stay focused on the tiny dots of bright lights against the sky as my nemesis rests his disgusting wet nose uncomfortably close to my nipple.

"I got you, buddy," I mutter, stroking his back. "But be warned, if you shit on me, you're going swimming again."

CHAPTER 30

Spencer

If this were a movie, I would've stormed out the night Nathan verbally kicked me out. I would've found the strength to pack my suitcase, grabbed Charlie, and disappeared from his life dramatically, hoping he'd ache for eternity from the misery of losing me.

But this isn't a movie. The flu is real. And my boss most certainly isn't miserable. I was powerless to do anything except sleep and heal as Nathan tended to me silently. Monday was bad, especially because of our fight. Tuesday was even worse. My fever nearly sent me to the emergency room. As angry as I was, I had to let Nathan be my knight in shining armor, getting Charlie sorted for school, and balancing around-the-clock care for me.

By Friday morning, finally my fever is gone and I'm able to see colors and somewhat taste coffee again.

Nathan and I hadn't talked about our big blowout. He hasn't mentioned me leaving again, and based on the way he so sweetly cared for me, I get the impression he's changed his mind. But at this point, Charlie and I need to leave for my sanity more than his. I didn't think it was possible to really fall for someone before getting physical. But here I am, feeling like a loser with an unrequited crush I can't shake.

I need space. I need a new home, and most importantly, I need a new boss.

Moving a little slower than usual, I walk into work after dropping Charlie off at school. My slacks feel saggy around the waist. The flu was a crash diet for me. I could barely tolerate water. Too wrecked to argue, Nathan was able to force-feed me a little broth. But after four days of a strictly liquid diet, my clothes are relaxing comfortably on my body again. It won't last. The minute I smell food, the weight will come right back on. It always does. This is the endless cycle of chasing something that's not meant for me. But I don't know how to quit.

How do you quit being so aware of all the things you aren't and don't have?

I call the elevator with a push of the button. After selecting the top executive floor, I wait for the doors to close, but immediately push the open button when I hear a distant, "Hold the elevator, please."

The doors don't obey, so I stick my foot in between, forcing them to reopen. "I've got you," I say to the man in a clean, beige suit jogging toward me. His blond hair is parted neatly and has so much gel it doesn't move despite his quick pace.

"Thank you." He hustles into the elevator.

"Sure. Which floor?"

He looks like a sales guy. He's probably on the eighth floor. "Same as you." He nods toward the already lit-up button. "Meeting my boss." He turns his head, and his smile instantly fades when he sees me.

My spine tenses as we both recognize each other at the same time. I furiously press the "door open" button, but they're determined to stay shut, and we ascend. I'm trapped here with the last man on the planet I want to see.

Casey Conrad.

Heart racing, fingers trembling, I look ahead, refusing to make eye contact. Like a muscle memory, my gut twists with shame, fear, and an overwhelming urge to flee.

"Spencer Riley," he murmurs quietly. "I had no idea you work here."

I try to say something. Anything. But this man knocks the wind from my lungs. My throat feels choked, my thoughts sputtering, I'm just trying to keep my head above water. Of all the times I fantasized about the day I'd see Casey again, it was never like this. I was rail thin, a total knockout, machine gun in my hands, relishing in the fear in his eyes.

I hate him so much, I can taste bile in the back of my throat.

I'm holding my breath, counting each blink. Only two more floors and I'm free. I can panic and fall apart anywhere except in his presence. If he could just stand there staying quiet like that, I might actually be okay... *If only.*

"Hey, I don't want any trouble," he says, as if dead set on my sabotage. "Last time I saw you, you almost got me expelled. But it's been years. We're cool now, right?"

My jaw doesn't *drop*. It unhinges and falls off. That's his narrative? *I* wronged *him*? I almost got him expelled?

He thinks we're *cool*?

The elevator dings louder than I swear it ever has, and the doors peel apart. Casey steps backward, holding out his hand, gesturing me forward. He ducks his head like a nobleman. "Ladies first, of course."

I try to exit, but my legs are frozen, outside of the trembling. The memories flash before me in the worst montage of my life. The jeers, the moos, the humiliation when the dean asked me if I knew how inappropriate it was to be sending boys naked pictures. The shock when people were more concerned about whether Casey could start the football season if I accused him of something. He hurt me, and public opinion chose the quarterback superstar. No one cared about the pudgy, vulnerable freshman who was borderline suicidal. I hung my head in shame as if it were my fault Casey violated what I thought was private intimacy.

I never felt safe with a man again. He tainted my relationship with sex. He stole my innocence in so many more ways than he could fathom. Desperate, I call on my mom to hold me steady. *Mama, don't let me cry. Please, don't let me cry in front of him.*

With a steadying breath, I will my feet forward. Tilting my chin up, I hold my head high, even though it feels awkward and forced. There are so many things I want to say to him. I should yell but the right words escape me. Glancing at his outreached hand, I'm transported right back to the worst moments of my life.

"You don't need to pretend to be a gentleman," I say in a hushed tone, more for my sake than his. "I know exactly what you are."

I walk away, not allowing myself to run. One step at a time, I put as much distance between me and Casey as I can. But with him in this office, it's not possible. There could be an entire ocean separating us, and it still wouldn't be enough space to put me at ease.

※

"We'd have to order the chloroform in small batches, collecting for a while," Dawn says nonchalantly as I blink at her in horror. Her sinister side is showing. "If we order a big vat, it'll raise suspicion."

"Dawn, we're not killing him."

She holds up her finger. "Another idea. We get him belligerently drunk, take him to the zoo, and give him a friendly hip nudge right over the fence into the alligator enclosure."

I tilt my head. "Those alligators are drugged. They have no appetite. And even if they did, Casey tastes repulsive."

Dawn cringes. "Speaking from experience?"

No. Judging by the look she's wearing, I know what part she's referring to. I actually never put Casey's dick in my mouth. It was my first time. I didn't know what to do. "I'm assuming deceitful weasel leaves a bitter aftertaste."

"Want me to go with you when you tell Nathan?" She finishes her salad, dropping her fork triumphantly into the empty plastic container. "I was starving." She pushes back from her desk, holding her hands to her flat stomach.

I poke at my Baja chicken salad with black beans, dried jalapeño peppers, and chipotle-ranch dressing. Normally, I'd dive in headfirst. I love when yummy foods hide themselves in salad. The chunks of cotija cheese should be more than enough to beckon my appetite, but nothing. I'm not sure if I'm still sick or if seeing Casey really shook me that bad.

"I'm not telling Nathan."

"Casey makes you very uncomfortable. He can't work here around you. If you're worried about who Nathan will choose—"

"I'm not." I meet her gaze, trying to stick the landing on my lie. Casey is a project manager helping with a billion-dollar new-build venture. I don't have that kind of experience. I'm replaceable. But hearing Nathan say that would break me, so I'm not going to give him the opportunity. "I contacted my old boss, Hank. He's using a temp assistant right now and would love to have me back."

Dawn frowns. "You're moving back to Miami?"

"I think it's best."

"For who?" she challenges. Sometimes I forget Dawn's a mom and her bullshit-o-meter is fully calibrated. "You can't mean Charlie because she has a best friend here, her grades are good, she likes school, and the girl is nonstop smiling. I know you can't mean Nathan, because whether or not either of you wants to admit it, he's far less of a brute with you around. And I know you can't mean me, Chelsea, and your other friends who treasure the moments we get to spend with you."

My lips flatten into a straight line. "You're guilt-tripping me?"

"I'm trying to get you to face your trauma. I don't want Casey to take anything more from you. If your mom were here, I bet you anything she'd tell you to stand your ground. You're strong enough now and you're not alone."

"Dawn, it's too late. I already quit." In a fit of emotion, I emailed Nathan this morning and gave him my two weeks' notice. I haven't gotten any real work done this morning. I missed four days. I should've been catching up on emails and tasks, but instead, I was scouring my employment contract trying to figure out when I need to surrender my SUV and how much of my advance I'll need to return.

Dawn's desk phone rings. A disappointed stare locked on me, she reaches for the receiver, pressing the speaker button with her pinky. "Office of James Hatcher. This is Dawn."

"Is Spencer with you?" Speak of the devil. Nathan sounds positively pissed.

Pausing, Dawn raises her brows at me, asking for permission to out me. I nod.

"She is."

"Why isn't she at her desk or answering her phone?"

"She's on her lunch break. Calm down, Nathan." Dawn flashes an angry look at the phone as if it's culpable for Nathan's grumpy mood. Except it's my fault.

"Tell her to come to my office as soon as you guys are done." He hangs up abruptly.

I shrivel in my seat, already regretting the mess I caused. "That doesn't sound good."

Dawn shrugs wordlessly.

"Are you mad at me too?" I ask softly.

"Yes," she answers plainly. "But it's because I'll miss you, doll. My daughter is in a phase of independence. She needs room to become her own person, and I think I've used you to fill a hole in my life. But I like to think you needed me too."

"I did... *I do*. We'll stay in touch. Nothing has to change."

"Of course." She shows me a weak smile because we both know it'll never be the same.

I stab my fork into my salad, forcing myself to take a bite. I'm going to eat this entire thing at the rate of a sloth. Because once lunch is over, I have no choice but to face the music.

That music? Nathan's fury.

CHAPTER 31

Spencer

To my great displeasure, when I get to Nathan's office, the door is wide open, and all I can hear is Casey's loud laughter. There's a wide smile on Nathan's face, which makes this so much worse. He's already chummy with the shit stain of a human being who shares DNA with a warthog.

I turn on my heel, trying to retreat. It's too late. Nathan spotted me.

"Spencer. *Come in*," he commands. "We're just wrapping up." Why does he always look so good when we have to have the hardest conversations? His dark blue button-down and tan pants are practically mouthwatering. I'll miss the view from my desk once I'm gone. If I'm being honest...I'll miss his company too.

I take a few reticent steps into the office, sticking to the perimeter of the space, as if Casey, who's looking way too relaxed in the sitting area, has an invisible forcefield around him.

Nathan gestures back and forth between me and Casey. "Spencer, this is Casey Conrad. He's helping me with the new hotel-casino on Sutton Street as project manager because we're on such a tight timeline. Casey, this is my executive assistant, Spencer. She's my right-hand woman, and also the reason all my folders and pens are pink and glitter-filled." Nathan shoots me a look, then continues, focusing on Casey. "Also, should you encounter her emotional support guinea pig, tempted as you may be, you are not allowed to kick it."

Casey laughs. "Why would I kick a guinea pig?"

"Beady eyes, oversized front teeth, annoying squeaking, sharp talons that cut little holes in your shirt when he clings to you. The list goes on. But the point is, I said *don't* kick him. He's part of our family now."

If Casey weren't here as an antagonist, I might've melted at Nathan claiming Spike, calling him part of *our* family. That was dang sweet. But I can't focus on anything other than the feeling of betrayal at my mortal enemy cozying up to my boss.

Rising and holding his hand out, he crosses the room. "Nice to see you, Spencer." He pumps his brows at me as he approaches, probably hoping I'll go along with the facade in front of the man who signs both our paychecks. Addressing Nathan, he reveals, "Spence and I met in the elevator this morning."

"I prefer Spencer." It's petty but the only way I can express my disdain. Don't call me nicknames. Don't ask me to lie for you. I clasp my hands behind my back, making it clear I have no intention of touching Casey, even as a formality.

Nathan furrows his brows, looking at me head to toe, confused at my rudeness. "How are you feeling today?" he asks softly.

I shrug. "Fine."

"Casey, why don't you go check on the zoning permits. I need to speak with Spencer, alone."

Casey catches my gaze with a nervous, pleading glance. "Absolutely. I'll make some calls while I head out for a coffee run. Can I get you guys anything?"

"No, thanks," Nathan says curtly. His eyes flash to the door, effectively dismissing Casey.

He closes the door behind him and locks it. "Sit down. Wherever you like."

I make my way to the sitting area and slump down on the far end of the sofa. I expect Nathan to sit in the singular chair across from me on the other side of the coffee table. It's better for eye contact. But he does no such thing. He sits right next to me and spreads his legs into a wide V so our knees are almost touching.

"I got your resignation." Wasting no time at all, he addresses the elephant in the room. Pointing to the wastebasket under his desk, he adds, "I filed it appropriately."

I flash him a sideways glance. "Did you print out my email, just so you could make a scene in front of me?"

"That's why I can't let you quit. You already know me so well." He smirks. "I meant to rip it up in front of you, but it was sitting on my desk and looking at it pissed me off. I tore it into confetti pieces."

"Real mature."

"So is running away." Leaning forward, he rests his elbows against his knees and audibly exhales. "You're under a very peculiar contract for exactly this reason. Have you thought about the consequences of leaving? Giving up the car? Forfeiting your advance? Reimbursing the company for your subsidized rent?"

"Yes, I have. I can handle it."

"And what about me?" He turns his head, meeting me with a weary expression. "Have you thought about me at all?"

All I do is think about you. That's part of the problem. But of course I can't say that. I put myself out there once, I won't do it again. Nathan wants a pet, not a relationship. I'm such easy prey. I need his help. I want his affection. I'm wrapped up so tight in his web. That's why I need to get away. To get my head straight.

"Do you know how many people would kill for this job?" I remind him. "You'll recover."

"I don't want people. I want you."

"Nathan, you don't know how to want me properly. You just know how to play games."

He's quiet for a beat. I stare out of the window at the Las Vegas skyline. I can't see the Strip from here, just blue sky and red earth. The side of Las Vegas most people forget exists.

"I don't apologize easily," he confesses, cutting the silence. "Another character flaw of mine? I hate to admit when I'm wrong. But all I do around you is say I'm sorry. And yes, *I was wrong*. I apologize for letting my emotions get the best of me earlier this week. I said things I didn't mean. I don't want you to go. I don't want secrets between us. Please don't take Charlie from me."

"Charlie?" My voice cracks. "You're worried about my sister?"

"Very much. She's important to you, so she's important to me. You mean so much more to me than you realize. My hesitancy is not about you. You have no idea how much I want to strip you naked and bury you into this couch right now. I want you to scream when you come. I want everyone in this office to hear how bad I fucking want you. But I can't...before explaining."

"Elise?" I bravely ask. I brace myself, expecting him to fly off the handle.

But he doesn't. He looks ahead, gazing through the window, lowering his head in a nod.

I already know his secret. It took me a while, but I figured it out.

I ruminated on this for weeks. Nathan's not on social media outside of the occasional feature on the company's page. James is always friendly to me, but I wouldn't dare betray Nathan's trust by going to his dad. Dawn and Chelsea are tight-lipped. Charlie knows something, I can just tell, but she's even tighter-lipped.

It was something my mom told me a long time ago that made me see what was always right in front of me.

Mom told me that when she passed, I would be angry for a while. She begged me to forgive her, but said it was okay to be angry at her for leaving us too soon. Sad, hurt, and distraught, I understood. But anger? It made no sense.

Mom explained that sadness trickles slowly, like a stream. It never really goes away, but it flows into other things and then morphs. The intensity ebbs and flows, never dissipating entirely. You have to make peace with sadness, because it never completely leaves us. Anger, however, is a bomb. It builds and builds and must be let out. It's the only way to be free of it. Following her profound advice, I did what I needed to after she passed. I took a self-defense class and bloodied my knuckles on a few punching bags. I even went to a rage room once. Over and over, I found safe outlets to vent out my anger, and just like Mom promised, eventually it diffused.

But Nathan must've never felt his anger like I did. It's the way he presses his lips together into a paper-thin line when he's trying not to say what he wants. The way his eyes glaze over and he detaches from the world when he gets caught in a memory. It's how he uses the silent treatment as a defense mechanism. When he was provoked enough at me to scream, instead, he told me to leave. He pushed me away because he doesn't know how to deal with the bomb that explodes in his chest every single damn day. Nathan's *so* angry, and he doesn't even realize it.

He's angry because he lost the most important person in his life. I can't tell him I completely understand, but I can try to. I know what that's like.

"Elise was my former assistant," he offers so quietly, it's almost a whisper. "But more importantly, she was my fiancée. We had a lot of the wedding planned, but never got a chance to..." Trailing off, he places his fist against his mouth, trying hard to stay composed.

I place my hand on his broad back, and rub small, soothing circles. "How did it happen?"

"Car accident. She was headed to the airport to pick me up. I hate driving but she loved it. She insisted she come get me instead of security. Elise didn't like having a lot of staff. She wanted us to lead normal lives. I used to have about ten people in my home at all times, and I got rid of them all. I told her she didn't have to but Elise cooked, cleaned, drove, grocery shopped. She even washed her car in the driveway instead of running it through a car wash. She found joy in being self-sufficient."

"My mom was like that," I say. "One of my favorite things about her." And it was the hardest thing for her to let go when her body got too weak.

"Elise would've liked you a lot. I think she would've liked you for me." I freeze when tears form in Nathan's eyes. It's not just that I haven't seen Nathan cry before, it's that I couldn't even picture it.

He looks so vulnerable. I wish I had a larger wingspan so I could wrap him up and hold him properly.

"I think if Elise were here, I wouldn't see you the same way. I'm not attracted to men in love."

"Do you get it, now? The problem?" He sits up straight, wiping away the few tears he let himself shed.

"Actually, no, I don't."

"Do you really want to be with a guy who is still in love with another woman?"

His words take my breath away. I never thought about it that way. As the realization moves through me, I know my answer. I find his hand and weave my fingers through his. "Do you want to be with anyone else while you're still in love with Elise?"

Nathan grimaces like he's in pain. "Before you came into the picture, Elise was the first thing I thought about when I woke up. She was the last thing I saw before I went to sleep. But these days, all I see is you."

I nod in understanding. "And you don't like that."

He cups my cheek with his free hand, stroking under my eye with his thumb. "It's a beautiful sight. But I don't know if I'm ready for anything more. I'm not sure if I ever will be. It's why I'm careful with you, Spencer. I don't let myself look at you or touch you like I want. I don't say all the dirty things I want to do with you. Things you'd love. Things that would feel so good, we'd both get attached. You're so young. I don't want my baggage holding you back. And I refuse to make you promises I can't keep. I'm not playing games with you, I'm just trying to put together an impossible puzzle. One that ends with you and me, but also—"

"You and Elise." I squeeze his hand, then bring it to my lips and kiss each of his knuckles. "I get it. I do. You're a good man for being considerate of what would happen to me if you led me on."

"Am I, though? A good man would let you go." He nods toward the wastebasket. "And I'm not doing that. I'll call your old boss's boss and buy the company right out from under him before I let you leave me."

Good luck. That would mean calling Dex, and I'm pretty sure he's just as rich as Nathan is. "So you want to keep me here, prisoner?"

"Like Fiona in that dragon-guarded tower. *Forever.*" He pumps his brows, adding a little humor into his response.

"Charlie made you watch *Shrek*," I intuit.

"Every. Single. One," he deadpans. "You were sick for twenty years, by the way."

"Be glad you didn't have to sit through *Puss in Boots*."

"Oh, that movie holds up. I like the Spanish cat. Actually, I like cats in general. I'd be okay with getting one if it wasn't for Spike. He'd look like Thanksgiving dinner to a calico cat."

My eyes pop wide. "You're worried for Spike's safety? Since when?"

He smooths his eyebrow with the edge of his thumb. "Monday night, after our spat, Spike and I came to an agreement. We're okay now."

I feel like there's more to this story, but there are more pressing matters at hand to discuss. "Nathan, I do still want to quit."

"No." He wraps his hand around my leg like it's a life-preserver ring. "What do I need to fix?"

"Casey." It just pops out. I didn't mean to go whining to Nathan, but it's the only real answer.

"He's a good guy. A little full of himself, but a hard worker. And you don't have to fetch him coffee." He releases me, then pats my leg, shrugging off my complaint.

"I slept with him."

Nathan goes stiff. His jaw twitches as his teeth grind together. I watch his Adam's apple bounce as he swallows hard. "You met him this morning. So you're telling me sometime before lunch with Dawn you let a stranger fuck you at work?"

"He lied. We met five years ago at UNLV. I told you I went to school here briefly."

He nods along. "You left after two weeks because your mom passed away."

Nathan was just so vulnerable, I want to be the same. But this is a different kind of trauma. One I'm not sure he'll understand. I'm worried I look silly or insecure—maybe I'm both. But all I know is Casey changed my life for the worst. After what he put me through, I don't view the world the same way. I never look over my shoulder because I don't want to catch someone laughing at me. It would've been easier if he assaulted me. People would get how wrong that is. But do people understand the gut-wrenching pain of public humiliation and how it scars you for the rest of your life? That's so much harder to explain.

"Casey was my first. He wasn't very nice to me. Even if my mom hadn't passed away, I probably still would've dropped out of school."

A new look crosses Nathan's face. A dangerous, madman flicker, very Dexter-esque. "He forced you?"

"*No.* No, no. It was consensual and I was of age. Barely, but still. He was the starting quarterback and I thought he was a good guy."

"Okay. At least I don't have to kill him. So, what happened? He slept with you and then never called you again?" Nathan relaxes back into the seat.

"Something like that." Except it was nothing like that. I would've gotten over a boy not calling me back. Instead, I fall right back into my usual rhythm with Nathan—lies and half-truths.

"I can't fire him for being a slut five years ago, Spencer. I kind of want to, but thanks to my dad he has some leverage over us. I can't even tell you what because I don't want you subpoenaed if it ever comes to that. Are you scared of him?"

"No," I say. "More like he should be afraid of me if we're in the break room alone and there's a kitchen knife in sight."

He blinks at me. "Noted. I'll keep him out of your way best I can. Will that work?"

"Yes." I try but I'm not even convincing myself.

"I'm here whenever you need me. I don't know exactly what you are to me, Spencer, but it's very important. Get used to being my priority." He kisses my forehead, and it breaks my heart. Crown the prince, because he just became a king in my eyes. A king that will never be fully mine because he lost his real queen.

I'm sick of life dealing me impossible cards. I want to talk to God or the universe directly and let it know it made a mistake. I cannot, in fact, handle anything on my plate, so it can cease and desist with testing my strength.

"So what now?" I ask.

"What's your dress size?"

My heart races like the Roadrunner fleeing from Coyote, preemptively sensing a dangerous trap. "Why would you ask me that?"

"My dad's fiancée is hosting a charity auction event on Saturday night. I want you to attend with me. It's a black-tie event and most of the people in attendance collect Maseratis like they're stamps. I'm not trying to sound like an ass, but I have a feeling you don't have a suitable dress in your closet." He touches my empty earlobes, frowning. "Did you toss the earrings after we fought?"

"Nathan, I would never throw those away." I touch his smooth cheek affectionately, and he nuzzles into my hand. "That's wasteful. I'd pawn them if I needed to."

He pulls away with a scowl. "That smart mouth. Anyway, I need to get a designer started on your dress today. What's your size?"

He simply wants a number to pass along to whatever designer he's going to bully into working forty-eight hours straight on a dress that probably costs more than my childhood home. He doesn't understand what a loaded question it is. Nathan might as well be asking me for my weight. And here I am again, naked in a poster displayed all over campus, my shame on display for the hungry lions to shred me apart.

Not using my brain, I lie, telling him two sizes smaller than I actually am. I haven't eaten all week, maybe I magically shrunk to my goal weight?

He thinks nothing of it. "Got it. And can you get a sitter for

Charlie?"

"I don't think so. My friends are out of town and Charlie's best friend has a different sleepover this weekend. I could ask Dawn?"

Nathan shakes his head. "She'll be at the event too. Okay, no problem."

Relief washes over me. I can't go and Nathan will never know my true dress size, unless he snoops through my closet to check my tags, but what kind of psycho does that?

"What's Charlie's size?"

"Ten in girls," I answer on autopilot, not realizing where he's going with this.

"Good. Family date night, then."

I should be panicking because of the mess I just got myself into. But my brain completely emptied when he said *family* date night. "Sounds great."

He raises his arm over the top of the sofa, inviting me to relax against his chest. I take in his office, trying to remember how long we have before the return window closes on this furniture.

"Are we ever going to redo your office?"

He laughs. "Eh, it's actually growing on me."

CHAPTER 32

Nathan

"Are there going to be celebrities tonight?" Charlie asks all bug-eyed. Her shin-length, dark blue, sequin dress makes her blue eyes look bigger and brighter. So she kind of looks like a lemur in the midst of all her excitement. The limo driver has had to circle the block three times now because she's so unwilling to get out.

"Maybe. None as big as Shaylin or anything... Spencer, are you okay?"

Spencer's sitting next to me, resting her forehead on the cool glass. Her long ball gown is stunning. It's pale pink with handsewn flowers decorating the bodice, round Swarovski crystals for the pistils. The dress hugs her curves and matches her pink diamond studs perfectly. I wasn't sure the designer could come up with something in time, but as soon as I sent over Spencer's size, the Italian legend happily informed me he had something spectacular in stock.

Spencer is breathtakingly stunning, even more so than usual. When she met me in the foyer after getting herself and Charlie ready, we almost didn't go. I wanted to break my rule right then, send Charlie to her room with noise-canceling headphones, and let the dam break. Such a pretty dress to tear to shreds, but who cares about hundred-thousand-dollar casualties when she looks like *that*?

The only problem is Spencer doesn't seem thrilled. She's been mostly still and quiet all night. Outside of adjusting my matching pink bow tie, she hasn't touched me. This isn't an official date, especially with Charlie in tow, but I thought she'd enjoy a night of luxury on my arm. I don't know what can happen between us but tonight was my way of showing everyone that *if* something new is going to happen in my love life, I choose Spencer.

"I'm fine," she mumbles, taking shallow breaths.

"You sure?"

She doesn't get a chance to answer because Charlie suddenly jumps in. "Have *you* ever met Shaylin?" she asks me.

I quirk my brow, stealing a sideways glance at Spencer, but she's turned her attention back to the window. "Your sister didn't tell you? We both did."

"*What?*" Charlie shrieks. "Are you kidding me? You met Shaylin and you didn't tell me?" Her shrill accusatory tone is at a decibel only dogs can hear.

"Damn, Charlie. You're going to crack a window," I complain.

A sly smirk spreads on her face. She holds out her hand. "Pay up."

Fuck. I forgot. I pull out my wallet and look through my bills, trying to find anything that isn't a hundred. I have one five-dollar bill. Charlie pouts as I hand it over.

"It's ten per cuss."

"Damn isn't that serious of a cuss word. I'm giving myself a discount."

"You can't do that. We had a verbal agreement."

"And what did I teach you about verbal agreements?"

She rolls her eyes, grunting. "They're seldom upheld in court. Follow up with a written contract and wet signature."

"Attagirl. And did you do that?"

She snatches the Lincoln out of my hand. "Oh, I plan to, Nathan. *I plan to.*" She looks at Spencer. "Now as for *you*. You met Shaylin and kept it from me? What kind of sister are you?"

"Can you yell at me later?" Spencer murmurs, pleadingly.

"Are you not feeling well?" I ask Spencer. Now I'm concerned. She's been off all night. "Do you not want to go? I can take you back home."

"No, no, of course I do. I want to support you and Julia." She glances at Charlie who is staring at her with daggers for eyes. "And I would also like to keep my head."

"What's wrong? You seem so upset." She pivots in her seat the way the Tin Man would move. I feel bad. She's probably scared of ruining the dress. "This dress is yours, by the way. You don't have to be so careful in it."

"Great," she mutters bitterly.

What the hell? All right, plan B. I'm just going to get her drunk so she lightens up. I grab the champagne bottle and fill our glasses again. Sneaky Charlie holds out her empty glass and I almost pour into her cup on autopilot.

"Excuse me, miss, your juice is over there." I point across the limo to the sparkling cider. "Would you like a swirly straw as well?"

Charlie pokes her tongue out at me. "I'm almost twelve. I think I should be able to have my first sip of champagne."

Spencer cuts her a look. "Over my dead body. You can have your first sip at twenty-one."

I wait until Spencer's head is turned, then mouth to Charlie, *eighteen*. I put my finger to my lips. Spencer's such a rule follower because she's terrified of Child Services, but I'll fly them to Europe. Perfectly legal there.

The limo slows to a halt, the back doors lining up with the red carpet leading into the venue. "Showtime, Charlie. We can't stall anymore."

She looks around, breathing in deeply, soaking up the ambiance of the limo one more time. "Bye, limo, I'll miss you."

Letting myself out first, I hold my hand out for Charlie, then for Spencer. She winces as she steps out. I glance down at her shoes, wondering if they're the cause of her sour mood. These heels really don't look much different in size and shape than the ones she wears to the office. That can't be it.

With Charlie strutting boldly in front of us, I hang back and hook Spencer's arm in mine as we approach the hotel doors. "Are you hungry?"

"A little," she answers.

"They're serving hors d'oeuvres, but I arranged a late dinner to be delivered to our room."

Spencer freezes, halting us both. "You got us a room?" She nods toward Charlie and lowers her voice. "What do you possibly think can happen with my sister here?"

I smirk. "I reserved the penthouse suite. Three bedrooms. We can eat, watch a PG movie together, then go to bed. All innocent." I grab her hand and run my thumb over her knuckles. "Or, we could leave one of those rooms untouched."

She scrunches her face. "I thought we weren't crossing that line. Your *rules* and all."

I lean back, admiring her from head to toe. I duck down to put my lips to her ear so no one else can hear the grizzly desire in my tone. "It's your fault. The way you look tonight... I think we're bound to break some rules."

"Julia," I bellow so loudly, I startle several guests. I've been looking for her all night. Finally spotting her in her gold, sparkling gown, I weave through the crowd, making my way to the host. Eyes wide in surprise when she faces me, she ends the call she's in.

"Nate! Sorry." She puts her palm to her forehead. "I mean Nathan. Your dad said you prefer—"

"Nate is fine." I hold out my arms, feeling awkward as fuck, but I'm forcing myself out of my comfort zone. "May I?"

"Of course." She hits me hard in the chest like a lineman. She's sturdy for her petite frame. I thought she'd bounce off of me, instead she sends me backward one step as she wraps her arms around my waist in a bear hug. "I'm so surprised you came. Thank you."

"It's a beautiful event."

She pulls away, a wide smile on her face. "Everything is falling apart." Her Vanna White smile is confusing. "I wanted tonight to be perfect, but—" She throws her hands in the air. Oh. I see now. She's smiling so hard so she doesn't cry.

I guide her by the elbow out of earshot of guests. "What's wrong?"

"I couldn't decide between the silent auction or selling tables. I opted for hors d'oeuvres and auctioning jewelry, but everyone's wallets are apparently glued shut. Everyone walked by the jewelry cases, yet no one's bid yet. I should've just done a five-course meal and charged per plate."

"I wouldn't worry too much. Once the liquor starts flowing—"

"We're already out of champagne," she admits.

Shit. "What else?"

"I promised everyone a performance." She glances behind her to the stage. There's a piano and four chairs. "There's supposed to be a string quartet from the New York Philharmonic and the opera singer Italia Lucci. I just got a call that all we're getting is a second-chair violinist."

"What happened?"

"Lucci got a better gig evidently. And I'm still waiting to find out why I only got a quarter of the strings I ordered." She forces out a deep, anguished breath.

"Anything else?"

"I ordered escargot with the caterers. The snails went bad, so they substituted Rocky Mountain oysters. I realize that's low on the list of concerns, but this is a fancy event. I didn't want to serve—"

"Cow balls. Got it. Where's my dad?"

Her eyes snap to mine. "Please don't tell him. I told James I had it under control. He offered to help so many times. Evidently your mom hosted events like this in her sleep. I'm failing at this."

I pat her shoulder, trying to provide reassurance. Then, I pull out my phone and text Byron.

> **Me:** I need you to hit every single liquor store in a ten-mile radius and buy every bottle of Dom Perignon in stock. Bring them to the back of the hotel.

> **Byron:** Moving now.

Except I spot Byron in his tuxedo tucking his phone back in his pocket and following a butler and a silver tray. Grinding my teeth, I text him again.

> **Me:** Great. Quit stuffing your face and move faster.

He looks up, searching for me around the ballroom. While I have eyes on him, he can't find me. Fearing my omniscient presence, he heads toward the exit.

> **Byron:** Roger that.

People used to cower around me, desperate to leap into action at my mere request.

Spencer has softened me up into a gummy bear to the point no one flinches when I speak anymore. I'm debating if that's a good thing.

"More champagne is on the way," I assure Julia. "Usually with silent auctions, they need someone to break the ice. Go put down my name as the starting bid for each piece of jewelry, anywhere from a quarter to half a million. In twenty minutes if there's no movement, double the bid under Dawn's name. If she actually wins anything, make sure to bill me. I'd like to keep my balls intact, thanks."

A smile overtakes face, even though she still looks on the brink of tears. "Why are you being so wonderful? I thought you hated me."

"Why would you think that?" I ask, knowing damn well the answer.

"I've literally seen you run away when I approached."

I cringe, rubbing the back of my neck. "I can be a tough case to crack. I'm sorry."

"If nothing else comes of this night, you speaking to me is a big win."

I hold out my hand and she proceeds to give me a firm handshake. Instead, I pull her hand to my lips and peck the back of it. "Cheers to fresh starts, right?"

She nods, her smile relaxing into genuine appreciation. "I'd love that."

"Just don't make me call you Mom."

She cackles. "Fair enough."

"And just so you know, you're not failing. You did a fantastic job. Look around. This place looks incredible and everyone is enjoying the attention to detail. My mother was fantastic at ordering things and bossing people around. Gun to her head, she could not tell you what was on the menu at any of her events. I'm certain my dad is already impressed. He loves you very much."

Curling her finger, she touches her knuckle in a dabbing motion under her eyes. "Please don't make me cry right now. My makeup is not waterproof, and I don't want to look like a wet racoon."

Her phone pings and she rolls her eyes at the text message. "Lucci," she grumbles. "Excuses, excuses. I only needed her for one song. She's on my shit list for life."

I nod toward the stage. "Is that piano tuned, or just for show?"

"I have no idea."

I'm taking a leap of faith which may cost me my life, but as much as I've put Julia through, she's been nothing but forgiving and kind toward me. I have to try to help. "After your opening speech, instead of announcing Lucci, just give me the stage."

"You can sing?"

"God no. But I know someone who can. Just do me a favor and tell everyone no recording and no flash photography."

"What?"

"Trust me?" I offer.

Twisting her lips, she debates it for a millisecond. "Fine."

It's an attempt to secure our new bond, more than actually having faith in my eleventh-hour plan. But it's something.

Now all I have to do is convince Spencer not to murder me.

CHAPTER 33

Spencer

There's not enough air in this room that's spinning. I gasp in short heaves, trying to fill my lungs, but my corset has a strict rule against breathing. It's *tight* tight. Two sizes too small. By some miracle, I was able to get the corset closed, but even the slightest movement and I'll bust free, ripping priceless couture to shreds. The dress is heavy with all the crystal embellishments, and barely an hour into this evening, even my bones are aching.

I'm in pain. I can't breathe. I desperately want to go home. *Stupid girl.* All because I was too embarrassed to tell Nathan my real size. I've been hiding in the corner of the room, praying for time to fast-forward.

I feel awful about this entire evening. Nathan has been every woman's dream. He's been polite, considerate, sexy, and smooth with every gesture. I, on the other hand, have been a cranky brat. It seems out of my control. My body is in shock, molded into a silhouette that isn't mine. Every time Nathan's told me I'm stunning, gorgeous, or he can't wait to tear this dress from my body, I know he's seeing what we both want me to be. Not what I really am. Upholding this standard is physically painful. And yet, I desperately want to be what he wants.

Something's changed between us since he told me about Elise.

He walks, always half a step in front of me, leading me, guarding me. Every time Charlie gets more than five feet away from us, his eyes latch on to her like a watchdog. He entered the ballroom tonight like he was attending with his most prized possessions—his family. Everything in me wants to cross the line with him. But...

There are consequences to falling in love with a claimed man. A man tethered to another woman by a tragically everlasting bond. Is second place good enough for happily ever after? Am I really content to share him with a beautiful ghost for the rest of my life? Is Nathan even thinking about forever? I learned the hard way that men transform into exactly what you want when they want something from you. Clever shifters with a total disregard for the consequences of their actions.

Probably because most of the time, they aren't the ones paying them.

"You all right?" a voice asks from behind me.

For a moment, I think it's Nathan, returning from wherever he whisked Charlie off to. Who else would find me in my hiding place?

"You look a little pale." Casey steps around me to face me. "Need some water?"

"No." Why is he still haunting me? Didn't I bury this memory five years ago? Maybe he's not the ghost I'm running from.

"You look good. Your dress and everything. You look like you've lost weight." Ignorance is truly a peaceful thing. Because the stupid, earnest smile on his face makes it seem like Casey thinks he just complimented me.

"Excuse me," I grunt out.

With tiny shuffles of my feet, I try to escape, but Casey wraps his mammoth hand around my wrist. "Wait."

"Let me go," I bark. But he doesn't. He tightens his fingers, a look of determination filling his eyes. "You're hurting me."

"Nate told me we should work in the meeting rooms downstairs moving forward. He's basically banished me from his office. Why is that, Spencer? We were cool until he spoke with you. What did you say?"

I successfully rip my arm away, but he only catches my other wrist.

"I need this job. This is my big break."

"*Let. Me. Go.*"

"Are you insane? You're going to try to ruin my life again over a stupid crush? Get over it. It was college and everyone was fucking around. I never liked you like that. I almost didn't graduate because you were so butthurt over it. It's pathetic that you're still holding on to a five-year grudge."

This is my moment. I should slap him. The blind arrogance. I want to do more. I want to grab the empty glass bottle off the nearest table and strike him across the jaw. I want to hurt him as badly as he hurt me. But I have too much to lose. *Charlie.* Assault is assault. I can't do anything except stand here and curse the injustice of the world that my only available weapon is words.

"You're a monster."

"No more so than you."

"How?" I ask indignantly. "What did I ever do to you?"

He finally releases me. I glance down at the red marks around my wrist and know in my soul if these don't disappear before Nathan returns, Casey is a dead man. "It was just a prank. Freshman hazing. You blew it out of proportion. You ran to the dean and nearly got me kicked off the team which would've let the whole school down."

"You were mediocre at best, Casey. Let's be honest. The team would've been fine."

"You bitch," he hisses.

We're interrupted when Julia grabs the microphone and offers her commencement of the event. She must deliver a beautiful speech in support of her cause because everyone is lost in thick applause, but not me and Casey. I'm deadlocked in pure hatred with the man who took my virginity.

I take the opportunity to tell him what I've wanted to for five long years. "Know what I did two days after my mother's funeral?"

Casey's anger sobers at the mention of my mom's death. "What?"

"I went to the clinic. The school nurse said I should get checked for pregnancy or an STD because the week you took my virginity, you slept with two other girls. And I'm willing to bet you didn't wear a condom with them, either."

Casey doesn't answer, but the way he hangs his head is confirmation enough.

"A princess, a jock, and a cow. Remember which one I was?"

"It was just a joke," he mumbles.

I can't hold back the tears. All I can do is keep my voice steady. "I spent my mother's funeral thinking about *you* and how you wrecked me. I never saw myself the same again. What you did traumatized me. I've played mental gymnastics every day since battling body dysmorphia. I starved myself for years, and when that wasn't enough, I put needles in my body to stave off the desire to eat. It almost killed me. But no big deal, because it was a joke, right?"

A piano sounds. It's a clean melody, the intro to "Hallelujah." Instead of jumping into the verse, the prelude repeats, a violin joining in and layering the melody.

"They played this at her funeral," I say to Casey.

"I'm sorry about your mom."

"You want to know what you did? You broke me when I couldn't afford to break. You marked me. *You damaged me—*"

I stop when a familiar voice rings through the microphone. It's enough to command my attention to the stage. I barely have time to register that it's Nathan playing the piano. I've never heard him play before, but the magic in his fingertips is swallowed up into obscurity when my little sister sings from her soul, looking like an angel with the spotlight casting a bright halo over her.

For once, I don't panic. I don't rush to do damage control. Paralyzed in place by this dress that's squeezing the life out of me, and the confrontation with Casey that has no resolution.

This isn't about revenge, or retribution. It's a realization that I'm stuck. I've been stuck.

I watch my baby sister on stage, but she's not a baby anymore.

Not remotely close. The chubby cheeks and wispy pigtails are things of the past. She looks like a woman, commanding the stage without an ounce of shyness. She looks happy as she dances over the vocals like music was created for her and her alone.

I tried to hide her. I attempted to instill the fear that lives in me. Fear of rejection. Fear of humiliation. I want to shield her from all the pain that kept me from living my own life. I tried to teach her to fear the stage because what if they laugh? What if they can't see she's worthy? What if she leaps, thinking she's a princess, only to find out she's the cow?

How could I do that to her?

And how is it possible that my eleven-year-old sister is so fiercely brave, she didn't buy into my bullshit for one minute? She's a diamond on stage, blinding us all with her radiance.

The song ends. The audience roars in applause. Filled with pride, I want to clap along, but the room rotates faster and I can't seem to put my hands together. My vision is so blurry I can't even *find* my hands. Air, I need air. Why won't my lungs work?

Casey garbles out something, but it sounds like he's underwater. I can't ask him what he said because I feel like if I open my mouth, if I *could* open my mouth, I might vomit.

Sweat drips from my forehead and melds with my tears.

The performance is over, yet the lights seem to dim even further.

Nathan is pushing through the crowd, everything around him going darker and darker but I see his gaze fixed in my direction. He's moving faster than my mind can comprehend. He glitches like a movie that's not buffering properly. Ten paces away, then two, back to five.

My hands reach out finally to grasp at anything as I fall to the ground. Faintly, there is the sharp tear of fabric, then silence, then blackness.

Then, peace.

CHAPTER 34

Nathan

Fuck, fuck, fuck. I slam my elbow into the up arrow. *Not fast enough.*

I growl in frustration as I make my way to the staircase with Spencer in my arms. Of course as soon as I turn around, the elevator finally arrives.

"For fuck's sake," I shout. I ignore the onlookers as I carry Spencer into the elevator. The moment the doors are closed I punch the "emergency stop" button. The alarm rings, jostling Spencer. She's not fully unconscious, just so woozy I don't trust she can stand.

The dress was too tight, suffocating her. How didn't I see it before? Of course that's what it was. She couldn't move. She barely spoke. Spencer's been in pain all night.

I watched her from the stage, talking to Casey, trying to calm the beast of envy in my chest. I played the piano from memory, my eyes in the crowd as my fingers glossed over the keys. Charlie was so excited to take the stage, but I wanted the song to be over. I needed to figure out why Spencer was crying.

"It's ripped," she whimpers.

The back clasp of the dress broke free and there's about a two-inch tear in the back.

Setting her down gently, I spin her around so she can brace herself. "Hold the wall, Spencer. It's about to be a lot more ripped." I grab both sides of the fabric and yank.

"No," she cries out. "Nathan, please don't. The dress."

I ignore her, continuing to split the dress apart. Fabric falls down to her ankles, and I see what's actually choking the life out of her. I don't know what the hell kind of contraption she's wearing, but the corset looks like it was made to crack her rib cage. It's sheer and thin, but the tightly sewn lining is squeezing her skin so hard it looks like she was poured into it.

"What is this?"

"Body shaper."

"Shaping you for what? Death?"

The sheer corset is held closed by about fifty metal clasps. No time. I wrap my canines around a weak spot in the fabric. I puncture the material just enough to get my finger through. Once I rip the top in two, it falls to the floor, freeing her breasts. Spencer gasps for air like she nearly met death underwater, and barely resurfaced in time.

As she catches her breath, I scour her bare back where the material cuts into her skin. Thick red lines are embedded in her flesh where the seams cinched her, creating a waistline several sizes too small. She's lucky she's not bleeding. Her flesh looks raw and whipped. I trace the lines with my fingertips and she flinches.

"I'm sorry." I stare angrily at the dress and corset at our feet, as if they forced her into this misery. "I'm going to kill that designer. He said this was your size."

Panting calmed, Spencer covers her breasts best she can with her forearms crossed, then turns to face me. "It was the size I told you."

"You gave me the wrong size on purpose?" I study the lines across her chest and belly. They are angry and deep, matching the ones on her back.

"A smaller size."

"Why?"

Arms still wrapped around her chest, she shrugs. "I didn't want you to know. I thought you'd suddenly be put off."

"Impossible. Spencer, you put a *guinea pig* in your front pocket and I still wanted to rip those overalls off your body a couple weeks ago. That should tell you how insanely attracted

I am to you." I trail my eyes over her lush, perfect body. "I see nothing here but what I want. Minus the pain. Don't ever do this again. Be honest with me."

"You want me to be honest?"

"Yes."

"I want you to stop looking at me," she murmurs ashamedly. "I know I look gross."

"No, you don't. You're so beautiful. Even when you think you're at your worst, I'm a man obsessed. Let me show you." I walk her backward until she's pressed against the elevator wall. I cloak her with my body, moaning in pleasure when I feel her soft curves press against me. "You're so sexy." I grab her hand and place it against my growing erection. "Feel that? This is what you do to me constantly. It's fucking torture, Spencer. Don't worry about the dress, it was always bound to come off." Leaning down, I nuzzle against her cheek. I tug on her earlobe with my teeth. "Should I fuck you right now? Will that help show you how much I want you? What if I can't wait to get to the room? Can I have you here?"

"My dress was too tight. I'm sweaty." She turns her head, unintentionally giving me access to her neck. I nip and kiss at the delicate skin close to her collarbone.

"I don't mind at all. In fact, I want to taste you. Would you like that? Can I lick your pussy clean right here, right now?" I graze my hands down her body. She refuses to untwist her forearms, so I skip her breasts for now. She flinches and tightens her midsection when I track my hands down her stomach. I cup her sex, grinding the heel of my palm against her. "I'm not a man who begs, but I'll beg on my knees for this, baby."

With my thumb, I find her clit through the fabric of her panties and she lets me massage little circles against her most sensitive spot, but it's when I drop to my knees and try to replace my thumb with my lips, she pulls back.

"Can we stop?"

God, no. Please no. I blow out a deep breath and reluctantly release her hips. "Yeah, we can stop."

I unbutton my jacket, shrug out of the sleeves, and sling it around her shoulders.

She clutches the lapels, closing the jacket around her body. "I'm sorry."

"Don't be. Bad timing on my part. I misread how to help." I've been craving Spencer's body since the night I met her, but I didn't picture it like this. Angry red slashes across her skin, tearstained makeup, the look of despair on her pretty face. Fuck.

Spencer's gaze falls down once more. She refuses to look at me. "I don't think you can help me. Just like I don't think I can help you."

"What do you mean?"

"Seeing Casey is drumming up a lot and I think...I need some space. I want to work on myself for a while. And maybe you should work on yourself too." She cocks her head, eyes still glued to the tile floor. "We're both broken, Nathan."

"I'm aware." I want to hold her, but her body language is telling me no. "But it might feel better to be broken together."

She wets her lips and rubs them together. "Or we'll just hurt each other until we're beyond repair."

I hook my finger under her chin, lifting her face until she meets my eyes. "Am I hurting you?"

She nods. "I know I'm never going to be the fantasy you've built up in your head. I can flirt and tease, but this? Passionate moments in the elevator, ripping off my clothes, saying these things that should make me wet, but instead they scare me."

My body stiffens. Her words hit me like a slap across the jaw. "I'm scaring you?"

"Because you want what I'm not. I have a very broken relationship with sex and my body. I ruined your night because I'm so stuck in my head. I just... I don't think it's going to change anytime soon. Especially not while Casey's here."

Reading between the lines, it kind of sounds like Spencer doesn't hate Casey. It sounds like there's still feelings there. Maybe I'm blind. All I could see was what I wanted, but maybe I'm not what she wants.

As a last-ditch effort, I grab her hand. I've been trying to do better and choose honesty when it's so much easier to be cold and callous. "Spencer, I'm at a fork in the road and the one that leads to you is bumpy, rocky, and flat-out exhausting, but it's the one I want. You don't need to be a porn star to captivate me. You already have." I run my finger across her bottom lip. "This sassy mouth of yours owns me."

"I wasn't sassy tonight."

"I know. And I missed you." Dropping my hand, I scrunch my nose at her. I'd put on a clown suit and perform as a one-man band if I could just get her to smile.

Her lips remain in a flat line. "I think...I just need to be your assistant. And your friend."

My heart sinks with a thud to the bottom of my chest. "That's really all you want?"

She nods with heavy eyes and a frown that doesn't match her words.

Of all the things I hoped for tonight, I never saw rejection coming. Then again, she has a way of blinding me—hyperfocusing on what I want. I didn't realize she was something I couldn't have.

"Okay. Have it your way."

"Are you mad?"

"No," I lie. "Why don't you and Charlie enjoy the penthouse tonight on your own? I have my dad's bachelor's party next week in L.A. I'll head out early tomorrow, get some work done while I'm getting his party ready. I'll be gone for a week, and when I'm back, we'll start fresh. Just boss and assistant. Friends. Sound good?"

"We live in Vegas. Isn't this kind of the hub for strippers and bachelor parties?"

"Believe it or not, there are strippers in L.A. too." I chuckle humorlessly as I push a button so the elevator resumes its ascent to the penthouse suite. The ride is mostly silent, a new awkward tension between us. But once the bell dings, she hesitates to step off.

"Two-nine-four-three is the door code. I'll go back downstairs and send Charlie up with your purse and such. Just call room service to order dinner, drinks, whatever you like. They'll bill me."

"Okay. Thank you."

When she still doesn't move, I ask, "Is something wrong?"

"Can I keep this for now?" She tugs on the lapels of my jacket.

"Of course. You think I'm going to parade you around in your underwear? Leave the dress, I'll clean it up. There should be robes in the hotel room."

Her smile is weak. "Thanks."

The elevator dings again and I have to kick the closing doors with my foot so they pop back open. "That's your cue."

She takes a step, then doubles back. "Okay. One more thing… When you're in L.A. at the bachelor party, are you going to…um… Well, you're going as single, right?"

No, she doesn't get to look at me with those sad puppy-dog eyes. She turned me down. She's the one walking away. "I didn't think about it, but yeah, I guess."

She swallows hard. "Should be fun."

I shrug passively. "Goodnight, Spencer."

Dragging her feet through the threshold, she trudges out of the elevator, leaving me alone with the tattered dress, corset, and the wreckage of tonight.

Of all the ways I thought tonight would end, the only thing I didn't prepare for was alone.

CHAPTER 35

Spencer

I've never done anything like this before in my life.

Fist raised, ready to knock, I nearly turn around, fleeing from Lennox's porch. I've heard girls do this: drop in on each other when they're in need, no apologies, just blind faith in the fierce bond that is sisterhood. I've just never had this before.

For five years my life has been filled with duties and obligations. Taking care of Charlie is what drove me. Work, school, and my sister are all I made time for, so while all my peers were bonding and developing lifelong friendships, I made peace with being alone. Even when I met Jesse, I felt alone. Actually, I think that's why I dated him for so long, and agreed to marry him. He didn't really see me. I was more of a consistent prop in his life. He didn't pay too much attention. He didn't want too much of me.

Nathan's his antithesis. The way he looked at me in the elevator last weekend set me on fire. All I could think about is how bad it would hurt if Nathan saw too much of me, and what if he woke up from whatever spell he's under. What if he saw me for what I am, and laughed?

I'm not crazy enough to think my boss would point and sneer like a grade-school bully. I'm *waiting* for him to see how mismatched we are. He's disgustingly rich, I live paycheck to paycheck. He's sexy, dripping with swagger. I'm constantly tripping over my feet. Nathan is built of bone and thick muscle, and I'm as soft as the Pillsbury Doughboy. I can't fathom what he sees in me. I don't know why he looks at me like I'm his sweet escape. It doesn't make sense, the same way it didn't make sense when the senior starting quarterback set his eyes on the nobody freshman.

I ran from Nathan because I was scared and that's what I do...

But I don't want to run away from my insecurities anymore, which is why I'm here. Sucking in a breath and holding it, I knock firmly on Lennox's door.

She answers and lights up, a surprised smile on her face until she sees the bag of Chinese food I'm holding. "Are you DoorDashing on the side?"

"No. Did you order DoorDash?" Shit. I didn't think of that. It's seven o'clock on a Friday night. I was just worried she wouldn't be home.

"We should've. Avery was supposed to make dinner." She raises her voice. "But three different types of dip isn't dinner," she calls over her shoulder.

Avery shouts something back I can't make out.

"Oh, I didn't mean to interrupt. Your husbands are here too?"

"Yes, funny thing about husbands—once you marry them, they're constantly around. Avery and I were just talking about how we need—" Stopping short, her features contort. She holds her belly, clamping just underneath her belly button.

"Oh my God. Are you okay?" In my panic, I drop the bag of Chinese food. "Is it time? Hospital?"

She exhales. "This kid has to cook for at least four more months. He's just trying to expand his real estate by rearranging my organs." Lennox flashes me a smirk as she points to the bag on the ground. "You may come in if there's lo mein in there."

"Yes," I giggle. "Two kinds."

"I'm kidding. You and Charlie are always welcome in my home. Where is she anyway? You guys are always attached at the hip."

"Birthday-party sleepover." In a show of solidarity, Claire refused to go to the birthday party that she got invited to but Charlie didn't. Miraculously, Charlie got her invitation the day after Claire declined. I am forever grateful to that little girl for being an angel when she should be in her brat era.

"Are you okay, hon?"

My turn to blow out a sigh. "I see you like a big sister, if that's not too much to dump on you. I always wish I had someone to be to me what I am to Charlie."

"Yeah, I get that. I'm an only child. I totally understand. You can talk to me about anything."

"Good, thanks." I bring in the food. "I'm here because I need to talk about sex."

I'm seated in a sofa chair as Avery and Lennox sit next to each other in the sectional, unsubtly nudging each other with their knees. They don't know who should talk next.

For the past thirty minutes, I've poured my heart out, explaining in great detail my awful introduction to sex at UNLV. I ran them through my awkward intimacy-scarce relationship with my ex-fiancé. Finally, I told them about Nathan, soup to nuts. The less-than-stellar start to our working relationship, our first sleepover, moving in, Casey showing up, all the way to my meltdown in the elevator when Nathan tried to go down on me. Then how I lied through my teeth telling him I wanted to just be friends.

I break the ice for them. "Do you think it's hopeless? Because he's been cold-shouldering me all week."

"How so?" Lennox prompts.

I glance through the window to Finn and Dex outside on the patio, buried deep in the Chinese food I brought. Lennox threatened lives if they finished off the pork lo mein, but in an attempt to evade the awkward "girl talk," they cloistered themselves outside with dinner and a six-pack of beer.

"He gave me the whole week off while he's out of town. I texted him and asked him how his flight was. All he said was 'fine,' then he warned me that IT was coming in to upgrade my laptop to a desktop computer later this week so I can have two screens. I haven't heard from him since. Do you think he's punishing me for rejecting him?"

Avery's mouth twists. "Babes, you told him verbatim you wanted a professional relationship. I don't think he's punishing you. He's respecting what you said."

I bite into my cheek. "I didn't mean it though. I really didn't. I care about him and I feel awful. After everything he shared about Elise, and how hard he's trying to work through everything to be with me, and I"—I groan in anguish—"I fucked it up so bad."

"Maybe a big romantic gesture?" Lennox asks. "I think I can get my hands on a jet that writes messages in the sky."

"Okay, Richie Rich." Avery scowls at her. "No. Something more sentimental. What's something Nathan really cares about?"

Good question. All Nate does is work. He doesn't like to drive. He swims for exercise. He cares about Charlie and her singing. "Oh! He likes piano."

"Maybe a little piano keychain or a music box that plays his favorite song?"

"Aw, that's sweet," Lennox adds.

"No. Jesus, stop," Dex gripes loudly.

We all whip our gaze through the large glass patio doors, surprised we could hear Dex's outburst. Finn's wearing a look of exasperation to match Dex's. They're both staring at us now.

"How are you eavesdropping?" Lennox asks.

"Windows are open, Len, and you're talking really loudly," Finn says. "We'd have to drive down the block to *not* hear your conversation."

They seriously could *not*. Oh my God. I've been chattering away like a monkey about every single one of my girl problems. *Oh, fuck.* I just accidentally overshared about my awful sex life with Jesse. I specifically likened him to a lazy gecko when he'd go down on me. I cover my eyes, convinced I'm going to die of humiliation. Yeah, that sounds about right. I was always destined for death by embarrassment.

Within seconds, they're piling in through the back door and join us in the living room. Finn sits and wraps his arm around Avery's shoulder, pulling her backward with him as he settles into the sofa-sectional.

Dex joins Lennox on the other side, with a small plate of food. "Here." He kisses her temple. "Feed my baby while you let the boys fix this." He says to me, "Please don't buy Nathan a piano music box. That's not how dudes' brains work."

Finn taps his nose twice and points to Dex in agreement. "Don't buy him anything. That's not what he wants. Nate and I have been buddies for a long time."

"You have?"

"Since college. We mostly lost touch after Elise died."

Avery runs her fingers affectionately through Finn's hair. "Who is Elise?"

"His assistant for years," Finn says. "Her ex was a dirty cop who beat her up for sport. It was so fucked up. Working for Nathan was her first real job because Peter wouldn't let her work. He didn't like her going out after he'd mark up her face. Nathan got caught in the middle. Even after she divorced Peter, he was still harassing her, so Nathan moved her and her daughter in with him. They were inseparable. Nathan dated around a lot before he met Elise, but she was it for him."

Avery presses her hand to her heart. "And she died?"

Finn nods. "Awful car accident. Nathan wasn't right for years. After her funeral, I didn't hear from him again until your birthday party. He called me for a business favor."

The night we met. House of Blues. Nathan was there because he knew Finn? He never mentioned it. "Wait. Elise's daughter died too?" I ask.

"Claire? No, she wasn't in the car. They took her from Nate when her mom died. She had to go live with her grandmother."

Her grandmother? I throw my hand over my mouth as that last piece of my déjà vu puzzle scuttles through my brain and slams into place. Claire looks so familiar because I saw her before. The little girl in the picture in Nathan's office. The beautiful redheaded woman and her almost-identical daughter. It's why Nathan's such a natural with Charlie. He's done this before. *Oh, Nathan.* He didn't just lose his fiancée. He lost his family.

My mind races, more of the story coming together. Ruby mentioned her son traveled a lot for work, which is why she took care of Claire.

"Finn, what happened to Peter?"

"Prison. After everything came out about him abusing Elise, he was sentenced. He just got out though. Nathan was pretty pissed about it."

Heart thumping against my rib cage, I sift through my memories like a mental scrapbook. I focus on every single time I've seen Claire. Were there any marks? Was she wearing heavy makeup to cover anything up? I can't remember anything concerning. Charlie has zero chill and would've told me if her friend was getting hurt. Maybe Peter was only abusive to Elise, but I'm furious at Ruby for lying to me. Charlie's been over there several times now. As her guardian, I had a right to know if she was around an abusive felon. I have to tell Nathan.

I have *so much* I have to tell him. Which brings me back to the conversation at hand.

"So, no presents?"

"Nope," Dex answers this time. "That's not what he wants."

"Then what should she do?" Lennox wonders out loud.

Finn and Dex exchange glances. "Which version are we doing? Are we giving general advice from guys and pretending like we didn't hear everything you guys talked about? Or do you want specific advice for your situation?"

Heat splashing my cheeks, I cover my eyes again. "Specific," I mumble.

"Send him a nude," Dex says simply. "*Ow.* What?" he adds after Lennox slaps him on the thigh.

"You Neanderthal. This is a man she's falling for, not a Tinder date."

"Not to mention, the last guy she did that for was a pig. It's not something she takes lightly," Avery says.

I sit silently as my friends run commentary about my love life as if they were announcers at the Super Bowl.

"Exactly," Finn chimes in. "It's a trust thing. If he opened up to you about Elise, he cares for you deeply, Spencer. And you in not so many words told him you don't trust him. If you give him what you gave Casey and let Nathan treat you better, that's all he wants."

"How do you know that?"

"I'm so confident, I'll punch Finn in the dick if he's wrong," Dex promises.

Finn's face pinches in offense. "The fuck?"

Dex shrugs innocently. "I'm trying to make her feel confident in your advice."

"Punch your own dick." He faces me again. "Ignore him. Listen to me. See this woman right here?" He jostles Avery goofily in his embrace. "Do you know why we're so close and I love her so much? Because we figured our shit out together. You don't need to be asking us for sex advice. If Nathan is your guy, then navigate this *with* him."

I shake my head. "I see what you're saying, but I really don't know what I'm doing. And I don't want to scare him off." The irony is that in an effort to not scare him off, I chased him away.

"Neither did I," Avery muses, slowly turning to smile at Finn. "But when you fall in love, it's not about being perfect. It's just having faith that even when you don't see the best in yourself, your person does. That's all it takes to make this work."

"It's that simple?"

"That simple." Lennox nods. "Believe us. We've already had our lessons in love. I'm sure there's more to come," she adds as she holds her belly, "but it all starts with being brave enough to trust someone with your insecurities. It's such a heavy burden to carry on your own. If you want a real, honest relationship with Nathan, then help each other figure it out."

I nod in agreement, questioning if I'm actually capable of that.

I'm good at burying things. I'm skilled at running and rebuilding. But can I trust someone enough to let them see all my ugly scars?

"Now that we've settled that, circling back to earlier, you said you had some questions about oral?" Lennox asks, entirely unashamed.

I've never seen two people jump to their feet faster in my entire life.

"Beer run?" Dex asks.

"See ya," Finn says by way of agreement.

I cackle as they practically trip over each other fleeing the room.

CHAPTER 36

Nathan

"Damn, Dawn. You're wearing the shit out of that suit."

Cigar in her hand, Dawn takes a twirl, showing off her sharp, navy-blue three-piece suit tailored to hug her slim figure. "I'm James's best woman, I had to bring my A-game tonight." She sits down at my table and tosses a coaster on the barrel table before setting her drink down. She's even drinking like the boys tonight.

"How'd I do?" I ask.

"On the bachelor party? Phenomenal. On keeping your dad somewhat sober? Big fail."

Dad's loud laughter bellows from across the room. He discarded his suit jacket somewhere. His face is tomato red and sweaty. There's ashes on his dress shirt from his latest cigar. He looks sloppy. And happy.

"When do the strippers get here?" Dawn asks.

Palm to the ceiling, I point at her. "Isn't that why you're here? Get back in your giant cake so I can roll you out for a proper grand entrance."

She raises her hand like she's about to backhand me. "Why, I oughtta," she says through a girl-like giggle. Ah, Dawn's drunk too. Everyone seems to be having a good time. Except me.

"Out of respect for Julia, there will be no dancers tonight. Just all of Dad's favorite things—bourbon, cigars, and a lot of old rich bastards." We golfed eighteen holes earlier this afternoon. Not my sport. I sat around in the golf cart with a beer, fighting the urge to text Spencer.

Another howl of laughter comes from my dad. I'm disturbed when I see the comedian causing his outburst. *Casey.* I really did like the guy until the charity event. Spencer's into him. I can feel it.

"What's wrong?" Dawn follows my gaze, trying to determine the sudden change in my demeanor.

"Casey's objectively a good-looking guy, right?"

"If you find gargoyles attractive, I guess."

"Someone's claws are out. What'd he do to you?"

Dawn rolls her eyes. "Best to keep my mouth shut. He's currently your dad's favorite pet." She grabs her glass and throws the rest of her drink back in one glug. She exhales with her mouth open, trying to soothe the burn.

"I've been dethroned," I mutter.

Dawn's lips curl into a sly smile. "You don't make a good pet. You talk back too much."

"I'll take that as a compliment." I pull two cigars out of my inside coat pocket before shrugging off my suit jacket. "Put that out." I nod to her cigar. She douses it in a crystal ashtray before taking one of mine.

"What is this?"

"Gurkha Black Dragons. They cost over a grand apiece. I was saving one for Dad, but I can't get him away from his puppy."

Dawn runs the cigar under her nose. "His loss."

I chuckle. "I brought more. It's all I'm indulging in tonight."

Dawn shoots me a sideways glance. "You're not drinking?"

I shake my head. Before I know it, I'm glaring in Casey's direction again. "I don't trust my temper tonight. Alcohol won't help things."

"She told you." Dawn exhales deeply.

"About Casey? Yeah. That's why she dumped me. Something's going on with them."

Dawn screws up her face. "Between Spencer and Casey? Not a chance." She hiccups once hard before pounding her chest with her palm. "Ah, fuck. One too many."

"It'd make sense. He's more her age. Less complicated."

She blinks at me. "What are you talking about? Spencer loathes Casey. What did she tell you?"

I drag my hand over my face, exhaustion weighing me down. This whole week has been a test of self-restraint. I can get over her, but I need more time. Maybe I'll hide out in L.A. for another week. "She told me he's stirring old feelings up and asked if we could go back to being...nothing. Boss and assistant."

Dawn's eyelids drop to half-mast. She smacks herself in the cheeks repeatedly.

"What're you doing?"

"Trying to sober up enough to see if I still want to do this." She teeters her head back and forth. "Yup. Too late. Nathan, Casey is stirring up feelings for Spencer because he's a traumatic trigger for her."

"No, she told me she slept with him consensually."

"And then he asked her to take naked pictures of herself for him. He and his dumbass football friends spread them around the entire campus with the word 'cow' painted on all of them. Thousands of students saw her butt-naked and made fun of her. Then she's the one who got scolded by school administration for inappropriately interacting with boys. If I were her mother, I would've taken those fuckers to court. But her mom couldn't even swoop in to protect her little girl because that very next week—"

"She died," I finish, a sudden nausea making my stomach spin.

"Five years ago isn't *that* long. She's still stuck in the worst moment of her life. Public humiliation does something to a woman. It twists her heart. Makes it so hard to trust again."

I feel my heartbeat in my ears. The room goes silent as I will myself not to move. *Breathe through the anger, Nate.* Just bottle it back up. I know I can't fix this. But I'm rageful with a deep-seeded fury that heats my body from the core. Adrenaline courses through me, taking over my limbs, and pulling me from my body.

I'm out of my seat, Dawn's empty glass in my hand.

Ignoring my better sense.

I'm across the room and my hand is around Casey's neck, slamming him against the wall.

Everybody's shouting at me, but I can't hear the words. I don't give a fuck. I've been so angry for so long. I want to choke the actual life out of him because whoever raised this piece of shit didn't teach him there are consequences to his actions.

Now, I'm his consequence.

I smash the cup against the wall, an inch from his ear. He whimpers like a little bitch when he sees the blood run down my hand, not understanding that it's mine.

"You're fired," I growl out, my face mere inches from his. "I don't employ scum."

I release his neck so he can breathe. "What'd she tell you?" he sputters out. "I didn't do anything. My buddies took my phone. It was just a joke, man."

"Even if I believed you, which I don't, doing nothing is just as bad. Did you pound the shit out of your so-called buddies for violating a young woman that way? Did you help pull posters down? Did you check on her? Did you fucking apologize? Did you do any goddamn thing the way a real man would?"

"Nathan, let him go," Dad says sternly.

I side-eye my dad, keeping Casey body-checked in place. I can't believe this punk ever played football for a Division 1 school. He looks pathetic and puny in my eyes. "Dad, stay out of it."

"Nate," Dad pleads. "We're all having a nice night. Don't do this."

"Tell my dad what you did to Spencer. Tell the whole room if you're so proud of it."

Casey clamps his jaws shut, unwilling to say a word.

"You want me to tell them?" I threaten.

He pulls in his lips. "I'm sorry, man. I'll tell her that I'm truly sorry."

I tighten my fist, wanting him to hear the loud crack of my knuckles. "No, you're going to stay the fuck away from her. Forever. Leave the city. Leave the state. I don't care. If you ever speak to Spencer again, I will break you, Casey. Starting with your face, then your wallet, your credit, your reputation, and anything else you give a shit about. I will hurt you like you hurt her just to prove a point. Don't drive me to extremes, because I love to keep my promises."

"Fine," Casey forces out. His cheeks are painted splotchy red. His embarrassment is only a small taste of what he did to Spencer, yet he seems like he's going to break under the pressure. "James?" He looks to my dad for help the very moment I step back.

"Casey, I don't know what's going on, but my loyalty will always be to my son. And if you hurt someone he loves, my hands are tied. I think you should go."

"And my job?"

"I don't see how—"

"Transfer him," I interrupt Dad. The suggestion comes from fucking nowhere, I don't even know why I'm doing it. I just do it. "You have up-and-coming projects in Orange County, right?" I ask Dad. "Assign him something else here. We'll pay for your move, whatever you need," I say to Casey.

Understandably so, Casey looks at me, his brows pulled with concern, trying to make sense of my confusing generosity. "Why the mercy?"

"I have no goddamn clue." I turn around to address the room. "I'm sorry, everybody, for my outburst. Please, get back to the party. Drain this entire cellar, on me."

Soon enough, a low rumble of chatter fills the space again. I look across the room at Dawn who stayed planted in her seat during the debacle. She gives me a subtle thumbs-up, her stamp of approval for avenging our girl.

Before heading to the exit, I pull my dad aside and try to offer my apologies for making a scene during his party. But he holds up his hands, stopping me.

"All this about a girl?"

"It's not like—"

"No, I hope it is, Nathan. You, flying off the handle, seeing red when someone wrongs the woman you've chosen to protect." He pats my cheek. "Feels good, doesn't it?"

"What?"

Dad grins, a bit drunkenly, but earnestly. "Falling in love again."

"I don't know if that's what's happening."

"Something's happening." He shrugs with a boyish smile. He's tipsy and wants to get back to acting silly, but I'm in no joking mood. I need to get out of his way.

"Goodnight, Dad. Have fun. *No strippers*," I say mock-sternly. "I promised Julia I'd keep you an honest man."

He snorts. "All right, son. Let me leave you with one more thing."

"What's that?" I ask, anticipating a corny dad joke.

"The best part about falling in love a second time is you have the chance to fix past mistakes. If you could've done anything different with Elise, what would it have been?"

I take a moment to really think. Our relationship was picturesque in my mind. I'd change all the pain Elise endured, but not anything about us. All I'd want is more time. "I wish we would've gotten married sooner. If she had to die, I wish she would've died as my wife. I still want Claire to be with me. I should've made that happen while I had the chance."

Dad yanks me into a hug. The smell of liquor seeps from his pores as he pats my back. "Then don't waste any more time, son. Go after what you want."

The minute I'm outside, I suck in a deep breath of California night air. This close to the water, I can almost taste the salty spray. I don't know why there's still a ball of lead in my chest. I confronted Casey. I solved the mystery of why Spencer panicked in the elevator. I don't think a man has ever treated her the way she deserves. She's been alone for so long, faking smiles. Maybe I make things too real for her, the way she does for me.

Real is messy and hard, but it's honest. And it's the only way forward.

Maybe it's time to lay all our secrets on the table, stop wasting time, and move forward together. I take out my phone to call her, but forgetting it was on silent, I'm met with messages from Spencer already.

> **Spencer:** *I don't know how else to apologize.*
>
> **Spencer:** *Or the best way to tell you how I really feel.*
>
> **Spencer:** *But please know, this is me trusting you...*

Then there's a picture that stops my heart. I have to blink several times to absorb what's in front of me.

She sent me a naked selfie.

Nothing's covered. She's offering me everything. Her full tits, dark, thick nipples, the smooth, tan flesh of her thighs, it's all a siren's call, and I want to crash my fucking ship into this beautiful woman. The only problem with this picture is that I can't spin it around and admire the view from the back.

I need to see her.

Right now.

I locate the blackout sedan Byron rented when we got to L.A. I punch in the numeric code to unlock the door and find the keys sitting in the cupholder. Not allowing myself to think about how much I hate sitting in a car, I start the engine and drive.

I'm not wasting any more time.

CHAPTER 37

Nathan

I park haphazardly in the roundabout driveway, leaving the keys in the car. My phone is going off like fireworks. From the notification previews it looks like Byron scolding me for taking the car without telling him. Hodge letting me know fresh surveillance will be ready soon. Dawn asking if I'm okay, wondering where I went. At the moment, I don't care about a damn message unless it's more from Spencer.

I bust through the house, making a beeline to the patio. I'm almost down the concrete steps and heading toward the guesthouse when I notice the blanket-covered lump on a pool chair a few paces to my right. *Spencer? Why is she sleeping out here?*

"Hey," I whisper, not wanting to startle her. She's sitting so close to the edge of the water, even a minor freakout would send her flying into the pool. I sit down on the pool chair closest, but my movement doesn't startle her. She's sleeping so deeply that if my entire body weren't coursing with adrenaline, I'd let my girl sleep. I'm too impatient to wait through her slumber. Purposely, I drag the chair closer to her, grinding the metal bars against the concrete to wake her.

I wait until her eyes fly open, round and startled. She blinks at me like she's seen a ghost.

"Good. You're awake."

The blanket falls to her waist as she sits upright. I survey her silky black pajama camisole wondering what in the hell possessed her to have a lonely sleepover with my pool.

"You startled me," she says.

"Now we're even." I grab my phone and show her the picture that nearly caused me a coronary. You can't shock a man like this with no warning.

"I'm sorry. I didn't know how else to—"

"Why didn't you tell me?" I can't sit here and listen to her apologize for nothing. She's misunderstanding why I'm here and what's going through my mind. I'm going to tell her everything. Tonight, I'm taking what's mine. But first, I need to know what she's thinking. No more secrets. No more surprises.

"Tell you what?"

"About Casey. I nearly ripped his head off tonight when I found out the real story." I thank my lucky stars we were in public. He should do the same. Had we been alone, my anger would've bested me. Casey might be taking a long nap in a shallow grave for his behavior.

"What do you mean—" She pauses. A quizzical look crosses her face. "Wait. How are you here? You were in L.A."

"I drove...fast."

"What time is it?" She peers at me, skeptically.

Ignoring the piled-up message notifications on my still-broken screen, I check the time. "Quarter past one."

I'm not sure if she's stalling with small talk, but she seems fixated on something I have absolutely no interest in. What I'm most concerned about is why she sent that picture. What she's trying to tell me. Where her heart is. Where her head's at. And the loudest question in my mind: Why are our clothes still on?

"You weren't on a date?" she asks out of left field.

Date? What the hell would I be doing on a date? "Of course not."

"You had a private block on your calendar," she explains, continuing with the third degree like she's trying to catch me in a lie.

I quickly explain that I had to switch the bachelor party venue. She thought the party was last night, when it was actually tonight, and vague on my calendar to surprise Dad. I'm distracted by my racing thoughts, ricocheting off the walls of my mind, so it takes me a moment longer to realize why she's asking so many questions. "Why? Were you jealous?"

A big part of me hopes she was. One, so I know she feels exactly the same as I do. Two, so I can easily put her mind at ease. She's the only woman that exists in my world. The only one who's been able to get through to me. It's Spencer, or no one. Plain and simple.

She confirms my suspicion with a sad little bob of her head. I try to find her gaze but she's staring at her lap. *Oh, sweetheart. Don't even go there.*

"If you think for one second I'd get over you that quickly, you must not know how I feel about you," I assure her.

She finally looks at me. Her light chocolate-brown eyes are glistening under the patio lights. "I thought I blew it and maybe you were trying to forget everything that happened between us."

"I couldn't forget if I tried. And I don't want to." I inch closer, craving her warmth. But I know once I get too close, there's no stopping me. I've waited too long. I'm going to take her right here on this pool chair, for starters. Round two in the bedroom. Round three in the shower. I'm going to love this woman until my body collapses. There's just one thing. "Where's Charlie?"

"A sleepover party she got invited to at the last minute."

Oh, thank fuck. "Good. I'm glad she's making more friends."

"Me too."

"Are you mad I pulled her on stage and asked her to perform at the charity event last week?" I ask.

Spencer assures me she's not. That's...new.

"You sure? Because this is a topic you get pretty huffy about... We share the same worries, Spencer. I promise. I would never put her in harm's way. Do you trust me?"

"I do," she answers so confidently, it's all the reassurance I need. My fingers itch to rip the blanket off her and pull her into my lap where I can hold her the way I desperately want, but she continues. "I mean with everything. I want to tell you the truth."

There's been so many secrets between us, I'm not sure which truth she's talking about. "What does that mean?"

"There's something else that happened with Casey but it was hard to talk about... Wait, you said you knew the real story."

Shit. *Sorry, Dawn.* I've no choice but to blow your cover. "Dawn slipped."

"So you know about the real reason I left school?"

I swallow the fiery lump in my throat as I'm reminded of it. It's not just the circumstance. It's picturing Spencer crying, alone, having her beautiful, healthy body shamed for reasons that only drunk, idiot college kids could justify. She was a woman before they could understand what that means. A real man sees curves and a plentiful body as sinfully seductive, something he can bury into and get lost in. The poor girl was beyond her years, lost in a pen of blind, shallow pigs.

Dawn said those posters read "cow." The dumbasses were so uneducated, they didn't know how to spell "queen."

"And now that it's all on the table, how do you feel about me?" Spencer asks. She takes in a deep breath and shows me a piercing stare. "Tell me the truth."

"You first... Why did you lie?" What she told me about Casey was a lie by omission, but still a lie. She had me thinking he was the better man, and I'd lost her to him somehow.

"Because I didn't want you to see my scars. I wanted you to see the good version of me."

"Spencer." My mind is jumbled, so many thoughts competing to be the first words out of my mouth. I don't know where to start. It's scary how quickly I got here again. Elise said something similar years ago. She didn't want me to see her scars. She felt weak and pathetic for staying with Peter for so long. I had to remind her over and over again she wasn't weak for staying, she was strong for leaving. Her scars were marks of her determination, survival, her will to live, and her everlasting love for her daughter. Her scars were admirable. Just as Spencer's are.

Now I've come full circle, once again falling for a woman who doesn't know her own power. She carries the world on her shoulder, and still apologizes when she barely stumbles.

"Why did you leave me on read? That hurt," Spencer says before I can collect a coherent thought.

Oh. She thought I was ignoring her? How could she possibly think I could ignore a gesture like that? "Casey was there. I just found out what he did and stormed out of the party when you texted me. I damn near had a heart attack. I couldn't think straight. I got in the car and started driving. I needed to tell you in person."

"Tell me what?" Her voice cracks as her eyes light up. She wants my confession as badly as I want to make it.

"That I know what this picture means. I know what it must've taken for you to send it after everything you've been through. I'll protect it. *And you.* You're safe with me."

She nods, mumbling in agreement, looking like she might cry if she tries to say more. But I don't want her to be sad. We've both been sad for so long. Right now, I just want her to feel good.

"It was a very nice picture." I try to layer a hint of seduction in my voice. It's been a while since I've done this.

"Are you going to keep it?"

I slide her a grin. "It's already my wallpaper."

We laugh together, but the lighthearted moment is quickly taken over by my *need* to touch her, now. I slide my hand up her warm skin, underneath the short sleeve of her top. I loop my finger underneath her bra strap, and her breathing immediately shallows. She grows tense and rigid against my touch. "This okay?" I ask as I peel the strap down slowly, giving her ample time to protest.

Instead, she nods shyly. It's not a matter of what she wants. She might be more anxious about how we'll get there. Nerves are apparent from her tense expression and ragged inhales. I trade her bra strap for her hand. After guiding it to my lips, I peck each of her fingers with sweet kisses. As much as I want to fuck her raw, *hard*, and unleash the months of frustration, I want to show her intimacy too. A little of what I need. A little of what she needs. We can meet in the middle. "Are you ready now?" I ask.

"For what?" Her eyes are transfixed where my lips meet her fingertips.

"A truce. No more games. No more lies. Just us giving this an actual try."

Her shoulders loosen like all the tension has fled her body. A soft smile touches her lips. "You're going to finally start being nice to me?"

"I didn't say that. I still plan on punishing you for teasing me with that picture." I mean to sound playful, but my cock twitches at the idea of bending Spencer over my desk and lightly punishing her bare ass. "You still have no clue what you do to me, do you?"

"I think I mostly infuriate you."

An unintentional laugh breaks free from my lips. In a way, she's right. It's so infuriating to lust for what you can't have. Tonight, that changes. I lean in close, breathing in her warmth. "How'd we get here?"

"Where?"

I stare at her plump, pink mouth that's just begging for my tongue. "With me needing your lips more than I need my next breath."

I smash my mouth on hers, a little more aggressively than I intended for our first kiss. I've tasted her before, but not like this, with her lips eagerly latching to me. She moans into my mouth as I weave my fingers in her hair.

I suck on her lips, feeling them swell from my passionate kiss, but it's not enough. I immediately need more. Bunching my fist in her hair I guide her head backward so she's presenting her neck. I kiss the tender, hollow space just above her collarbone. Her pulse thrums against my lips. My cock is unhinged, punching against my zipper, demanding to be freed. I know how this is going to go. I'm not anticipating a marathon even if I practice my best restraint. *Three years.* She'll have to forgive me if the first time I feel her, I'm overwhelmed. The least I can do is ensure she comes first.

"Stand up and drop your panties." I kick back my chair as I

rise. I give her plenty of room to stand, but she doesn't. Scooping under her elbows, I pull her up until she's on her bare feet, her toes polished in light pink. I tug free the tie on her pajama shorts and look at her expectantly. She still doesn't move. "Going to make me do all the work, hmm?" I hastily slide down her shorts and underwear. Before I can glimpse her, she covers herself with two hands.

"I didn't realize I'd be seeing you tonight," she whispers sorrowfully.

I peel her hands away and replace them with mine. I cup her sex protectively, not allowing her to hide. With my ring finger, I stroke against her crease glistening with her slick arousal. She whimpers and leans forward, her forehead resting against my chest.

I tease her entrance, swirling my finger around her opening, tapping playfully against that door. "Aren't you glad I'm here?"

"Yes, but…I'm a little prickly. Can you give me a minute to run inside and freshen up?"

"I cannot." I drop to my knees, unbothered by the hard cement pressing against my kneecaps. Preemptively securing her wrists in both my hands, I graze my lips back and forth against her mound, just a few inches above her clit. "Does it look like a little stubble bothers me? Be bare, be hairy, I love it all, baby. Just let me taste you."

Hands clamped tightly around her hips, I guide her backward until the back of her knees hit the chair, causing her to fall into a seated position. I swivel her legs around so she can lean comfortably against the back of the chair.

"Put your heel right here." I tap one edge of the chair before settling between her thighs. "Good girl." I tap again, on the other side. "Now your other foot, right here."

She throws her arms over her face, burying her eyes in the crook of her elbow. "Like this?"

"Almost. *Relax.* You look so beautiful. Fuck, your pussy is perfection. I need to see all of you. Let your knees fall to the side."

"Your dirty talk sounds an awful lot like instructions at the gynecologist."

Reaching up, I pop her lips with one finger. "Keep running your mouth and I'm going to fill it. Understand?"

I was only teasing, but her lips part and she sucks in a short breath. Her eyelids flutter as she bites down on her bottom lip. "Okay."

"Do you like when I'm harsh with you? Is that your kink?"

She shrugs. "I'm not really sure what I like."

"I hate to ruin the mood," I say, raking the inside of her bare thigh lightly with the backs of my nails. "But what did your ex do for you?"

"What he liked," she answers. "He'd mostly just—"

"No. Stop. I don't give a fuck what he liked. If he wasn't serving your needs, he's useless in this conversation. Forget him. I'm here now."

She nods, avoiding my gaze, going shy on me again.

I figured she was a little inexperienced. Spencer's never given me vixen vibes, but I didn't realize her needs were so neglected. "Let's start here. I want you to picture two scenarios and tell me what sounds better."

She takes in a shaky inhale. "Okay."

"What if I trail soft kisses from your neck to your thighs? I'll be gentle over your tits and nipples. Then, I'll tickle you a little when I dip my tongue in your belly button. But when I get to your clit, I skip over it. I'll tease you, blow on it, but I'll kiss around your pussy, touching you all over except where you want. I'll massage your thighs, while telling you how wildly sexy you are. I'll spend time with every single inch of your body before I finally suck on your little button and slowly build you up to sweet relief. How's that sound?"

She swallows, hard, and nods. "Yeah, okay. Do that, please."

"Don't you want to hear scenario two?"

"I guess?"

"I flip you over like a pancake on this chair. You put your

cheek against the chair, chest down, ass up, and I swear on my life, Spencer, if you drop those hips I will punish your ass with my hand. Except that'd probably only get you wetter, wouldn't it? You'll be dripping, *begging* for my cock, but I'm going to make you wait while I play with your body however I want. I bet you're so tight, I'd have to spit on your pussy over and over before you're lubed enough to even take my fingers. And when you're thoroughly spent from riding my hand, barely able to move, that's when I'm going to flip you back over and fuck you until your eyes roll back in your head. My way. My pleasure. Is that what you want?"

I was betting on tender romance when it came to Spencer, but her toes only curled around the bars of the chair when I started growling at her, describing ways I would use her for my pleasure. I push her knees apart wide and touch the entrance of her hot sex where a single drop of her arousal invites me. Her body is telling me *exactly* which scenario she wants.

I lick the tip of my middle finger and flick against her clit. Her hips buck at the stimulation, her back arching. "What's it going to be, Spencer? Do you want to make love, or fuck?"

She can barely speak through her rasps, but she manages, "Whatever you want."

"What I want..." I push my longest finger inside of her, groaning when I discover she's even tighter and wetter than I could've dreamed. She's going to show my cock no mercy. "...is for you to come."

"Okay, I can do that." Her determined reply confuses me for a beat. But when I gently work a second finger into her pussy, she lets out a sort of bizarre squeal. She moans loudly, and pairs it with a few "oh, oh, ohs." I stop pumping my hand and look up. Spencer's eyes are clamped shut tightly as she performs like she's auditioning for a bad porno.

"What the hell are you doing?"

She peeks through one eye. "It felt really good. I came. *Hard.* Your turn." She tries to scramble back upright, but I push her back down against the chair.

"You came," I deadpan.

"Yes." She blinks.

"I don't think we're defining that word the same."

She gives me innocent doe eyes. "What? I had an orgasm."

"Really."

"Yeah... A big one."

"*A big one*?" I bite down on my smirk. "Like an earth-shattering, sight-blinding, leg-shaking, euphoric-wave-of-pleasure kind of orgasm?"

Spencer thinks she's such a good liar, but that sudden aggressive eye twitch sells her down the river every time. "Yeah, Nathan. Can we move on? Do you want me to suck your dick?"

I'm no longer smiling. "No, I want you to get up." I climb off the pool chair and offer her my hand. As soon as she's on her feet, I jab my finger toward the main house. "Inside. Go to my bedroom."

"My room is closer," she points out. I realize the guesthouse is *right there*. It's not where I want her.

"I need you in my shower." I pick up her bottoms from the ground. When she doesn't move, I swat her bare ass and she squeals. "Move it, Spencer."

She does, scurrying a few quick steps so I'm out of arm's reach as I trail behind. *For fuck's sake, baby.* I thought we were done with all the fibs. Her ex may not recognize, or care, when a woman has a real orgasm, but I do.

I'm going to set the new standard right now.

With me, Spencer's not going to fake a goddamn thing.

She won't have to.

CHAPTER 38

Spencer

I'm trying to guess Nathan's next move, but I can't fathom why in the world he threw one of his nice goose-down pillows in the corner of the shower. Double doors wide open, we're both standing in the center of his enormous walk-in shower.

He led me through his bedroom, into his impressive master bathroom, which is senselessly large. The crown jewel of the bathroom is this space, enclosed by frameless, crystal clear glass. The recessed lighting, dimmed above my head, glows against the thin streaks of gold accents in the floor-to-ceiling tile.

I assumed he wanted us to get naked and have sex underneath the rainfall showerhead. I don't like how my hair looks when it's soaked, but then again, I don't like being paraded around naked, either. I'm having a hard time understanding why Nathan looks at me like I'm his prized possession, so wanton and alluring. But I already pushed him away once because of my insecurities, and it was followed by a miserable week of regret. I won't do that again, so I'm plunging into the deep end, letting him take whatever he needs.

"Take your top off and sit down." He points to the pillow he positioned.

I do as he says, tossing my shirt through the doors so it doesn't get wet. Fighting the overwhelming urge to cover my body, I step backward toward the pillow, but Nathan grabs me by the hand and yanks me close. Hunching over, he buries his face in my breasts, sliding his tongue between my cleavage. One at a time, he swirls his tongue around each of my nipples, before releasing me.

"Fuck, baby. You really think you can handle me?"

Hand around the small of my back, he draws me closer, his thick bulge pressing against my belly. I wedge my hand between our bodies. Mapping out his length, I stroke him through his pants, base to tip. "You're big," I admit. "But I can handle it."

"Prove it," he grumbles against my ear. "If you want my cock buried deep inside you, show me you can handle it." I paw at his belt buckle but he steps back before I can loosen it. "Not yet. It's going to be so good, Spencer, I promise you. But you need to earn it first."

"Earn it? How?"

He points again to the pillow, and I roll my eyes. "Make up your mind. That's where I was headed before you mauled me. You're getting in your own way here."

I spin around and Nathan jerks me backward, my back to his belly. He cups my tits and growls into my ear, "I can't wait to fuck this smart mouth of yours."

Smack! He sends me off to the corner with a firm swat to my ass. I'm tempted to linger because I want another. *Why does that turn me on so much?* The impact makes me out-of-control hungry for him. It feels so damn good to be *handled*.

I sit down on the pillow, my self-consciousness causing me to cross my legs.

He scowls, points at me with two fingers, then splits them open in a V—a wordless command for me to spread my legs. It's clear sex with Nathan is never going to be lights-off missionary, under the covers. This man is going to be my awakening.

I hike up my knees, opening my legs. His eyes are glued between my thighs as he licks his lips. I want his tongue more than anything. I want to be greedy for once and hold his face between my legs until I'm thoroughly sated, but Nathan doesn't join me. Instead, he grabs the detachable shower wand.

There's a loud hiss as he turns on the water, then quickly toggles the showerhead through different settings. He flicks past mist, rain, percussion massage, and lands on what has to be turbo power wash.

After checking the temperature, he flicks his wrist, sending a splash of water in my direction. My face pinches as the warm water hits my body. "What're you doing? How come you're still dressed?"

He lifts one shoulder and drops it. "Do you want me undressed?"

"Seems unfair that I'm naked and you're not."

"I'll compromise." He unbuttons his shirt and discards it near my top, but leaves his pants on. His muscular bare chest and his deeply defined abs, are enough eye candy to distract me for about ten seconds. But then I want to see more.

"Now take off your pants," I demand.

He sprays me with the water again, snapping his wrist so the burst of water arcs and rains over me. "Watch your tone. This isn't your show. It's mine."

"I'm sorry—"

"No. I don't want you to apologize to me. Just be my good girl and do what you're told."

I don't know what game this is, but I love it. He's so deliciously gruff and bossy. I can't get enough. "What do you want me to do?"

"First, tell me the truth. Did you come earlier by the pool?"

"Yes—"

With his perfect aim, the forceful stream of water lands right on my clit. "*Ah*," I wail at the intense, unexpected stimulation. My knees clamp shut and he lowers the wand again.

"Legs open, Spencer. Do not make me tell you again."

"Okay." I part my thighs, bracing for more overwhelming pleasure.

"I'm going to ask you again, but this time don't lie to me. Why'd you fake an orgasm out there?"

My head falls back as I fix my gaze on the recessed lighting. Nathan is relentless when he wants to get to the bottom of something. Fighting is no use. "I wanted to make you happy. I can't come from sex with someone else. It's not you, or any other man. I'm just difficult. My body's broken I think."

He smirks. "No it's not."

"*It is.* Believe me... It's never worked even once. Not even from oral. That doesn't mean I can't have fun though. I just can't seem to finish. But I still want it to be good for you."

Pressing his lips together, he shakes his head. "You've never had a man make your pleasure a priority. That's the problem. But I'm your problem solved, baby. Watch."

This time he teases me with the water, aiming for my inner thighs, edging closer and closer to my clit, but not committing. I thrust my hips forward and open my legs wider to give him an easier target, except he's missing on purpose.

The warm water taunts me. It feels so good beating into my skin. *So good, but not good enough.* I groan in frustration. "Nathan, *please.* Put it back."

"Good girl, that's exactly what I want." He takes a step closer, the pressure of the stream more intense now. "Beg me if you want to come."

"Please," I sing out shamelessly. "I want to."

My breath goes ragged, short rasps of anticipation as he moves closer, *closer*, torturously slow. "Remember, legs open. If you want to show me you can handle my cock, I want you to focus on staying spread for me, just like this."

I nod eagerly. "Yes. I got it."

"Yes, *sir.*" He lifts his brows. "I'm your boss in the office, *and* whenever you're naked. Clear?"

"Yes, sir," I answer obediently. Then, I'm richly rewarded. He concentrates the water right against my center, and immediately the tension beneath my navel begins to build. Rapidly. Faster than I can control.

"Oh...fuck," I groan. I try to absorb the pleasure, grinding my ass and heels hard against the floor. It becomes apparent why the pillow is necessary. I'd break my back against the hard tile wall and floor with the way I'm arching my spine. It's bearable for about ten more seconds and then the sensation strengthens past manageable.

Whimpering, mewling, crying, gasping... I can't think.

"You're doing such a good job, baby. You're so fucking beautiful. Almost there, aren't you?"

I bunch up my fists, refusing to close my legs. I want to. I'm way overstimulated. My toes have gone numb, my thighs are so ignited, they're useless. All I can do is sit here and allow the blinding surge of pleasure to build and build until I detonate.

"Oh my *fuck*," I scream. I don't even recognize my own voice.

I don't come just once. Hot, powerful peaks of sensation slam into me over and over in rapid succession, multiple climaxes rendering my limbs totally limp. My knees fall outward, my legs boneless. Nathan shuts off the shower, mercifully. A second later though, he's kneeling in front of me, assailing my still-sensitized clit with two deft fingers.

He flicks at my swollen bud a few times, torturing me with post-orgasmic ministrations. Then, his fingers thrust inside of me. He doesn't pump into me like I expect him to. Instead he curls them, shifting the tips of his fingers side to side...exploring, searching...

Satisfied with whatever he's found, he begins to stroke my inner wall causing a new sensation to unroot. A coil of heat unfurls *right* where he's touching. *Oh no. No, no.* "Nathan," I whimper. "Wait. Stop, I'm going to—"

Too late.

I'd blame it on the shower if I could, but it's shut off, dangling in the corner lifelessly, as I drench Nathan's hand. I clench but I can't stop what's happening. I'm helpless as he works my body over like he knew all along what I was capable of.

"That's it. Such a good job spilling on my fingers like this. Now I know what you look like...feel like..." His fingers slide out and he pops them into his mouth, sampling me. "...and taste like when you come. So don't ever shortchange me, baby. I need you weak with pleasure every time we fuck."

Weak, I am. My brain and body are rended. He catches me before I slump over and cradles my shoulders in one arm. His other hand brushes up and down my trembling legs. Tiptoeing up my thigh, he moves in for my clit. Powerless to fight him off, I turn my head and bite his nipple. "Don't," I simper. "Do not touch me there. It feels so good, it hurts."

He chuckles, jostling me in his arms. My body feels too heavy to move, so I simply fall against him, knocking him backward. He steadies his back against the shower wall and pulls me half onto his lap. Nathan looks down at me with pride and adoration, like I did something much more impressive than sit here with my legs spread while this man set fire to everything I believed about sex and orgasms.

I let out a soft, bemused hum of satisfaction. "It's kind of funny."

"What's that?" he asks.

"In a roundabout way, you're my first."

"First orgasm you didn't give yourself?" Nathan smirks.

"That too. But I mean this was the first time I really enjoyed myself. I didn't know it could feel like this. Is sex always this intense for you? Or is this new?"

His sexy, alpha demeanor has calmed. Mission accomplished, he goes back to a sweet marshmallow. "Everything is new with you. I think the intensity of sex depends on how much you care about a person. Obviously, we're explosive."

I nuzzle into his lap, his semi resting against my cheek. A reminder. "Hey, it's your turn." No way he's allowed anywhere between my thighs right now. I'll implode. But I can put him in my mouth. I reach for his damp pants, soaked in splotches from the shower.

He takes my hand, stopping its explorations. "Another time."

"You don't want me to?" I peer up at him, curious.

He rests his head against the wall, looking completely satisfied even though he never got relief.

"Spencer, I know this is a tough lesson for you, but sometimes it can just be about you. You can be the star and center of attention. You can take what you want without worrying so much about everyone else." His head descends to kiss my cheek. "This one was just for you."

CHAPTER 39

Nathan

My phone lights up with a bright glare. *Dammit*, I left it on the dresser. It's on silent but keeps going off, making my dark bedroom look like a rave. Carefully, I drag my body away from Spencer. She's in such a deep sleep, she's not remotely disturbed when I climb out of bed.

Grabbing my phone, I pad quietly out of the room. Thanks to the blackout shades, I had no clue it was already morning. Hodge has been calling every two minutes since six forty-five this morning. My stomach twists as I call him back. It can't be good news if he's blowing up my phone.

"Hey, boss."

"What the hell's going on? Eight missed calls."

"I found something you need to know, but because of who is involved, I didn't want to email. No paper trail."

"Talk," I grumble as I open my fridge, fishing out the jug of orange juice before grabbing a small glass.

"Ruby met with that contact again. I didn't recognize him at first, but I asked another PI buddy of mine. It's Zavala. An enforcer for the cartel. They send him all over to collect serious debts."

"Serious debts?" I fill my small glass to the brim, as I try to unpack Hodge's sobering update.

"A lot of cash or heads. Whatever they can pay with."

"Why the fuck is Ruby meeting with the cartel?"

"I'll do more digging, but probably because she's trying to pay off something Peter owes. I bet he went to prison owing them.

They got impatient, started harassing Ruby."

"Who lives with Claire," I grind out. "They can't harass a single grandmother and little girl."

"I don't think his family situation is consequential."

My blood goes hot with anger, and dread. Violent drug cartels don't get their reputation for mercy. Whatever Peter got himself into, he got Ruby and Claire involved in as well. "I remember Elise telling me Peter was an inside man for some crime organization. Is it possible he folded and told LVPD something that put his entire family at risk?"

"Not likely," Hodge grunts. "Snitches are dealt with swiftly. There are cartel enforcers in every prison you can imagine. If Peter were a snitch, we'd know because he'd be dead. I'd bet my life this is about an unsettled debt. Ruby's been hitting the ATM almost every two days, collecting cash."

After a small sip, I slam my glass down on the island. "You're just telling me this now? I told you to alert me of anything significant—"

"I didn't think anything of it until the fourth or fifth time, boss. She's an old lady. Cash is a thing of the past for us, but baby boomers still like to fill their wallets with bills and butterscotches. I just ID'd Zavala this morning. I'm piecing this all together as you are."

"Tail them both," I order. "I want daily reports now. I also want you to keep an eye on Claire. If anyone suspicious sneezes within a mile radius of her, I want to know about it."

Hodge sighs into the phone. "I mean..."

"What? Spit it out."

"What's your budget for this, boss? I'm one man. I'd need at least two more guys on payroll to keep up with all of them."

Why is this man testing my patience so early in the morning? "Hodge, let me be clear, when it comes to Claire, I have no budget. Got it? Just get it done. Eyes on everyone. Call me daily." I hang up, fully aware of my misplaced aggravation. I grit my teeth, picturing Peter's face. How much more damage can this fucker do? How is his tyranny transcending Elise's death?

"Good morning."

"What?" I snap. I spin around to see Spencer cowering in place. "Oh shit," I breathe out.

She's only wearing my shirt from last night and her black panties. She must've just rolled out of bed and heard me on the phone. "Sorry, I didn't—" she starts.

"Shh." I take two paces forward and wrap her in my arms before she can retreat. Rubbing her back soothingly, I murmur in her ear, "I'm sorry. *So sorry*. I got a call that pissed me off. Didn't even realize who I was talking to when you came in." I kiss the top of her head repeatedly, inhaling the sweet strawberry scent of her hair.

"It's okay," she whispers.

"It's not okay. I won't allow myself or anyone else to ever speak to you in that tone." I hook my finger under her chin and guide her gaze upward. "Okay? I didn't mean to make you feel bad."

She smirks. "I snuck up on you. Next time I'll approach with snacks. Maybe hold out my hand so you can sniff it first."

"So I'm an animal now? Hilarious." I tap the tip of her nose and she scrunches her face adorably. She looks so satisfied this morning. I like this look on her.

"What was the call about? Do you want to talk about it?"

"No." I regret my answer immediately. I've been carrying this on my own for so long, but I'm not sure how to lean on anyone else.

Her smile is half-hearted, but she nods as she pats my elbow reassuringly. "Okay, no problem. Can I make you some breakfast?"

"Wait." I follow the intuitive tug in my gut. I need to tell her. "Yeah, I want to talk about it."

We're both surprised. After a beat, her expression works its way back to neutral. "That's great too." She hops up on the kitchen island and lets me wedge myself between her legs.

I hold on to the outside of her thighs, steadying myself. "I had a daughter once. I don't know how else to explain it. You actually know her. She's friends with Charlie."

Spencer ducks her head. "Claire. I just found out she was Elise's daughter."

"You did, how?" I tilt my head, trying to remember who said what. I don't think I ever mentioned Elise had a daughter. It's not information I offer up easily.

"I talked to Finn."

"You went to my friend for details about me?" I'm taken aback. That was audacious. Then again it's Spencer. And I guess I have been a closed book.

She pokes out her tongue. "You're cute, but not cute enough for me to stalk you like that. Finn and his wife are good friends with my old boss, Lennox, and her husband, Dex. I just found out about Claire last night. I wanted to tell you, but there wasn't much time for heavy conversations last night."

"How are you feeling, by the way?"

She pumps her eyebrows. "Rested and ready for more lessons...*professor*."

My hand scopes up between her thighs. "Yeah?"

She clamps her legs shut tight, preventing me from reaching my intended destination. "First, let's talk though. What happened with Claire, I don't fully understand. Why did they take her away?"

"Elise and I were engaged, not married. I always intended to adopt Claire, but getting Peter to sign away his rights was a long battle we were preparing for."

Spencer blows out a heavy breath. "I hate to say this, but logic tells me... I mean Peter seems like he has the kinds of *hobbies* that are money motivated. You're not exactly strapped for cash. You couldn't pay him off?"

I tuck her hair behind her ear. "You don't think I tried that? Peter had a sick obsession with Elise. I don't understand his sociopathic behavior, but he wanted to own her at all costs. Not even money could dissuade him. And Claire was a pawn in his game to keep Elise within arm's reach. He didn't care about her, nor did he want to take care of her."

"Then I don't understand. Why didn't Claire stay with you after her mom passed?"

My throat closes with anguish. "Ruby," I manage.

"Ruby?" Spencer asks in a high octave. "Sweet grandma *Ruby*?"

I gulp down my disgust. "Ruby has a hard time seeing her son for who he is. An addict. An abuser. Her perspective is the world happened *to him*. She doesn't expect him to take any accountability for his actions. When he hurt Elise, she told Elise to be a better wife and try not to provoke him."

"What. The fuck. Who says that to a woman?"

"Peter was all she ever had. I think she needs him to stay a saint in her eyes. And now, Peter's out of prison, and his past is catching up to him. They're getting involved with ruthless crooks. Claire might be in danger and I don't know what the hell to do."

Spencer smooths the worry wrinkles on my forehead with two fingers. "You miss her enormously, don't you?"

"I do. But I imagine she hates me now. I told her I'd come back for her and I can't figure out a way. When it comes to family law, money has no persuasion."

"What if I invite her over to see Charlie? You guys could talk."

My palms rest heavy against the tops of her thighs, almost squeezing, like holding on to her is grounding me as I continue down the list of why nothing about this can be handled with reason or fairness. "Ruby is her legal guardian and has made it clear I'm not to have any contact. If she were to find out... And besides, I don't want to use Charlie. I could never do that to her."

God it feels good to talk about it though. It feels good to talk to *Spencer* about it. I've been holding this all in for so long, I needed the relief. This helps. The care and concern in her eyes are genuine. The way she's running her fingertips through my hair, comforting me.

"You're a good man, Nathan. One who's been through more than his fair share of pain. I'm so sorry."

I cup her chin, steadying her face. I sweep her lips in a gentle kiss. "I'm in less pain these days."

"Am I one of the reasons for that?"

I kiss her again, this time with more lust. I pull her bottom lip between mine and savor the feel of her softness—her warmness. "You're not just a reason. You're the only reason."

Reluctantly breaking our kiss, she grabs my cheeks in both hands. "Thank you. For seeing me, even when I didn't see myself."

My lips brush her forehead. "We're going to be okay."

Spencer nods in agreement. "Anytime you want to see Claire, you let me know. I'm not afraid of Ruby's reaction. My loyalty is to you. Say the word and I'll bring her here."

"Let me think about it." It's so tempting, but I'm still not sure how Claire feels. *Three years.* She's not a little girl anymore. I don't know what she remembers or what she thinks of me now. "Hey, this is random, but have you ever seen Claire with a golden locket?" I pat my chest where it used to hang on me. "It's small and the chain is kind of thick. I know it's a long shot but—"

"Nathan." Spencer's eyes water, the reflection of the morning sun gleaming off her pupils. "Is it a locket in the shape of a heart? You gave that to her?"

I nod, hope swelling in my chest.

"She's never without it. I know that locket well by now."

Tightening my jaw, I try to control the tremble of my lips. All the emotion I've been suppressing for years erupts from the depths I thought I buried them in permanently. "Thank you for letting me know," I say, weakly.

"My poor guy," she whispers, touching my cheek. I meet her gaze and she drops her hand. "Or, I didn't mean *my* guy. I meant... well, actually I don't know what we are. It was just an expression..."

"Just an expression? So you don't want me to be *your* guy?"

"No, I do. I mean, not yet. Unless you want to? Yes, if you want to, but if not...that's okay too." Her eyelids squeeze shut. "*Oh my God,*" she mutters to herself.

A crooked grin creeps over my lips. "You done?"

Eyes still closed, she nods. "Embarrassing myself? Mhm."

I take her by the hips and scoop her off the counter. She lands softly on her bare feet. I undo the singular button that's holding my shirt she's wearing closed. Her breasts pop free and my mind goes blank. All the worry, all the stress, the pain—it's lighter around Spencer. It's easy to feel happy even in the midst of disaster.

"Come." Clasping her hand, I pull her down the hall back to my bedroom. "Let me show you how *yours* I am."

CHAPTER 40

Nathan

"What time do you have to pick up Charlie from the sleepover?" Already shirtless, I shove my shorts down and fling them over my shoulder.

Spencer's seated at the edge of my bed, heels hanging on the adjustable bed frame. "About noon. Why?"

"Because I'm going to take my time with you."

She shrugs out of my shirt. She doesn't seem so shy this morning. "You can do whatever you want to me." She bats her lashes.

Pushing her backward on the bed, I plant my knee between her legs. "Good to know." I palm her tit in my hand, massaging her soft flesh. She moans when I roll her nipple between my thumb and forefinger. I tighten my grip until she lets out a high-pitched squeak. Releasing her, I suck where I pinched, lapping away the pain. I treat her other nipple the same way as the first. I'm testing how I affect her. Learning how she likes to be handled.

"Can I tell you something?" Her tone is full of tepid nerves. She's quick-witted in any other circumstance, but when she's naked, she gets so submissive. I have her exactly how I want her. *Mine, mine, mine.* She's at my mercy, just like I'm at hers.

"What?" I breathe against her ear, as I tug on her panties. She obediently bridges her hips, allowing me to discard her underwear.

"I want to be good at this for you. And I don't want your approval out of pity. I want to make your head explode like you did mine last night. One for one. Every orgasm you give, you get."

I smirk, staring into her blazing eyes, full of some fierce determination this morning. "Under that logic, you technically owe the showerhead a bust."

"Nathan, I'm serious. What do you like?"

I climb off of her and roll over flat on my back and tuck my hands behind my head. "For starters, I want you to ride me."

She obeys my request like it's a demand. Hiking her leg over my hip, she rubs her warm pussy against my briefs. I spring to life, bucking my hips, grinding my cloth-covered cock against her crease, craving her heat. She pushes down my waistband, freeing the crown of my cock.

Fuck.

My thighs tense as my tip gets a teasing taste of her wetness. It's taking all my willpower not to lift her up and drop her on my cock, burying deep inside her in one thrust. That's all it'd take for me to explode inside of her, coat her walls, leave my mark, and claim her. *Goddamn do I want to.* But I made myself a promise.

"Spencer, when I said ride me, I meant my face." I lick my lips. "Right now, baby. Sit it on my face."

She hesitates, her eyes pooling with concern. "Um, I don't— *Ah!*" She yelps when I grab her roughly. Hooking my arms firmly under her supple thighs, I yank her up until her pussy crashes into my face. I position her so her clit is resting on my upper lip. I slide my tongue inside, letting her sweet tang drip into my mouth.

Spencer's silent now. She's too focused to protest. My cock hardens even more when I feel her subtly buck against my mouth as I fuck her with my tongue.

"Oh good girl. Just like that."

She stills. My praise is spooking her. She rises to her knees, trying to lift her weight from my face. "I'm sorry. I'm going to suffocate you."

"Then I'll die a happy man." I grab her hips and guide her back down. Squeezing her ass, I encourage her to grind against my face. I moan, permitting her to enjoy the ecstasy of my attention, everywhere. Once she succumbs to the position, she rolls her hips eagerly, her range of motion allowing my tongue to barely tickle her asshole.

The way she shudders is a clear invitation. She wants me to guide her. To show her everything. To relish every single part of her with animalistic need. I throw her to the side, press her legs together then bend them out of my way. "Hold your knees," I tell her as I lift her ass. My tongue goes exploring over every fold. Nothing untouched. I lap at her from ass to clit, over and over until her legs start to shake.

She whimpers out something I can't understand.

"Stubble... It's your fucking stubble. *So good*," she pants.

Cluing in, I rub my rough cheek against her clit and it sends her into hysterics. She cries out as she comes hard, unabashed, screaming obscenities as she bunches the comforter in her fists.

I rip off my briefs. Desperate to catch the end of her orgasm, I plunge into her. *Oh fuck, way too tight.*

I let out a roar-like groan. Her gasp is fearfully dramatic. I went too far. I meant to be gentle and give her time to adjust, but I lost my head. "Are you okay?"

"Yes, yes, fine," she assures me. "You're so big."

"Does it hurt?"

"Yes, but in a good way. I'm so full. I'm ready. Fuck me, please."

Doubting my better sense, I take her command. I drag my cock out slowly, and thrust into her again. She clutches my ass in her hand, inspiring me to go deeper. She bucks her hips, begging for friction. I know she wants more, but she's so tense, I'm going to split her in two if I fuck her the way I want. The way she's squeezing the life out of my cock, I know any sudden movement will cause her serious pain. "Slow down. Relax for me."

She drops her hips to the bed. Her tits rise as she takes a deep breath.

"There you go, sweetheart. Slow is good too." The saliva pools in my mouth and I angle my head to let it free right over her swollen, pink clit. It drips over both of us, making my movements smoother. "There it is. How's that?"

She answers with a throaty moan. Her whole body in a cathartic trance as she melts into the mattress and lets me work her over with long, languid pumps into her throbbing heat. There's not a proper word in the English language to describe her pussy. *Good* is an insult. *Paradise* falls short. "Baby, *baby*, goddamn, you're my fucking angel. But stop moaning like that, you're going to make me come."

She can't stop. Between her whimpering and gasping, the way her mouth stays open and her expression is twisted up in uncontrollable, needy greed, I can't hold on any longer. I pull out at the last minute, coming on her stomach.

We breathe in stillness for a while. Her eyes fall shut, as she escapes into her personal euphoric sedation. I roll over and lie down next to her, searching for her hand. I weave my fingers through hers and hold her tightly.

"What's going through your head?"

"Right now?" she murmurs, hoarsely.

"Mhm."

"I can't tell you." Her voice cracks. "It's too soon. It'll scare you away."

I smile to myself, assuming what she means. I thought sex with another woman would be wrought with sadness and remorse. But I don't feel anything right now except calm. Outside of my physical satiation, I'm relieved it feels different. Sex with Spencer has nothing to do with past intimacy. It gives me sincere hope that falling in love again doesn't mean I'm replacing Elise. It means I'm living again, which is what I know she wanted for me.

And even if I can't do it for myself, I can do it for Spencer. Even if I'm scared to dive in, this woman deserves a man who wakes up with gratitude every day. One who decorates her, head to toe, in rare jewels. A man who defends her honor and becomes enemies with the ones who've wronged her. She deserves a man who hates rodents but nearly gave a guinea pig mouth-to-mouth because he loves her so fucking much, it inevitably spills over into every other interaction.

And maybe there's another guy out there who is just as worthy...

Maybe worthier.

But we'll never find out. Because I'll be damned if I ever let go.

Spencer squeezes my hand twice. "Still with me?"

"Yeah, I'm here."

"What's going through *your* head?"

Rolling onto my side, I nuzzle her neck, then plant a soft kiss on her temple. "Can't tell you. It'll scare you away."

CHAPTER 41

Spencer

"Charlie!" I shout down the hall.

"I'm almost ready!" she yells back. "Chill."

The nerve of this kid. I'm ready to go. Spike is ready to go. Charlie, as usual, is holding up the entire operation spending an extra twenty minutes in the bathroom this morning carefully putting on her new makeup. I think Nathan sexed me into a blissfully permissive state, because on Sunday I took Charlie to Ulta and told her she's now allowed to wear mascara. I didn't anticipate how much time a few swipes of mascara would add to our morning routine.

There's a light knock on the front door of the guesthouse, surprising me.

It can't be Nathan. He left early this morning to meet with someone named Hodge. I remember specifically because I told him Hodge would be a cute nickname for a hedgehog. Nathan then told me if I brought any more rodents into his home, he was going to spank my bare ass. I pretended to scowl, but good grief, that threat does things to my insides. A part of me wants to provoke him into delivering, just to see.

We fucked all weekend. We also had sex. I think we also made love. I shamelessly let Charlie have her iPad and junk food for an entire day so Nathan and I could steal away and explore each other's bodies. I wasn't ashamed or clumsy. I stay focused on feeling good...on making him feel good, and just like my friends advised, it fell into rhythm. I'm not sure why I always thought hot sex was about attractiveness and technique. Turns out, it's about trust.

When I open the door, I'm greeted by a man in a black suit and sunglasses. He looks like he just stepped off the set of *The Matrix*. "Hello?"

He peels off his sunglasses and flashes me a toothy grin. "Hey, Ms. Spencer. I'm Miller. Mr. Hatcher sent me to take you to work."

I squint in confusion. "Uh, I think we got our wires crossed. I take my little sister to school, then go to work."

Miller nods. "Yes, ma'am. I'm tracking. First to Beaumont Middle School, then to Brickstone Headquarters. Also, let me know what time you'd like me to take you to lunch or pick something up. I'm told a 'Mr. Spike' needs baby carrots promptly at noon. I was hoping you could provide clarity on that. How many baby carrots, and who exactly is Spike?"

I blink at him, trying to absorb the nonsense information he just dumped on me. I jut my thumb over my shoulder to Spike's carrier on the coffee table. "Spike is a guinea pig."

"Ah," Miller breathes out. "Okay, that makes more sense. I was confused by this morning's email."

"Pardon me, but I'm still confused. Who are you?"

"Your driver." He smiles. "And task master. If there's anything you need, I'm at your service."

Okay, this makes more sense now. Nathan hired me my own personal Byron. "Thank you very much, but I'm okay. Charlie and I have a routine. I'll talk to Nathan when I get to the office today."

Charlie sneaks up behind me and peers at Miller. "Oh my God, are we taking a limo to school?" She bounces on her heels.

"No. We're taking our SUV as usual. And you need to wipe off that blue eye shadow stat. *Go. Now.*" I point to the bathroom, sending her off with my best I'm-not-taking-your-shit-today face. I turn back to Miller. "Tweens. Give them an inch, they take a mile, you know?"

He nods and smiles again like he's obligated to. "I'll have to take your word for it."

"Are you out of a job if I tell Nathan I don't need a driver? I already have a company car but I don't want you to get let go. I'll put in a good word, I promise."

"Uh..." He scratches the back of his head, the tip of his nose puckering before he continues, "About the company car..."

I've been stewing the entire way here. Even Charlie sat in silence as Miller dropped her off in front of school. Spike didn't release a single squeak. Clearly my sister and her guinea pig could read the room.

I storm through the front doors of the office, making a beeline to the elevators. I punch the elevator button with the heel of my palm, unnecessarily aggressively. Now Spike releases a weak *mweep, mweep*, politely letting me know he does not appreciate the bouncy ride, a consequence of my anger-fueled power walking.

The first thing I notice when I get upstairs is Nathan's doors. I can't see him through the crystal clear glass. Instead, some kind of foggy window film has been installed as a privacy shield. I grumble, annoyed, knowing I can't just burst into his office and rip him a new one. After setting Spike down underneath my desk and promising I'll free him soon, I reach into my desk drawer searching for a sticky note. Nathan will absolutely come looking for me any minute now, and when he does, he'll see a note on my desk that says I went car shopping since he felt the need to confiscate my company car.

I open the second drawer of my desk and snag a pink sticky note. I'm stabbing my pen into the innocent paper when I notice my mini donuts are missing. Opening the drawer wider, I lean over in my chair, ensuring they didn't roll into the back.

No. They are most definitely missing. They were sealed, so there's no way maintenance came by and tossed them. Maintenance never goes *in* drawers, unless there was an ant infestation or something. I quickly check my other drawers and see the contents untouched. That's so strange. Who would—

Oh, you've gotta be fucking kidding me.

I clutch the pen so hard in my hand I break off the clip.

That does it. I don't care if he's in a meeting.

After flying out of my office chair, I burst into Nathan's office. He's at his desk on a call that he promptly ends when I enter.

"Good morning, gorgeous." He flashes me his stupid billion-dollar smile. I want to use his perfect teeth as target practice at the moment.

"Was I interrupting?" I glare at his phone.

"Nothing important. And even if it were, you're welcome to interrupt me anytime. I love that dress on you. Hugs your body just right." He raises his brows. It dawns on me why my boss had his office doors frosted. Foolish decision. The only thing he's getting behind closed doors is my wrath.

As I glance around, I notice subtle changes. The pink furniture is still here, but the pillows have been replaced. The rug is gone. The pink wallpaper on the accent wall has been stripped. "You're remodeling?"

"In stages. I would've asked for your help but..." He gestures around the room. "We tried that once already."

Approaching the opposite side of his desk, I jab my finger toward his face. "Stop smiling."

"Hard to do around you, pumpkin. What's wrong?"

"You have to ask?" I'm seething, further provoked by his joyful nonchalance.

"Yes. Which is why I did."

The smug bastard is relishing my attitude for some reason. I hate how sexy he looks in...everything. *Ugh.* "You took my company car. You can't do that. It's part of my contract."

"Pretty sure *not* fucking your boss is also in your employment contract, but we did a lot of that over the past couple days."

I narrow my eyes at him, daring him to get on my angst level. "That's most definitely not outlined in my contract. I checked. And you need to take me seriously right now."

He pushes back from his desk, folding his arms over his chest. "I upgraded your transportation to a personal driver that can provide you with security and give me some peace of mind. Now that we're together, your safety is my priority. Charlie's as well."

"When did you decide we were together? Were you going to inform me of that or simply continue to make life decisions on my behalf?"

"Life decisions? It's just a car, Spencer."

"*Just a car*?" I ball up my fists like a cartoon character who's about to explode. "Spoken like a man who has never had less than twenty dollars in his bank account and in shambles about how to afford groceries for the week. A car is a big deal, Nathan. *Huge deal.*"

"All right," he says calmly. "I have a team coming in today to move your stuff and Charlie's belongings into the main house. I didn't want you to have to lift a finger, but now I'm thinking that's also going to piss you off."

I curl my fingers into claws like I could squeeze his head right off. "You're unbelievable. And do I get my own bedroom, or are you going to keep me in a cage in your oversized closet?"

"What has gotten into you today?"

"You stole my snacks!" I blurt out. My head rolls back, my gaze to the ceiling. *Dammit.* I really thought I was handling this argument intelligently until that little outburst.

Nathan's smirk is back. "Is that a deal breaker? Do we have to break up, or can I just replace your snacks? Also, what snacks did I steal?"

"How can we break up? We're not together!"

Anger flits in his eyes. "Stop saying that."

"It's not because I don't want to be, Nathan. But we have a hell of a lot of stuff to figure out. I have to find a new job—"

"Why?"

"This isn't professional anymore." I indicate his office doors. "And I *know* why you got the glass covered up all of a sudden."

He pumps his eyebrows, full of flirty energy. "Smart girl."

"I'm not just a sex toy for your leisure. I'm a woman, and a momster—yes, that's a mom and sister combined—and I need to know that my dating life won't negatively affect my responsibilities. I don't want to keep starting over in life. If you continue swooping in, saving the day, throwing your money around at problems like they're silly, when you eventually get bored of me, I'll be left with nothing. Charlie will have *nothing*."

"How could I get bored of you?" He balks in surprise. "You keep me on my toes, Spencer Riley. For example, I thought we were going to have a pleasant Monday, with me getting to enjoy my girlfriend not only at home, but at the office too. Instead, she's here first thing in the morning, complaining about all the thoughtful things I've done for her, accosting me about nonsense."

"*Nonsense*? You know what." I raise my hands in the air. "Let's take a breather. Your assholery is full throttle." I stride toward the door.

"Don't walk away from me."

Ignoring him, I yank the door ajar, but he's in front of me in a blink. He pushes it back closed, steps in front of me, blocking the handles with his body. "Sit down," he growls. "You try to flee again and I'll pull that skirt up and punish your bare ass. Got it?"

"It's cute you think that's a threat."

"Not a threat. It's a promise." He reaches behind his back and locks the door. "Take a seat. Let's talk."

I match his glare. "What happened to my mini donuts? Two packs. They were in my desk drawer."

Nathan issues a humorless laugh. "Why? Were you particularly attached to donuts for some reason?"

"Perhaps."

His eyes shift from their usual bright blue green to a stormy gray, looking angrier by the second. "Why? Were they a trophy of some sort? Like some sleazy guy wrote his number down, trying to seduce you with some cheap-ass donuts?"

Admission. He took them. "They were a thank-you gift."

"Thank you for what?"

I lift my chin, challenging him. Clearly I'm dead set on self-destruction today. "For handling his pump."

"What the fuck did you just say?" Oh, now he's mad. Really mad.

"I said I handled his pump." I hiss out a breath of frustration.

I need some space. I don't know how to sort through this. Nathan is being protective, but too controlling. If he were my husband, sure. I'd love a man taking any and all measures possible to protect me, but we still haven't established if we work. Not only are we from very different worlds, there's the matter of Elise. As much as I want him, I can't be Nathan's permanent stand-in. We need more time.

"You want to explain that to me in layman's terms? What *pump* are you referring to?"

I roll my eyes. "Move," I grumble. "Your overbearing, bosshole behavior isn't charming this morning. I want to go." I reach through the space between his elbow and side, intent on unlocking the door and leaving the scene. He catches my hand, threading his fingers between mine, squeezing tightly.

"Couch. Now."

"I said I want to go."

Ignoring my protests, he tows me toward the office sofa. "Strike one was saying we weren't together. Strike two was trying to win an argument by leaving the room. Strike three was that smart mouth of yours, insulting me. If my feelings for you are overwhelming, bummer. Make your peace with it, pumpkin, because they aren't going anywhere."

In a fluid motion, he sits on the larger sofa, then shuttles me down over his lap, belly first. I grunt when my stomach hits the outside of his thigh.

Oh no. But also...

Oh fuck, yes.

He plants his forearm across my upper back, forcing my cheek deeper against the velvet cushion. "Nathan, what are you doing?"

He hikes up my skirt, exposing my ass and thong. "Keeping my promise."

CHAPTER 42

Nathan

Spencer's quivering in my lap. Her ass is bright pink on both cheeks.

I smack her again, brightening the mark. Her skin is hot to the touch. I wanted to stop four swats ago, but she's mewling like a cat in heat.

She gasps. "Oh, fuck. *Again*."

"It's supposed to be a punishment. You like this?"

She buries her face in the couch. "No," she muffles.

"Liar." *Smack!*

This time she yelps too loudly. I have to stop what I'm doing and reach around to cover her mouth. "Hush, Spencer. Take it quietly. We're at the office." I give her a light, warning swat and she spreads her legs so my next smack lands between her thighs.

As soon as I free her mouth, she pleads with me. "Then hurry up and make me come."

"Greedy little thing. The other part of your punishment is I'm going to leave you wanting. Next time you say something ridiculous like 'we're not together,' remember how this feels."

"I didn't—"

"Shush. The damage is done." I guide her off the couch, onto her knees. "You hurt my feelings."

Her long, thick hair has mostly fallen loose from her low ponytail. Her eyes are watering, eyeliner slightly smudged. Her cheeks are glowing red. "Sorry," she offers. At first I think it's genuine, and I mean to tell her I'm only teasing. But then she opens her sassy little mouth again. "My mistake. I did not know bossholes came equipped with feelings."

"Are you trying to provoke me? Isn't your ass raw enough?"

She smiles like a vixen. "I can take it."

"Can you? Open your mouth." I unbuckle my belt. There's a loud *whip* when I pull it free in one sweep, letting it drop by Spencer's knee. "You do the rest."

Her eager hands are fumbling with my pants button. I flinch when she unzips me, worried she's going to nick me in her haste. She manages to get my cock free, rock hard, with a single drop of precum dressing my tip. "Deep breath, baby." I wrap my hand around the back of her neck, drawing her closer.

After a few fortifying breaths, then one long pull of air, she opens her mouth wide. I dive into her throat with zero restraint. *Fuck, that's euphoric.* It's wet and warm, just like her pussy, and my head is spinning seeing her pretty face right there on my dick. There's not a part of this woman's body that doesn't feel like utopic bliss. As much as I want to rest here, I pop out of her mouth as quickly as I plunged in.

She sputters and gasps, drool coating her lips. Panting, she demands, "Again."

"Slow down. Breathe."

She swallows another mouthful of air, then attacks me with her lips. She's done this for me before, but tentatively. Her tongue danced delicately around my shaft, like she was afraid of offending my cock. Today she's latched on and hell-bent on sucking me dry.

"*Slow, slow, slow,*" I beg. She's fucking me with her mouth like an expert and I'm losing control of the situation. She swirls around the tip, shamelessly pressing her tongue against my hole. I take calming breaths, trying to prevent my balls from tensing too tightly, but when her gaze flashes upward, landing on me, it's too much. It's the most arousing sight—her big beautiful eyes tear-streaked from strain, mouth full of my throbbing cock. But it's when she moans, mouth stuffed, sending vibrations up my shaft, I have to throw my hips backward. I slide out from between her lips with a soft pop.

"What?" She wipes under her eyes and sniffles. "You were close, I could feel it."

"You didn't come."

"I thought that was my punishment. Or is your memory impaired at the moment?" she snarks.

I brush the hair away from her damp forehead, and tuck it behind her decorated ear, the pink diamond studs still in place. "You know that sassy mouth drives me crazy, don't you?"

She nods with a warm smile.

"You're always one step ahead, something up your sleeve."

Her smile shrinks a touch. "Am I too much?"

"Maybe for a weaker man. You're perfect for me." I fist the tip of my pulsing cock. "Climb on, baby. They were empty threats. I want to feel you come."

She tugs up her skirt with urgency, drops her thong, and straddles my legs. I brace her by the small of her back, planting her down onto my cock. We both moan in agonizing relief. Filling her is so much pleasure, but at the same time, not enough. Gripping her ass, I try to guide her movements, but her range of motion is limited because she's trying to hold her weight on her knees.

"Spencer," I rasp into her ear.

"Mmm, yes, so good," she mewls, but it's disingenuous. I know this because when she's lost in pleasure, her face locks in shock, eyes wide, jaw slackened, like she's surprised sex is so enjoyable. Instead, right now, her brows are furrowed in determination.

"What's wrong?"

"Nothing," she insists.

"You don't like this position," I state firmly, not giving her room to argue.

She rests her forehead on my shoulder. "I feel awkward."

"Because you're not relaxed."

She shrugs. "I'm smothering you like this. It's hard not to notice. Do I feel too heavy—"

"Stop." I shush her. "Get out of your head. You don't feel like anything but so fucking good. Try this." I unbend her legs, one at a time, so she's resting on her heels instead of her knees. I hold out my hands as handles. "Hold tight."

She lifts up and slams down on me, feeling the full impact of my cock. No words, just groans of pleasure as she slides up and down my pole like a seasoned performer. *There's the look I was waiting for.* Her eyelids are heavy, lost in the ecstasy.

"How's that, baby?"

She answers by picking up the pace, using me for her pleasure. Her low groans evolve into loud shrieks. I thrust my hips, slamming into her hard. Spencer belts out an alarming cry and I have to place one of her hands on my shoulder so I can cover her mouth.

She shakes off my hand. "Sorry, sorry," she says quietly between gasps, still riding ferociously.

"No apologies," I remind her. "You ready to come?"

She nods with fervor. "Please."

"Please, what?" I buck my hips hard, getting deeper than before.

"Sir, sir, sir," she rushes out.

"Good girl." I cup my hand over her mouth again. "Now scream."

I pummel into her with wild abandon, fucking her like a madman possessed. She doesn't just scream, she bites the inside of my finger, trying to stifle her sounds. I come hard, spilling deep inside as she continues to ride me through my release.

Gripping her hips, I slow her pace as I flinch at the extra stimulation.

"I liked that position." She settles back on her knees on top of me.

"Me too." I guide her off my lap to the side, but when she leans down, reaching for her underwear, I kick them aside. "You didn't finish."

She blinks at me. "But you're done..."

"Spin around. Grab the back of the couch." I fetch a few tissues from my desk before returning. "Spread your legs."

She shimmies her knees apart, and my cum seeps out of her. I catch my release with the tissues, wiping away the excess. She starts to close her legs as if we're done. I have to pry them back apart. I sit with my back resting against the edge of the sofa, head between her legs. Curling my arms around her plentiful thighs, I direct her pussy to my tongue.

She resists. "Nathan, you just came in me."

"Sit," I growl out while I spread her legs wide until her warm clit finds its home on my tongue. The little I didn't wipe away, I clean up with my mouth, unapologetically. It's a new level of intimacy for her, but soon she'll get used to no secrets, and absolutely no shame between our bodies. I suck and nibble in rhythm until I feel her thighs start to tense. Her toes curl against my shoulders, and while she comes quietly, her body dances—writhing, bucking, and riding the waves of her climax. When she's done, she collapses to the side, too weak to speak or stand.

I pull up onto the couch. Lifting her head, I slide in beside her, my lap as her pillow. I stroke her hair sweetly, eliciting more of those satisfied sighs and sedated purrs.

"You still mad at me, pumpkin?"

"Yes."

"What was more offensive? The car or the donuts?"

"The combination," she murmurs against my leg.

"Let's go shopping for a car if that makes you feel more secure. One that's all yours, in your name. Even if you leave me, it's yours to keep."

She rolls in my lap, looking up to meet my gaze. "Me leave *you*? You don't honestly worry about that, do you?"

I trail my finger gently from her hairline, over the bridge of her nose, then grazing her lips. "You keep saying we're mismatched, but I think you're confused as to who has the upper hand."

"Why? You could have anyone you want."

"I'm a selfish man. I want the woman who didn't give up on me, even when she should've. I want the one I don't deserve."

Her eyes shimmer with a medley of emotions that she doesn't

reveal with words. She rolls back over, facing away. "When I move into your bedroom today, I want the bigger closet."

I chuckle lightly, causing her head to bounce. "Steep ask. Something I'd only do for my girlfriend."

She's quiet for a beat. Her shoulders rise and fall heavily against me. Then finally...

"I'm your girl, Nathan. I'm not going anywhere."

CHAPTER 43

Spencer

"Miller, I say this with affection, but your days are numbered, buddy."

He glances to the passenger side of his blackout sedan. "Ms. Spencer, you realize even after your car arrives, I'm still assigned as your security detail. But it's nice to know I'm growing on you."

"Aww." I chuckle. "You know I adore you. I'm just not sure why Nathan thinks I need a babysitter."

As promised, Nathan bought me a car after our confrontation in his office last week. We swept through three fancy dealerships, but I'd grown quite attached to the Lincoln. I wanted the exact same make and model but in a pearl color. I was more than willing to settle for black when they didn't have it in stock, but my boyfriend said "settle" is no longer a word allowed in my dictionary. My pearl Lincoln is being shipped from Florida and should be here in a couple days.

I couldn't be the girl who used her new, rich boyfriend to buy her something as substantial as a car, so I created a repayment plan, *interest-free*. I'm not ridiculous, there are some perks to dating a billionaire I'll indulge in. Maybe feeling a bit guilty for his controlling mishaps over the past few weeks, Nathan was a total gentleman about the idea of me slowly buying my car from him. He only rolled his eyes once when I made him sign the repayment agreement.

The loud school bell rings and Miller rubs his hands together. "I'm feeling good today. It's my day for the win."

I scoff. "Fat chance."

Over the past week, Miller and I have developed a new game at school pickup. Whoever spots Charlie first, wins. According to my sister, Claire's missed a lot of school lately, so she's been forced to branch out. She's become quite the social butterfly, and it's hard to guess which crew she's coming out with. The choir kids made sense. Even the cheerleaders were in line. Miller and I were both alarmed when she was lurking around the giant oak tree in front of the school with the goth kids. I swear to God if she asks me for permission to get something pierced, I'm going to start attending school with her every day.

"How come she never hangs out with the jocks?"

I love my little sister so much, but when it comes to sports, she's about as graceful as a duck in a diaper. "She's more the artist type."

Knock, knock, knock.

Miller and I both leap at the loud pounding on my passenger window. My heart screeches to a halt when I see Ruby's flushed face trying to peer into the vehicle. The car windows are tinted past regulation, so I have no idea how she spotted us. Lucky hunch?

"I'll handle it." Miller switches off his playful demeanor and goes James Bond-dangerous in front of my eyes.

"No, no. Roll down the window," I say. "She's a friend." *I think.* I'm honestly not sure how I feel after learning what Ruby did to Nathan...and Elise. It's hard to see her the same way.

"Spencer." She exhales my name in relief. "I was going to call you." Upon closer inspection, her eyes are slightly swollen, weakly supported by puffy bags beneath them, and not a lick of makeup. She looks like she's lost a significant amount of weight since the last time I saw her. Her hair is slopped up in a messy bun, very unlike her. She's also wearing black sweatpants with a baggy, black T-shirt. Never once have I seen Ruby in anything other than clean slacks and some kind of floral blouse. If the hairs rising on the back of my neck weren't warning enough, her current state is a very loud cry for help.

"Ruby, are you okay?"

She pats the windowsill, then rests her hand over it. "Fine, just fine, dear. Is this your boyfriend? He's handsome."

Miller salutes her with two fingers but stays silent, waiting for me to take the lead. Something tells me I should keep Ruby in the dark about my relationship with Nathan, so I let her assume whatever she pleases as I sidestep the question. "I heard Claire's been sick."

Ruby diverts her gaze, making her lie so obvious. "Yes, well... She's at school today."

"Oh, good. Bell just rang. I'm sure the girls will come out together shortly. I was actually going to ask you about inviting Claire over soon, but I wanted you to know I moved—"

"That's perfect. Is tonight okay?"

I shoot Miller a glance through my periphery, wondering if he also picked up on the desperation in her voice. He arches one brow indicating we're on the same page. I turn back to Ruby. "It's a school night."

"I know. Um, it's a big favor, but I was hoping you could keep Claire for a couple days. I have to go out of town for an emergency. Could you get her to school? She has lunch money for the week, but I'll reimburse you for everything else."

"Oh, well, we'd love to have her, Ruby. Are you sure everything is okay?"

"It will be." She forces a smile, but it comes out pained. "I wouldn't ask you if I had anybody else."

It takes all my strength *not* to ask where the hell her dad is in all this. "Sure. How long?"

"Is through Sunday okay? I should be back by then."

I don't even know if I've weighed the magnitude of this. I'm flying by the seat of my pants, here. Nathan and Claire, reunited? Is that a good idea for anybody? He never gave me his blessing. But I'm powerless not to do something. It's clear Ruby is distressed, and Claire too, by extension.

"When are you leaving?" I ask. "I can come by and pick Claire up tonight if that makes things easier for you."

Ruby looks over her shoulder, warily. "Can you take her now? I have a bag packed for her in the car. I also brought Babe if you wouldn't mind keeping an eye on her too?"

"Ruby?" I reach out to place my hand over hers. "Are you sure you're okay? If you need help—"

She shakes her head so vigorously she's going to give herself whiplash. "You taking care of Claire is all the help I need, I promise. Thank you for worrying about me, dear, but you needn't. I'm just going to run to the car and grab Babe and Claire's things. I'll be right back."

Ruby dashes away to her red hatchback parked on the other side of the street.

I turn to Miller as soon as she's out of earshot. "That was weird, right?"

He nods in agreement. "People only act like that when they're being watched...or chased."

Step one—get the girls home safe. Step two—call Nathan. He'll know what to do.

"Who is Babe?" Miller asks with a hum of light curiosity.

"Spike's lady friend."

Miller exhales out a weighted breath. "Boss is going to love that."

"I don't think he'll care, actually."

Nathan and Spike have made their peace. Tolerating Babe for a few days shouldn't be a problem. He might not even notice...

There'll be a far more distracting presence in his home.

CHAPTER 44

Nathan

Two quick knocks sound from my office door before Dad barrels in. "Working hard or hardly working?" He tosses a manila folder on my desk, then plants himself in the chair opposite me.

"What answer do you think I'm going to give my boss?"

"You look tired," Dad says. "Too much on your plate?"

There's no way in hell I'm going to tell my dad that I'm probably looking worse for wear because Spencer and I are having sex twice a day, every day. "Just this timeline." I drag my hand over my face, feeling my thick stubble which probably accentuates my exhausted appearance. "Dad, I don't care if every permit, inspection, and transaction goes flawlessly from now until opening, there's no way we're getting this hotel built and opened in a year."

"Okay. How about another year?"

"That might save me from a stress-induced early grave," I say.

"You got it."

"But I thought you wanted it opened as soon as possible so your investment wasn't dangling."

He dismisses my worry with a carefree shrug. "You're too young for gray hair. My money can sit tight another year." Dad nods to the folder. "That might help."

Dragging the folder in front of me, I glance over the stack of paperwork. "A partnership agreement with Harvey Corp?"

"I'm taking the old bastard out tonight for dinner and his signature. We're going to celebrate our first joint venture."

Leaning back in my chair, I fold my arms across my chest.

349

"You're not exactly one to play nice in the sandbox. Why are you suddenly sharing your toys with your competitor?"

Dad laughs. "I'm getting too old for rivalries. They're tiring. It's time for Senior and I to bury the hatchet and see if partnering gets us further than sabotage. We still need a project manager though since you exiled Casey."

He arches his brow like I did something wrong, but I regret nothing. Casey got off easy. I should've decked him in the jaw. "I want to work with Spencer on this. Not as my assistant but as project manager."

To my annoyance, Dad frowns. "She's inexperienced. This is a huge undertaking."

"We'll get her all the support she needs. But she has good judgment and a keen eye. I think this would be good for her."

"All right. I trust you."

"Thank you. And I was thinking, maybe you and Julia can come over this weekend. If we all beg, I might be able to convince Spencer to make these Cuban egg rolls."

Dad's expression twists, conveying his trepidation. "Cuban egg rolls?"

"Shouldn't work, but totally does. It's fan-fucking-tastic." My desk phone rings and a familiar number flashes across the caller ID. "Speak of the devil."

I pick up the receiver and lay it to the side. "Hey, baby, you're on speaker. Tell my dad how you make those Cuban egg rolls with that dipping sauce that I'm convinced has crack in it."

Baby? Dad mouths at me, waggling his eyebrows.

"Hi, Mr. Hatcher. Um, can we talk about egg rolls later, Nathan? I need to talk to you about Ruby." Spencer's tone is off—urgent and panicked. "Should I call back?"

"No, go ahead. My dad knows everything."

Dad goes alert. He sits up straight, staring at the phone intensely, like it's a pot about to boil. "Are you okay, Spencer?" he asks, inserting himself into the conversation.

"I'm okay. But I don't think Ruby is. She ambushed me and

Miller outside of Beaumont at pickup. She asked me to take Claire for a few days while she goes out of town."

That's not good. "Did she say why?"

"No, not really," Spencer answers. "She just said it was an emergency."

"I have a tail on her. I'll call and figure out what's going on right now. Thanks for telling me, Spencer."

Fully in go mode, I nearly hang up on Spencer before she's ready. "Nathan, wait. Claire... She's here at your house. Is that okay?"

My heart knocks heavily inside my chest as the situation washes over me. The last time Claire was in my home was not a pleasant memory. I wonder what she's thinking. "Of course it is. How is she—"

"Perfectly fine. The girls are getting changed to go swimming. We're sending Miller out for pizza and ice cream. I think Ruby didn't realize tomorrow is a teacher work day. The school is closed, so if it's okay with you, I'm going to take tomorrow off work and hang out with them."

"Yeah, I think that's a great idea. Maybe I should..." I place my fist to my lips, debating how to ask the nerve-racking question on my mind. Except I don't have to, because Spencer reads me better than anybody and answers the question I didn't ask.

"Claire's walking around this place like it's filled with happy memories. She showed Charlie which room used to be hers. She's so smiley and at ease... She wants to see you, Nathan. She's missed you very much."

All I can do is bury my face in my hands. I'm filled with relief and simultaneously overwhelmed with guilt. She needed me, *she missed me*, and I wasn't there.

"Nathan's really happy to hear that," Dad says when I let the silence carry on too long.

"Just do what you need to. Call about Ruby. I'll take good care of the girls until you get here. We'll save you some pizza, okay?"

"Thanks." My voice cracks, and I clear my throat. "I'll see

you soon."

Spencer ends the call, and after replacing the receiver, I dial Hodge, also on speaker. He answers immediately. "Hey, boss. Finally. I called you half an hour ago."

"Sorry, I was working. Didn't hear my phone. Where's Ruby?"

"That's what I was calling about. I have my guy Terry on it. He's following her. He thinks Ruby's driving for the border. She loaded up a few duffel bags of cash."

"She's going to get herself killed. I need to stop her."

"If she gets to Sierra Vista, border control is bound to have some questions about why she's headed to Mexico with random bags of cash. I have a contact there. I can see if we can hold her up."

"Do that, now. Get your guy Terry to location share. I'm on the way."

"Roger that, boss. Stay tuned."

The room falls silent until I roar out, "*Fuck*!" in frustration. "Dad, if she enters Mexico—"

"She's not coming back," he finishes. "What the hell has she gotten herself into now?"

"I know you don't want me getting involved, but I don't have a choice. Don't try to stop me. I have to find out."

As much as I despise Ruby, she's Claire's grandmother. While she's been vile to me, she's been kind to Claire. Basic humanity doesn't want me to see Ruby ripped to shreds by a violent cartel. Not even Ruby should have to pay for Peter's crimes.

Dad shakes his head somberly. I expect him to lecture me about letting the authorities handle it and to keep myself uninvolved, but after studying my resolute expression, he says, "*We* have to find out."

"Dad, you don't have to—"

"Nathan," he interjects firmly. "Ruby's trying to keep her kid safe. And so am I. You go, I go. End of discussion." He pulls his keys out of his pocket and dangles them in front of me. "Come on, I'll drive."

CHAPTER 45

Spencer

As soon as I wake up, I check my phone. Nothing.

Nathan didn't come home last night. He warned me he'd have to cross state lines. I'm worried for him. I'm worried for his dad. And Ruby.

I pity her, truly. Only a mother's love could be blinding enough to see Peter for what he could be, instead of what he is. I hope I'm never in that position with Charlie, but if it were to come to that, how would I behave? Would I continue to protect her to everybody else's detriment?

Nathan's bed is far too big for one person. It's uncomfortable lying here alone. Or maybe that's the worry. I forgot that love has an ugly partner—fear. Once you have something you care about, you realize what it would mean for someone to take it away.

There's a soft knock at the door. Probably the girls politely requesting I get the hell up and start on breakfast. Claire and Charlie eat nonstop. After pizza last night came popcorn. Then strawberries and pretzels with chocolate dip. Then dry cereal as a late-night snack. They're so teensy, I don't know where the hell they're putting it.

"Come in."

Sitting up, I swing my legs over the side of the bed. I stretch my arms overhead and take in a deep breath to fill my lungs.

"Spence?" Charlie asks from the door. She's still in her pink-and-teal llama pajama set. They're so cute, if they were remotely close to my size, I'd steal them.

"Good morning. Are you guys up?"

"I am. Claire's still sleeping."

I pat the bed, inviting my sister in. She scuttles in with quick feet, then leaps freely onto the mattress, landing next to me with her arms spread out. It doesn't jostle me. Nathan's bed is that special kind of memory foam that absorbs movement. "Someone's in a good mood," I say.

"I can't believe I get to have three sleepover nights with my best friend. That's like the lottery. We're going to do manicures and pedicures today. Can we borrow your purple polish?"

"Sure."

"And the clear glitter?"

"Why not."

"And we'll base coat and top coat. *Oh!* And we need rose petals for the foot soak."

"Charlie," I grumble, tapping my temples with two fingers. "I'm going to need thirty minutes and two cups of coffee before you start being a handful this morning, okay?"

"Okay," she says through a giggle.

"I love how happy you are though. How's Claire doing? Did she mention anything about Nathan?" Sue me. I need a little intel from my sister.

"Not much. She said they used to be like best friends. Nathan almost married her mom. Did you know that?"

I bow my head slightly. "I did."

"Claire said something..." Charlie sits up, and a cloudy, sorrowful expression ages her young face. "It made me wonder..."

"What, babes? What did she say?" Pivoting, I turn my knee, facing Charlie.

"*On Mom*, you can't say anything to Claire."

"*On Mom*," I swear.

"I was showing Claire our scrapbooks. She really liked them. I told her we do that to keep Mom close by. I told her we could make one for her mom too. So she could keep her close."

I cup her face, stroking gently against her cheekbone. "I did a pretty good job with you, know that?" I wink. "You're a very sweet girl, Charlotte. Don't ever lose that."

She gives me a half-smile, one cheek bunching up into a perfect sphere. "Well, Claire said we can't because she doesn't have so many pictures of her mom. Her grandma doesn't like a lot of pictures of the past. She doesn't even like to take Claire to her mom's gravestone."

It's becoming increasingly more difficult to like Ruby. Ripping Claire from Nathan was shameful enough, but keeping her from the memories of her mother? It's heartless.

"I was thinking," Charlie continues, "Nathan probably has some pictures of Claire's mom, right? What if we asked him for some and made Claire a scrapbook she could keep here and look at whenever she wanted to?"

I need to tell Charlie that after this weekend, when Ruby finds out where her granddaughter has been staying, who I'm dating, who Charlie calls friend—we might not get to see Claire anymore. But I just don't have the heart to ruin such a sweet morning. "I love that idea. I'll talk to Nathan about rummaging up some pictures."

"Okay. Thank you."

I beam at my baby sister. "Mom would be so proud of you, you know."

"I try," she sasses.

I let out a breathy chuckle. This girl is powerless not to ruin sentimental moments with her snark. I giggle again when I remember Nathan saying the same thing about me. Guess it runs in the family. How'd we get here? We didn't *need* Nathan to be a family, but it sure feels better now that he's here.

"Pancakes?" I ask.

Her eyes bulge. "Can we go big with the toppings? Strawberries, chocolate chips, *and* whipped cream?"

I match her buggy stare. "And powdered sugar and sprinkles too?"

Her fists go high in the air. "Yesss! Are you going to eat with us? Or are you still on your diet?" She pouts her bottom lip.

"I'm taking a little break from dieting. What do you think?"

"Good. You cook better when you actually taste your food."

This girl. "All right, out." I point to the door. "I'm right behind you. Go get the piggies fed. And Spike needs a bedding change today, don't forget."

"I'll do it now," Charlie answers.

"Put Spike in his own carrier while you clean. Don't put him with Babe, okay? They can't share a cage." Charlie goes still. The look she gives me is the same one she had a year ago when she accidentally purchased seasons one through ten of *Friends* from the digital library. Over two hundred dollars was charged to my credit card—nonrefundable. I swear it's my mom's scold that comes out of me. "What did you do?"

"*Nothing*," she whines. "We let Babe and Spike play together last night. They're already in the same cage."

"*All night?*"

"Yeah," Charlie squeaks.

Welp. Too late. Babe's pregnant.

The girls are tag-teaming breakfast dishes, flinging soap at each other, making more of a mess than they are actually cleaning up.

"Enough," I playfully scold. "Finish up already. Sun's high enough. Let's get changed and in the pool." It's the best way to wear them out. When they're swimming, their diva demands are curtailed. I'm looking forward to a morning of sunbathing by the pool, listening to the screeching and splashing of best-friendship until we break for lunch. I'm praying Nathan's back by the time we fire up the outdoor stove for grilled cheese paired with virgin piña coladas.

The doorbell chimes, echoing in the living room and kitchen with a loud, resonant ring.

"I'll get it!" Charlie belts out.

"Halt, missy." I stop her. "Don't even think about it." I make my way to the door and point Charlie down the hall. "Go get your swimsuit on, nosy. You know you aren't supposed to answer the doorbell."

She scoffs. "When it wasn't our home," she mutters. "Now it is."

Another conversation I have to table for now. Charlie's living out a Cinderella story, but she has to understand Nathan and I just started dating. This is still *his* home in which we're guests. I'm not going to rush into forever this time. Not because I can't picture my life with Nathan. *I can.* But I want to savor this. I don't think I've ever really fallen in love before. It's creating a shift, where my happiness matters just as much as Charlie's. Being self-full is a new concept for me, and I want to take my time, approach this with care. I want Nathan and me to build something solid and everlasting together.

I open the front door expecting Miller who drops by daily to check on us. Instead, there's a man I don't recognize standing on the stoop. He looks homeless. His beard is unkempt and patchy. Thick in some places, sparse in others. His red, long-sleeved shirt and dirty jeans have holes in a variety of sizes.

"Who are you?"

"Peter," a small voice says from behind me. Claire approaches us, but stays mostly hidden behind me, an obvious display of fear and apprehension.

"It's *Dad*," he growls out. "Get your shit. We're going."

His breath is rancid. Not just morning breath after coffee, it smells like rotting. He tries to smile, and there's the source. Several teeth are missing, and the swelling and discoloration on his gumline is screaming for emergency dental attention.

I turn around, blocking Peter's view of Claire's face with my back. I raise my brows, wordlessly asking if she's supposed to go with him. Taking the cue, she widens her eyes with a pleading look and subtly shakes her head. I nod, concluding the most dramatic game of charades I've ever played.

"Go find Charlie, and get changed for the pool, sweetheart.

I'll talk to your dad and see if you can stay to swim."

With my permission, she flies down the hallway out of sight. My mama-bear instinct kicks into high gear. I wheel around, ready to give Peter a piece of my mind for showing up in this state. Not just his tattered clothing and dirty mouth. His eyes are bloodshot and he's swaying in place like he's drunk or high. He's out of his damn mind if he thinks I'm letting him take Claire anywhere.

"Peter, you need to go."

My intuition tells me to shut the door about two seconds too late. Before I can lock him out, Peter digs into his pocket and produces a handgun. He points it between my eyes. "I'm not going anywhere without my fucking kid."

CHAPTER 46

Nathan

Ruby stopped late last night just outside of Tucson at a seedy-looking motel. We caught up to her in the middle of the night, but I was not about to knock on her door at midnight. The way she's behaving, she's scared, paranoid, and not in her right mind. I don't want to frighten her into a heart attack.

Instead, we waited all night, dozing off in our vehicles, until she emerged from the motel, dressed in all black, and opted for breakfast at the small diner across the street.

Dad and I are in his Jaguar. Terry, one of Hodge's PIs, is in a plateless sedan behind us. We're all watching Ruby through the diner window. "I'm going in alone," I announce.

"I don't think that's a good idea," Dad answers.

"Dad. Trust me." I step out of the car and head toward the restaurant. Dad must have faith because I don't hear footsteps behind me. A polite *ding* announces my entrance. I bypass the hostess stand, giving a curt nod to the waitress. "Meeting someone," I say, and proceed to Ruby's booth. She's buried in her phone and doesn't notice me until I plop down across from her.

Shock blanches her face the second she peers up.

"Good morning, Ruby. Where are you headed with three black duffel bags full of cash?"

No longer surprised, she's angry. Her eyes narrow to pin-sized. "I *thought* you were having me followed. Peter warned me. I should've listened."

"Ruby...I'm tired of this war. Aren't you? Don't we all want the same thing here?"

My statement gives her pause. She opens her mouth like she was armed with a comeback, but I took her off guard. "No. We don't. You want Peter in prison, or worse."

All true. But that's not why I'm here. "I want Claire safe and happy."

"You want to take her from me too," Ruby whispers.

She looks so weary. Not at all like the calculating villain I remember from the past. She's frail, her blue veins pressing against her thin, pale skin. How could I not pity her right now? "We could've done this together," I say. "Did you ever consider that?"

She wets her dry, cracked lips. "How so?"

"I can't forgive Peter. But I could've forgiven you. You let Elise down in so many ways, but you could've had a fresh start with Claire. I didn't want to own that little girl. She wasn't part of a power struggle. Did you ever stop to think that I wanted a relationship with Claire not just to spite you? Why wouldn't you want your granddaughter's life filled with even more love and support after she lost her mother?"

She drops her head, unable to meet my gaze. "Elise kept her from me. You guys wouldn't let me see my only grandchild."

"Ruby, wake up." I raise my voice a notch higher than restaurant level. "Elise kept Claire from danger. You are so delusional about Peter, you'd rather him hurt his family before admitting he's a monster. You made the choice to alienate your grandchild when you swept abuse under the rug like it was nothing."

Elbow planted on the table, she holds her forehead. Tears fall from her eyes and splash onto the speckled white table. "It was the drugs," Ruby whimpers. "It's not my Peter. It's the *drugs* that make him crazy. It's not his fault."

No, fuck that shit. Unless she's tying him down and jabbing the needle into his arm, it most certainly *is* his fault. Not saying he doesn't deserve help, but he sure as hell never deserved Elise, and he doesn't deserve a relationship with Claire. Not then, and not now.

I take a deep breath. Yes, that pissed me the fuck off. No, anger doesn't get to run the show anymore. "Let me help you, Ruby."

"You can't. It's gotten too out of hand. Just let me do what I need to."

I lean into the table, lowering my voice. "Being?"

She sniffles. "They just want their money. Once they have that, they'll leave us alone. If I go to the police, they'll hurt everybody. I couldn't do that to Claire—"

"You already did," I grind out. "Up until this point, you have already made every single poor decision you possibly could. You're not fit to raise Claire. You don't know how to prioritize her well-being over that pedestal you still have your son on."

Ruby cries harder which brushes against my heartstrings, but doesn't completely tug. She needs to face the music. Actions have consequences. "I don't have enough. But I thought if I gave them something..."

"Peter's debt?" I ask. "How much?"

She forces herself to look at me. "With interest, five hundred thousand."

"And how much do you have?"

"Twenty-eight thousand, cash."

I exhale sharply. "Ruby, if you go to Mexico with less than ten percent of what Peter owes the cartel, they will kill you. Claire will never see her grandma again. But that won't be enough. They'll come after Claire."

Ruby's bottom lip trembles. "The things they threatened if we go to the police..." She shudders violently. "I can't even repeat it. Peter wants to run."

I shake my head. "Where? They'll find you."

"I know, I know," she sobs. "That's why I drained my savings. I took a second mortgage on the house. If I give them a deposit, they'll know we're trying."

"Trying isn't good enough."

She slams her fist on the table. "I haven't slept. I can't eat. I can't think. How did it get this far? Claire and I were fine until—"

"Peter got out of prison?"

Ruby nods, a disturbingly sad frown sweeping over her face. "I'm scared. Of them...of him."

Hot anger pumps through my veins. More and more it seems like Peter disappearing would be the solution to everybody's problems. I'm tempted to just feed him to the drug lords he stole from. If I knew their cruelty would end there, I would. But Ruby and Claire will never be safe until the debt is paid.

"I don't know what to do, Nathan. I'm sorry."

"Ruby, look at me."

Her eyes lift to meet mine, guardedly. "Is this the part where you swoop in to save the day, yet again? Just like with Elise?"

"Elise saved herself. Crediting me with that is an insult to her memory. Leaving Peter, taking Claire, starting over on their own, was the most difficult thing she ever had to do. And she did it for her daughter. You could at least show some respect for that."

She bows her head. "Okay. I know."

"You're going to pay off Peter's debt on my dime. Text your contact and let him know we'll set up a drop, untraceable. We'll double what he owes if they can ensure they never contact your family again and will never sell to or through Peter. I'm not in the business of trusting the integrity of drug lords. I have guys who can handle it. After that, you need to wipe your hands clean of this whole situation. Tell Peter's parole officer he's back on drugs, and then *let him go*, Ruby."

She stares over my shoulder, her open emotional wounds written all over her face. "I don't have a choice, do I?"

"You do. I'm simply asking you to make the right one."

Her eyes land on mine. "Why are you doing this for me? You hate me."

"There's a stipulation."

She sucks in her lips. "You want Claire back."

"I want you to let Claire choose. If you're giving her a better home than I can, so be it. But if she wants me... Let her go, too."

"And never see her again?" Ruby's eyes fill with tears.

"No. I don't want to take anything else away from her. As long as Peter's not in the picture, you can see Claire as much as she's okay with. If you cut that tumor known as your son loose, you can still be part of her life. Birthday parties, holidays, whatever you like. When it comes to Claire, it should've never been a situation of either-or."

She doesn't take long to weigh her options. "She'll choose you, Nathan. I know it. Just..." Tears pouring, she clasps her hand over her mouth, catching her sobs. "Don't cut me out again."

"Don't give me a reason to."

My anger with Ruby has cooled, but only some. Part of me wants to embrace the frail, elderly woman who looks as helpless as Spike did in that pool, minutes from death. But I still need time.

At least, this is a start.

"I'm going to call one of my PI guys. He has contacts that are familiar with the cartel and how they operate. He can help us arrange a safe drop."

"Okay." Ruby sniffles.

"Stay here... Maybe order us some coffee?"

She nods eagerly.

Exiting the booth, I dial Hodge who answers on the first ring.

"Hey, I need you to—"

"I don't know what happened, man. I just got another car. I'm on my way to your place right now. I bet that's where he's headed."

I exit the restaurant, hot Arizona air blasting my face. "What the hell are you talking about, Hodge? We just caught up with Ruby in Arizona."

"*Shit.* You're not with Spencer and the girls?"

"No." Dread pours over me like heavy cement. "What the fuck? Explain."

"I was following Peter. I went into a gas station to piss, and when I got back, my tires were shot out, and a bucket of paint was thrown on the windshield. Peter's onto me. He lashed out."

Of course Peter clued in that he was under surveillance.

Ruby just confirmed that moments ago. That's not the part that's making my stomach turn inside out.

Peter shot out Hodge's tires, meaning Peter has a gun...

He knows I'm having him tracked...

And I haven't heard from Spencer all morning.

CHAPTER 47

Spencer

"Put that the *fuck* down," Peter snarls at me when I reach for my phone.

I freeze, holding up my shaking hands.

I had no choice but to let him in. Gun to my head, he walked me backward into the kitchen. The girls have the good sense to stay hidden in their rooms. I pray Charlie locked the door. I've already resolved that if Peter turns his back and heads down the hallway to find them, I have no choice but to attack. There's a kitchen knife in reach. I'll have to be quick and precise. The space between his neck and shoulder. If I plunge it deep enough, it should make him drop the gun.

I am scared shitless, but my purpose is clear.

The girls survive. Whatever it takes.

"Turn it off," Peter continues. He takes a step forward and stumbles when his knees buckle. I flinch and an involuntary whimper escapes me. Not only does he have a lethal weapon, he's too inebriated to operate it. He's just as likely to kill me by accident.

"Why?" I ask. I know why, I'm simply buying time to think.

"Just do it!" he shouts, practically foaming at the mouth.

"Okay, okay." I hold down the correct buttons to bring up the "end call" screen. I hover over the "off" button and pretend to swipe right, proving to Peter I'm following directions. If he was remotely sober, I'd never get away with it, but taking advantage of his impaired state, I swipe right on the Emergency SOS call instead. I've never used that option and I have no clue what's to come. I flip my phone over and try to lure Peter away from investigating further.

"Peter, can I make you some coffee? If you want to take Claire, it'd make me feel better if you had a nice hot cup of joe first."

"Coffee?" he grunts out.

"Yeah. How do you take it?" I keep my voice steady even though my entire body is trembling. "Cream? Sugar?"

"Just sugar."

"Okay, I have plenty of that." My chipper tone is a survival tactic. Borderline denial, but it's serving me. I walk back by the kitchen island to subtly inspect my phone. I check a cabinet underneath the island for coffee mugs. Again, high-as-fuck Peter is unsuspicious of why coffee mugs would be where we keep the pots and pans. I can't flip it back over to see if it connected. That *would* likely tip him off.

Hunching over so my mouth is near the speaker, I say loudly, "Peter, do you want to put the gun down? *Please.* You're scaring me."

I say it more for the emergency operator who I pray is connected on the other line. But I look up at Peter to gauge his reaction. There's a detached, cold look in his eyes. Like his soul has left his body. "I don't think so," he slurs, tightening his grip around the gun.

"What are you on? Meth? Coke? Or are you just drunk?"

Again, not for his benefit. I'm leaving breadcrumbs. "Shut up," he snarls. "Quit askin' questions. Get my coffee, get my daughter, and stop talking."

His nose starts to drip blood. He wipes it away with his dirty sleeve.

"Can I get you some tissues?" I try to retreat from the room.

"You bitch. Don't move!" Something's escalating. Like the drugs are on a time release and I have a feeling what's bad is about to get much worse. I throw a Hail Mary knowing this is the best I can do. I can't best him physically; he's quite large. Not to mention, I don't know how to use or disarm a gun.

"Peter, do you know where you are?" I speak slowly and clearly. "This is 14289 Pelican Way in Las Vegas. This is Nathan Hatcher's house and you're trespassing. He's going to be very upset that you're in his home uninvited, threatening to kill his girlfriend, her sister, and her friend. *Three people in the house.*"

Too obvious. *Dammit.* Peter's eyes light up with rage. He grabs my phone off the counter and chucks it at the wall, shattering it. Then, he turns on me, gun aimed. I step backward but my back hits the ledge of the island. I have nowhere to go. I'm hyperventilating through my nose now. Hot tears fill my eyes and I do my best just to focus. I look for anything within arm's reach that's a weapon. But he's too close. I don't know what to do. I fixate on the pistol, wondering if I can snatch it. It's so risky, but what choice do I have?

The girls survive. At all costs.

I stretch my wobbling fingers, preparing to lunge, knowing without a doubt this is going to end up with a bullet in my belly, but I have to try.

Boom!

The front door breaks open and all I hear is, "Ms. Spencer. *Down!*"

I dive away from Peter, dropping to my stomach, hitting the kitchen tile so hard my tooth drives into my lip. The metallic taste of blood is on my tongue when I hear gunshots. A body hits the ground beside me, and judging by the smell, it's Peter. There's a tussle as someone wrestles Peter's firearm away, sliding it clear across the room.

I look up to see Miller rushing to my side. A familiar face is all it takes for the floodgates to break wide open. He helps me up but I collapse again, letting loose an ear-splitting scream, and I can't stop. I wail and screech, releasing all the tension that barricaded in my body.

"Is he... Is he...?" I bumble out.

"Not dead," Miller answers. "I popped him in the thigh. He's in shock. Probably a drug reaction. He looks like he's on everything in the book."

Police sirens wail in the background, getting closer. *Relief, relief, relief.* I really wasn't confident it would end like this.

The moment I can feel my legs again, I break free of Miller's steadying embrace, and dash down the hall as fast as my feet will carry me. Ten paces, then I bank left. I jiggle Charlie's doorknob, but it's locked. *Yes. Smart girl.*

"It's me! Spencer. Open the door, girls. We're safe. Everything is okay."

The handle turns within a second, and I'm greeted by two tear-streaked little girls, red-faced, looking a word past terrified. I hold them both, one in each arm as I sink to my knees. It's an awkward hug, but I refuse to let them go. I hold tightly like they are my lifeline.

"You guys did so good," I whisper. "You did everything exactly right. We're okay. Everything is going to be okay."

"Is my dad okay?" Claire asks with a sniffle. She pulls away to meet my gaze.

"Claire, *oh, sweetie.* I'm sorry, he needs a lot of help. He's going to be okay, but he's going to have to go away again. He did a really bad thing just now."

She wipes at her eyes with both palms. "You're talking about Peter," she says quietly.

"Yeah."

"I meant my dad," she says weakly, gripping her locket in her fist. "Is he here?"

My heart disintegrates like ash in the wind. It tears me apart, and I can't hold back my sobbing. Charlie wraps her arms around me tightly to comfort me. I kiss the top of her head over and over again. How long has this little girl been hurting? Silently missing her mom and the man she still knows as dad.

She's been in too much pain for far too long.

"Yeah, hon. Nathan's on his way, I'm sure of it." If Miller's here, Nathan's been alerted. "Your dad is coming."

CHAPTER 48

Nathan

I arrive to fanfare in front of my home. There are so many police cars blocking my driveway, we had to park fifty yards down the way. Fuming, I leave my dad in the dust, making a beeline to my house, vowing never ever to leave my girls again.

Miller already told me they're okay, and Peter is on his way to receive treatment where he'll be handcuffed to a hospital bed before they drop him back in a cage where he belongs. He should be grateful. Prison protects him...from me.

I trudge forward, making plans. Security will be tripled. Spencer, Charlie, and Claire will have personal security details on them at all times. We're installing a panic room and a panic button. Every inch of the property, inside and out, will have security cameras. I will hire armed guards to perch at every entrance to our home. Snipers on the roof, too.

In about a week when I've calmed down, I'll think of more reasonable security measures, but as of right now, my girls are on lockdown.

"Are you Mr. Hatcher?" one of the policemen asks, falling in stride next to me.

"Yes. This is my residence." I don't slow my pace. If he wants to talk, he needs to keep up.

"We've already taken a statement from your wife and daughters, but we need one from you too, if you don't mind." I halt, turning my head to observe the squirrely cop. He looks a little new, probably more concerned with procedure than reading the room. He called Spencer my wife. Claire and Charlie, my daughters. That'll be misrepresented on his report...

But I don't correct him, because I like how it sounds.

"Anyone who stands between me and my family at the moment is going to see a very ugly side of me. So, all due respect, Officer, please come back later."

I storm off, up the stairs, through the stoop and into my home. A small forensics team is working away. They've roped crime scene tape around the entry pillars to try to block off my kitchen. There's a little blood splatter, probably from when Peter got shot. Spencer's phone is shattered in pieces by the far wall.

Miller called me the second everyone was safe and gave me the rundown. Peter crashed his car through the main security outpost, deactivating the gate. He left his car and walked the half mile from my property entrance, to my home. Spencer opened the door and had a gun pointed at her head. Every time I picture her face, I nearly collapse. She must've been so scared. But my clever girl somehow managed to alert the authorities. Miller beat them to the house by minutes. From what I was told, Spencer kept him calm, kept him talking, and bought precious time until help could arrive. She saved their lives.

I wouldn't have survived losing them.

She saved my life, too.

"Spencer?" I bellow out. I bet she's in the bedroom. I make my way down the hall past all the strangers in my home who I want *out*.

A door opens behind me with a small squeak. I look over my shoulder to see big, green eyes and long, bright red hair. It knocks the wind out of me. She looks so much like Elise, it stuns me into silence.

"Hey." Tears dripping down her face, she forces a small smile. "I thought I heard you, Dad." She scrunches her toes into the hardwood floor. "Can I call you that, still?" She sucks in a small breath.

It feels like I float to her. *I blink.* I'm on my knees. *I blink again.* She's in my arms. *One more time.* I'm sobbing into her hair. "You call me what I am, princess."

She blubbers into my neck about how she missed me and how she begged Ruby to let her visit. I can't even think straight enough to form independent thoughts. I have to piggyback off all her sentiments. Everything she says, I add "me too."

This hug feels like home. This little girl feels like a promise. I am never letting her go again.

Claire pulls away before I'm ready. She has to push hard against my shoulders to put any space between us. Silently, she wrestles out the long chain from underneath her shirt. The heavy, heart-shaped locket swings like a pendulum in her hand. She shows me proudly. "I kept it safe." I duck my head and Claire loops the chain over my neck. "You can have it back now."

The words of my promise to her from years ago echo through my mind.

I wouldn't give it up without being sure I'll get it back. Keep it safe for me. I want it back when you come home.

"You're home now, Claire. They can't keep us apart anymore."

She wraps her arms around my neck and squeezes tightly. "Home," is all she murmurs, over and over again. "*Home, home, home.*"

CHAPTER 49

Spencer

Two months later

I feel Nathan's eyes on me as I stare into the cage. "What do you mean, '*how did this happen?*'" I ask.

"I mean two days ago, there were two pigs in this cage. Now, how are there seven?"

I glance at him like he's dim-witted. "Nathan, please tell me I don't need to explain basic biology to you."

"Pregnancy is *nine* months, Spence. We've had both of them for two months now."

We're standing in the "guinea pig room" as we've dubbed it. Babe and Spike need so much space, I talked Nathan into giving them an entire room all to themselves. We built quite the spectacle. They have their shared home. Spike has a man cave. Babe has a she-shed. These piggies are living the good life.

I stare at the new babies, squealing at the top of their lungs, begging for mama's milk. Two of them look exactly like Spike. Only one of them is caramel colored with a white mark on its head like his mom. One is albino, and there's one all-black guinea pig that I already named Onyx. *God, they're cute.* The symphony of squeals will get old really quick, but there's something so uniquely precious about seeing a family of piggies together like this. The babies have created a cuddle circle, only breaking free to take turns at Babe's milk.

"We have to get rid of them before the girls see."

He's not wrong. Claire and Charlie are going to fight tooth and nail to keep every single baby. Not happening.

"Hey, know what we should do?"

He pretends like he's put off by the sight, but Nathan wraps his arms around my shoulders, pulling me tightly against his side. He presses his lips against my temple. "What's that, baby?"

"We should host trivia at the party tonight, and the winners get a guinea pig."

To my surprise, Nathan nods in agreement. "Fantastic idea. Worst party favor ever. It will guarantee we never have to host an event like this again."

I chuckle heftily.

After months of searching for a nice venue to host the rehearsal dinner, we settled on Nathan's estate. A venue would've been easier. It's taking a team of thirty to prepare his mansion for his dad's dinner tonight. I'm thrilled, on the other hand. It's a black-tie affair, and this time I have a dress that actually fits me. Charlie is performing a full set. A mini stage with professional acoustics is being installed by the pool so she can wow the whole crowd with her angelic voice. I even wrote a speech for Nathan to share tonight. Touchy-feely stuff isn't his forte, so I gallantly stepped in to write all the beautiful words I know he's feeling.

"Can we keep one?" I ask.

"We can keep two," Nathan says. "The mom and the dad. The rest have to go."

"Oh, Nathan...*please*. Let me keep Onyx."

"Woman," he says, flashing me a stern look. "You did *not* already start naming them."

"Of course not. *Snickers, Mars Bar, Biscuit, Ghost,* and *Onyx*." I hurry out their names under my breath.

"You're worse than our girls."

I flash him a toothy grin. "The thing is, if we keep Onyx, we kind of have to keep Ghost too. But those piggies are mine. The girls will each want one of their own. And we can't possibly exclude just one baby. That's so cruel."

He blinks at me. "They. Have. To. Go."

I circle my fingertips around his chest between his muscular pecs. I've learned this is an erogenous zone for Nathan. He melts when I touch him here for some reason. I'm not above using my feminine wiles to keep my piggy family together. "Which one do you think is cutest?"

"I know what you're doing, by the way..." He lets out a grouchy grumble, but eventually points to the corner of the cage. "Which one is that one?"

"Mars Bar."

"He's all right. He's the only one who walks normal instead of freaking out and scurrying around like a roach."

"Oh my *God*," I exclaim. "How cute would matching shirts be for all of them?"

"For fuck's sake," Nathan mumbles, shaking his head.

"C'mere," I say, luring him to the only couch in the room. I wait until he sits to curl up next to him. I rest my ear against his chest, feeling the loud thumps of his heartbeat. "How are you doing? The hearing is coming up soon. Anything on your mind?"

It's been a heartbreaking two months for Ruby. Peter went back to jail. He's never getting out. Ruby has decided to move away from Las Vegas, somewhere on the East Coast. She wanted to start fresh. Honoring her promise to Nathan, Ruby gave Claire a choice...

But it wasn't much of a choice. Nathan's name was on her lips before Ruby could barely get out the question. Their bond is deep and unbreakable. Even after three years, they remained loyal and hopeful. It finally paid off. Now, we're all a family.

"It'll feel good once it's official. I can't forget the past. I'll never stop thinking about how easy it was for them to rip Claire away from me. I just want to sign the papers so I don't have to live in fear."

Reaching up, I cup his cheek. "It'll be done soon. Claire will be all yours."

"Not just Claire," Nathan answers. "I worry about you too.

And Charlie. Can I ask you something?

"Anything."

"Hop up for me." He squeezes me in a reassuring hug, before pushing me off of him. He darts out of the room, then returns in a flash with a scrapbook in hand. At first I assume it's one of ours, but then I realize we don't own a purple scrapbook.

Nathan resumes his position right next to me and hands me the book. I run my fingers over the beautiful etched flowers, layered in a collage-like fashion over the various purple hues. "This is stunning. What is this?"

"Charlie inspired me. She said these scrapbooks really help you guys. I thought it'd be good for Claire."

I nod. "Charlie had the same idea. They're how we stay connected to Mom. There's something about a picture. Memories warp and fade. Sometimes I can't recall the times before my mom got sick. When she's stuck in my mind as frail and so ill, I forget we had a life before that. The photographs help me remember. Emotions twist the narrative based off where you are in life, but photographs keep the memories honest and alive."

Nathan stares at me with bleeding adoration. He couldn't control his smile if he tried. "I'm so glad you wrote my speech for tonight."

I chuckle. "You and Claire have been working on this together?"

Nathan bobs his head. "It's been a trip down memory lane."

"How's the journey?" I stare into his eyes, always light these days. Even when we have these difficult conversations, they never lose their little spark. Whatever was missing, Nathan got back.

"Bumpy," he claims. "But therapeutic. Things that Claire remembers, I don't. There are some things I recall that she can't. Together we're piecing it all together."

He reaches over my lap and pulls the book open. The first page holds a photograph I'm familiar with. No longer hiding in the broken piano bench, Elise and Claire are basking in a field of flowers, their smiles glowing against the black page. "They are stunning, Nathan."

"So are you." He cups his fingers underneath my chin, guiding my gaze toward him. "You know that, right? This book doesn't mean—"

"*Nathan.* You don't have to do that every time. Your heart is big enough for all of us. I'm not jealous of Elise. She's part of our family too."

He lets out a low hum. "*Our family.* I really like that, Spencer. I love you."

It's not the first time he's said it. It's not the first time I've returned the sentiment. Movies used to tell me that "I love you" was supposed to be some big parade. Flowers, fireworks, and big to-dos. But when you love someone from your very bones, when your heart only beats properly when you know they're safe... There's no gesture that can do it justice.

I love you isn't a theatrical declaration.

It's just the truth.

"I love you too, babe."

I continue flipping through the pages, one by one. I glimpse a lot of firsts for Nathan, Elise, and Claire. It's like watching their story come to life. It's bittersweet that Elise found love, only to leave it too soon. But at least she had it. I'm so glad that after Peter, Elise had the kind of love she deserved.

When I flip to the next page, there's no picture. Just four photo corners surrounding an empty rectangular space. Beneath, a caption reads: *The day she said yes.* "What is this? Are you missing a picture?"

"Claire's idea. We're manifesting. The moment hasn't happened yet."

The "*she*" isn't Elise... It's me.

I sit upright, meeting him with big, round eyes. Excitement flutters in my chest as my breathing quickens. "Nathan Hatcher, are you proposing to me?"

He holds up both hands. "Whoa, calm down. Yes."

"What?" I balk, instinctively smoothing my hair and wetting

my lips. I'm still in pajamas this morning, but who cares. It's fine.

"But," Nathan adds loudly, "not today. Not like this. But yes, Spencer Riley-Brenner. I want you and your sassy mouth forever. I'm sure of it. I'd put a ring on your finger today, but the girls will kill me. It's sweet. They want to be very involved in the proposal plans." He raises his brows. "Expect a balloon arch and colored silly string."

Joy bubbles up in my chest and spills out as laughter. "I'll take it."

"What I wanted to ask you earlier... When I make you my wife, can I adopt Charlie, too? I've had my legal team look into the logistics. There are some hoops to jump through, but with your okay—"

"You have my okay." I try to smile at him, but I'm overcome with emotion. "Thank you."

"What's wrong, baby?"

I hold my face, enjoying the energizing feel of cool fingertips against my warm cheeks. "Since my mother died, even through my past relationship, I always had this familiar feeling. And now it's gone."

Nathan's face fills with concern. "What aren't you feeling? What am I not giving you? If you tell me, I'll try—"

"Nathan, the feeling was *alone*. And now it's gone."

He pulls my hand from my face and kisses each of my knuckles, dolling out extra kisses on my ring finger, like he's making a promise. "Never alone again," he murmurs.

We enjoy the sweet quiet for a while, just sitting together, enjoying each other's warmth. But a commotion from the guinea pig cage disturbs the serenity.

"Spike," Nathan gripes. "Leave her alone, man. She just gave birth."

He scolds Spike who is trying to mount Babe, but struggling to get around the babies who are providing a protective shield around their mother.

"She's in heat again."

"What? No way. She just popped out a litter."

I rack my brain trying to remember the details from the guinea pig documentary Charlie made me watch. "Pretty sure she can get pregnant again in just a couple hours after giving birth."

The smile falls dramatically from Nathan's face. "You're kidding me."

"Nope."

Nathan rises in an instant. He flings open the cage and scoops Spike right off of Babe's back. "Oh hell no, you horny little rat. Our entire home is going to be crawling with your spawn." Nathan waltzes out of the guest room with Spike in hand.

"Where are you going with Spike?"

"He's grounded," Nathan calls back. "Separate rooms from now on."

I hold my ribs as I giggle, feeling gleefully full in all the right places.

All the hurt, all the hell, all the broken pieces... We all had to brave the storm until perfect timing brought us all together. We couldn't have done it on our own. We needed each other to heal the ache. All the broken moments were waiting to be pieced together just like this.

Our odd little family, stitched together by chance. By choice.

Our perfect, happily ever after.

Nathan

Four Years Later

"Dad," Claire hisses from across the dining table. "Don't you think that's enough questions? Aiden can barely eat."

The large square table in the formal dining room can seat twelve people easily. Even so, we're usually clustered close, only taking up two sides with my pregnant wife right next to me, my daughters sitting together on my left side. But today the table is far more full than I prefer. Claire and her date are sitting next to each other. Charlie and her date, adjacent. I blinked and my girls are suddenly teenagers, heading to prom.

I always thought I'd be a cool dad, especially because my daughters are adopted. Our bonds started with friendship. I thought I'd be evolved enough to respect two young ladies becoming women, but *nope*. I was wrong.

Very wrong.

All I can think of is driving my foot up both of these suckers' asses. I was eighteen once. I know exactly what's on their minds, which is why I insisted on doing the pre-prom dinner at our house so I could intimidate their dates properly. I even offered up the finally constructed and operational hotel-casino that Dad, me, and Spencer busted our asses over for three long years. I gifted Serendipity's Ballroom A as the venue for Charlie and Claire's high school prom this year.

The school was so blown away by my generosity, they didn't

pry into my ulterior motives, which was an excuse to chaperone tonight. I claimed it was for quality control purposes as Serendipity has only been operating for less than a year, but let's be honest–I want to keep an eye on how close these kids are dancing. I am not above pulling the fire alarm and ruining over a hundred teenage girls' updos if their hands get too curious.

"Sorry, Aiden," I reluctantly acquiesce. "Please enjoy your steak." I gesture to his untouched dinner then turn my attention to Charlie's date. "So, Mitchell, are you looking forward to tonight?"

"Yes, sir." He nods eagerly. His fair skin and blue eyes are a stark contrast from Claire's date, Aiden, who is dark-haired with deep brown skin.

"And explain to me why you couldn't find a date your own age, and decided to ask Charlie to prom, who is two whole grades behind you?"

"Dad. Stop!" Charlie shrieks.

"Nope. Fair question," I answer.

"Spence...*help*," Charlie pleads, making bug eyes at her big sister, begging her to rein me in.

Mitchell clears his throat and nervously straightens his bow tie.

"Nathan," Spencer grumbles out in a tepid warning.

"What?" I ask, feigning innocence. She lifts one brow, daring me to continue being an ass. "Fine. What I meant, Mitchell, is how did you and Charlie meet?"

"Um... Well, sir, Charlie and I met through swim class. Electives aren't grade specific so we were on a relay team together. We've spent a lot of time getting to know each other–"

"In your bathing suits?" My jaw tightens as I imagine wrapping my hands around his throat.

"*No!*" Mitchell squabbles out, fear exactly where I want it–in his eyes. "I mean, yes, we wear swimsuits to swim class, but I didn't ask her out just because I've seen her–" He stops short of concluding his thought and hangs his head. "I think I need to be done talking now. Aiden looks full if you want to ask him more questions."

"Dude," Aiden protests, then quickly shoves another bite of steak in his mouth so he's busy chewing.

"Here are the rules for tonight," I begin, deepening my voice. "No drinking, no drugs, curfew is ten o'clock—"

"Eleven," Claire chimes in, reminding me of my promise.

"Fine. *Eleven*. You guys are welcome to come back here and use the pool, but I want you all swimming in long-sleeved wet suits, fully zipped up. Clear?"

Spencer pats both hands on the table and scoots her chair back. "Kids, go ahead and finish eating. But save room for dessert. I made churro cheesecake. And don't forget, we only have forty minutes before Finn gets here to take pictures."

The girls still need to put their dresses on. They had dinner in jeans and T-shirts to avoid accidentally staining their couture gowns.

I didn't have to teach Claire and Charlie humility and modesty. It's in their bones. Despite our wealth, my daughters never come to me with greedy hands. But we pulled out all the stops for this milestone in their lives. Between their dresses, shoes, jewelry, the makeup artist, and private limo, I could've bought them each a mid-trim sedan.

I'm about to dive back into my meal when I glance up to meet my wife's scowl. She has both hands on her hips. "Sweetheart, can you help me with the cheesecake?" Spencer flutters her eyelashes at me while a creepily sweet smile expands on her face.

Ah, fuck. I'm in trouble. She only smiles like that when she's trying to keep her composure.

I push back from the table and follow her down the hall to the kitchen. I've barely turned the corner when her finger jabs me in the chest.

"What is your problem?" she asks. "You said you were going to behave tonight."

"I was behaving."

"You grilled Aiden like you were trying to get a confession

out of him."

"I did not."

"You asked him if he was involved in any offshore investments." Spencer folds her arms across her chest.

"His dad is a junior partner at Drexol Holdings. They just had a huge scandal with illegal offshore shell companies. I was simply asking–"

"He's *eighteen*."

"Exactly. He's an adult. Old enough for a credit card. Old enough to invest. Way too old to be dating my kid."

"They are two years apart, Nathan."

"Two years too many," I insist.

"Your hypocrisy is stunning, truly. I'm ten years your junior, Grandpa."

God, she's cute. Even when she's making fun of me. I crack a small smile. "Real funny. Pregnancy has made you glib." I put my hand on her belly, hoping to feel a little kick, even though she's told me time and time again it's too early.

"I've always been glib. You, however, have gotten very grumpy in your old age. Are you shocked that your fifteen- and sixteen-year-old girls are interested in dating?" She pretends to gasp in horror.

"It's not that. Boys his age only have one agenda. When I asked you out, I was a man, fully capable of paying for dinner, and taking care of you and your family."

Eyes wide like an owl, Spencer scoffs. "*Asked me out*? You tortured me as your assistant for a few weeks, locked me away in your guest room, then spanked me in your office. Not exactly the courtship of fairy tales."

I wince with a flicker of remorse. "There was way more to the story than that. And I've spent a lot of time trying to make up for–"

She bursts out in a chuckle. "*I'm kidding*. I love our story. How much we've grown together. You're a good man and I'm head over heels in love with you, over the moon that I'm carrying your son."

"I love you too, baby, I just–" I halt, frozen by shock as her words seep in. *Son?* She's carrying my *son*?

"Whoops. Did I let that slip?" The look on Spencer's face, sly and proud, tells me she meant to spill.

My hands are around her stomach immediately. "When did you find out?"

"I couldn't wait. I'm sorry. They emailed me the blood test results. I had a whole cute thing planned with a piñata to tell you, but it's not as easy as you'd think to hunt down all-blue candy. Everything is blue raspberry flavored, which let's be honest, is just garbage and I–"

"Are you happy?"

Her smile is soft and sweet. "Are *you*?"

I nod. "*So happy.* But boy or girl, I don't care. I'm just happy this is happening with you." I pull her hand to my lips and sweetly kiss her palm. "I hope he gets your smile, your wit, and your fierce determination. I hope he gets your big heart too."

She issues a small hum of appreciation, as her hand cradles my cheek. "You're sweet."

"What do you want for our son?"

She pops her shoulders playfully. "I want when he's eighteen to *not* be interrogated in his girlfriend's home after he brought her such a pretty corsage and has been nothing but a gentleman all night."

"You think I'm being unreasonable?" I ask.

"I think you love your girls very much." She scrunches her nose. "And yes. Very unreasonable. But you're justified. I know it's hard to watch them grow up. But this is a big moment for Claire and Charlie."

"Prom?" I ask, skeptically.

"This is where young women learn how men should treat them. These boys have called you 'sir' all night. They chose to sit through a very uncomfortable dinner with their dates' family instead of pre-gaming with Burnett's and Red Bull at some house party. And by the way, the swim class thing? Charlie isn't a strong swimmer. She was getting harassed for constantly causing her team to lose the relay races. Mitchell's a captain on the team. He'll probably end up in the Olympics one day. He asked for Charlie to join his relay team instead because he can easily even the playing field and make up for her lost time. *He's protecting her.* It reminds me of something you would do."

I wrap my hand around the small of her back, pulling her in close. My lips brush against the top of her sweet-smelling hair. Ever since Spencer got pregnant, she complains that her shampoo reeks. It's hormones. She still smells like strawberry pie. The smell that makes me feel like I'm home.

"Okay. If I want the girls to have a good experience tonight, what should I do?"

"Don't go to their prom," Spencer explains simply. "Give them space and an opportunity to make good choices."

"Okay."

"Curfew at midnight," Spencer continues.

"I can do that."

"And if they choose to swim... I mean, who, outside of Dex, has spare wet suits lying around?"

I bark out a dry laugh. "All right, all right. Just promise me you'll never leave me. I think you're the only reason I don't make an ass out of myself daily."

She nuzzles deeper into my embrace. "*Thank you.* I'm so glad to be getting some credit finally."

Leaning away, I hook my finger underneath her chin. "So just you and me tonight, huh?" I show her a salacious grin. "What ever shall we do?"

Spencer shrugs, her eyes glinting with mischief. "I don't know, Grandpa. So many possibilities. Want to go sit on the porch and yell at kids to stay off our lawn? Or maybe we hit up Golden Corral and complain that we missed the early-bird special and now the brisket is far too dry, and there wasn't enough cobbler to go around. *Oooh*, I've got it. Let's go to the post office and bitch about the never-ending rising costs of stamps."

"*Mean*, woman. You're just mean."

We both burst into raspy chuckles that echo in the kitchen. "I'm sorry, my love," Spencer says quietly. "How can I make it up to you?"

I nod over my shoulder to the fridge. "That churro cheesecake is a fantastic start. But if you're really sorry…" I trace my fingertips lightly over the curve of her ass. "It's been a while."

She backpedals once. "I know. I just feel…off. I mean, I'm only twelve weeks pregnant," she says, grabbing underneath her arms and squeezing where it's soft. "I already know I'm going to gain a lot of weight. My mom did too with Charlie. Genetics, I suppose."

I step forward, closing the space she introduced. "You are so beautiful. Now more so than ever."

She places her hand against my chest. "I'm serious, Nathan. I'm struggling with this."

I want to tell her she has nothing to worry about, but I don't want to negate her feelings. "How can I help?"

"I don't think you can. I just don't feel sexy. And while we're on the subject, I don't know what kind of fucked-up sorcery this is, but how come when wives get pregnant and extra jiggly, their husbands tighten up even more?" She runs her hands down my torso. "See? You almost have an eight-pack all the sudden. How is that fair?"

"I have an idea that might help, but I need you to trust me. *Really trust me*."

Her gaze flicks upward to lock on mine. "I trust you with my whole heart."

"Then let's eat this cheesecake, get these kids out the door, and then later tonight, when I get you naked and alone, I want to record you."

She looks at me like I just suggested we go commit some felonies for fun. "You are unhinged."

"Just your face, baby. I want you to see what I see when I look at you. When I'm making you feel good, when you're happy, and satisfied, it's beauty like I can't explain. You're always gorgeous,

Spencer. But when you're with me, *all mine*, it's something I can't describe." I kiss her forehead, then each cheek, before I rake my lips down her neck, feeling the warmth of her delicate skin. "I will always want you. And the days you're feeling insecure, tell me. I know it's hard to share this stuff, but be honest with me. Whenever you forget who you are and how I see you, I'll always be here to remind you."

"Thank you. It's not hard to share with you. You make it easy." She half-smiles, a glint of flirtation in her eyes. "So, sexy selfies are really your kink, aren't they? Thank goodness I had the good sense to lock you down with one of those four years ago."

A rumble erupts from my chest, breaking free as playful laughter. "Only with you, pumpkin. All I want is you."

She weaves her fingers in mine, the large, pink diamond ring on her left hand pressing hard against my knuckle. "No need to pine too hard. You've got me, Nathan. Forever."

THE END

ACKNOWLEDGEMENTS

The entire *Lessons in Love* series has been a healing process for me. Each of these stories represents a challenging life lesson I learned the hard way. Bringing these characters to the page was so therapeutic, and sparked my own journey of self-love. To see this series come to a close is surreal, freeing, and heartbreaking for me. I want to live with these characters forever, and thanks to the amazing readers, their stories live on.

My first big thank you is to my editor, Michelle. You explored every single nook and cranny of this story with me. From the moments of doubts, big questions of why, the nonstop writing and editing sprints, you were there for me every single step of the way. There aren't enough words in the world to show my gratitude. Thank you for safeguarding the most sacred, treasured pieces of my creativity and helping me make them shine.

To Mr. Cove, thank you for tolerating me through the ups and downs of writing fever (and real fevers). You are my rock. My forever. You are the source material for every single happily ever after I write. Thank you for never changing on me, but instead, growing with me, babe. I love you.

To Team Kay–Tatyana, Trisha, and Brooke, my favorite found family and my partners in crime. You amazing, strong, beautiful, creative women encourage me every day to be my goofy self and keep scribbling these love stories down on page. Thank you for your fierce loyalty and friendship.

To Kristin, thank you for your unwavering support. Your beautiful designs are always the biggest source of my inspiration. This series started it all, and while I'm sad to say goodbye to

Lessons in Love, I'm so excited about all the adventures we're about to embark on together.

To Meredith and the entire Page & Vine family, thank you for your faith in my stories and for bringing the Lessons in Love series to bookstores and to so many new readers. I am so grateful for all your support.

To Judy, another huge thank you, not just for your keen eye and manuscript polishing superpowers, but for being so amazingly supportive. I appreciate you so much.

To all my readers, in a world filled to the brim with incredible stories and authors, thank you for choosing to spend your time with me and my characters. I hope Selfie brings heart and healing into your day, and I hope to see you on the next adventure.

ABOUT THE AUTHOR

Kay Cove is a contemporary romance author, who crafts plot focused stories with sassy heroines and dirty-talking MMCs, full of witty banter and situations that force flawed characters to grow. She likes to challenge herself by writing in a variety of sub-genres.

After a career in corporate HR, she ultimately decided to pursue her dream of becoming a published author. Born in Colorado, Kay currently resides in Georgia with her husband and two sweet and rambunctious little boys.

ALSO BY KAY COVE

Lessons in Love
Camera Shy
Snapshot
Selfie

Real Life, Real Love
Paint Me Perfect
Rewrite the Rules
Owe Me One
Sing Your Secrets
First Comes Forever

Paladin
Whistleblower
Tattletale
Snitch - Coming 2026

STORIES WITH IMPACT

WWW.PAGEANDVINE.COM